The Day:

THE SUN RISES

GRACE FINLEY

Printed in the United States of America
ISBN (Kindle) 978-1-953781-18-5
ISBN (Paperback) 978-1-953781-19-2
ISBN (Hardcover) 978-1-953781-20-8

Finley Books | Phoenix, AZ
www.FinleyBooks.com

FINLEY BOOKS

PHOENIX, ARIZONA

"But the Lord is with me
like a mighty warrior..."

–JEREMIAH 20:11

part one

1

indebted

"What are you working on?" Essie asked, rounding the kitchen table where her dad sat typing on an old laptop.

"The next sermon series."

She nodded, moving to the refrigerator. She filled a short glass with lemonade and shuffled her feet in his direction. She furrowed her brow as she took a sip. "You seem to be the lead pastor, Daddy. I'm old enough to remember when you referred to yourself as the *backup* pastor."

"Pastor Caleb started another church on the other side of the Ark."

"He couldn't take the pressure," she said, pursing her lips. "Those pews have been *full*."

"It's not a competition."

Her eyebrows jumped playfully. "This *is* what I'm saying."

"Caleb is a great pastor."

"Ain't no pastor like the Daddy I've got."

He shook his head, his cheeks tightening. "You're in a good mood."

She smiled broadly, her eyes dancing to the front windows and back. "Josh is taking me on a date."

"You've been going on quite a few of those."

"He decided a few weeks ago that there's a 'wooing' process that needs to take place."

"'Wooing'."

"Yes. It's a weird word. Is 'courted' better? I thought it sounded too medieval."

"Well, whatever the word, it sounds like a good idea," he said with a smile. "So, where are you two going today?"

"He said something about a miniature golf establishment being renovated?"

"Sounds fun. Try and take it easy on him."

"Take it *easy*? I've never played."

"Yeah, but your competitive drive tends to nullify any learning curve."

"I'll refrain from victory dances," she said with a shrug, taking another sip of lemonade. "But I can't promise I won't partake in friendly wagers or smack talk."

"Well, can't say he didn't know what he was signing on for."

"I was just going to check on the animals, get things tidy. He should be here soon."

"Want some help?"

"Nah, you work on your victory sermon." She placed the glass down on the table, moved to give him a side hug, but he stood abruptly, wrapped his arms around her. "Sono così felice per te, mia bellissima ragazza." *I'm so happy for you, my beautiful girl.* "Have a wonderful time. Ti amo, ti amo, ti amo." He kissed her repeatedly on the top of her head.

Essie hugged him tightly. "Ti amo, ti amo, ti amo."

Matteo kissed her once more. "Are you sure you don't want help?"

She nodded. "If we're not back before sunset, will you feed the animals dinner? I'll set everything up."

"I'll feed them. Go have fun."

Esther squinted into the glare of the midday sun as she jogged down the porch steps, pushing her sunglasses on her face. Hwin whinnied when she saw her approach and Bree tossed his head high in the air, trotting enthusiastically toward the fence. He lined up his back longways along the fence.

"Hey, Narnian. We'll go on a long ride tomorrow, okay? I promise."

Bree neighed, bumped the fence with his haunches.

"Hey, *you're* the one who doesn't let other people ride you. I'm sure Teo would be happy to, but you'd have to be as sweet to him as you are to me." She climbed up on the first post, patted the Percheron's thick neck.

"Have you been playing in your water, Hwin? It's all *muddy,*" Esther said with a pout. She hopped down, moved to the gate, noticing Bree's wobbly gate as he followed along beside her. "You've got a mud pie in your hoof, don't you?"

The horse snorted.

She reached for the hoof pick dangling on a key ring on the outside wall of the barn.

"Alright, Buddy. You know the routine."

Bree readjusted his weight and tenderly lifted his front hoof, like a dog begging for a treat.

"Ow, there was a rock in the middle of all the nasty mud. That didn't feel good, did it?"

He dropped his muzzle beside her, nudged her cheek.

"Yeah, you're welcome. Is that better?" She stood, patting his side. She was about to affectionately scold Hwin when a sudden breeze sweeping dust into the air caused the hair on the back of her neck to stand on end.

Esther heard the tires creep across the gravel driveway at the same time as Bree. She speculated it could be Josh arriving early until Bree immediately took a rigid stance, ears alert. The moment she tried to step around him to look, he released a low squeal and moved to block her path.

A heavy vehicle door slammed.

"Would you be Esther Nat-a-lee?" a man's voice asked. He had a hint of a southern accent.

She stroked Bree on the chest, ducking under his neck. "She's out on an errand. Can I help you?"

The man looked a little more polished than she'd expected. He was about 6 feet tall, mid-forties, and was dressed like he was on his way to a golf tournament. "*You* are Esther Nat-a-lee."

She couldn't stand it. "Na-taw-lay. It's Italian. But no, she's not here."

He nodded calmly, furrowing his brow. "We're going to need you to take a ride with us, Esther Na-taw-*lay*."

She took a step toward the fence bordering the next paddock, tucking the hoof pick in her fist.

"Afraid it's not optional."

Bree sidestepped, once again putting himself between her and the man at the fence. He backed them both toward the barn.

"Take it easy," a voice said in a coaxing tone, suddenly behind them.

In the time it took her to glance over her shoulder and back, the man at the fence had been joined by two additional men, each with a poorly concealed handgun. She glanced toward the Percheron horse, strategizing a way to grab Bree's mane and hoist herself onto his back. Even if she managed the maneuver, Bree likely wouldn't be able to scale the fence, even with a running start–unless she aimed for the section of exterior fence he had begun to loosen when he expressed his discontent if she took one of the other horses for a ride.

The leader clucked his tongue impatiently. "This ends with you in the back of that ve-hic-le. Why don't you just make it easier on everyone and come quietly?"

Essie thought of her dad inside the house. He would have noticed the SUV pull in. What would happen to him if she managed to escape?

He'd want you to run.

Bree released a breathy snort, tapped the ground with his hoof.

It happened quickly. The man in the barn slid open the gate, scraping the flooring, which alarmed Bree. The men on the outside of the fence used this distraction to scale the fence. Seeing no alternative, Esther burst out of her rigid stance and took off running, Bree close alongside.

She jumped toward the water trough, managed to make enough contact with her boot along the metal corner to gain altitude. She landed with a huff on Bree's back, her hands gripping his mane, her positioning not entirely stable. She felt her body edging to the right and threw her weight forward, trying to stay on.

A gunshot triggered Bree to rear back, beating his front hooves in the air. Additional shots echoed across the ranch. Bree released a scream and his body started to tumble.

The moment her body made impact with the ground and Bree landed on top of her, she felt her back snap, heard the crushing of her pelvis, her ribs, her knees. Her skull rattled. She couldn't take a breath.

Through blurred vision, she watched Bree toss his front leg upward, felt him roll his neck toward the sky, desperate to get up.

Three gunshots came in close succession and proximity and Bree no longer moved.

Essie's ears were ringing. Her head swirled. She didn't know what the men were saying, but it was apparent they were arguing with one another.

She wanted to look toward the house, but she couldn't get her neck to rotate. She couldn't get it to move at all.

When the men gathered over her, she closed her eyes. Her mouth was filled with the taste of metallic mixed with dirt; she had to repeatedly swallow to try to keep her throat clear, but even that was difficult.

She had just registered the words "dead or alive," when she felt her body being tugged forcibly from beneath Bree. It was being done in a careless fashion; first by the neck, then by her shoulders, which cracked repeatedly with the movement, pulling loose from the sockets, twisting with unnatural ease. Clearly keeping her body in one piece was not a priority.

As soon as the compression of Bree's body was eliminated, the severity of her other injuries became more apparent. She still couldn't move, but her body now seethed with pain.

One of the men scooped her up, thoughtlessly folding her body, the motion causing a stabbing sensation in her torso accompanied by a popping she could both feel and hear. Her abdomen immediately filled with warmth and she silently assessed that a broken rib had probably punctured an internal organ. Maybe a lung.

She began choking on breaths. Her mouth released a constricted cough and through the grit in her eyes she could see the resulting blood splatters coating the shirt of the man carrying her. They were just rounding the corner from the barn when a handful of gunshots rang out. The first was loud and booming and resulted in the collapse of the man carrying her. She felt her body tumbling to the ground in suspended animation.

The second and third shots fired one after the other, but she couldn't tell where they hit. It sounded like they'd ricocheted off metal. The final two were muffled and originated over her shoulder.

She landed on her side on the gravel driveway. The force of her head slamming into the ground caused a ripping sensation in the opposite side of her neck. Her cheek settled onto the ground at the same moment her eyes managed to focus on the shape of her dad standing by the porch steps. For a brief moment, she felt relief.

And then she realized he was falling.

Even with the distance between them, she could see that the light had already gone from his eyes.

2

winston's rats

five days later...

"You are proposing we devote our limited resources to try to track down one girl?"

Luther narrowed his eyes. "That *girl* has saved hundreds of thousands of lives. *Minimum.*"

"A fact that we're only just learning because you kept us in the dark, Dr. Graham. A fact we haven't begun to wrap our minds around."

"I was protecting her. She went through tens of thousands of hours of torture to save as many people as possible and she asked for *nothing* in return. Trying to protect her was the very least I could do."

"We have an appropriate level of personnel investigating."

"Your calculation for an 'appropriate' level should factor in that she saved the lives of half the people in this room, along with your families."

Grainger dropped his chin regretfully. "Be that as it may, she is *one* person, Luther."

"No one here is denying that she's had an impact for a girl of her age," Jonas said, lifting his eyebrows conclusively.

"Of her age? How many lives have you saved, Jonas?"

"Well, I—"

"The question was rhetorical. You're the only person on a prophylactic dosing of the 'immunity booster'."

Jonas's jaw dropped open.

"She's a hero, Luther," Grainger said firmly. "I'm glad this was finally brought to light so that we can honor her, celebrate her contributions and impact."

"We won't be able to honor her or celebrate her unless we take immediate action to find her and bring her home." He spoke forcefully, jabbing his fingers into the table top.

"As we've *already* said, we're just learning about this. We have people investigating what happened. They have an expedited reporting timeline."

"When?"

"Friday morning."

"In two days," Luther said in disbelief.

"Yes."

He shook his head. "Would that be an acceptable timeline if this was your daughter?" He motioned toward Chip Elwes, who was looking very tired. "It's been *five* days."

"With all due respect, Dr. Graham," Grainger began, clearing his throat. "This girl *wasn't* your daughter, or even a relative."

Luther recognized his use of past tense.

"More like a lab animal by the sound of it. I don't think a *father* would subject his daughter to what you put her through," Jonas said, rabid suddenly. He peered down at his row of colleagues. "Chip, would you put your kids through what Luther here put this girl through?"

Luther tensed his jaw.

"She asked him to do it," Sadie Parker said solidly, returning to the chamber from an urgent phone call with her husband. She moved behind the other chairs to her place next to Jonas. As usual, she wore a bold patriotic blue. "I apologize for my tardiness."

"It's understandable," Jonas remarked. "I forgive you."

"Oh, I was talking to Dr. Graham. Your opinion means absolutely nothing to me, Jonas."

Jonas leaned to his opposite arm rest. "Very mature, Sadie."

She glared over at him with intense repulsion. "I don't agree with you even still being here, for the record, *and* for Dr. Graham's information." She shook her head angrily. "It's my understanding that we're to discuss plans to locate and rescue Esther Natale–or Essie. You said she goes by Essie?"

Luther stared blankly at the space before him, picturing her the last time he saw her: waving from the passenger seat of Josh's truck as they drove away on a date, a huge smile on her face. Matteo said she'd finally overcome her insomnia. She'd started singing in church again. She'd made her peace with the past. She was happy.

The image of Essie smiling as she and Josh left for a day of fishing was replaced by the scene he'd found at the ranch: Essie's colossal horse, Bree, who she'd nursed back to health when he was rejected by his mother as a foal dead in the paddock. Matteo Natale, the best friend he'd ever known, Essie's dad, shot dead.

"*Luther*," Sadie coaxed softly.

He stood, tensed his jaw, planted his feet on the floor, and stared down Jonas Miller. "You kidnapped a 20-year-old girl."

"I did no such thing."

"You murdered her dad in front of her."

"I–" Jonas stuttered.

"Mistakes were made," Grainger remarked, nodding regretfully. "On *both* sides."

"You don't get to speak," Kyle Geoffreys bellowed, pounding his fist on the table top.

Chip peered over at his colleagues, looked up at Luther sympathetically. "Dr. Graham–"

"My name is Luther. I don't give two shits about being called doctor. My *name* is Luther."

"*Luther*, we are investigating what's happened to Essie, and once we have more information, we'll see what options we have."

13

"You don't understand. If we don't–" Luther was finding it difficult to take a full breath. "We have to go in and get her. *Now*."

Grainger shook his head. "You know we can't do that. We're assuming she was taken outside the Ark and any action on our part to find her will equate to an act of war."

He felt like he had to tell them the implications; it seemed like the most surefire way to get them to act, but doing so would put Essie in greater danger. He had already thought of how he could attempt to explain how Essie's cellular structure, her body's capabilities, could be used for both good and evil, comparing it to oxygen. He'd explain how oxygen on its own is life-sustaining. It's vital. You can combine oxygen with hydrogen and create water–or you can combine oxygen with hydrogen and make a bomb. While he felt like that explained it in terms they could understand, he wasn't sure that was the messaging he wanted to convey, calling Essie a potential bomb. They'd say she was a threat. Some of these people would consider the feasibility of eliminating oxygen from the earth because it could potentially be used for harm.

Luther took a deep breath. "What about your contacts at the White House?" Luther asked, speaking to Jonas directly. "The ones you coordinated her kidnapping with?"

Jonas shook his head, looking away.

"My understanding is that they've severed communications for the time being," Sadie replied, lifting her eyebrow for confirmation from Jonas.

Luther shook his head. "So you gave her up for nothing, just as they knew you would."

Jonas shook his head. "I will not have us waste any more time on this issue. We have more pressing matters to discuss, most notably *millions* of Ark residents."

"'*Waste* any more time'?" Sadie asked in exasperation.

"There's no point in spending more time on this. On figuring out where she is or figuring out a rescue plan. There's *no point*." His voice was tight.

"*Why?*"

Jonas took a deep breath, gnawing at the inside of his cheek.

"Jonas? If you have information, you *need* to tell us. We're all you have; your Gowon allies have left you hanging out to dry."

He nodded, looking on the verge of tears. "I didn't have all the information. Before we arranged–" He looked up at Luther, shaking his head.

Sadie narrowed her eyes upon him, a fearful expression on her face. "*Jonas.*"

"We shouldn't spend more time on this because the girl in question–Esther? *Essie?* She's dead."

Luther felt his chest constrict.

Jonas picked up the stack of papers before him and tapped them on the desk to straighten them. "So, you see, it doesn't make sense to spend any more of this council's time on this. We have other things to discuss." He set the stack of papers down conclusively, putting up his hands. His voice was softer when he spoke again. "This was a tragedy, but we have other things to discuss."

Silence swelled in the chamber.

"How do you know she's dead, Jonas?"

"The men who carried out the mission wore body cameras. The footage was cast back here."

"I want to see the footage."

"Luther, what's done is done."

"Well, it seems some members of this council have no idea *what's* been done. If one of us authorized this, it's as though *all of us* authorized it. Are all of *you* confident that Jonas, Grainger, Mays, whoever else conspired in her kidnapping, did the appropriate thing?"

"Show us the footage, Jonas," Geoffreys muttered angrily.

He sighed, scrolling on his device.

"*Now.*"

"The question is if the girl is dead, *correct*? There's no reason to subject the council to more gruesome images than necessary." He screen-mirrored from his device to the wall-mounted monitor in the chamber.

Luther rotated to look at the side wall, where a projection of Jonas's phone home screen briefly appeared, showing his wife, Hailey, with their 18-month-old twins.

Jonas switched to a video player app. "We'll limit it to proof of death."

"*Jesus*, Jonas," McNeary grumbled.

Jonas lifted his hand in apology.

The video began as a closeup of Essie's face as she was laid on the open tailgate of a pickup truck. Her skin was coated in dirt and streaked with blood. She had her eyes squeezed shut, a single stream of tears running from the corner of her eye. Her lip quivered.

"You *authorized* this?" Sadie yelled, then clasped her hand over her mouth. "*Jesus Christ*, look at her Jonas!"

Jonas glared at Sadie. "Yes, I authorized this *precisely*. What do you think? No. Absolutely not. I did not want her killed. I did not order *any* of this."

The camera shifted as the man stood in the truck bed. This provided an overhead shot of a truly horrific sight. What had not been apparent by the closeup view was how disfigured Essie's body was, the least of which was her left arm, which was hanging loose from the socket. The underside of her arm and the cross tattoo were twisted outward, the bones in her arm, her elbow clearly crushed. Her whole body had a flattened appearance, like it lacked any remaining structure to give it shape.

And yet the man leaned down, seized hold of her shoulders and dragged her into the truck bed.

A sharp cry cut through the air. Essie opened her eyes suddenly, her expression startled.

Sadie clasped her palm over her mouth, slowly shaking her head, tears brimming her eyes.

"*God dammit, what the hell are you doing?*"

"*You said to get her in the truck.*"

The camera aimed at a middle-aged man in a polo shirt, his sunglasses propped up on his head.

"Do you see her arm? Does that look normal *to you?"*

The image whirled, landing back on Essie, whose mouth had fallen open.

"I'm not sure if you've noticed, but her whole body looks like that. Where am I supposed to grab?"

Her mouth slowly closed and opened again, as she seemed to be trying to pull in a gulp of air.

"If we're bringing her in dead anyway, should we just shoot her and put her out of her misery?"

"I doubt Gowon's going to appreciate a point blank bullet in his daughter's brain."

"Yeah, but the rest of her injuries are fine, right?"

"As far as I'm concerned, none of this would have happened if that effing horse didn't fall on her."

"Well, you're the one who shot the horse; what did you think was going to happen?"

A rapidly expanding pool of blood began to fill in the grooves in the truck bed liner beneath Essie's body.

"Shit."

"She's bleeding out. It shouldn't be long now. Just leave her."

The camera panned down to Essie's face. A tear had stopped halfway down her cheek. She stared blankly ahead. Her pale lips were parted, but she no longer sought air.

*   *   *

Luther gathered his belongings from Security with automation, walking quickly toward the parking lot.

The moment he stepped outside, his legs began to waver. He stumbled forward, dropping his bag, his phone, everything he'd collected in his arms, and fell to his knees. His chest heaved and he found himself choking on sobs. He shook his head repeatedly, unable to reconcile in his mind what he'd just seen.

It's better that she's dead, he thought insistently.

It wasn't a comfort. Just the fact that his mind had tried to reason with him mere minutes after seeing her die made his breathing exponentially more strained, made his heart feel like a lead weight in his chest.

It suddenly occurred to him that the last thing she'd said to him was "Love you, Luther." She'd just hugged her dad goodbye and had been so excited to see Josh pull into the driveway, but before scooting off to greet him, she'd thrown both arms around Luther's neck and told him she loved him.

When he'd first brought her to his mom's house when she was two, he'd still needed to keep up appearances at the lab. He'd accepted evening assignments, which helped enable him to keep up with his other classes, and be there with Essie, as he tried to find a placement for her. For those couple of weeks she lived with them, she slept in his room, she'd worn his old clothes, he'd read to her before leaving for his shifts. One evening, she was wearing his Spider-Man pajamas, her hair still damp from her bath, split into two thick braids. She sat beside him on the couch, "crisscross applesauce" (as his mom had taught her), as he read her a rhyming board book that had been a favorite of his. He knew he needed to keep some separation emotionally from her so he was seated forward, leaning over his knees, trying to establish some physical separation. As he read to her, he noticed her nudging closer until finally her head rested against his shoulder, her small hand tenderly draped over his arm. He continued on since he wasn't far from the end of the book. As he closed the cover, he peered over at her. She lifted her big, round eyes to gaze up at him, blinking slowly. He felt the corners of his mouth pull upward.

"I have to go to work, Evin."

She nodded, running her palm over his arm in a soothing manner, taking a deep breath as she did—something she would have seen his mom do. After a quiet moment, she released him and scooched herself back on the couch.

He knew he'd need emotional resiliency if he'd have any chance of accomplishing anything he set out to do, of saving any of the babies. It was going to take everything out of him; he couldn't get too close. But then he considered where she'd come from, what she'd endured, and it suddenly felt very selfish to keep himself distanced. It was for this reason that when he stood and said goodbye, he leaned in and kissed the top of her head. She'd locked her eyes upon him and given a faint, hopeful smile.

Traffic continued to trudge forward on the road that ran alongside the Council Hall. He could hear the sound of children playing nearby, birds in the trees overhead. The sky had an eerie appearance with thin streaks of clouds, a haze filtering the sunlight.

It was at the moment he felt his heart twist and writhe in his chest, and he felt like he would never take a full breath ever again, that his sat phone chirped on the ground beside him.

3

in this storm

The coffee maker beeped three times, signaling that it was powering down. Gabe stepped over to the machine, filled a mug, then poured the remainder down the drain, rinsed the carafe.

Fenway suddenly scuffled across the hardwood floor, tail wagging wildly. Josh allowed the Shepherd to jump up and rest her paws on his legs, but he was visibly unsteady as he emerged from the second bedroom at Luther's cabin, where he'd spent the last few nights, recovering from a concussion, along with a dislocated shoulder.

"Easy, Fenway," Gabe coaxed.

The dog whimpered, buried her muzzle into Josh's shirt, trying to decipher the different smells attached to the fibers of his clothes.

Josh scratched behind her ears, his eyes brimmed with tears.

"Mom would want me to make you eat something."

The way Josh continued to stare straight ahead gave the impression he was seeing something very different than the Shepherd, the hardwood flooring beyond. Despite having had several showers, he still had the appearance of being coated in dirt as a result of road rash that had just begun to scab. Tears rolled down his cheeks. Josh made no move to wipe them away, even as the salty stream settled into the raw scrapes on his face.

Josh had knelt next to Matteo briefly at the ranch to check for a pulse, despite his wounds being incompatible with survival, then turned his attention to the driveway. He hadn't noticed previously that the orchard pickup was missing, that an SUV was parked in its place, one of the tires blown to bits. It took him a brief amount of processing time to remember that the truck had a GPS tracker, something Luther had one of the Dannys put in place "just in case."

Moments later, Josh was back in his own truck, running the red light to make a left hand turn on Chesapeake. According to the receiver he had retrieved from his glove box, the pickup was driving east on the same road about five miles ahead. Based upon the landmarks in the vicinity, it seemed they were most likely going to a small airstrip.

Josh made several call attempts while in pursuit. First, he called Luther, who did not answer. Next, he called Miles, who did. He immediately went into action, saying he'd call Danny to get surveillance activated and shut down the airfield. To his surprise, Josh called Gabe next. The thought had occurred to him just beforehand to call his dad, but one consideration of having to tell him in rushed words that his best friend was dead made him quickly reconsider. He sent Gabe to check on Matteo, just to be sure, not able to let the reality of Teo being dead blur his thoughts.

Josh was a mile away from the airfield when Miles called back.

"The airfield's been shut down for years, Josh. We haven't even used it for Ark operations. No one should be there."

"They just turned in. I'm ½ mile out."

"Are you armed?"

"I just have my sidearm."

"Dammit. Danny's launching a drone right now. We can't get ahold of Luther. He had a meeting with the council and they don't allow comm devices in there. His phone's probably ringing in some security bin. We're trying to get through directly to the council chamber."

Josh narrowed his eyes as he reached the start of the airfield security fencing. "There's a heavy jet parked on the runway."

Miles conveyed the message to Danny. "You can try shooting out the tires, but they're probably too thick. Drone is two miles out."

As the airfield came into full view, Josh could see the orchard pickup truck parked at the bottom of the airstair just being closed. His eyes panned over to the airfield gate and he slammed his foot onto the gas pedal. By the time the truck barreled through the gate and sped toward the jet, the aircraft was creeping forward.

"Josh?"

It was all happening too fast. The jet was accelerating; there was no way he could get in front of it to be able to try to take out the landing gear, nor was he confident he could. He tried to keep the truck parallel with the plane as he pulled out his sidearm gun, struggling to roll down the window.

"*Josh.*"

He pulled in his breath as he raised his chin, wiping roughly at his tear-stained cheeks.

"I made coffee if you'd like some," Gabe said, offering a mug.

Josh nodded, accepting it in his right hand, his left arm guarded against his stomach. "Where's Luther?" he asked, voice gritty, glancing around the same cabin where Essie had spent so many hours during the Phoenix Initiative antidote runs. He could feel her presence, he could visualize her lying in that leather recliner.

"He had a meeting with the council this morning at 7. I'm not sure how long it was going to be, especially if they were planning to interrogate him again."

The last time Luther was summoned to visit the council was the day Essie was taken. All communication and recording devices were strictly forbidden and confiscated prior to stepping into the council chamber. He suspected after that they'd scheduled the session at the exact time of the kidnapping so he wouldn't have a chance to issue a warning until it was too late.

Josh tensed his jaw.

The sound of the key code on the door lock snapped them both to attention. It was 8:20, which meant his meeting with the council lasted no longer than half an hour.

Luther pushed open the door, took in the sight of them, the corners of his mouth lifting in an indiscernible way; whatever it was, it was decidedly *not* a smile. He set his keys down on the table by the door, removed his shoes on the rug, but took pause as he removed his jacket, squeezing his eyes closed as he moved to hang it on the hook.

"*Well*?" Gabe asked. "Did you find out anything?"

Luther shook his head and crossed slowly to the kitchen.

"They were involved, Luther. They had to have been. *Where did they take her*?"

Luther took a steadying breath, dropping his chin to his chest as he leaned against the kitchen counter. "I don't know how to say this to the two of you."

Gabe's chin swiveled to Josh to see if his brother was getting a better read on Luther.

Josh stood as stiff as a statue, deep set brown eyes reflecting the sunlight pouring through the kitchen window.

Luther pulled in his breath in a great heave, putting his hand to his face. "Essie died." His voice broke, his nostrils flaring. He gasped as the reality struck him square in the chest. He leaned more heavily into the counter to keep his balance, shaking his head, releasing several huffs of air, appearing incapable of taking in a breath.

Josh's eyes had become unfocused. He stared straight ahead, not blinking, hand still gripping the coffee mug.

Gabe took a step forward in protest. "You said her condition—you said her body could—"

Luther gave a hard shake of his head.

"But *Luther*—"

"Gabe, she had a two *thousand* pound horse crush her spine. She was also shot. She didn't make it to wherever they were taking her; she didn't make it alive off the ranch." Luther's voice had tightened and become

23

incrementally louder. He forced himself to take a breath, trying to suppress further outbursts. "I'm *sorry*." He reset himself. "I'm sorry."

No one spoke for a few prolonged moments.

"They're lying," Gabe growled suddenly, his face pale. "Essie, she can't be—"

"The truth is, she'd prefer this to—" Luther interjected, hesitating before continuing.

"Oh come *on*," Gabe bellowed. "She would *not* want this. You're actually going to stand there and claim *what*, that this is for the best?"

"You think she'd prefer to endure whatever Gowon's people had in store for her?" Luther's body turned rigid as he wiped roughly at his eyes.

"How did they *find her*?" Gabe demanded. It took the expanding silence that followed for him to arrive at the answer. When he did, his shoulders slumped with the weight of it: "The blood sample at the hospital."

Luther lifted his eyes.

Josh continued to stare across the room toward the window, the forest beyond, saying nothing.

"The reason she was at the hospital was because of me. I insisted that she go, I'm the one—" Gabe stopped speaking abruptly. "Oh, *God*."

"Don't do that," Luther said, his voice lacking conviction.

Gabe shook his head forcefully. "But what you *said*–about her body healing itself?"

Josh's jaw tightened as his gaze lifted to the open study and the leather recliner.

"Gabe."

"They lied about being in contact with Gowon. Why wouldn't they lie about this?"

"I saw her, Gabe," Luther stammered, eyes wide. "I *saw* her."

Josh suddenly made direct, unwavering eye contact with Luther, his eyes asking the question he couldn't verbalize.

They'd been sitting in the barn at Natale Ranch when Luther had shared the real reason Essie's body could heal itself so effectively, that all her body's stem cells were pluripotent, always at the ready to defend against any threats. At the time of that conversation, her body was regenerating organs. Luther had marveled at the potential, at the seemingly limitless capabilities of her body; they had both expressed concern about the danger she was in, simply by existing. They feared what would happen if that knowledge wound up in the wrong hands.

And it had. Their worst fears had been realized.

Luther gave a short shake of his head. "It wasn't enough, Josh. No one could survive what happened, not even her."

Josh's gaze shifted to the study again, to the recliner, his posture starting to deteriorate.

Gabe dropped onto the couch, buried his face in his hands.

The room filled with an uneasy silence.

Josh shifted suddenly, his movements difficult and stiff. He set the coffee mug firmly on the counter, picked up the keys for the orchard pickup, his own truck having wound up in a crumpled heap of metal in the overgrown brush that lined the abandoned airfield. "I'm taking the truck."

Gabe nodded shortly. "I'm sorry, Josh," he said in a low, pleading tone.

Josh gave a nearly imperceptible shake of his head and moved toward the cabin door. Fenway scurried to follow, her muzzle repeatedly drawing upward to get a read on his face. He paused as he pushed open the screen door, reconsidering something. He seemed to be wanting to ask a question.

Luther braced himself. Would he ask to see her himself? Would he demand to know who was involved? Would he ask if she suffered?

Luther felt compelled to console Josh by telling him how much he knew she loved him, but the moment he let the thought resonate, the moment he realized he would be conveying the sentiment because Essie was dead, he once again found it very difficult to breathe.

Without another word spoken, Josh let the door close behind him. He started the ignition and the truck rumbled past the front porch and down the dirt road.

The cabin was quiet for a long enough time that a patch of clouds had drifted overhead and given a strong threat of rain...and rolled out again.

"Someone needs to share this information, Gabe," Luther finally said. "To your parents, to her friends, the church."

Gabe pulled in his breath. "I'll take care of that." He rubbed the tears roughly from his face.

"Please don't blame yourself," Luther said flatly. Dutifully. Because Essie would want him to say it. Even if he disagreed. The experience of standing in his cabin, delivering this message to Gabe was surreal, like an out of body experience. The returning disbelief that she was dead acted like a numbing agent; he could hardly perceive his own body.

"I injected her with a literal bomb, I put her blood sample out there. They would *never* have known who she was if not for me. If she'd never come to Denver, she'd be alive right now. If it weren't for me, she'd be alive right now." His voice caught.

Luther took a deep breath. "It's *my* fault, Gabe. I should have never—I should have done a better job protecting her." He was about to admit more—that he should have never stepped aside and let the council seize control, he should have seen the Arks through, ensured things went according to plan–but he was distracted by his sat phone chirping in his pocket.

Danny.

Luther glanced up to the drive and cleared his throat. "You can take my SUV so you have a vehicle, but would you mind dropping me somewhere on your way?"

*　　*　　*

Danny had a very disheveled appearance when Luther arrived, uncharacteristic for him in all the years he had known him. His dress shirt was heavily wrinkled, like he'd been sleeping in it and the buttons were misaligned. His hair wasn't combed and cowlicks forced this hair in all directions.

When Luther stepped off the elevator in the main security and technology hub for the Northern Ark, Danny was waiting for him near the elevator bank. It was unlike Danny to be distracted, always a task-focused person, but his attention was fixed on the window of the unoccupied conference room across the corridor. It required the second chime of the elevator indicating it would be making its ascent to break his attention away.

Danny swiveled his chin toward him. "I've been calling you," he said in an accusatory tone. "Have you been with the council all this time?"

"No. I had to make a stop. Is this conference room free?"

Picking up on something in Luther's tone, Danny narrowed his eyes. The chatter of his colleagues echoed down the hallway and he gave a short, tense nod, then wheeled himself toward the room. Once the two men were inside and the door was closed and the privacy windows were activated, Danny silently pulled up a screen share on the monitor. There was a lot of code; Luther wasn't quite sure what they were looking at.

"I need to tell you something first, Danny."

Danny frowned, gripping his phone in his hand. "This is important."

"So is this."

Danny dropped the phone into his lap, rotated his wheelchair to face Luther, then conclusively clicked the brakes into place, lifting his eyebrows impatiently.

With Danny always being a bit unpredictable with his emotions, Luther prepared himself that he might not have much of a reaction. He tended to be logically-minded. He tended to work through difficult to process situations or tragedies by studying them methodically.

Luther was sparing with details and allowed the silence that followed.

Danny furrowed his brow, eyes wandering around the room as though working through a challenging mathematical equation. He started and stopped speaking a number of times, pausing each time with the same confused expression on his face.

"It's a lot to process."

"It's not that. It just doesn't make sense." He frowned. "God gives a purpose to any bad thing that happens and Essie being dead serves no purpose." There was an unfeeling way he said the word "dead;" Luther understood why some people were put off by Danny's tone at times.

"Danny, not everything has–"

"Purpose? *Yes*, it *does*. Sometimes it's hard to see, but it's *always* there, Luther." He fell silent.

Luther no longer wanted to continue this debate. "What did you have to show me, Danny?" he asked quietly.

Danny looked down at his phone with increasing introspection. "You received an encrypted message from an operative within Gowon's special guard."

"It came to me directly?"

"I thought it was unusual because you weren't the one to recruit him and from what *I* know, you've never even met." He frowned, uncertain of his assessment. "Being on the special guard assignment, the idea was that we'd use his placement for access to Gowon in the event we took a more *offensive* approach. Which doesn't seem to be in the nature of the council," Danny said, shaking his head.

"So he's been pretty much dormant then, as an operative?"

"It would have been too dangerous to try to leave. The special guard is essentially a one-way endeavor. People don't retire from their post with a pension."

"Nobody does," Luther said darkly. "Has he ever provided information of value before?"

"'Value' is subjective. He's provided intel, but it hasn't been utilized. This is the first time he's sent something like this though. All messages are encrypted, but this has extra protection. There's no accessing the message or the file without a password."

"I can't say I know anyone on the guard. Who recruited him?"

"Boulder."

Luther lifted his eyes. Boulder was the code name for Demetri Malick, Annette's personal guard. He'd been the intermediary to communicate with Luther. Seventeen years earlier, Demetri became involved in his efforts to save children from the government experiments, but at the time, he still had a wife and child to worry about. When Luther began the operation, accessing the lab's dark web auctions, he was limited to the babies that were rejected from the experiment. This number had decreased significantly once the researchers decided they could have some use for the organs of the rejected babies, particularly those who possessed the cellular structure at least in specific organs or in their bone marrow. At the very least, they could harvest stem cells for various medical applications.

Demetri's role began by simply adding findings into the child's case file that made them undesirable for any research interests of the lab, namely that their cellular structure had normalized to specialized functions or they had the markers for various abnormalities so they would be rejected and put up for auction. With Demetri's help, they saved 319 babies who would have otherwise been harvested for parts. At the time, he considered Demetri Malick his strongest ally, which is why he had asked him to be Annette's guard.

It would be reckless for Demetri to recruit spies and risk his cover.

"This is someone who worked with Boulder in the STRONG lab."

Luther frowned. "Why do you say that?"

"It's in his file, for one thing. But then I noticed the encrypted file name. On the surface, it looks like a random system generated file name, right? What made me think the numbers were actually a date was because if it *is*, that date was two weeks before my birthday." Danny raised his eyebrows. "That's why I kept trying to reach you. I thought this message *had* to be about Essie. Because if *that's* a date, that was the day–"

The day I met Essie, Luther said silently. He took a steadying breath. "What's his name? The operative."

"Call sign is Babel. Name is Marcus LaCroix."

4

anomaly

seventeen years earlier...

If someone had put the saline solution back in its proper storage cabinet, Luther wouldn't have had any reason to open the door. If he had never opened the door, made from reinforced steel with a wheel locking mechanism, much like you might find on a submarine, he would have never heard the blood-curdling screams. If he had never heard the screams, he would have never seen the pair of feet, barely the length of his thumb, protruding from what could best be described as medical shackles around her ankles. He would have never known a child, not even three, to have needed to be restrained so thoroughly.

In addition to the clamps around her ankles, there were metal restraints over her midsection just above her diaper and another set of clamps just above her elbows.

A blindfold was reinforced over her eyes and muddy-colored hair was impossibly tangled and matted around her head. Her starfish hands were clenched tightly into fists. Her body was rigid, braced in pain.

A timer on the wall shelf indicated a duration of 17 hours, 31 minutes.

Her throat gargled and the tautness of her jaw told him she was grinding down on her small teeth.

It was apparent the diaper had not been changed in quite some time, brownish green liquid seeping through the elastic leg bands. He would believe her last change corresponded closely with the timer duration.

The vitals monitor flashed, silently alarmed that the young subject's last blood pressure reading was 170/119 and her pulse was 140, body temperature 105.4.

It was just as he considered that he should consider that she needed medical intervention that the readings began to fall. Her body settled suddenly, her legs long and loose, her palms wide and open, and her vitals eased to normal ranges over a matter of sixty seconds. The timer stopped and, in the silence, he could hear her concentrated breathing.

Suspecting at any moment someone would be returning, Luther stepped back through the reinforced steel door and sat down at his workstation. He stared at the oval orb before him and the shape within.

The thirty-two-week-old preborn child, a boy, struggled to sleep, his face tense. The use of sound generation of a heartbeat had failed to have the intended impact of simulating a natural womb for this child, as it had in others. He had all the indicators for being under severe stress.

Until tonight, Luther had convinced himself the study was something benign. Yes, the children were born from artificial wombs, but there was a good reason for their usage. Childbirth was a high risk for both the baby and the mother. Artificial wombs would offer convenience to couples, equal reproductive rights, and allow closer monitoring and better detection of any abnormalities. Babies born from artificial wombs would be categorically healthier.

He glanced around the warehouse-sized room full of glowing orbs. He thought of the toddler strapped to a metal table just on the other side of the wall and marveled at his own naivety.

Luther recalled making the case to his mother when he first learned of the course offering. She had closed her eyes and reached for her cross pendant, running it between her fingers. "Something changed for me the first time I felt you kick, Luther. I still felt like a child myself when I got pregnant, but I felt that kick--" She paused to gaze at him. "I told you: 'I don't know how, but I'm going to make a good life for us. I will always protect you.' I told you I loved you more than anything or anyone and it was the truth. We had so much quality time together those months I was pregnant."

"People adopt, momma. They love their kids, too."

"What does that do to the baby? Being grown in a lab?"

His mother's words echoed in his head as he watched PI-07-13-X3 curl his head over his torso, hands at his ears as though defending against a loud noise. Babies in the artificial wombs did not face the uneven and often unhealthy nutrition of a biological pregnancy, so they were all quite lean. This boy was no exception, his narrow arms punching at the spongy walls of the translucent womb from his tightly curled position.

Luther turned off his task light, then after checking the lab for any other technicians, he began to sing a nursery rhyme in a soft, low voice, a childhood favorite. It took persistence with the chorus, but the child relaxed, the monitors showing his heart rate slowing a bit. He found himself studying the gentle slope of his nose, how he crossed his tiny feet when he slept.

The course work was advertised in the medical school curriculum as being focused on embryonic development. For seven months, he had worked in the first-trimester lab. There he had appreciated the regimented dispensing of what the research leads referred to as 'immunity boosters,' the balanced nutrition, and the more promising start it afforded babies. He hadn't considered what happened to them when they reached the next developmental stage.

It was just two days ago that he was reassigned due to a staff shortage in the advanced groups.

The hallway door flew open, bringing in a gust of humidity and nicotine. Nita was putting in her earbuds, gnawing on a wad of gum as she returned from her meal break. "You alright, new guy?" She asked, raising a thickly penciled eyebrow. She had struck him as a woman of harsh extremes, given her affinity for sharp edges in her appearance. Her makeup was heavily applied, lips outlined with triangular tips and painted a dark purple. Her hair was bleached white, the roots left a midnight black. Her exposed shoulders jutted out from beneath her tank top, her shoulder blades looked downright lethal.

She narrowed her eyes, set beneath fuzzy tarantula lashes. "Did the bulb go out? How can you see over here?" She switched on the fluorescent light and the baby stirred, flipped away from the bright light. "Ugh, they get so creepy when they're older."

Luther looked from Nita to the baby, recognizing for the first time, the broad, sort of goofy smile he wore when he slept.

"What were you doing?" she asked distrustfully.

"I was following the protocol. I had taken a sample--" He motioned to the petri dish and vial filled with the baby's blood on the workstation.

"Oh, that one's just for parts now. We're not doing any more samples or including the data. You don't know the codes on the specimen sheet?"

"I guess I don't."

"Any specimen identified as an anomaly is excluded from the Proto-Immune Experiment. One lab's trash is another lab's treasure though."

"Meaning what exactly?"

"*Meaning*, a specimen with undesirable traits is useless to us, but another lab facility could use it for parts or whatever."

He looked closer at the baby, at his rounded features, his crossed feet. "Anomaly?"

"Did you not notice the flattened nasal bridge, the epicanthal folds, the stubby body?"

Luther took in the features as she pointed them out. "I'm sorry, I wasn't going into Obstetrics or Pediatrics. I didn't notice that anything looked off."

"Down Syndrome."

"Oh," he replied flatly, still not convinced.

"Yeah, probably a donation from an in vitro couple. They usually have spares after they're done having kids. There's another one a few pods down with Spina Bifida that'll go to one of the Franken-labs." She walked past him to the same door where he'd just emerged, casually climbed through, clicking her gum between her teeth as she returned. She placed the bottle next to his computer without comment. "How many more do you have to do?"

"Four more."

"That should be enough saline then. I'll have Facilities restock supplies next shift."

"Oh, is that storage back there? No one showed me."

"Not really. They're wrapping up the previous phase of the genome building experiment. There's just one specimen left."

"How many did they start with?"

She pulled out an earbud, resolving that she would be required to interact with another human for a bit longer. She attempted to mask her annoyance as she swept greasy hair from her eyes. "Uh--two dozen at least. God, that was a racket back there for a while. It's a good thing these are noise canceling."

He could hear the little girl's shrieks echo in his ears. Since her blood pressure had stabilized, she had been silent. "What are they testing on? Dogs?"

Nita glanced back toward the door then narrowed her eyes at the translucent orb in front of them, the baby within. "You're working on one. Well, not *that* one, but--" She motioned to the row of identical orbs. "We have a batch in the next lab nearly ready to start the experiment. At this point, they're just testing the limits of that one."

"Testing the limits?"

"Most subjects admitted into the experiment didn't make it past the first few tests. They're just throwing everything they have at it now to end the trial."

"By end, do you mean—?"

"If they're going to move forward with the project, *that* won't be the poster child, no pun intended." For a moment, he saw her tough facade shatter as her eyes floated over to the row of artificial wombs, the children within.

"Why?"

"Not *diverse* enough," she said distantly. Her eyes rested on one specific orb, her breaths thickening. She dropped her gaze and cleared her throat. They stood in silence for a few moments, Nita distracting herself with readings on the baby Luther had been working with, showing more interest than if she believed he was worthless. "It'd be bad PR. It's why for future batches, they're requiring racial or ethnic mix so we don't waste time."

He pictured the child's pale legs and feet tinged with a sickly gray hue, how as she recovered and the blood flooded back into her toes, they turned a rosy pink.

"It's still pretty amazing what they accomplished." Her drawn-on eyebrows did not match the enthusiasm her words were attempting to convey.

The outer door opened, and a pair of young men appeared. One was scrawny with dark haphazard hair and seemed to struggle with growing a beard. He sipped a whipped cream topped coffee beverage. The other appeared a bit oversized for the doorframe and had a slower pace to him.

"'Nita, you're looking lovely," the scrawny one said.

Her face hardened in an instant. "Screw you, Marcus."

"What'd I say?"

She looked across Marcus to the other man. "I borrowed some saline. We were out."

"No problem. We have more than enough." He pointed toward the door she'd left ajar. "Noisy?"

"I just got here. It's been quiet though. New guy?"

"Luther." He corrected, but no one seemed to care. "Haven't heard anything."

"*Good*, maybe it finally died." Marcus laughed as though he had made a joke.

"Kind of not the point of the experiment, dipshit." The taller man shook his head and extended his hand. "I'm Demetri."

"The point was to build immunity or something?" Luther asked, accepting the handshake.

"Yeah," Marcus snickered. "More like making a mutant species."

"This is a big breakthrough though? What Nita has told me?" Luther offered. "Genome building or something?"

35

"Yeah, we can't announce the greatest advancement in genome research with *that* as our subject." Marcus glared toward the back room.

"The government building a super-race of white people? Yeah, that doesn't scream Nazi," Nita chimed in. "Although, wrong hair and eye color I guess." The simple acknowledgment that the child had eyes and hair had seemed to have given her pause, her hand suspended over the Petri dish.

"Doing all this testing on a colonizer *is* slightly satisfying."

"How is she a colonizer, Bro?" Demetri asked.

Nita sprang into action, dropping the dish into the trash.

"*It* had ancestors that enslaved my people and stole this very land we're standing on from the Indigenous."

"She has only ever seen the inside of this lab. Also, you've seen that she's female. Why must you call her 'it?'"

"They're all just numbers to me."

"So, you're square then? Now that you've gotten to torture her since birth?" Nita's voice was tight and angry, but Luther doubted it was entirely related to his aggression toward the young test subject.

Marcus laughed. "No, it's screwing with me because it won't die."

She shook her head, putting a palm toward Marcus and addressing Demetri. "What was this round?" Nita asked, checking her phone.

"Pancuronium bromide and potassium chloride," Demetri said, raising his eyebrows.

"That's what they use for lethal injections," Marcus explained proudly.

"They use a sedative, too, typically," Nita added.

"To make lethal injections seem more humane. They don't do shit once the real drugs kick in."

"Let me guess, you had an ancestor who was a serial killer who got the death penalty and you're still upset?" Demetri muttered.

Marcus shrugged. "I *may* have."

"She recovered from a lethal dose of cyanide in 18 hours," Demetri said, checking his watch. "If she's recovered already? That'd be something. Especially since Lisbon has actually been giving her immunosuppressants."

"I thought the idea was to boost immunity?"

"It *was*," Demetri said flatly.

"I don't know where you'd go from a lethal injection," Nita remarked.

"Maybe pour acid on it. See if it melts."

Luther could not tell if Marcus was serious, but by the way Demetri turned and walked away, he believed he might be.

Nita rolled her eyes as she spit out her gum and pushed it into the bottom of the worktable. "You're like little boys burning ants under a magnifying glass."

"At first it was interesting to test how much it could take, but if nothing will kill it, we'll have to just toss it in with the others. Let nature run its course," Marcus sighed.

"By nature, he means big man-made flames," Demetri clarified, moving toward the back lab.

"Same thing."

"It's really not." There was an exaggerated groan from the door.

"Is it dead?"

"Nope and it's your turn to change her, Marcus."

"Screw that. Bring on the flames."

"Dr. Lisbon said to keep her alive. For you it won't be bad; no worse than your apartment."

"Well, I'm not doing it. I'll work on the B group today. I nominate New Guy."

"You nominate New Guy for what?" Luther asked.

"Cleaner of literal shit. Congrats."

Nita shrugged in response to meeting Luther's eye. "Better you than me."

*   *   *

Luther closed the heavy metal door behind himself at Nita's request, the pungency of feces finally reaching her nasal cavities. She had given him specific instructions: Unlock subject from the table, take subject to the recreation room, change diaper, lock subject in the recreation room. He doubted silently if any room here would meet even low expectations for something called a 'recreation room.'

He found his hands shaking as he unlocked the clamps, trying not to accidentally pinch her skin or apply pressure on her small body. She had flinched when his skin first made contact, so he started to speak lightly under his breath, narrating his actions, so she was aware of his location and intentions.

"I'm just going to get these restraints off you--those don't look very comfortable."

She breathed steadily. With the blindfold over her eyes, it was difficult to tell if she was awake.

"That's better. Now we're just going to get you cleaned up, little one." He decided using the word "we" might intimidate her, so he back-pedaled. "My name is Luther. I'm going to help you." He froze as he heard the words out loud. In the glimmer of time the words ran through his mind, he had thought he meant he would help her feel better in the present moment, but as he finished releasing her from the cold metal table and she turned a listening ear toward him, he realized he meant the words in a far more daunting way.

But how could he possibly help her? They said she already had a death sentence. Obviously, this work was secretive. He couldn't just walk out the door with her--and what was he to do? Raise this pale-skinned child as his own? He stared at his auburn fingers resting against her wrist. Even with her hands coated in grime, there was a stark contrast. If nothing else, it would be highly suspicious that a young black man like himself, in the middle of medical school, would suddenly be the sole caregiver of a toddler who clearly did not share his DNA.

Even so, he watched his fingertips trace the imprint the steel restraints had left upon her arms. It was surprising that there weren't deep cuts where the edge of the steel had pressed. His eyes fell upon the data matrix tattoo on her forearm. He took a breath and heard himself say: "I will help you escape this place, little one."

38

There wasn't a detectable shift in her body, but he sensed when her attention sharpened. As he lifted her small body off the table, he felt her arm tighten around his shoulder.

The recreation room was the first door on the right. He had low expectations for its appearance and amenities, and it still managed to fall far short. The walls were lined with padding except for a large copper-tinted airplane-style window. It failed to provide much natural light. There were a few gym mats and ramps set up on the floor, and three deflated beach balls scattered around the room.

In the far corner of the room, there was a large muddy stain. He didn't want to venture a guess at what may have caused it.

"Okay, the bathroom's in here," he narrated. "I wonder what toiletries they've left for us, a fine establishment such as this."

To his surprise, there was store-brand baby shampoo/wash on the metal counter. The bathroom was tinted yellow by the lights and smelled strongly of cleaning products. He located the storage for what turned out to be three scratchy hand towels. He braced her over his hip, noticing that the greenish-brown ooze from her diaper was starting to slip down her leg.

"Hold on tight. I'll lay a towel down." She squeezed her arms around his shoulders, and he felt overwhelming grief as her face dug into his neck.

The thin loop towel was a pitiful barrier over the unforgiving tile floor. "I'm sorry. This isn't going to be very soft." He glanced up toward the recreation room, considering moving her to one of the pads.

"I can use potty," her small voice whispered.

Luther arched his neck to look at her face. She had pushed the blindfold up to rest on her forehead. Shadowed by the mask, her eyes looked to be a pale shade of hazel. The cheek facing him had a hint of a dimple.

He felt compelled to compliment her, tell her what a pretty girl she was, how well she spoke, but all of this was overshadowed by the fact that all that stood between her and death was him.

He found his chest tightening, his airway constricting, and he determined any focused attention on her angelic features would distract him from what he needed to be doing.

"Can you stand?"

She released a light "uh-hmm" and slid from his arms.

"I'm going to take off this diaper, but I'm going to need to clean your skin before you sit down, okay?"

"OK."

He retracted to the sink and was thankful the water turned warm quickly. He pumped out some baby wash and lathered the rough towel, making a mental note to scrub gently. "Here we go," he said, squinting his eyes as though the action somehow offered her more privacy. As he wiped the sludgy excretions from her skin, he found his eyes welling with tears. Part was certainly due to the odor, but he found his heart aching hopelessly, wondering how he would possibly be able to save her.

"Alright, little one. Go ahead and have a seat."

She did as instructed and he stepped to the other side of the heavy bathroom door.

"*New Guy*," Marcus called in a sing-song voice from the hallway.

Luther stepped out of the bathroom to find Marcus hanging drunkenly by the doorframe.

"Don't bother cleaning it up."

"Why?"

"Lisbon just stopped by." Marcus made a kaboom noise followed by the fluttering of his fingers. "That's supposed to be flames," he said with a laugh. "Come on, man. I get to do the honors."

"Give me a few minutes."

"*Okay*, but there's no point. Dead colonizer walking." He peered over Luther's shoulder, pressing into the balls of his feet, looking for the girl with seditious interest.

Luther felt like the air had been vacuumed from his lungs. He turned slowly toward the bathroom, stepping in slow motion inside once he heard the toilet flush.

Her lack of muscle mass made her look even younger than she was. She wore a dirty t-shirt that hung off her like a dress and she stood in front of the sink, stretching to reach the faucet. Her hair, coated in grime and sweat, reached the bottom hem even with its impossible tangles. In the vanity light, there were glimmers of other shades beside the mousy brown. Her nose was small and rounded, her full pink lips pulled up naturally at the corners. After successfully rinsing her fingertips, she turned to face him. Her eyes met his gaze with a raw hope that seemed to cut right through him. She took a deep breath. "I going with you?"

In his heart, he couldn't bear the thought of handing her over to him, but when Marcus returned to claim her, a heavy voice in the back of his mind softly instructed: *Let him take her.*

With no intention to do so, Luther stepped aside, opening the path to the bathroom.

The image of Marcus slinging two-year-old Essie over his shoulder like a sack of rice was one that had haunted him every day since. Luther had promised to protect her, to save her, and he had put up no defense. Meanwhile, Essie *had* put up a fight. She had twisted and writhed, screamed at Marcus as he carried her away, as though she knew what awaited her, which, if he'd talked about it in front of her before, she probably did.

Luther didn't have to witness what came next to know it was horrific. He had made his way to his locker and retrieved his coat, resolving to never return to the lab. He would have to try for the rest of his days to forget what he had witnessed.

Then the voice returned. *Go to her.*

Luther had been confused but stood and rushed to the door. He found his way to the furnace room without ever being shown the way. The door flew open just before he arrived and Marcus rushed out, seemingly unable to catch his breath. He burst through the stairwell door without noticing Luther was there.

Luther made his way inside, the room particularly sweltering since the furnace hatch had been left open. The room was empty aside from a banker's box far too small to fit even a petite child.

41

Open it.

Luther feared what he might find inside the box, but his heart inflated upon seeing her vivid, silver eyes looking up at him. Marcus had been unapologetic in his delight of seeing this girl burned alive just minutes earlier, as she represented all he hated. Luther couldn't imagine what had sent Marcus running from the room. The only remaining step was to toss the box into the flames.

*   *   *

"Luther?" Danny repeated.

There were tears welling in Luther's eyes. His breaths had quickened. He could hear Marcus's sadistic voice echoing in his head, delighting in Essie's suffering.

If Marcus was working for their side, *if* Demetri truly believed Marcus had a change of heart, of mind, *if* he was a force of good, there would only be one reason Marcus would reach out to him directly. There would be only one reason he'd use that date as a code.

"'New Guy'. Try all variations. With a space, without a space, capitalized–"

"Got it."

A gray circle swirled on the screen, then a progress bar. Suddenly a video began to play, heavy metal music blaring, lights flashing.

Danny muted the sound. "What the *hell*?"

The camera was looking into a concrete cell, likely through a two-way mirror based upon the tinting, the subtle reflection. A figure passed through the room briskly, then immediately crossed through again going in the opposite direction. The timing of this seemed to indicate the space was not very large, if they were indeed walking from one wall to the other.

The camera was angled toward the floor and slightly too zoomed to allow them to make out any features except that the figure appeared to be wearing a medical gown. They must have had their arms crossed in front of them since only the fold of the fabric at the shoulder was visible. They paced four times, back and forth, back and forth, back and forth, back and forth, then disappeared from the camera frame for several moments.

The shadows on the floor indicated movement along the right wall. There didn't appear to be any natural lighting in the room, so the shadow was distorted, generated from the overhead tube lighting, which continued to flash intermittently.

The figure stepped back into view and moved toward the wall opposite the camera. With the additional spacing from the camera, they could see a bit more of her upper torso, her shoulders, her wild, tangled hair.

With her chin still lowered and arms squeezed over her chest, she turned to face the two-way mirror. She slid her back along the wall and sat on the floor, knees drawn up to her chest.

She released her arms at her sides and took a steadying breath, her hair creating a thick veil over her face.

Luther narrowed his eyes. *Look up, look up, look up,* he encouraged silently.

She lifted her left hand, forcing a section of hair from her eyes, tucking it behind her ear. It was enough of a motion to show part of the intricate cross silhouette tattoo on her forearm.

She wrapped her arms around her legs, leaned forward, and rested her chin against her knees.

When she looked up, revealing the silver shimmer of her eyes, Luther felt his heart inflate in his chest.

Then he noticed the overt tremor in her hands, the quiver of her lower lip, the tormented gaze in her eyes.

He thought of Essie at the tender age of two, with her round, hopeful eyes, her full pink lips that pulled up naturally at the corners despite all she'd gone through. He remembered how overwhelmed he felt looking into her face, wondering how he could possibly keep his promise to help her, to get her out of the hell that surrounded her. He felt helpless when she had been standing right before him.

Now, she was sitting in a concrete cell thousands of miles away. If her mouth pulled upward at all, it was due to pain or pressure in her ear drums from the volume of the music.

He   could   see   no   hope   in   her   eyes.

5

paul

one month earlier...

The Worship Band had just finished the last song before the sermon. An associate pastor was talking about a fall festival the church was putting on with other churches in the area as an outreach to those living in the Northern Ark. The specific focus was on those who were living within the Ark, but not by choice; they'd simply become residents by living within the territory when borders were constructed. The majority of the Northern Ark, aside from some urban areas on the eastern side, had been less densely populated and very few people had actually chosen to leave. Most had substantial homesteads and were fairly self-sustaining, so they chose to stay, but the churches felt it was important to continue to build the sense of community in the area. Matteo had already convinced Luther to sign on for the baseball tournament they'd be having.

Anticipating there'd be more instances in the other two Arks of people wanting to relocate back to the States, Luther had ensured there were processes in place to allow this. There had certainly been cases of Gowon loyalists being relocated in the other two Arks, some turning their situation into primetime interviews, inventing stories of deplorable conditions and chaos, meant to villainize the Arks, in addition to making them seem weak. It was a tightrope act the Gowon Administration was performing and based upon recent developments–a surge of people attempting to immigrate *to* the Arks, an increase in looting of government facilities, and general civil unrest–an act they weren't performing very well.

Matteo placed his guitar on its stand and fixed his microphone wire around his ear as Isaac finished talking about other activities going on, including an end-of-summer bash for the youth. He then presented Matteo, who had his brow deeply creased, shielding his eyes with his hand, as though blocking the sun. He gave a wave toward the choir loft. "I guess we're now offering balcony seating," he said with a lift of his brow. "God loves a full house, y'all." He smiled as there was some applause and hoots from the congregation. He chuckled, twisting his expression. "I can't pull off a 'y'all,' can I?" He winced. "I am going to *hear* about that from my daughter. She's back working with the littles today–but later, I'm sure she'll just shake her head–" He demonstrated her slow, disapproving head shake. "--and say 'but-a-Daddy-you-are-Italian-you-a-enunciate-each-a-syllable-and-a-use-punctuated-hand-a-gestures." He frowned. "I don't sound like that, do I?"

There were some low murmurs, then Luke burst out with: "It's-a-me-Pastor-Natale."

Matteo grinned, rubbing his chin thoughtfully. "Alright, so a couple weeks ago, I talked about Jonah. Let's see, I described him as *being*–

"The worst," Thomas muttered.

"Yep. Jonah's the *worst*. In that sermon, I talked a little about how God often uses unexpected people to carry out His plans. Think back on Jonah. God selected him to convey a very critical message to Ninevah, this city of lost souls who were sinning left and right, committing evil acts, etcetera. He needed to compel them to repent and be saved. Now, God doesn't have, like an HR council making these decisions, but imagine if He did. God says: 'Ninevah needs to repent or it'll be lost forever.' You, on the council, are like: 'Yes, so it has to be the *right* prophet to convey the message.' God says: 'I agree, and I know exactly who it should be.' You say: 'Great, who?' God says: 'Jonah. *He's* the man for the job.' And you're like–" He winced, squinting one eye. "'*Is he* though?' If God had a council He had to report to, which is ridiculous, but if He did, God would have found Himself stuck in red tape, they'd be calling for a vote of no confidence, saying He'd lost His dadgum mind.

"Aren't we glad God doesn't have to report to a council or a board? Aren't we grateful that God acts from His own wisdom? He *knows* us. He knows what we're capable of. 'I can do all things through Christ who strengthens me.' Right? Still, we do that ourselves, don't we? We question what God asks of us. We love God, we want to serve God, we raise our hands in worship, we love the fact that through His Son, we have the gift of eternal life—because that's *just* awesome, but God puts a path before us and says this is the path you need to take and we stop and go: '*Is it* though?'

"I got some complaints about my Jonah sermon–Cliffhangers? Not very popular. And for that, I apologize, but the truth is, we don't know what became of Jonah, if he changed his ways, or if he continued to sulk on the mountain for the rest of his life.

"Today, I'm going to tell you about Paul. Jonah was the worst prophet; Paul was the worst *sinner*. Also? Paul's story doesn't end on a cliffhanger, so put your mind at ease.

"So, who is this Paul? Well, he's thought to have contributed nearly one-quarter of the text of the New Testament. Yes, someone considered to be the greatest sinner–greatest being bad in this scenario–went on to write one-fourth of the New Testament.

"Was he really that bad to begin with though? *Yes.* Yes, he was. Before his conversion, Paul was known as Saul of Tarsus. He was a man of zeal, but his zeal was misguided. He *fervently* persecuted the early Christians, *believing* that he was actually doing God's work. He was responsible for the suffering and death of many believers. Saul's heart was filled with hatred and his actions were driven by ignorance." He paced to the right, pausing to smile at a newborn being snuggled a few pews back. He blinked a few times, frowning, looking away. "Saul killed Christians, thinking he was doing God's work." He paced to the opposite side.

"But then, on the road to Damascus, everything changed. In a blinding moment of revelation, Jesus Christ appeared to Saul and spoke to him. This encounter not only blinded his physical eyes but opened the eyes of his heart. In that instant, Saul realized the error of his ways, the depth of his sinfulness, and the magnitude of God's love and forgiveness. 'I once was *blind*, but now I—*see.*'

"Saul's conversion was a profound turning point. He was struck down by grace and emerged from that experience a changed man. He became Paul, a fierce advocate for Christ, a tireless missionary, and a prolific writer of epistles that now form a significant part of the New Testament. Paul's life became a living testimony to the transformative power of God's love.

"Paul himself acknowledged his past as the greatest sinner, but he also celebrated God's mercy that lifted him from the depths of darkness to the heights of divine purpose. In his letter to Timothy, Paul writes, 'The saying is trustworthy and deserving of full acceptance, that Christ Jesus came into the world to save sinners, of whom I am the foremost'. This admission of his former sins is not a declaration of defeat, but a proclamation of victory through Christ.

"Paul's story teaches us several invaluable lessons:

"Number 1: No one is beyond redemption: Paul's transformation serves as a reminder that no matter how far we've strayed or anyone else has strayed or how deep we've fallen into sin, God's grace is sufficient to lift us up."

Matteo raised up two fingers. "Number 2: God's grace is boundless: Paul's life underscores the immeasurable depth of God's love and the extent to which He is willing to go to bring us back into His embrace. Did God *need* to redeem Paul, previously known as Saul, who murdered Christians?" He shook his head. "Absolutely not. This probably would have been one of the instances where even good Christians would be calling for Paul's head, quite literally." He frowned. I think I've lost a few people, who might be thinking I mean that Christians should accept *any* evil that's done against us. No. Absolutely not. *But*, if God believes someone who has done wrong against me can be saved, who am I to say

God is wrong?" He glanced around at the congregation. "Honestly, it might be a situation where God says someone can be redeemed and I think: '*Can he* though?'" He rolled his shoulders. "I need to stop doing that with my neck, I'm going to pull something."

A couple of congregation members laughed appreciatively.

"Yeah, you get it. I used to be able to do all sorts of crazy stuff, now I tweak my neck and my friend asks what'd you do and I have to say: 'I sipped my water too hard' or 'I stretched and yawned at the same time.'" He sipped gingerly from his cup.

"Okay, number three: Our past does not define us. I *repeat*: Our past does not define us. Just as Paul's past as a persecutor did not dictate his future as a servant of Christ, our mistakes and failures do not determine who we can become in Christ. Some of us are making mistakes, failing *right now* as believers, and that's okay. It just means you need to turn your heart more fully to Jesus, let Him guide you.

"Number four: We are instruments of God's grace: Like Paul, we too can become vessels of God's grace, spreading the message of redemption and hope to a world in need. If you've never experienced something for yourself, it can make it very difficult for you to be able to explain it well, right? Or relate to other people who have gone through it? No one wants to experience loss, but it gives you a better understanding, an empathy for others when they're experiencing loss because you've been there. So, you can imagine a person is a much more powerful voice for God if they can say, I've been a sinner, I've *seen some stuff*, I've done some stuff, and following God is *so much better*. I've talked about churches I attended growing up where the pastor was up in the pulpit, arms raised in the air, perfectly crisp white robes condemning the congregation as sinners. I've said it before, I'll say it again: I'm a sinner. I'm not close to perfect. I've seen stuff. I've done stuff. I am no more worthy than anyone else here."

He allowed the silence to stretch.

"It got real, real quiet," he said, giving a friendly smile. He pointed vaguely toward the right side of the congregation. "Some of you are, turning to your neighbors going: 'what do you think he did?'" He cleared his throat. "The idea is not to cross some threshold that suddenly makes us worthy. As people, life has its ebbs and flows. You don't reach a point where you're immune to sin, but that's the beauty of the new covenant, of the mercy of Jesus: we don't *have to be.* He loves us as we are. He doesn't want to leave us as we are though. He wants to use us to do His work. Alright, back to the list. What are we on–five?"

He raised a hand in the air. "Number five: Transformation is possible. That's what we were just talking about. Paul's journey from sinner to saint reminds us that transformation is possible through a genuine encounter with Christ. It might not be something so dramatic as encountering Jesus and having a literally blinding moment, but *maybe* it is. I've talked to people who have had this sort of epiphanic moment. It can be sudden, or it could be more subtle where the Holy Spirit is guiding you in a particular direction, down a particular path. But whatever the experience is for you? Don't doubt the wisdom of God. Try to resist the urge to think that you could possibly know better. It might not make sense. You might hear God, through the Holy Spirit, telling you to do something and you might think: 'That's just a *bad* idea.'" He chuckled. "My daughter likes to say my childhood was a simpler time– and she's probably right. I remember seeing a t-shirt back in the day that said: 'That's a *terrible* idea. What time?' Maybe try to have that attitude when God challenges you to do something that you just don't want to do. If you're going to trust anyone, let it be God."

*   *   *

Danny patted Luther on the arm. "If you have what you need from him, I need to walk him through getting the cameras and satellite connection set up. It'll take some time."

Luther nodded, inputting a final message into the secured chat with Marcus LaCroix. He pushed his chair back from the table, an uneasiness churning in his stomach. He stood, aiming himself for the door, suddenly desperate for fresh air.

"Hey, Luther?"

He eased to a stop. "Yeah, Danny?" he answered quietly, running his palm over his head.

"*This* makes sense."

He swallowed hard. "What does?"

Danny pointed toward the monitor. "He's looking for redemption for what he did all those years ago and now he's being given that opportunity."

Luther peered over his shoulder, nodding slowly.

Danny typed out a message with impressive speed. "And *you* need the motivation of Essie being alive to do what *you're* meant to do."

He took a steadying breath. "And what am I meant to do, Danny?"

Danny was distracted by the message he'd received and was digging through his desk drawer for one of his many notebooks. Once he'd found the one he was looking for, he tested his pen's ink on a scrap post-it before scribbling himself a note on a fresh page. Then and only then did he look up. "You're meant to lead."

Luther considered this, his heart tensed. It was just as he was about to question Danny's assessment that he heard the same voice he'd heard all those years ago, that told him to let Marcus take Essie, then directed him to find her only after allowing the time for Marcus to break her tiny body. Now it simply said one resounding word: *Yes.*

He took a deep breath. "Call me if you need anything."

Danny nodded.

"Did you have dinner? I can get you something."

Danny reached down and opened the door on the mini fridge under his desk. "I have some snack pack things in here–cheese, crackers, cashews, tuna packets–lots of high protein, high fat, 'brain food' in case I'm caught up working long hours."

"That's smart."

"Of course it is. Essie stocked it for me." He focused his eyes on the monitor and swallowed hard. He typed another message, then slumped his shoulders, dropping his hands to his lap. "I'm not very good at friendships, Luther." He lifted his eyebrows, glancing toward his screen. "But Essie's my friend."

Luther nodded slowly.

Danny shook his head, blinked quickly and sat up straighter. "Go get some sleep. I have work to do."

Luther took long, focused breaths as he walked out to the parking lot. Gabe had returned his SUV at some point during the day, apparently having figured out something with other available vehicles.

A few weeks earlier, when Luther had been baptized for the second time in his life, Matteo had gifted him a large cross decal that resembled the one from his own pickup truck all those years ago at the diner, the decal that Luther took as a sign from God that Matteo was who he should entrust with Essie.

It had been an inside joke since Luther tended to re-tell the story so many times, perplexed by receiving such a sign from God.

Seeing the cross decal on the back of his own vehicle had entirely different meaning now:

He'd entrusted Matteo with Essie, but Matteo was gone now.

The responsibility fell to him again.

Luther reached for the side of the 4Runner as the weight of the realization struck him in the chest. He leaned against the door, taking a steadying breath. He closed his eyes and began to pray.

6

day twelve

Miles lifted his eyes to the monitor as he saw the first movement from Essie in 18 minutes: a shift of her hand. It had been contorted in an unnatural position since she had been dropped on the concrete floor of her cell. The movement had been small, just a rotation of her wrist, but it was enough to catch his attention.

Miles was both relieved to see movement from her and terrified of what they would inflict upon her next.

The last time Miles saw Essie at the northern Ark, they'd gone out for breakfast after meeting up at the gym.

The gym had an unassuming storefront, but inside was a vast expanse of state-of-the-art training equipment, full boxing arena, ninja warrior course, and a lap and diving pool. Josh had told him about the mixed martial arts "club" Essie was a part of, but it seemed she had taken up additional fitness endeavors. From his comfort zone on the treadmill, he had watched her start with a max-incline warmup run, followed by a vigorous 45-minutes on the rower. She'd then taken a few turns through the ninja course, including something called a "warp wall," done a few rounds in the MMA ring before finishing up with some weight training.

They were there for nearly two hours, he had blisters on his heels, and he had sworn off the treadmill, while the grueling workout had seemed to energize her.

Afterwards, they sat out on the patio of a brunch restaurant with their glutinous breakfast plates and Miles had teased her, but with genuine concern, that those monsters (her MMA opponents) were going to mess up her pretty face. He'd reached out and touched the swollen, bruised skin on her cheekbone, where she'd taken a kick to the face during her last fight.

"Aww, *Joely*," she had said dotingly, "you said I'm *pretty*."

He grinned. After initially being resistant to hearing his first name, having been named after his dad, he had actually grown fond of her calling him by the name, as she only used it when she was being exceptionally affectionate with him.

"Oh, stop. You're a friggin' knockout and you know it."

"Pun intended?" she asked, taking a sip of orange juice.

He frowned.

She sat across from him wearing a baggy t-shirt over a pair of jogger sweatpants. He'd been in a bit of shock when he first saw her at the gym, as she'd been wearing a tight crop top and baggy tropical print shorts that had maybe a 4-inch inseam, lined with bicycle shorts beneath. The outfit emphasized the curved chisel of her muscles and he'd honestly been startled by the strength in her legs, arms and abdominals—even in her feet.

"I know you're the baddest fighter in there—"

"Just to clarify, does 'baddest' mean *worst* in this context?"

"No," he said shortly, lifting his brow. "Those guys who look like they bench press tractors? You don't fight *them*, do you?"

"Of course not. They help with skill-building though, pointing out where we leave ourselves open."

He nodded. "'Baddest' means best–and I mean it. You're amazing. No one has your reflexes or speed."

She puffed out her lower lip, her most overt way of accepting a compliment.

"I know there's some sort of therapeutic outlet, stress relieving element in it for you–"

"*But?*"

Something about her baggy shirt, her hair tied haphazardly on top of her head, a plate of indulgent breakfast foods before her reminded him of one of his earliest memories: sitting with his sister as they each shoveled brightly colored cereal into their mouths at the kitchen table.

"*But* I just don't want to see you get hurt. You are literally my favorite person in the world."

Essie had grinned tightly at him, her cheeks puffed out with food.

There had been a week's time between when Essie was kidnapped and when they'd secured the video feed. The day they acquired the feed, both he and Luther had an outward gasp in response to her appearance, which had deteriorated quickly in that time, even since the video was taken by the contact inside, the one who alerted Luther that she was alive.

She'd lost a visible amount of weight and muscle tone. Her skin was pale and most of it appeared discolored and bruised.

Her hair was dirty and knotted and hung limply against her cheeks. A trickle of blood had dried, just visible beneath her nostril.

She had been seated in a solid metal chair bolted to the concrete floor in the medical chamber. A metal clamp was secured around her midsection. The blood stains on the medical gown near the clamp indicated she had been there for some time and/or had put up a significant struggle. Luther had speculated after that there might be blades in the clamp that were digging into her skin and causing her to bleed, noticing small tears in the fabric later.

Her arms were not restrained. Based upon the proximity of the table before her, it seemed they intended for her to place her arms upon it, but she kept her hands lying slack in her lap.

The day was spent with Esther being offered "positive reinforcement" in exchange for giving specific responses to prompts. These were seemingly ridiculous tasks; one involved her being shown an apple then being instructed to describe it as an orange, another involved memorizing and repeating phrases that made no logical sense, such as: "The dog flew under the ocean."

The positive reinforcement offered was simply reprieve from constant pain, a robotic AI voice providing instructions such as: "Complete the task correctly and the pain will stop for ten minutes. If you do not complete the task correctly, the pain will intensify for ten minutes."

The pain the voice spoke of was in the form of electrical pulses delivered through a band attached over her temples. Luther had muttered expletives when he saw it the first time, which Miles thought included some ill-feelings about "Communist China."

Essie had twisted in her seat in response to the pain, her frustration building for the restraint, for the device. She was fidgety and agitated, her upper body shivered spontaneously and one or both feet tapped nearly constantly, but she said nothing the entire day.

The full physical torture began the next day.

Her captors used tactics historically used in advanced interrogation, only she hadn't been asked to divulge any information. She had been waterboarded, electrocuted, burned with a flat iron, and in the most recent session, beaten ceaselessly until she'd lost consciousness. Each session began with at least an hour in the Sim, though they hadn't yet secured footage from the non-standard program sessions to be able to draw any conclusions as to the purpose. What they knew was that the non-standard sessions were more advanced. They used a person's thoughts and memories to create complex situations and scenes. They went far beyond a dream-like state; it was a full-sensory experience that aimed to override memories and manipulate thought processes.

If the insider was sharing details about the nature of these sessions with Luther, he hadn't passed along that information to Miles. All he knew was that it wasn't a standard program, as they had used in Mandatory, and the physiological monitoring was more extensive, as there were sensors fixed to her temples, her chest, and her wrists at all times.

Luther had shared limited information about the individual who had enabled their surveillance access, saying they had long sought redemption, having previously been a strong supporter of Gowon's "causes."

"They're still working for Gowon?"

"That's how we're able to have the feed, Miles. He turned to our side a long time ago."

"But how do you know he's loyal to us? To her?"

Luther had said nothing in response.

"Did he kill people for Gowon?"

"Yes."

"Under the Sim?"

"No," Luther said solidly, fixing his eyes upon him.

Miles hesitated to ask additional questions about the insider. "So if you have this person on the inside, you know where she's being held."

"Yes."

"But you won't tell me."

"There'd be no purpose in telling you."

Miles shook his head, gnawing on his lip. "This is what we did in MET, Luther. We got people out. Let's pull a team together, go in, and get her."

"The people you helped weren't being held in heavily guarded, high security facilities. I'm sorry to say it this way, but the people you rescued didn't mean anything to Gowon. *She* does. She is *very* important to him. I'm not questioning your skills in any way, but going in will take planning and coordination and resources we don't have right now."

Miles had sank a bit in his chair.

"I know this is tormenting to see her there, but we'll have *one* chance to get to her," Luther said, nodding thoughtfully, adding no additional explanation.

Staring at her on the monitor, Miles shook his head. "And there's no way we can tell Josh that she's alive?"

Luther released a sigh. "Josh is doing *what* right now?"

"I don't know, *mourning*? Holed up in his cabin?"

"He's quiet."

"He's probably suicidal right now, but yeah, *quiet*."

"Do you really think Josh would commit suicide?"

Miles considered this. "No. He'd never do that to his parents." He took a breath. When Gabe told Miles that Essie was dead, Miles had immediately gone to find Josh. He thought maybe Josh would have disappeared into the woods to avoid seeing people, but he knew he needed to, at least, try to find him. He and Josh had been friends for 15 years, but he realized as he made the drive that he wasn't going because he was checking on his friend. That was part of it, but his main motivation was because Essie would want him to. As he pulled into the scouts camp, he was surprised to see the orchard pickup parked in front of Josh's cabin, to then find Josh sitting beside the creek near the cabin, staring at the rushing water.

Josh said nothing when Miles arrived. He said nothing when Miles sat down on the ground beside him. Tears filled his eyes and occasionally streamed down his face, but for the three hours that Miles was there, Josh didn't say a word. He just sat and stared. So Miles did the same.

Luther furrowed his brow.

"He wouldn't," Miles affirmed again. "But I wouldn't put it past him to become a recluse alcoholic. Or maybe that's what I would do if I were in his shoes."

Luther nodded. "If he knew she was alive, what would he be doing?"

Miles swallowed hard. "*Not* being quiet."

In the five days since they'd acquired the video feed, Miles and Luther had switched off keeping watch over her, for no other purpose than to know what was going on. It was a small comfort to know that, in a way, she wasn't entirely alone, though it didn't do her a whole lot of good; she had no way of knowing they were watching her or that they were planning to rescue her at some point.

According to the person inside, Essie had been subjected to a sensory deprivation chamber for the first 48-hours after her arrival. The next 48-hours were solid heavy metal and flashing lights. The following day was spent entirely in a standard Sim program where she was forced to watch and listen to children, babies, and animals being tortured to death. The standard programs weren't as immersive as the non-standard programs;

they were essentially like being dropped into a 4D documentary without any influence on what happened, but the additional sensory outputs made the experience more intense, smells in particular. She'd been back in sensory deprivation, abandoned with the images, the sounds, the smells from the Sim program for the two days before they'd acquired the feed.

Essie's breathing deepened, apparent in the heavier rise and fall of her back. She blinked slowly.

The door inside her cell opened.

"Not wasting any effing time," Miles muttered, taking a deep breath.

She didn't attempt to look to see who was stepping inside.

Miles squinted, the polished appearance of the man out of place in the setting and among the guards and scrub-clad captors. "Oh, *Jesus*," he growled suddenly, pulling on a headset. He watched as Samuel Gowon himself stepped into the cell, peering down toward Essie's face with keen interest. This went on for long enough that Miles began to think the feed had frozen—until he saw Essie's continued slow, rhythmic blinking. She appeared to be staring in the direction of Gowon's shoes.

Gowon gave a very subtle gesture, then turned abruptly out of the room. Within seconds, guards had swept into the space, gathered Essie by the arms and dragged her down the corridor. Miles switched feeds to the main medical chamber, where they arrived a few moments later. There were two angles provided by cameras in that particular room. One was overhead, giving a bird's eye view; the other was positioned in one of the two-way mirror wall panels directly before the main testing environment, which housed a viewing gallery with views into both the medical chamber and her cell.

They dropped her into the metal chair, securing the contraption's abdominal clamp. Essie coughed roughly, wincing as they bound her wrists to the arm rests using magnetic cuffs. Another subtle movement from Gowon and the guards forced her knees to the sides of the chair, secured her ankles to the back chair legs by similar contraptions. The vulnerability of the position was further emphasized when the medical gown was ripped from her body.

"What the hell are you doing?" Miles whispered, switching to the wall panel view as one of the guards was blocking the overhead shot. Essie was positioned directly in front of the camera, which was angled upward toward the ceiling, for the moment, providing her a bit of modesty. He'd seen her fully naked several times at this point, but he still tried to focus his attention elsewhere. It was the very least he could do.

It was the closest look he'd had of Essie's face in two days. Her entire left cheek was streaked with blood, and her eyes were severely bruised, her lip split, and there was an unnatural swollen shape to her right cheekbone. She breathed as steadily as she could manage and avoided looking forward at her reflection and whoever might be beyond it. She focused her shadowed eyes slightly off-center, probably looking at the reflection of something behind her.

He thought of her sitting across from him at breakfast. They had sat on the patio since it was a very mild day. As the sun crept upward in the sky and beams of reflected light blasted her in the face, he offered his sunglasses. She had smiled tightly and declined, pulling a pair of mirrored wraparound sunglasses from her gym bag.

"Wait a second. Those are *mine*."

"Yeah, well, finders keepers."

"Where did I leave them?"

"In my truck. Like months ago. I keep meaning to give them back to you, but I keep forgetting and then I keep finding opportunities to wear them."

He chuckled, enjoying the general idea of Essie going about her day, running errands, wearing something of his. "Glad they could be of service."

"I'll give them back," she said grudgingly, "but can I wear them for breakfast? Remind me when we leave."

He nodded, pressing his lips together. "You know what? You hang on to those."

"Oh I can pick up a pair."

"From where? The food mart? Those are good ones. They're military grade. They'll protect your pretty eyes from the UV rays."

She grinned. "I'm old enough to remember when you said my eyes were creepy."

"I believe that was when you were selling me on the zombie baby story–and you were actively trying to make your eyes bug out of your head."

"Fair." She slipped them on, lifting her eyebrows.

"See, most girls would put those on and it'd look like she was trying to be Robocop or something, but look at you. *Adorable.*"

He had recognized a constant tremor in her hands before; now he could also see an involuntary quiver of her lower jaw and there was a spontaneous twitch in her left eye, an ever-present tear in the corner.

"Oh God, Essie, I'm sorry," Miles whispered, running his fingers along her cheek on the screen.

She took a deep breath, her eyes easing into an unfocused stare. Her blinking slowed.

Gowon sat in a sterile looking chair facing her, on a diagonal from the viewing gallery, which allowed Miles a side look at his face. He crossed his leg diagonally over his knee and gazed at her. "I'm told you worship God, that you were brought up in a church."

She tightened her jaw, attempted to swallow.

"Now that you've gotten some space from that *environment*, I'm curious, how's your faith holding up?"

Miles saw her lift her eyes toward the President. Only a narrow rim of silver was visible, as her eyelids were swollen, her pupils were dilated, and the whites of her eyes were bloodshot, but there was an intensity in her stare, unexpected given the state of her body.

Gowon nodded. "I explored church teachings at one point. Call it curiosity. People cling to their faith, don't they? It's really quite something." He paused to consider his word choice, holding up his hand, index finger raised. "It's really quite...counter-intuitive."

Essie appeared to be trying to slow her breathing again. The tension in her expression began to ease, but her eye continued to occasionally twitch.

"Their world is torn apart and they praise their Almighty, raise their hands up to He who controls *everything*?" He twisted his face in mockery. "You see how completely illogical it is?"

She stared at him.

"You must feel some doubt? I mean to say—where is your god now? If he loved you, wouldn't he reach down here and save you from any more suffering?"

It was nearly imperceptible, but Miles thought he saw her shake her head.

"What power does he really hold?" Gowon asked, his eyes gleaming over her naked, bound body coated in dirt and sweat and dried blood. He lifted his manicured eyebrows. "Who is more powerful in this room? Your god? Or *me*?"

She did not move.

Gowon tilted his chin, eyeing the elaborate tattoo on her forearm. "It's difficult to let go, isn't it?" He gave a small, sinister smile. "But you will."

Essie closed her eyes for a prolonged, steadying moment. Upon opening them again, she pulled in her breath with unintended intensity, startled by the proximity of a second man directly before her. She dropped her eyes briefly to something the man was holding that Miles was unable to see. The man sat on a rolling stool and Essie diverted her eyes back to the off-centered place on the mirror, her gaze quickly turning glassy and unfocused. Her breathing stretched.

"You may have been able to escape into your mind up until now, but your mind *will* betray you–and then you'll have nowhere left to hide," Gowon said silkily, still seated. "It would be far less painful for you if you'd simply—let go."

She gave no indication she'd heard him.

At the restaurant, Essie lifted the sunglasses to rest on her head. A foreboding group of clouds had drifted in front of the sun about halfway through the meal. A breeze was causing a fluttering of the strands of hair that had managed to escape confinement in her messy bun.

She listened intently as he told her about his childhood aspiration to be a sports announcer. When she had encouraged him to show off his skills, he had started to narrate breakfast, specifically providing commentary about how she ate so "ambitiously."

She'd needed to stop eating abruptly and had burst into suppressed laughter, her entire face turning red, cheeks tight.

The surge of exhilaration of having brought a smile to Essie's face, of making her laugh, was unrivaled by any other feeling he'd ever experienced. He was unconvinced that any better feeling existed in the world.

Gowon lifted his brow. "You can comply willingly and live–*or* you can comply *unwillingly* and die, but only after I'm very sure I've extracted every *last bit of usefulness* from you," he said, enunciating each syllable. He tilted his chin. "Perhaps I've been thinking of this all wrong though. Perhaps you're already to the point where I shouldn't be persuading you with the chance to live, but with the chance to die?" He furrowed his brow. "Or are you not quite there yet?"

It was as the second man centered himself before her, hand grazing her thigh that the quiver of Essie's lower lip intensified. She turned her chin to rest on her shoulder furthest from Gowon, trying to brace herself for what was about to happen.

Gowon leaned forward, trying to steal a glance at her face through her veil of muddy hair. "You've chosen this path. Remember that."

She closed her eyes.

Miles switched to the overhead view. "Oh, *shit*."

Despite all the advanced technology throughout the space, the man sitting before her held a medieval looking tool in his grasp. The handle was a solid, coated wood, the top forged from iron.

"Here, you've been faithful to this *all-powerful* god, you've obeyed his commands, you've kept yourself *pure*. And as soon as I give the word, your sacrifice will be for nothing."

Essie's lip quivered.

"Ask him to help you. Ask *your god* to protect you from what's about to happen. I want to hear you *beg* your god to save you."

She didn't move. She didn't speak.

Gowon lifted the corners of his mouth, watched her suppress signs of fear. "*Where* is your god?"

She squeezed her eyes shut, taking another deep breath.

Gowon nodded to the man positioned before her who propelled his arm forward.

Essie's chin jolted upward, the air knocked from her lungs.

Miles pulled off the headset, pushed himself back from the monitor. He stood, circled around his small workspace, arms resting on top of his head, and released a primal yell, his voice echoing around the cavernous server room. He slammed his fist into the side of a metal filing cabinet, immediately reeling his hand back in regret. He yelled out again.

"'Be strong and courageous. Do not be afraid; do not be discouraged, for the Lord your God will be with you wherever you go.'"

He could hear her voice speak the words. They were sitting out in the barn at the ranch, lounging against some bales of hay, waiting out a thunderstorm.

"That's your favorite verse?"

She shrugged. "It's hard to pick just one favorite, but that one is pretty powerful. That we're not alone, that we have no reason to fear." She'd gotten up to tend to Eustace, a very vocal goat who was batting his leg outside his shared stall. She released him, which temporarily quieted him, until he'd decided he wanted to go back in the stall, bleating angrily at her. "Well, fine," she said calmly. "Go back in."

The goat scurried back into the stall, then, taking in his surroundings, turned back to the stall gate and began bleating loudly to be let back out.

"He just can't make up his mind, can he?" Miles observed.

Essie shook her head. "I'm telling you, buddy, you're better off with your friends in there."

"You should listen–she's very wise."

Eustace rammed his small horns into the gate, pawing at the ground with his hoof.

"Fine, but I'm not putting you back in," Essie said, opening the gate just wide enough to allow him to escape.

"Should we close the big door?"

"He won't go out in the storm," she said, returning to her hay bale.

"So do you really fear nothing?"

She frowned and was about to speak when Eustace suddenly bleated toward the rain, turned around and complained to the humans. "What? Am I to blame for the rain, too?"

The tan goat shook off the mist from the rain, scurrying deeper into the barn. He continued to bleat as he circled around the space in front of his stall. He finally laid down, settling his muzzle so he was staring across at Essie.

"As you were saying–" Miles prompted.

She frowned, visibly getting her mind back on track to what they had been talking about. "Of course I'm afraid of things, *but* reminding myself that God has already won, that Jesus has already paid the price and no matter what may happen, Heaven is at the end of my path? It comforts me. It gives me courage."

Miles dropped back in his chair, clambering to put his headset back on as Essie rotated her chin to face Gowon.

Her eyes were filled with tears, but she established unwavering eye contact with him, her breaths staggered, jaw tight, her mouth twisting in pain. "It bothers you that you don't understand." Her voice was a strained whisper, her split, chapped, bleeding lips barely moving as she spoke.

It was the first time Miles had heard her speak in the five days they'd had the feed.

"*What* don't I understand?"

"God's love."

He sniggered. "*What* love? Your god has abandoned you."

She shook her head, swallowing hard. "He's here suffering with me."

Gowon uncrossed his leg, straightened up in his seat. "*Is* he now?"

Miles leaned forward.

"It will never be enough. You'll always feel empty inside no matter what you do."

"*Essie*, don't," Miles pleaded. He wasn't sure of her intent, but he knew challenging Gowon in any way could only make her situation worse.

"You'll never find the peace you're looking for this way. You'll have no peace while you live and no peace when you die–" She managed to get out the word "*unless*" before he interjected.

"Well, *you*—" Gowon began, lifting his brow in amusement. "—will have no peace *until* you die," he murmured coolly, the corner of his lip stretching upward. "But you're *far* too valuable for us to let that happen for a *very long time*." He nodded to the man still seated before Essie.

The man tightened his grip on the wooden handle, using both hands. There was a loud, clinking sound, like armor locking into position. Then he pulled forcefully backward on the handle.

Essie hurled forward with the movement as far as the restraints allowed, crying out in a hoarse shriek as the device was extracted.

Miles snapped his chin away, wincing. By what he could gather, the clinking sound had been a switch causing directional blades to fan out from the iron, the jagged teeth of the blades designed for maximum damage.

There was substantial blood covering her legs, the chair, the floor when Miles once again set his eyes on the monitor. Her chin rested on her chest, but her mouth remained ajar, her face braced in pain. Slowly, she lifted her chin and met Gowon's eye.

This continued for a few prolonged moments, her breaths heavy.

Gowon broke eye contact first, lowering his eyes to her naked body, staring until he saw her flinch involuntarily. He gave a light, victorious smile as he rose from the chair.

He had just reached the doorway when she quietly said: "I'll pray for you."

Gowon chuckled silently to himself but did not turn around or even peer over his shoulder. "Do the procedure again."

"Sir, she's already lost a lot of blood–"

"*Do it again*," Gowon said tensely, then left the chamber.

*   *   *

"Tell me we have a plan to kill him," Miles demanded of Luther the moment he arrived back to the surveillance room.

"Who?" Luther asked, his eyes swollen and exhausted.

"*Who*? Gowon."

"Eventually, yes."

"Well I'm going to respectfully request you move up the effing timeline. Move it up whatever priority list you have. *He needs to die*," he said, his voice growing thick.

Luther placed his hand on Miles's upper arm. "What happened?"

Miles shook his head. The air conditioning unit powered on and as the cool air struck his cheeks, he realized they were soaked with tears. "He was there, Luther. With Essie."

Luther's eyes jolted to the monitor. Esther had been provided a fresh gown, which was already saturated with blood. It appeared there were attempts made to wipe her face, but her tangled, grimy hair continued to stick to her cheeks. She was sitting cross-legged on the concrete floor, leaning forward over her knees, shivering, though she seemed to be trying to disguise this with a subtle rocking motion. "What *happened*?" he repeated.

"He came in after she spent the morning being beaten unconscious. When she came to, he had her raped with a god damn medieval gardening tool. I couldn't figure out why she would sit herself on the floor after that—and then it dawned on me that she's sitting on the concrete because it's cold—"

"To help with the pain," Luther murmured.

"*Tell me* there's a plan to kill him."

Luther frowned. "He had her *raped*?" The look on Luther's face almost made Miles regret his coarse wording. But no. Any way he could manage to explain what he'd witnessed would feel like a euphemism. Luther was clearly at a loss for words, confusion filling his eyes.

67

"I don't want to describe it, but it was vicious. There was so much blood, so much—*flesh.* It felt–*personal* and sinister as hell. He mocked her faith. He said that her keeping herself 'pure' was now a waste."

Luther blinked slowly, pressing his lips together.

"Does he not *get* that being 'pure' is a very different thing than–" Miles tensed his jaw, looking away.

"He doesn't understand any of it, Miles. It's outside the limitations of his narrow comprehension," Luther said quietly, pinching the bridge of his nose. He took a deep breath and looked up at the screen. "Her tremors are getting worse."

Miles narrowed his eyes. "Of course they are. She's being *tortured.*" He wanted to point out the obvious, that she was also actively bleeding, but stopped short.

Luther swallowed hard. "How was she? I mean, *obviously*—"

Miles shook his head, took a deep breath, and told Luther about the beating, how she had lost consciousness. He described how Gowon had her tied to the chair, stripped naked, how he had then questioned her faith, and tried to convince her that God had abandoned her. "He shouldn't care *this much* about her faith," Miles said angrily. "That has *nothing* to do with what the son of a bitch is looking to accomplish so why does it matter so much to him?"

Luther gave a small shake of his head.

"She was trying to save his soul, Luther. In the midst of this."

"What do you mean? She *spoke*?"

Miles nodded. "She told him that he'll never 'find the peace he's looking for.' She started to say *unless* he repents, but he cut her off."

Luther focused his gaze on Essie, who had rested her head against her folded leg, jaw chattering.

"When he started to leave the room, she told him she'd pray for him. She was entirely serious, Luther. She wasn't mocking him. She meant it."

Luther nodded slowly.

"So he had her raped again." Miles rubbed roughly at his face, his movements sharp. He sniffled loudly. "Why would she do that? Why would she say that?"

Luther shook his head, swallowing hard. "Could you *imagine* if Samuel Gowon turned to Jesus?"

Miles shook his head repeatedly. "*No.* He is the devil incarnate. The man's killed tens of millions of people. More, probably. *No.* I know God says no one is irredeemable, but just *no.* That man should not be strolling around Heaven. Absolutely not."

Luther took a deep breath. "The other thought I have is that she could be trying to provoke a response from him."

"What do you mean?"

"Gowon has been known in the past to have a short fuse when out of the public eye. He despises Christianity. She may have been trying to trigger his knee jerk response."

"Why?"

"She wants him to kill her."

Miles swallowed hard, stunned by his blunt word choice. "I know they're torturing her, but do you really think she *wants* to die?"

"Wouldn't you? If you were her?"

Essie sat upright, resituating her arms around her knees again and resuming a gentle rocking motion. There was an edginess to her movements, the look in her eyes.

"Yeah, but–"

"She had gotten Josh to agree to shoot her if she was captured on the way to the Ark."

"Wait, *what*?"

Luther nodded.

"We both pulled our guns, but it was to shoot the guy who was taking her. It wasn't–" He frowned. "You're telling me that he was going to–She made Josh agree to *shoot her*?" He considered Josh's strange attitude toward Essie. He'd interpreted it as Josh being angry with her, but that wasn't it at all.

He was scared to death that something would happen to her.

Miles watched Essie pause the rocking motion. She tensed her face, a thought, a memory seeming to pass before her. She winced and continued the rocking motion, shivering as she did. "What does Gowon want? I thought maybe we missed what his demands were in the week before we got the footage, but he's *not* asking for information."

"No."

"He also made it *very* clear earlier how valuable she is to him, that he wouldn't let her die until he could—'extract all usefulness'? What is *useful* about what they're doing to her? I don't get it. What's the point of all this? What are they getting out of this?"

Luther sighed. "He's trying to break her. Her mind, her body, to some degree."

Miles narrowed his eyes. "Break her 'to some degree'? What does that mean? For what *purpose*?"

Luther took a long inhalation.

"Luther? I adore this girl. She's family to me. She's the love of my best friend's life. *Why* is this happening to her?"

Luther took a seat in the second task chair, motioned for Miles to sit. His eyes flitted up to the screen several times before finally speaking.

"A few decades ago, the basis of a lot of scientific research was the use of stem cells. It was used in regenerative medicine, in vaccines. It sparked a lot of controversy because the most useful stem cells were harvested from aborted babies."

"I'm sorry, I don't have the strongest science background, Luth. I was homeschooled by my sister."

"Stem cells are cells that can help regenerate or repair organs and tissues in the body. Embryonic stem cells are adaptable and prevalent. They're called 'pluripotent,' which means they can divide into more stem cells or they can become any type of cell in the body, which makes sense because the baby's body is still developing."

"Do adults have stem cells?"

Esther rocked herself up to her knees, crawled onto the concrete slab serving as her bed and tugged the thin blanket around her body. She curled her knees up to her chest, her jaw still chattering.

There was a pool of clotted blood left behind on the concrete floor.

It appeared to take tremendous effort for Luther to peel his attention away from the screen. He began to speak in an automated manner, eyes still fixed on Essie. "There are a lot fewer stem cells in adults and they're not as useful or versatile. They're specific to wherever they are in the body. There was a lot of research where scientists were trying to reprogram the genetics of adult stem cells to behave more like embryonic stem cells."

"So the cells could turn into whatever they needed to be?"

"If they could reprogram the genetics of adult stem cells, it would essentially allow the body to heal itself. In theory. In practice, there were a lot of risks. In some people, reprogramming cells in this way led to rampant tumors, genetic mutations. Researchers tried isolating the reprogrammed cells to target specific areas of the body, but this didn't work very well either. It was like upgrading one component in a computer and nothing else. It was an all or nothing situation–upgrade everything or the entire system would get overwhelmed and crash. The problem was that they couldn't figure out how to upgrade every cell in the body."

"What does this have to do with Essie?"

Luther furrowed his brow. "Researchers decided to try to reprogram genetics from as early an age as possible. They started doing treatment from early in pregnancy. The initial run of the experiment used natural pregnancies. That's when Essie became a part of the program. After that, they moved to artificial wombs since it was much easier to do more involved work with the babies without having to deal with a mother."

Miles had become slack-jawed.

"The reprogramming efforts caused major issues with the growth and development of the babies. The researchers couldn't keep up with the body's instinct to have the cells become specialized, many of the babies ended up with aggressive tumors–the long story short of it is that most of the babies weren't given the chance to be born. Those who *were* allowed to be born lived very short, very painful lives." He nodded slowly. "Essie is the one exception. She retained the same level of stem cells with the same versatility as embryonic. She survived every test, every experiment they subjected her to."

Miles blinked slowly. "So Essie's stem cells have been reprogrammed to act like the pluripostal ones?"

"Pluripotent. Yes."

Miles narrowed his eyes. "So how did that work with the antidote testing? Wouldn't her body respond differently than a normal person?"

"The antidote was derived from antibodies in *her* plasma. The reason it was so effective is that her blood stem cells are *also* pluripotent. When used in treatment, they act as carriers of the antibodies that treat the condition *and* the cells in the patient, in turn, mimic their behavior temporarily."

Miles gave this some thought. "She's the source," he finally concluded. "She's the only reason we have an antidote. *Isn't* she?"

Luther nodded.

"So to be able to generate the antidote you'd need antibodies, which would mean she'd have to be exposed to whatever the threat was, *right*? To trigger her body's response?"

"Yes. At the time, that's what we thought."

"So she willingly subjected herself to–what?"

"Toxins, diseases, viruses."

He furrowed his brow. "How long does it take her to recover?"

"Hours. Typically anywhere from 6-14 hours to regain consciousness, days to fully recover. The body shuts down nonessential systems if it's fighting something off. That's why people tend to sleep when they get the flu."

"Was it—I mean, it sounds painful?"

"'Like being burned alive, drowned, and ripped apart, all at the same time,'" Luther echoed. "That's what she said–unintentionally after the first test. She was still pretty out of it. She tried to downplay what it was like once she knew I was more than a little reluctant to continue."

Miles swallowed hard, eyes brimmed with tears. "She willingly endured what amounted to torture?"

"120 times. That doesn't account for what she endured as a child." Luther watched her attempt to fold herself to better fit beneath the small, thin blanket. "She didn't know *why* it worked, just that it worked. I actively tried to keep her from figuring out the full potential of it."

Miles narrowed his eyes. "Why?"

"I mentioned that in previous research, the induced pluripotent stem cells had the potential to mutate and cause tumors?"

Miles nodded. "You said it would overwhelm the body."

"It's different from what she generates. The antibodies and stem cells–they're more, let's say, *natural*. The way induced pluripotent stem cells were used before was very jarring; it felt invasive to the body of whoever they were injected into. Hers don't."

"You implied that this could be used in other treatments."

"It has the potential to be used in regenerative medicine, to heal damaged organs, make transplants unnecessary. It has the potential to reverse brain damage, cure cancer, infertility, repair a *spinal cord*," Luther said, raising his eyes pointedly to the screen.

"And she knows this?"

Luther sighed. "At this point, yes. She had suspicions before because of what happened to her at Calvary. I tried to keep her from understanding the full potential, but she would know now."

Miles frowned. "Calvary?"

"Her childhood church?"

"What happened to her at Calvary?"

Luther sighed and described how when Essie was sixteen, her church's Children's Ministry was attacked, that terrorists had thrown in a sarin gas canister and barricaded seven kids with Essie inside. He described how she sealed up the supply closet from the outside to protect the kids, but by that point, the gas had reached her. She started experiencing all of the effects and at one point, she thought her spine snapped. After collapsing on the floor, she crawled to the canister and threw her body over it.

"To keep the gas from getting to the kids," Miles concluded.

Luther nodded.

"Did the kids survive?"

"Yes. You know two of them."

Miles dropped his shoulders, releasing a huff of air. "Thomas and Renee. She--" He shook his head. "Did she know at the time that she'd survive it? She couldn't have, right?

"She didn't know what her body was capable of, no."

Miles exhaled deeply. "So she sacrificed herself to save the kids."

Luther nodded.

"Why didn't you tell her? Once you knew this?"

"If she knew, she never would have stopped—doing the antidote runs, draining her blood to be used in transfusions. Miles, she *never* would have stopped. And if she didn't stop, eventually she would have been discovered."

"And wound up like this."

Luther gave a small nod. "I've tried to keep this exact situation from happening."

Miles nodded, eyes panning to the monitor. "So she *did* live in a government lab as a baby."

Luther frowned. "*Yes.*"

He sighed. "She made jokes about it. She said they were creating–" He stopped short, searched the tabletop for the tissue box. Once he'd mopped his eyes and smothered his nose, he continued: "How did she get out of there? The lab. How did she get out?"

Luther took a deep breath. "The primary researcher rejected her from the program when she was just shy of three years old."

"*Why?*"

"Because of the color of her skin."

He frowned. "Is something *wrong* with her skin?"

Luther tightened his lips patiently. "Because she's Caucasian, Miles. They wanted more 'diversity.'"

"Are you *serious* right now?"

"Yeah."

Miles rubbed his eyes. "And what happened? Did they stick her in foster care?" He frowned, remembering the conversation where Essie talked about how Luther had taken care of her before she was adopted by her dad.

Luther gave a pained expression. "They didn't treat the children like children, Miles. They removed any rights they had. They were classified as medical research property. The government had legally changed the definition of when a baby's considered human so it was easy for them to do with them as they pleased."

Miles narrowed his eyes.

"'Once the birthing person *accepts* the birthed fetus.'"

"What the hell kind of *nonsense* did your generation come up with, Luther?" Miles asked angrily.

Luther lifted his brow.

"What happened to the kids when they left the program?"

He cleared his throat. "No one left. When the babies and children died, they were cremated."

"But she didn't die. You said she was *rejected* from the experiment."

"To them, it meant the same thing."

Miles pinched his eyebrows together.

"Their records at the time showed she was 'destroyed.' One of the lab technicians brought her to the furnace where she was meant to be—"

"*Burned alive?*"

"Yes."

Miles had stopped blinking. "You saved her."

Luther slowly nodded.

"So—wait. Do they know *who* she is? That she was from their experiment?"

Luther nodded.

Miles took a breath, let his eyes drift over to the monitor. Essie turned over to her left side, facing the door. He switched to the security panel feed, which had automatically switched to night vision mode when the overhead lights turned off at 10pm.

Her eyes blinked slowly as she stared into the darkness, her mouth moving as though speaking. He pulled on his headset, strained to hear her.

"Is she praying?"

"I'm not sure. They've had death sounds blasting since they dumped her back in there."

Luther took another look at her on the monitor. Besides the twitch in her left eye, which had been becoming more prevalent, he wouldn't have thought she was being subjected to the sounds of human and animal torture.

Miles listened a bit longer, wincing, then gave up, removed the headset and tossed it on the desk.

"How long has this been going on? With the audio?"

"Five hours?"

Luther shook his head regretfully.

"What does Gowon want with her?"

Luther took a deep breath. "Gowon is very interested in tapping into the brain. Having pluripotent stem cells in the brain allows for a certain *pliability*."

Miles frowned.

"He wants to reprogram brain cells." *Among other things,* he added silently.

"How does 'breaking her' help what he's trying to do?"

"The body has certain guards against threats. Hers in particular. If the brain has a fear response, certain systems go into action. He can't do what he wants to do if the defenses are activated. It's like with hypnosis. If the brain is 'open' or suggestible, thoughts, actions can be influenced or controlled."

"So he *wants* her to be a shell of a person."

Luther took a deep breath and nodded. "Her and whoever else he wants to control."

"Which is everyone."

"Yeah. With the antidote, the cells of the person receiving the injection temporarily mimic her cells, which helps to make it more effective. What he wants to do is to reprogram her brain cells, then extract her cells, replicate them, then create a serum–"

"And use that to hijack everyone else."

Silence filled the room, both men turning to the monitor where Essie seemed to be gazing in their direction, still saying something too low for them to hear.

"Luther, why did you choose me?" Miles asked quietly, raking his fingers through his blonde curls.

"What do you mean?"

"I mean, for *this*. The only people who know about Essie are you, me, and Danny, correct?"

"Yes."

"Why did you trust *me* with this?"

Luther swallowed hard. "In MET, you showed better instincts than anyone. You're strategic and logical. You're strong."

Miles glanced up at the monitor.

"I was also at your baptism, Miles. I know what she means to you."

Miles pressed his lips together, tears filling his eyes. He gave a short nod.

7

500 miles

The memorial service for Matteo Natale was held on a Saturday morning. The maximum occupancy of the church was 410. Three times that many people came to pay their respects. People had filed into outer aisles, into the choir loft, many remained in the lobby and the courtyard outside, intending to listen to the broadcast of the service through the speakers and on the monitors placed just for the occasion.

Sara had maintained a clear aisle, keeping all standing attendees behind a specified grout line on the tile floor. She paced along the line, taking several steadying breaths as her eyes scanned the front of the church, assessed the placement of Teo's portrait on its stand, and ensured people were finding their way to their seats.

She turned on her heel and startled, finding herself facing the casket, which had been placed on a podium in the center of the lobby, just outside the Sunday School classrooms. She took another focused breath, gathered herself, wiping roughly at her eyes, suddenly locking eyes with Luke. She pursed her lips, her eyes filling with tears.

As she took in the sight of Miles, Josh, and Gabe, who would be serving as pallbearers along with Luke, a squeak emerged from her lips and her mouth twisted as she tried to suppress sobs.

She checked her watch, nodded, and stepped toward the four men. She secured her hand tightly around Luke's arm.

"Remember, the casket is going to be empty," she whispered, careful that no one around them would hear. "Just try not to make it obvious."

Miles gave an uncertain nod, glancing up at the other men.

"It's almost time to get started," she said, squeezing her nose with a tissue and rushing away to find the music director.

"Teo will have a public gravesite," Gabe explained quietly to Miles once she'd gone, nodding toward the swarms of people who were in attendance. "But we decided he'd want a private burial place–next to Essie."

Gabe chose not to clarify further, that they didn't have a body to bury in Essie's grave, that they'd be forced to bury mementos of her instead, that they were meant to be gathering items to contribute.

Josh turned his chin toward his brother as he spoke, but didn't make eye contact, finding it difficult to breathe. His head began to swirl.

In the sanctuary, the pianist began to play.

*　　*　　*

four days later...

Josh had actually considered not attending Essie's funeral and instead trekking out into the woods for the foreseeable future.

He sat on the porch swing at his creekside cabin wearing his plain black suit staring into the trees, unable to wrap his mind around what was to take place.

How could he be expected to say goodbye to her when he hadn't settled his mind to believe that she was dead? When he could still feel her presence? When it felt that at any moment, she'd pull up in the driveway, or suddenly be sitting alongside him? There were mornings he'd be sitting on the porch and his mind would decide she was still sleeping inside; he'd expect the groan of the front door at any moment and for her to pad over to him in one of his oversized t-shirts and a pair of socks, snuggle in beside him.

It had been some time since she'd spent the night. Her insomnia, the reason for the sleeping arrangement had resolved spontaneously–once she'd recovered from the "bunker buster," once they'd finally declared their love for each other, once she'd started singing in church again. She'd finally been able to sleep at night without an "emotional support human," as she dotingly referred to him. Her mind, her heart was at peace. She was happy.

He was happy.

There was a hollowness to the world around him now. He struggled even considering the reality that he'd never hear her voice again, never hear her laugh again, never hear her sing again. She'd never settle into the nook of his arm or nuzzle up against him again. He'd never get to watch her reading, her expression reflecting her engagement with the storyline. She'd never settle her gaze upon him in that way she did that made it feel like there was no one else in the world but the two of them. He'd never get to experience their back-and-forth banter, have her tease him, or speak in her flirtatious, doting little voice.

He was not ready to attend her funeral. Attending would require some acceptance about the situation. It was simply not possible that she was no longer in the world and yet the sun still rose each morning, set each night, that the moon and stars shimmered in the sky at night, that the birds still had the audacity to sing.

The fact remained that he had no choice. He had to go. It was for Essie. He *had* to go.

His mom had arranged everything, purposefully keeping things simple and small (probably with much encouragement from his dad): a short, private service at the overlook closest to the Natale Ranch.

Where she told him she loved him. Within feet of the tree stump where she had stood, her arms about his neck and told him she wanted to marry him.

Matteo's body had been cremated and his ashes would be buried during the service. Essie's gravesite would be beside him, despite having nothing to bury. Luther hadn't said specifically and Josh hadn't asked, but he assumed that there was specific scientific interest in her, even after death. He couldn't think of her body being subjected to further study, further prodding. He hated the idea of burial and he hated the idea of cremation, but this scenario felt infinitely worse, where there was no end, no peace.

He knew it was just her body. His mom tried to comfort him that *she*, that Essie's soul, was in Heaven, but it plagued his mind to think of her body being considered "scientific property," being picked apart, being bastardized for whatever "research" they felt compelled to conduct, with whatever their intended goals.

Despite previously holding a public funeral for Matteo, the private service would be for both of them. His mom had suggested everyone share their favorite stories, their favorite memories. He understood that she meant it to be cathartic, but he couldn't think of any memory he wanted to share in that setting. He feared sharing it there would forever entangle the memory with the funeral, with her death, with Teo's death. If he left the memories alone, it almost felt like she lived on in them and if he focused enough, imagined the scenes clearly enough, it would almost be like he could visit her in his memory.

That and he would never succeed in being able to explain things to do them any sort of justice. They wouldn't hold the same significance to anyone else.

Saying nothing, sharing nothing didn't sit well with him either.

He had considered talking about the last thing she said to him. It had been on the two-way radio the afternoon she was taken. She'd spent the morning at the gym and having brunch with Miles. Josh had needed to make rounds with a few veterinary cases so they'd planned a mid-afternoon outing. He had selected mini golf for their date, at a place that had been elaborately renovated to be a Hawaiian theme and was operated by the extended family of one of the ranchers he worked with a lot. Golfers even received leis when they arrived. He knew Essie would get a kick out of it.

When he'd described it for her, she joked about wearing a grass skirt and a coconut bra, saying she could attempt a hula dance to distract him and gain a competitive advantage, but then admitted that she'd probably end up injuring herself.

He had laughed as she went on about it–a very tight laugh that resided deep in his stomach. It was the sort of laugh he'd only experienced as a result of something Essie had said.

"I love you so stinkin' much. You know that, right?" he had managed to say.

"You know *what*, you better!" she exclaimed. He could hear the smile in her voice. "After all you put me through, *waiting* and *waiting* for you to finally figure out something you knew *all* along, that you love and adore absolutely everything about me–oh wait, that was me, wasn't it? Thank you for that, by the way."

"Thank me for what?"

"Waiting. For me to get myself together."

"I'd wait for you forever, Essie."

"Well, that doesn't seem very fair."

"There's nothing I wouldn't do for you. You could put a thousand-mile road before me and tell me you were at the end of it and I'd walk it to get to you."

"You wouldn't run?"

"I'm not a *machine*. A thousand miles is a long way," he teased.

"I feel like there's a song that conveys this sentiment. It has a catchy hook."

"I know the song."

She began to string together the melody out loud.

He grinned and began to sing softly: "'*When I wake up, well, I know I'm gonna be, I'm gonna be the man who wakes up next to you...*'"

"Well, don't stop," she said with a laugh.

"*You're* the singer."

"Who says there can only be one singer in a relationship? I'd love for you to sing to me, Josh West."

"You would?"

"Uh, *yeah*, I really eat that stuff up."

"What stuff?"

"You talking in that funny accent, you singing to me? I *love* it. It makes me feel all tingly and happy."

He grinned. "That's good to know."

She hummed more of the melody, then softly sang the chorus from The Proclaimers song: "*I would walk five hundred miles and I would walk five hundred more just to be the man who walked a thousand miles to fall down at your door.*"

And then, simultaneously, they both burst out with: "*da-da-da, da-da-da, da-da-da-da-da-da-da-da-da-da-da.*"

She laughed. "So you're picking me up?"

"Yep. At about 3:30, if that works?"

"Are you feeding me?"

"*Obviously.*"

"K. I'm going to go check on the animals and get stuff set for them."

"I'll see you soon."

"Yes, you will."

He remembered smiling widely at the excitement in her words. "I love you, Essie."

"I love you."

The last words she spoke to him were "I love you."

He swallowed hard, his eyes burning as he stared through the trees to the creek.

Josh thought of standing on that overlook facing the reality that Essie was gone, that he couldn't simply call her or drive over to see her, and the gaping hole in his heart grew larger.

He fidgeted with a bouquet of wildflowers he'd picked for her gravesite, checked his pocket for the letter he'd written for her that would be buried at the site. He had nothing else to bury; there was nothing of hers he was willing to part with.

He pulled in his breath and stood.

*   *   *

eight days later...

Josh heard the crisp blade slicing through wood as he made his way back from the lake. Fenway perked her ears, taking a solid stance between Josh and the noise. He encouraged her to continue forward around the next bank of trees and found his dad in the process of building a substantial pile of firewood outside the cabin.

Fenway released a low, nervous growl.

"It's okay, girl," Josh murmured, continuing forward.

"Looks like the trout were biting today," Luke said, motioning to the mesh bag Josh carried.

Josh nodded, lowering his eyes as he approached. "What are you doing out here, Dad?"

"Chopping firewood."

"I see that. Thanks, but you don't have to do that."

"Your mom had some things at the house she wanted to give you," he said, motioning toward the box placed by the front door.

Josh did not want to consider what awaited him in the box, the memories that would undoubtedly drown him in grief.

"You're really out here by yourself these days."

Josh took in a breath, glancing around to the vacant cabins. "The guy who lived across the way went into military training and the couple in the other cabin are expecting twins so they moved somewhere bigger."

"Miles should move out here. He's never liked that apartment, right?"

Josh thought of Essie scrubbing Miles's bathroom, lecturing him about keeping up with the cleaning. He'd moved into what she called her "socialist utopia apartment" when she'd moved out to live with her dad at the ranch, housing assignments becoming scarce.

She'd done her best to try to make the apartment feel like a home for Miles, but he'd always found it too confining and lonely, preferring to spend time at Gunner and Gabe's complex, or at the ranch. He wondered briefly if Miles had felt more attached to the apartment now, since it was something that he'd acquired from her.

"I don't see much of him."

"What's he doing?"

Josh considered the question. "I really don't know, Dad."

Luke secured the ax on the chopping stump. "It might be good–for the two of you to hang out?"

"Like I said, I don't know what he's been doing. Other than–" He stopped himself from saying *attending funerals*.

Luke peered up at the sky. "We're supposed to get a cold snap this week."

"Thanks for chopping some wood then. I appreciate it."

Luke took a breath. "There's not a great way for me to ask how you're doing."

"You already know the answer."

His dad nodded. "I know you need your space right now. It's just–I think your mom and I would both feel better if—"

Josh lifted his chin.

"If we knew you weren't—looking for a way out of your pain."

He narrowed his eyes. "You think I'm planning to kill myself?"

Luke lifted his shoulders. "You two were inseparable. You had this connection ever since you were little. You told me when you were fifteen that you–"

"I *know* what Essie means to me, Dad. I don't need you to tell me. I feel it. Believe me. I *feel it*," he said tightly, his voice cracking.

The sound of the nearby stream echoed through the trees and filled the space between them.

"Even though it feels like we can't possibly move forward, we have to. We *have to* move past this."

Josh pulled back his shoulders, anger building in his chest. "'Move *past* this'? It's been *days* since it happened, Dad. Not months, not years."

"I know, Josh, but–"

"You want me to *move past this*? Move past *her*?" Josh shook his head, clenching his jaw. "Essie was kind and generous and good and if not for her, more than half of the people in the Arks would be dead. Hannah, *none* of the babies would even have been born—" He pulled in

85

his breath. "--and they killed her. Viciously and—" His voice caught. "They *killed* her."

Luke nodded slowly, though his brow furrowed in confusion.

"I'm not about to move past her, Dad. I'll probably never move past her. But I'm working and I'm here. I'm staying busy. I'm doing the best I can to just exist right now."

Luke continued to nod.

"If it's something you and mom need to hear to feel better, then fine. I have no intention or plan to kill myself."

"*Josh–*"

"Have I thought about it? *Yes*. Will I do it? No. *Why*? Well, I don't like the idea of putting you and mom through that, honestly, but mainly? Because *Essie wouldn't want me to*." He didn't realize until he'd gotten the words out that he was shouting. His voice echoed against the trees and river rocks.

Fenway released a small cry and scurried up toward the porch. She laid across the top step, resting her muzzle over her paws, panning her eyes over to the pair of men to keep watch over them, but pointing her snout away.

Josh felt guilt rise up in his chest–toward his dad, toward Fenway. He tried to absorb it, but it lingered. He picked up a stray piece of wood and tossed it toward the pile of firewood. "I'm doing the best I can. I'm not just going to move past it though. It's not a matter of willpower. 'Sometimes the only way out is *through*.'" The words had flown out of his mouth before he'd known he'd thought them. He thought of Teo giving the sermon when he'd used those exact words. He was talking about grief, sharing publicly for the first time his own experience after his wife died.

Josh felt his body stiffen as his heart was struck with the fact that Teo was dead, that one of the last things Essie saw, if not *the* last thing, was her dad being shot to death.

Luke moved to steady Josh as his body heaved forward.

Josh braced his hand on his side and stood upright again.

86

"You don't have to go through it alone though, Josh," Luke said softly next to his ear.

Josh shook his head, taking a step away. "I think it's better for everyone that I keep my distance."

"It might help if you talked to someone, if you prayed, hell, I don't know. Teo was the one—" Luke stopped short, wiped roughly at his eyes, his breaths becoming airy and staggered. "I know Teo would say that this isn't the time to turn your back on God. This is the time to open yourself up *more* to God."

Josh scoffed, turning away.

"Look, I know you're angry–"

He spun back on his heel to face his dad. "What are you going to tell me? That God is going to make something *good* out of this? Out of Teo's death? Out of–" He shook his head. "She *was* the good. Essie was *all* the good in this world and *He let her die*. How could He do that? *Why* would He do that?" He stood as upright as he could manage and lumbered toward the cabin. He stopped abruptly, his cheeks streaked with tears, his voice unsteady: "You asked me if I'm angry?" He turned on his heel. "Yeah. I am. I'm really *fucking* angry at God right now. And I really don't feel like praising Him when He *could have* saved her." He fanned out his arms. "*Okay*? That's where I'm at with this. And yes, I realize she wouldn't want me to be angry with God *either*, but I just can't seem to help it right now."

"You want to know the truth?" Luke asked quietly, closing the distance to Josh. "I'm angry, too. At God. For taking away my best friend. For taking away–" He took a breath, eyes flooding with tears. A breeze filled the space between them and when Luke spoke again, his voice was more measured. "I don't understand it, Josh. I don't know why this happened. I don't know what God's plan is here."

Josh shook his head.

"You're not the only one who loved her. It's not the same kind of love, I know, but–You're not the only one mourning her. She was Teo's daughter, but I loved her as if she were my own."

Josh took a steadying breath.

"When Hannah was born, people said things about your mom and I finally having a daughter, but the truth is, I kind of felt like I already had one."

Josh lifted his eyes. His dad looked so much thinner and weathered in just the past few weeks. He felt compelled to step forward and hug him, but he felt like that act would release all of the emotion he'd managed to hold inside.

He couldn't let the dam burst. He'd never recover from feeling everything at once.

"You don't *have* to go through this alone, Josh. I don't *want* you to go through this alone."

Josh nodded slowly, then turned toward the cabin. "Thanks for the firewood, Dad."

He intended to go immediately inside, but as Josh crossed the porch, his eyes panned over to the box his dad had brought for him. He paused mid-step, the screen door leaning against his shoulder. He found himself staring at an envelope sitting on top, addressed to him. There was no doubt in his mind that the handwriting belonged to Essie. He took a deep breath and allowed the screen door to close with him outside. He turned slowly, lifted the letter from the box and took a seat on the bench swing.

The world around him turned silent. He vaguely observed when his dad pulled out of the driveway, but he could hear nothing but the beating of his heart echoing in his ears. He ran his fingertips over the imprint of her writing on the envelope, tracing each letter. He had always loved how his name looked when she wrote it. There was a whimsical way she created her J's, how she mixed cursive and print. She enjoyed the loopiness of the *o's* in cursive, but preferred a printed *s*, a loop added on the tail to make it blend better.

He turned the envelope over, startled to find a Post-It over the seal in his mom's tightly woven script:

Luther wanted to make sure you got this. I love you. -Mom

He wiped at the corner of his eye, gazed out into the forest, the emotion he'd managed to suppress starting to break through.

Josh,

When I was little, my dad and I had this ongoing conversation about Heaven. What it would look like, feel like, be like. I had decided and he'd gone along with the idea, that places would exist from our memories and experiences and we could go and relive those moments, just as they were. It was my theory that God gives us little moments of Heaven on earth so it made sense to me that we'd be able to reclaim them there. I actually drew a map of Heaven, taped extra pages to it as new places were added. My dad kept it tucked away ever since I was young and recently I spent some time wandering through the Heaven I'd created. I came to the same conclusion that my dad and I had during our conversations: It's the people who make the places, the experiences, the life special. So even if I get the Heaven I've dreamt up in my mind, so much of it will be empty until the day everyone else is there, too. And you, Josh West, live in so many places in my Heaven. I'd say all, but there are places and experiences I didn't get to share with you. I will someday. And you know what? You'll get to do the same—with things you experienced up until now without me—as well as the things you experience after I'm gone.

It's such a bittersweet thought. I wrote that and then I felt a burning in my chest. An ache. I don't want there to be life apart from you.

Josh, if something happens to me, if God calls me home sooner than we'd like? Know how much I love you. Know that there is nowhere I'd rather be than with you, wherever that may be. I hope I've made that as clear as possible so you don't actually need this letter to resolve any doubt.

So what is the purpose of writing this? Well, maybe it's actually for me. Maybe it's so I know that if I don't get to speak the last words I would have chosen, I know you'll have this.

Okay, so you may have noticed this paper is wrinkled and my writing got wonky above? Well, that's because Miles ripped the page away to see what I was writing and—well, #1, he's upset with me. He doesn't like the whole idea of a just-in-case letter. #2, he wants it written that if something happens to me and you eventually move on with someone new, that he subsequently gets first dibs on "Heaven me." I have to be honest—this is not something I thought I'd have to worry about in eternal life.

I'm not going to tell you what to do in your life, Josh. What I will say is this: follow God's guidance, wherever that takes you and to whomever He leads you. You know me well enough to know what my thoughts would be in any given situation. Live your life and live it well. You had a few years of life before I came along and you were already a radiant beacon of light in the world. Remember who you are. When you're feeling sad? When you're missing me drooling on your shirts and not securing the lids properly on jars, remind yourself who my best friend is and all he has to offer to the world.

No matter what happened to me, Josh, remind yourself that no evil can reach me in Heaven. Picture me lying on the grass under the tree at the farmhouse reading a book. Picture me floating in the stream, probably with more garments than I actually typically wore—though, now I wonder if it's a Garden of Eden situation in Heaven? If we go back to not being ashamed and we all run around naked? That'd be weird.

[Respectful pause as you resolve the whole naked scenario.]

Picture me in your favorite memories...because that's where I am. I'm convinced there will be some variation of your cabin there and I can hang out on the porch swing reading, expecting you to turn up from fishing at any moment.

I imagine that's what it'll be like for me: Savoring the best feelings of my life, the best memories, along with everything Heaven offers, but also, looking forward to one day getting to share it with you, looking forward to the moment I see you again and you can tell me all about your wonderful life.

I love you.

Love,
Essie

8

the book of job

seven years earlier...

Matteo shook out his clear umbrella over the potted plants next to the front door, leaned it against the wall. He pushed open the door, met with a quiet stillness.

"Daddy," Essie began in her questioning tone, "in your *professional* opinion, what in the Sam Hill is going on in the book of Job?" She was folded into the end of the couch, leaning toward the table lamp. Her forehead was deeply furrowed, eyes narrowed.

"You have an afternoon to yourself and you take on the book of *Job*?"

"Evidently," she muttered, propping her chin up against her fist. "People claim I'm a 'bright girl,' but I make some very questionable decisions. I've been so caught up in it that I forgot to start dinner."

"We have leftovers from the two *other* dinners you made this week."

"*Oh.* Well, hallelujah."

"I won't soon forget this lack of initiative though."

She smirked. "Yeah, yeah, I'm a slacker. When you were thirteen, you were walking ten miles to school in the snow."

"Barefoot."

"The lack of footwear is a new detail."

He shook out his damp hair, smiling. "I'm going to clarify for my sake that the making dinner thing is very much appreciated, but it's not expected. You're thirteen, kiddo."

"Consider it clarified," she said, taking a deep breath. "Can you try to help me make sense of this now?"

"Tell me about what you know from reading what you have so far. How far have you gotten in the book?"

"I finished it."

He nodded, impressed. "It's a tough one to get through."

"You're telling me. I need to read some *Captain Underpants* nonsense after that."

He sat down in the chair across from her, smiling lightly. "Give me your synopsis."

"Job was faithful to God. God knew that." She took a deep breath, clearly angry and frustrated. "Satan thought that the only reason Job worshiped God was because of the blessings God had bestowed upon him. He claimed that if all of that was taken from him, he would curse the name of God. So God agreed to let Satan torture him—which is my *first* issue with this book."

Matteo nodded, suppressing any commentary.

"So Job loses everything. All his possessions, his family, all ten children killed. Like, seriously? Ten children? Dead. But apparently that's not enough. Satan covers him with boils and does everything short of killing him since God had told Satan he wasn't allowed to do that. Which is my second issue with this book. Seriously, *so many* issues."

Matteo pressed his lips together, patiently waiting for her to continue.

"He's living at the dump basically, he's just a broken, broken man—except for the fact that he continues to praise God." She ran her palm across her face, shaking her head. "Daddy, I get that there's suffering on earth and it's Satan's work. People are quick to blame God when they're in pain, when they're suffering even though Satan's to blame for the wicked in the world."

"But?"

Her eyes glistened in the dim light. "But it *bothers* me that God allowed Satan to do all of this to Job, who was absolutely loyal to God. He actually *invited* Satan to torture him."

"I'm a pastor and this book makes me very uncomfortable."

She took a deep breath. "What was the *point* of Job's suffering?"

He frowned. "Do you know how many sermons have been done about Job, trying to make sense of it, make it show a purpose, make it feel less—"

"Horrific?"

Matteo nodded. "I'd like to hear what you think."

"I think the Old Testament is absolutely terrifying and I much prefer the hope and miracles of the New Testament starring our Lord and Savior, Jesus Christ."

He suppressed a smile.

She sighed. "Satan is the author of suffering. *Not* God."

"Yes."

"God is the good in the world, the love, the families, the friendships, the blessings; that's all God's doing, His influence."

He nodded.

"Satan and his demons influence people to do evil. All the pain, suffering, disease, death; that's Satan." She frowned. "So Hell is basically *this* world, but without God. Not to veer off subject, but Hell isn't necessarily a literal burning wasteland; it could just be *this* world without God."

"Yes."

"That feels so bleak. I think of that and I feel hopelessness in my heart. Like I know the visual of lakes of lava and the world literally aflame should seem like the worst possible thing, but imagining this world *without* God feels worse to me." She frowned, shaking her head. "So Satan is throwing everything at Job to break him, to make him turn away from God. He's literally torturing him—his heart, his mind, his body— everything short of actually killing him."

Matteo took a breath and nodded.

"God could have stopped it."

"Yeah. He could have."

Her shoulders fell. "How could He watch this happen and do *nothing*? God calls us His *children*. I mean, if this was happening to me and *you* could do something, you'd do it. You wouldn't just let me suffer." She was getting more animated with her hand gestures, but suddenly froze as she motioned to her dad, her brow furrowing.

"I can see you formulating a theory, but I'll just chime in and say, yes, I'd move heaven and earth to get to you."

She dropped her hands to her lap. "This has something to do with Adam and Eve, right? Suffering, sin, evil exists because they couldn't follow one rule: Just don't eat from that one specific tree. Not *all* the trees, just that *one*. Was that really too much to ask? It's like God tried *everything* to make sure they didn't sin. 'Okay, I have to put temptation in here *somewhere*. There, that tree. They have other apple trees. There's no possible justification for eating from that one tree.'"

He shrugged. "Satan got a hold on the world."

"I hope that was a really good apple."

"Yeah."

"They're not always good apples. That's why we have the expression 'bad apple.' Some have like, *very* little flavor and a grainy, gritty texture." She frowned. "But I guess that represents sin well. The temptation sells the sin, but in the end, the sin doesn't live up to how the temptation felt. I'm sure some sin feels, you know, worth it at the time, because people see others sinning and think, hey, that looks like something I should *also* be doing, but in the end, it's meaningless and isn't fulfilling and–" She shook her head. "Tangent. The long story short of it was that Job did nothing to deserve what Satan did to him."

"No, he didn't."

"God wouldn't let Job suffer just to stick it to Satan, right?"

Matteo remained quiet.

"I guess that *would be* demoralizing to Satan. And in this world, God lets it rain, figuratively speaking, on everyone. Believers and non-believers."

"Yes."

"Suffering can lead people closer to God."

Matteo nodded.

"It can teach people things, though I don't see the lesson in this for Job. After Satan's first pass at him, if he was remaining loyal to God, you would hope *that* would be it, that he would have proven himself." Her shoulders sank. "I guess with the world being what it is, some suffering doesn't necessarily have a point. It just is. Right?" She gazed across the room toward the kitchen, remembering suddenly that they were meant to be having dinner soon.

"Let's finish this. You're working through it. I can see it."

She took a deep breath. "We can't understand all suffering. It doesn't appear to have a point, but if you think about this story in today's terms—maybe it's silly to think like this, but I think of Satan having like, demon foot soldiers. Well, not foot soldiers, more like spirit demons, moving around, spreading evil and wicked thoughts. I think of someone who's suffering like Job not yielding to the temptation of renouncing God and I think of the demon recoiling and maybe shriveling up and dying shouting '*nooooooooooo*' like some doomed villain in an animated movie–"

Matteo smiled lightly at her enthusiastic gesturing.

"That's okay to wish for Satan and his demons to suffer, right?"

He shrugged.

"It's a gray area probably. We shouldn't wish ill on anyone, yada yada. *Anyway*, some suffering I suppose we can't understand, but there might be a purpose we can't see. *Or* it may just be how it is because of the nature of the world once sin came into it. *But* God still gave His promise and He still blesses us while we're here."

"Yes."

"He didn't exactly reward Job, but He did bless his life after this. Job lived a very long life after his health was restored. He went on to have twice his wealth, which, you know, *is* what it is. He gave him ten more children. He didn't resurrect the children who died, which He proved He *could* do, but I get it. That would be undoing what Satan had done and–" Essie took a deep breath. "This is just a tough story to wrap my mind around. Giving him ten new children doesn't take the pain away from losing the others."

Matteo shook his head. "No, it doesn't."

"He wished he had never been born," she murmured, lifting her eyes. "When Satan was torturing him? Job *wanted* to die." She could see the moment his expression faltered. In a quiet voice, but maintaining her gaze upon him, she asked: "Do people who commit suicide go to heaven?"

The muscles of her dad's face twisted a bit as the memories came rushing back. He'd put enough years, enough life between himself and the day Rachel killed herself that he first images, sounds, smells that came to mind were not of the moment he found Rachel's body in the bathtub, but of their life before that. Their childhood. Her laughter. How she liked to use the river stones that made a surreptitious path across the river near where they grew up as her own balance beam and depending on the water level, if there had been high rainfall, could make it appear she was walking on water. He thought of how she would lose herself in a dance, closing her eyes delicately, stretching her elegant arms toward the heavens, seeming to float just above the ground. How she indulgently took in the scent of roses, her favorite flower.

"I'm sorry, Daddy," Essie whispered.

He shook his head. "It's a big question."

She nodded.

"What do *you* think?"

"I don't know the Bible like you know the Bible." She met his gentle, patient gaze. "Suicide is a sin. But it's not an *unforgivable* sin. The Bible says that if you commit one sin, it's as good as committing them all. Not that we should then have a free-for-all, but it *does* say that. All people are sinners."

He lifted his brow.

"Salvation isn't contingent on anything but having faith and trusting in Jesus for salvation, accepting Him as Lord and Savior. That's the *only* requirement. No one enters the gates of heaven except through the Son. The repentance of sins and acceptance of Jesus covers all sins, past, present, and future–as long as the trust and faith in Jesus remains."

Matteo's lips pulled upward, though there was sadness building in his eyes. He stood and moved to sit beside her on the couch.

"So I think it's not a matter of what sin was committed, no matter what it was. I think if they had trust and faith in Jesus, they'll be saved like every other sinner."

He placed his palm over her hand that rested on her knee. "And there you have it."

She pinched her eyebrows together. "Daddy?"

He nodded lightly, encouraging her to ask the question she was afraid to ask, the question he'd considered in some way every day since Rachel died.

"Do you think Rachel went to Heaven?"

Matteo took a steadying breath. "Rachel and I met at Sunday School. She was very faithful growing up. She loved Jesus, praised Jesus. She sang louder than anybody during worship songs–" He winced. "--not a great vocalist. But she believed, she was passionate in her faith, she was baptized when she was eight, she planned to go into the Ministry." He straightened his posture. "She went through a lot once we got a little older. Her parents died suddenly and she had to move away to live with family she didn't know very well, who were *not* Christ followers. She was mistreated and abused." His jaw tightened. "When we were able to reunite permanently, things got better, she came back to the faith, she got baptized again." His voice trailed off. "When we lost several pregnancies, several babies, she fell back away from her faith. She couldn't understand why God would let her go through so much, why He would let her suffer again." He wiped roughly at his eyes. "For my own sake, I wish I didn't know the answer to your question."

Essie furrowed her brow.

"She left a letter. In that, there was no ambiguity. She said very clearly that she thought it was foolish to believe, to have faith in God if He would allow such pain and such suffering."

Tears were brimming her eyes. "You suffered, too. And she–she made it *so* much worse." Her voice was tight, anger seeping into her tone. "In her last opportunity, in her last words to you, she–"

He nodded. He could see her suppressing a lot of what she wanted to say, her lips firmly pressed together. "Essie, you can say it. You don't need to hold back."

She winced. "I don't want to hurt you."

"I can take it."

She turned her chin away, tears streaming down her cheeks. "You named me Esther *for her*. Because *she* liked the name."

He nodded. "I did."

"*Why*?" Her jaw tensed.

He cleared his throat, gathering himself, piecing together the words in his mind. "Rachel reached a point where she could no longer see any good in the world. Satan had gotten a hold on her mind and on her heart. For a long time, her single beacon of hope had been the idea of having children, of having a family.

"When I saw you, I was entirely overwhelmed with love and hope and some fear, honestly, because I literally had no idea what I was doing."

"You did pretty well for not knowing what you were doing."

He gave a light smile. "In your sweet face, your big, hopeful eyes, I saw all the good in the world that Rachel had no longer been able to see.

"I named you Esther to honor who she was before Satan got his hold. I thought that, in a way, I was showing her that good still existed in the world, but *Essie*, the good you embody every day? Your kindness, your selflessness, the light you shine on the world? Is far beyond anything she could have possibly imagined. Anything I could have possibly imagined."

She frowned.

"At first, I *did* think of her when I said your name or heard your name. For that reason, there was a time I regretted choosing it."

She blinked slowly.

"But now? When I hear your name, say your name, I just feel the tremendous love and goodness and grace of God. No sadness. No pain. Just goodness and love."

Essie abruptly seized hold of his cuffed sleeve and began blotting her eyes. She broke down in sobs the moment she felt her dad's hand brace the back of her neck and fell into his chest, hugging him. "I'm sorry you went through that."

He kissed the side of her head, smiled affectionately into her mane of wild hair. "I suffered, but then God blessed me so much more than I deserved."

*   *   *

The stream that ran through the West's farm was approximately fifteen feet wide. Not exceptionally wide, but not small either. Unlike many waterways on other farming properties in the area, which were essentially dug out ditches filled with mucky, questionable water, the stream was lined with rocks and was natural to the environment, a side passage of the Jameson River, which flowed directly from the Rockies. During storms and inclement weather, the streams could develop a moderate current, but on a typical day, it offered a calm, gentle flow of freshwater.

Sara and Luke had chosen to homeschool Josh and Gabe. With this autonomy, they were able to adjust schooling schedules to coincide with farm work, fair weather, poor weather, and pretty much anything else that happened to come up.

If the boys found themselves occupied by schoolwork or farm tasks, the farm offered plenty of sights and activities to keep Esther occupied. One of her favorite places was the stream, particularly on warm days. Her latest read, Pride and Prejudice, *sat under a tree by the grassy shoreline. She had been keeping the cover hidden from Luke, as a complicated love story would be just the thing he'd poke fun at, albeit in an affectionate way.*

Bree quietly grazed near the tree, swishing his luscious white tail to shoo away any lurking flies.

Esther had decided against wearing her clothes in the water, fearing the chill of the wind on the long walk back and had undressed down to her underwear and a sports bra. The heat of the sunshine on her back was warm, but the mountain-sourced stream was still quite chilly and it took her breath away as she submerged her body up to her shoulders. She waded a few strides across into the sunlight, released her feet from the basin and began to float.

Her long, unruly waves soaked up the cool water and billowed out around her head. She could feel the tension in her body, still trying to maintain some sense of control. She took a deep breath and focused on relaxing her body, muscle group by muscle group. She slowed her breathing, listening to the individual breaths seeming to echo in the water, the gentle sound of the water lapping against the river stones.

The sun began to warm the skin of her arms, her stomach, her cheeks.

She felt no muscle aches from the earlier exertion mucking stalls. She didn't feel her body at all.

And then she heard the murmur of a voice in her ears:

It's better not to feel.
It's better not to think.

Essie opened her eyes to find the sun still shining brightly overhead. Her chest constricted with tightening breaths. She tried to relax again, tried to slow her breathing, feel the sun, feel the water.

There was a prickle on the back of her neck, a premonition, like something out of a horror movie.

Her eyes flew open at the same moment she felt a hand clasp over her mouth and her body being pulled underwater.

9

juxtaposition

Luther heard a deliberate cough echo from the living room just as he stepped out of the bathroom, an oversized burgundy towel wrapped about his waist. He stepped with some trepidation toward the bedroom door.

"Luther, it's Sadie," she called out. Her dark eyes lifted as he stepped into the doorway, but she turned away, seeing the state of him. "I'm sorry to intrude. I–I shouldn't have–I'm sorry. This isn't appropriate of me."

"It's fine, but you could have knocked," he said in what he hoped was a light enough tone, scanning the room for anyone else that might be with her. He lifted his hand to scratch his head, inconspicuously tapping the communication device over his ear, which would activate his microphone and alert Danny. Luther found himself briefly distracted, noticing he'd left out a collection of maps and blueprints on the kitchen counter.

She turned back around. "I need to talk to you. I wasn't even sure where you lived, but Danny gave me your address and the door code."

There was a crunching noise in his ear, followed by the echo of a sip from an aluminum can. "You're going to want to talk to her, Luther," Danny said, matter-of-factly. "I'm in the middle of something right now."

"*Okay*," Luther murmured tentatively, deactivating his microphone. "I just need a minute to get dressed."

Sadie nodded, distracting herself with the details of the living room, examining what little personal items he had on shelves.

When Luther stepped back into the room, fully-clothed, she didn't look up right away, eyes fixed on a framed portrait of his mother, Loretta. He moved toward the kitchen, gathered up the maps and blueprints and dropped them into the large trash bin.

"Luther, I'd like to help you," she said finally, looking up. "In any way I can."

He leaned on the kitchen island. "Help me with what exactly?"

She sighed. "We'll save a lot of time if we don't do this."

"If we don't do what?"

"Dance around, trying to coax some information out of the other. I'd prefer *not* to waste the time or energy."

"Okay."

"You don't have to share all the details with me, of what you're doing, but I know we could be more effective if we put our heads together, if we work together."

He nodded.

She furrowed her brow, showing the least amount of confidence he'd ever seen from her. "We're of the same mindset, Luther. We have the same goals. We want the same things, as far as I can tell. The problem is, we each have information we're terrified to have come to light because if it does, it puts those we love in danger."

Luther narrowed his eyes, wondering what skeletons could possibly lurk in the closet of Sadie Parker, who prior to the Arks, was the most formidable political threat to Samuel Gowon. Or *would have* been, if fair elections were held. She was poised and natural and relatable. She refused corporate donors, published her bank statements and tax returns, and quietly gave away her entire political salary. She was also involved in her church, from community events to the food pantry to being one of the leaders of the women's life group. What was more was that while Gowon berated opposition "leaders," often using air quotes, he hadn't so much as mentioned her. Luther assumed it was because Gowon was intimidated by her.

Press corps reporters had started to ask unscripted questions, straying from the usual, but only Christopher Loop had questioned Gowon specifically about something Sadie Parker had said. In these few instances, Gowon would reply with his own question, something unimportant like: "She's from Montana?" or take the opportunity to make a comment about "preferring the weather in Montana right now," when the District was facing storms or oppressive heat. He'd then act as though there'd been no question, that he and the press had been having a conversation that had naturally progressed to talking about Montana and he was simply getting them back on track.

"I guess I'll go first?" She took a deep breath and spoke in a steady, measured voice. "Well, *this* is where I tell you that my maiden name is Gowon and that my younger brother, Samuel, has killed at least ten times more people than anyone else in the history of the world."

Luther blinked.

Sadie perked a dark, defined eyebrow. "Should I continue?"

He nodded.

"Have you read his recently published 'autobiography'?"

"No," he lied.

"I don't blame you, to be honest," she said with a frown. "The book really falls more into the fiction category. It's difficult to stomach a genocidal maniac portraying himself as a humanitarian. But whoever *actually* wrote it really does try." She had become uneasy, plagued by her thoughts. "It *would be* beneficial to scan through it if you plan to take him on. It's surprisingly insightful to figure out his current motivations."

"I'll consider it."

She cleared her throat. "It's *especially* insightful when you consider the previous draft. He sent it to me to get my thoughts. To my old Senate email address," she added, answering his unspoken question, then went on, realizing there was more to explain. "He's been trying to reconnect for twenty-three years. He does that sort of thing. He sends me–or *sent* me–things, trying to get me to speak to him."

He lifted his brow. "The two of you had a falling out back then?"

"We did. He's killed many people or *ordered* many people to be killed I suppose. When he was younger, he had a more hands-on approach. One of the first people he killed was our younger brother, Seth."

Luther frowned.

"Samuel performed experiments on Seth to try to 'cure' him and he took things too far."

"To *cure* him."

"Seth had Down Syndrome."

Luther thought of Timothy, who had the markers and all indications of having Down Syndrome. It was what had gotten him rejected from the STRONG experiment. "How exactly did he try to *cure* him?"

"He said he had a theory about deep brain stimulation being used as a cognitive therapy, to expand the capabilities of the mind. He used a version of electroshock therapy. He recorded it," she added, swallowing hard. "Seth was awake for it. He begged Samuel to stop. He was sobbing. Samuel wouldn't stop." She furrowed her brow. "It caused a stroke. If Seth had received medical treatment sooner, there's a chance he would have survived–"

Luther felt his stomach turn. "He didn't try to get him to a hospital?"

"Samuel let it happen. He sat down and *watched*, like he was mesmerized by what was happening. It was only once Seth was dead that he called for help. He made up a story that Seth wanted to see his lab, that he'd needed to take a call or something, and that he found him unconscious." Sadie pressed her lips together, suppressing something internally.

Luther frowned, motioning toward the couch. "Why don't you take a seat? Would you like something to drink? Bottled water? Bourbon?"

"While bourbon is tempting, I make a point not to drink. I'd take water though. Thank you." She moved toward the seating area, sat herself at the edge of a couch cushion.

Luther stepped over to the refrigerator. With the door shielding his face from Sadie, he took a couple of deep breaths as he reached for a bottle of water. He sighed as he turned back for the living room. "When did this take place?"

"This was when Samuel was in sophomore year of college. Seth was 11," she added, compressing her lips.

"How did you find out the truth?"

"Our mother did. She knew he was lying. First, he told his story about finding Seth unconscious. The autopsy showed brain abnormalities consistent with electro-convulsive therapy. There was also an excess of glutamate. Samuel then pivoted and made the claim about his 'theory' of ECT as a cognitive treatment for Down Syndrome. He pleaded with our mother that he was trying to help Seth. Samuel then tried to justify what he'd done, saying that it was for *her*." She twisted off the bottle cap and took a long sip. "*That* broke her."

"Where were you during all of this? What's the age difference?" Nothing in the autobiography had so much as mentioned an older sister, nor had any campaign efforts.

"I had already graduated college at that point and moved away. My husband and I were living in Billings; I was pregnant with our oldest son." She nodded slowly. "My mother called to tell me. She was strangely calm. She told me that Samuel had murdered Seth and that it was her fault. I didn't–I was working in a busy hospital at the time when she called, there were interruptions, chair alarms going off, I couldn't really process what she was saying. And then she told me that she was going to kill herself."

Luther narrowed his eyes.

"I thought I'd misheard her, but then she laid out her plan, that she was going to go see Samuel. She'd decided to use a cyanide capsule because it would be quick and she didn't like the idea of handling a gun. She said she was going to tell him that she'd seen with her own eyes what he did to her son–there was surveillance in the lab–she was going to tell him she saw what he did and then she was going to kill herself. I tried to convince her to stop and think about this, to get help. I mentioned that I was at work, but to let me call her back in just a few minutes." She frowned. "She apologized. She actually apologized. Her voice was light and she said she didn't mean to interrupt, but that she couldn't possibly change her plans since she was already at his office, about to go inside.

"To do what he did to Seth–he was not a well person, but he *adored* our mother. She knew what she was doing. She didn't know what he'd become, obviously, but she knew it would cause damage he'd never recover from."

"What about your father?"

"He started drinking after Seth died–and couldn't seem to stop. Samuel had him killed before he ran for office. They were never very close."

Luther leaned forward, frowning. "How have you gotten where you are?"

"Why wouldn't he have just killed me, too?"

He nodded.

She shrugged. "Most people assume he doesn't feel remorse–and for most things, I suspect he doesn't. He's killed nearly 100 million people. They were ants to him." She drew her eyebrows upward. "He's never gotten over what happened with our mother though. That she knew what he'd done. I believe in his twisted mind, he believes he was doing good. That he has done good.

"I think when and if he ever accomplishes what he set out to do, he wants to be able to show me and say 'See? Look at all the good I've done.'

"And it sounds ridiculous when I consider what he's done, naive probably, but I honestly think he still cares about me, which is why he's removed all traces of me from the final book. I think he had me included and sent me the proof, intending to force me to act, to speak to him."

"Have you?"

She shook her head. "I've gotten very good at ignoring his attempts to bait me."

"When he's been questioned about you, he doesn't defame you like he does others."

"No."

"Because he's protecting you."

The silence stretched.

"I don't imagine people would allow for much explanation if they found out who I am," she said quietly.

"Probably not." He took a deep breath. "It's difficult to find any sort of commonality between the two of you."

It wasn't true. He could see something about her refined features, the chisel of her chin, the rate of her blinking. He'd always respected Sadie Parker and shared the values she represented, but he could find traces of Samuel Gowon in her appearance, in her mannerisms. It didn't mean anything beyond what it was, but he couldn't help but feel a bit uneasy by the resemblances, even if they were superficial.

"You said we want the same things," he said delicately.

"Yes."

"What is it we want?"

She didn't hesitate. "To bring us back to the foundation of the country. To limit government. To secure personal liberties and rights and religious freedom. To make being a senator, a congressman, a President, a civil service, not a way to get rich. Most pressing of all? We both want to overthrow the Gowon regime and begin to reclaim our country."

He nodded slowly. Despite it sounding too good to be true, he believed her.

"When the Arks came to be, I was optimistic that they would be the way forward and then the cliche politicians got their hands on the wheel. They considered themselves first."

"What did you do before becoming 'Senator Parker'? You mentioned a hospital?"

"I was a social worker in a pediatric hospital. This was before socialized healthcare, before death panels or whatever they call themselves: healthcare decision advisory boards, was it?"

108

"Something like that."

"After my mother's death, I quit my job–seven months' work in exchange for a six-year degree, probably not the best return on investment. My husband and I bought some land and had our babies. I stayed home with the kids and homeschooled."

"Does Owen know about your family?"

She appeared impressed–and pleased–that he remembered her husband's name. "I met him in high school. He's been there for me through all of it. You have to remember, Samuel didn't even step into politics until 10 years ago. He was funding most of the programs and research, but no one knew much about who he was."

"What made you decide to run for office?"

"Why not keep my quiet life?"

"Yeah."

"My babies weren't babies anymore. Their friends were being pulled into Mandatory and they weren't coming back. Children we'd known their whole lives. Gone. I had to do something."

"They don't know? Your kids?"

She shook her head. "They couldn't help but be suspicious when they weren't called up for Mandatory."

"How did that conversation go?"

"It didn't. I lied, Luther. We told them there must have been an error."

"That's risky though. If Gowon called you out?"

"I suspected he wouldn't." She shrugged. "Even evil doers like him can have a weak spot."

Luther took another deep breath. "Does anyone else know?"

"No."

Luther frowned. "Why did you tell me?"

She winced. "I told you so you'd trust me, though hearing how I presented all that, maybe I had the opposite effect."

He shook his head.

"I want to help you, Luther. Truly."

"With what specifically?"

"You should lead. You're the one who made the Arks possible. You orchestrated resources and moved people and designed counter-efforts against the government. *You* should see this through."

He took a breath.

"While I haven't seen him face to face in over 20 years, I know Samuel better than any living person. He's shown that in whatever way he's capable, he cares about me."

Luther nodded slowly but was uncertain what he was supposed to infer from that statement.

"That could be helpful if there was a need for leverage."

"*Leverage*," he echoed slowly. "Threaten your life, you mean?"

"You might feel differently about using the tactic once you hear what I have to tell you."

"And what is that?"

"I believe Essie Natale is alive."

His breath caught in his chest. "Why do you believe that?"

"She's what he wanted to create–or at least some aspect of what he wanted to create. If he made these efforts to get her, there was a reason. If she was killed, his response would have been—" She winced. "We would have felt it. Those who struck the deal with him, arranged things, would have felt it. I assume he would have had the kidnappers killed regardless of what happened; he was never going to let them live. But it just doesn't make sense: the most important person in the world to him arrives dead and he takes no further action? He gives the silent treatment? It doesn't add up."

Luther lowered his eyes, reeling all she'd just told him, wondering if he was willing to risk trusting the sister of Samuel Gowon, of all people. "You started off this conversation implying that we both had information to share with one another. What is it you hoped to learn from me?" he asked quietly, looking up.

She frowned. "*Oh.*" She glanced down at her hands, pressed her lips together. "To be completely transparent with you, I anticipated after sharing what I did–I thought you might feel compelled to tell me–

110

Luther, I wasn't entirely forthcoming. I'm not wagering a guess that she's alive. I *know* Essie's alive."

The muscles in his shoulders stiffened. "How do you know that?"

"I have a contact at the White House. I say 'contact,' but they just reached out. It's a known asset. I tried to verify who it is, but the Ark asset profile is classified. I had to reach out to Security, who wouldn't tell me a name, but told me that the message originated from the White House."

"That's how you got in communication with Danny?"

"Yes."

This eased something in him—it hadn't occurred to him before that there's no way she should have known who Danny was.

"The ID stamp on the classification belonged to Danny."

He nodded.

"I mentioned to him that I wanted to talk to you about the communication and it would be helpful to know who had sent it specifically—and he still wouldn't tell me. I'm a persistent person though. He finally told me 'Bluebird.' 'Just tell Luther it's Bluebird.'"

So, Annette knows. Luther nodded encouragingly. "The message was about Essie?"

She swallowed hard. "'Tell Luther E is stateside and active. Location unknown.'"

"Is that all it said?"

Sadie nodded, her eyes widening. "You knew already, didn't you? You don't seem—"

He furrowed his brow, considering lying, but knew he had already given himself away. "I did."

"I got that message and suddenly understood why you were being so quiet. What kind of situation is she in?"

"Literal torture."

"He doesn't care about 'optimizing the genome' anymore then."

"No."

*　　*　　*

SecureChat Session-user7741db9gp46

You got my message.

>Still trying to decide what your intentions are with the message.

You cut off communication.

>That doesn't explain why you would involve Hathaway.

Thought you needed an ally.

>I didn't realize you were acquaintances.

We never met that I recall.

Creature values so few things. If push comes to shove, I wanted to make sure you had an option.

>Hathaway made the same suggestion.

Really?

>I'm not really in the business of using human

bait.

I didn't have a choice. You weren't going to take action without motivation.

Like I said: human bait.

Do you think that was easy for me? I get nothing from this.

I don't understand how sacrificing E was the only option. Or an option at all.

You would have never considered stepping up otherwise.

Luther slid back from the computer, taking a steadying breath, resisting the urge to explode at Annette. While she had a point that he'd taken decisive action as a result of Essie being taken, he could not, absolutely *could not* wrap his mind around the idea that a parent would sacrifice their own child, that she would offer Essie up on a silver platter to Gowon, knowing what fate would await her.

The truth was, Annette was highly-intelligent, but lacked a scientific mind. She hadn't thought to question the generic explanation of hyper-immunity. In her defense, he hadn't shared anything about the significance of Essie's cellular structure.

The Arks come first. Millions of people come before one single person. No matter who that person is.

"Lord Jesus, give me strength," he murmured.

She didn't understand the consequences of her actions. She may not have known that Essie's dad was murdered as a result, and she might not care; she didn't know about his friendship with Matteo and he certainly wasn't about to tell her now. She also didn't know the full extent of Essie's unique cellular characteristics. If he explained it to her and she suddenly understood what could result from her "choice," what would be the point?

It might set her off. She might do something that would compromise Essie's rescue.

Do you know where?

Yes.

What I saw said 'Area 51,'
but it seems strange that they
would go to New Mexico.

You said you have one
mission at this point.

I did.

E is not your mission.

Is she okay?

"Is she okay? Of course she's not effing okay."
Danny peered over the top of his trio of computer monitors.
"I didn't mean to say that out loud."
"She actually asked that?"
Luther lifted his brows.
"Essie evidently got her intelligence from somewhere else. Nurture won out."

Of course she's not okay.
That was stupid.

I'll get to her as soon as I
possibly can.

Do you think she'll understand?
Why I did what I did?

Luther scratched his neck, exhaling deeply.
"What now?"
"She wants me to make her feel better."
"She said that?"
"Not exactly, but it's what she wants to hear." He sighed. If he told
her the truth, she'd be disheartened. She might try to intervene. She
might not follow through with her mission–and they really needed her
mission to be successful.

I doubt she'll even care how it
happened. She'll just be grateful
to be safe. As far as I'm
concerned, there's no reason she
needs to know all the details.

You did what you felt like you
needed to.

If I had acted sooner, you
wouldn't have felt forced into
action.

You're trying to make me
feel better.

Just stating facts.

It's bad then.
For her?

Yes.

You'll be able to get her?

Yes.

When you see her, will you
tell her I love her?

I know that sounds
pathetic after what I did.

Maybe you can show her.

How?

Do you still have your offshore
account?

Yes. Do you need money?

For her future. I don't want it
tied up with anything else we're
doing. I want the transactions as
far from me, from you as
possible.

She can have all of it.

Let me get some more plans in
place then I'll reach out with
more information.

116

Thank you.

10

by the sword

Everyone falls into rhythms, whether they intend to or not, whether their tasks vary a bit from day to day, or not. After enough time, there are patterns, predictable sequences, grooves of normalcy, where any variance from the usual rhythm feels uncomfortable.

Esther had committed herself to memorizing the habits of her captors, learning the transitional points in their routines, like a zoo animal testing for weaknesses in an electrified fence.

There were three crews: "medical/science" staff, guards, and custodial staff. Each of the crews had unique schedule sharing and overlap. "Medical/science" staff arrived between 6:21 and 6:28am. Never later. There were three who rotated the earliest shift. She'd assigned them all nicknames, as she felt learning their actual names showed far more respect than they deserved:

Buzzkill was a very solemn young woman whose skull was shaved in geometric patterns on the bottom half. She had a single column of long blonde hair she typically put in a top knot. Her skin was too snug over the bone structure in her face and she had piercings in her chin and brow. She had an apathetic, disinterested way about her, typically not swaying very far from her baseline mood throughout the day.

Hillbilly Bob was a balding, middle-aged man with a thick southern accent who always seemed to be gnawing on something—gum, food, sometimes just the inside of his cheek. He reminded her of a cow chewing the cud. Unsettling further was the way in which he'd stroke her arm or her forehead and speak in a higher register, as though trying to settle a spooked animal.

Second Act Doctor Wu was coolly sinister and confident, never addressing her directly, always speaking in terms of "the test subject" when dictating his research notes. Like his namesake in the first *Jurassic World* movie (his first act taking place in the original *Jurassic Park*), *Second Act Doctor Wu* was quiet but arrogant and carried an abundance of self-importance and greed. He was obsessed with his "work." If there was a discovery to be made, he wanted his name attached. While the other two would have Essie taken back to her cell when the sessions ended, he would have her remain in the chair, watching him mull over his thoughts, just in case he had something come to mind he wanted to immediately investigate, checking her pupil dilation, or her pulse, or if he wanted to see what happened if he doubled a dose of something. Inefficiency angered him.

The afternoons were far busier in the lab. Based upon conversations she'd overheard, the staff who only worked afternoons/evenings had spent mornings in lectures, which correlated with their younger ages.

Bobble looked like a more effeminate version of a Harry Potter/Ron Weasley *Goblet of Fire* mash-up. He wore round glasses that severely magnified his blue eyes, had a mop of red hair, and was constantly in everyone else's way.

Gollum was an emaciated looking girl with pale, nearly translucent skin, thin white hair, and protruding eyes that didn't seem to blink enough.

Kamala was inept, cackled a lot, and everyone hated her.

The supervising "scientist," *Palpatine*, was a gangly man in his late fifties/early sixties who spoke in an expectant, grating tone and typically kept his back turned to her. He constantly wore a nondescript, indulgent smirk, like he was enjoying every single aspect of his work. His seniority seemed to preclude him from any menial tasks, which probably added to his overall job satisfaction. Even if one of the others had done all the prep work, he got to be the one to initiate programs, inject serums. He did this with a psychedelic glint of enthusiasm and anticipation in his eyes, further heightened when she had an outward, involuntary physical response to an experiment.

There were six guards, restricted to staying in the corridor unless in the process of dragging her from her cell to the lab or the lab to her cell. They'd twice been required to shower her, both times when *Palpatine*'s sensitive olfactory system couldn't handle the stench any longer.

The guards seemed to understand that their presence was probably not essential, given the security measures in place, given the weakness she demonstrated, given that she had to be carried from place to place.

Two guards were on duty at a time, one in the corridor, while the other, she surmised, was manning the structure's exterior door. Typically, they traded off every hour. Each of the guards had a different way of dealing with the monotony of standing in a confined space for an extended period. It was fairly easy to figure out who was on duty based upon gait patterns, affinity for humming, gnawing on fingernails, etc.

Night guards tended to wander away from their posts. There had been several late-night hours when she was certain she was alone. Despite none of her captors being a comfort, the isolation when no one was around actually made her captivity more debilitating, left alone to her thoughts, her fears in a dark, windowless, underground room. It felt like she'd been buried alive.

It made her think of a television adaptation of an Edgar Allan Poe story, "The Cask of Amontillado." In it, a man named Montresor believes another man, Fortunato, has insulted him. Montresor, played by the dad from *Home Alone*, leads Fortunato to an underground prison of sorts and proceeds to bury the man alive by building up bricks to block his only way out, cackling maniacally as he works. Just as he leaves, he feels what might be pangs of guilt in the form of shivers but decides it's just due to the cold of the night.

Essie had stumbled upon the video as she sat in one of the media booths in the library in the Wests' hometown. It had been left behind on the shelf above the disk player.

As the credits rolled, she immediately pulled the disk, put it in its case and exited the booth. She tucked the case behind some documentary videos on the movie shelves, hoping to spare anyone else from accidentally viewing it.

She'd then sought out Josh, who was working on one of the computers, midway through one of his virtual classes. Essie had sat sideways in one of the armchairs situated behind him, her arms empty, her mind plagued with the images from the video, disconnected memories, with a general feeling of uneasiness.

It was a story, she told herself. It was fiction. She'd never found herself in the situation depicted and yet she felt herself able to empathize with Fortunato's situation, able to relate to the hopelessness he must have felt when the last brick was laid.

Josh had inexplicably turned around, headphones on. He caught her attention, frowned and silently asked if she was okay.

Being thirteen and not fully understanding what it was she was feeling, remembering but not at the same time, she had generically shrugged her shoulders.

Josh glanced to his left and found the next workstation occupied, however, the study space that lined the right side of the computer area was free. He strained to tug out a chair and dragged it around to the space beside him.

He paused to reply quietly to a question posed in his online class, then perked his eyebrows at Essie, patting the chair seat.

I'm fine, she mouthed, then added *Edgar Allan Poe* with a roll of her eyes, as further explanation of her foul mood. The last bit clearly had not translated to Josh, who furrowed his brow.

He patted the seat again, his eyes round and insistent.

She swung her legs down, stood, and plopped herself grudgingly in the chair beside him. She gave a moody, *okay, now what?* gesture with her hands.

He shook his head, put his arm around her shoulder, pulled her against him. He kissed the side of her head, laughing silently when her wild hair became tangled in the headphones' microphone. Once he'd freed her, he pulled her close again, ensured his microphone was muted, and whispered: "Who's getting their butt whooped in–" He checked the computer clock. "--17 minutes?"

"It's an author and he's been dead for decades. Maybe centuries."

"I assumed that might be the case. *Still*." He slid the Post-It stack in her direction and offered his pen. Then, taking on a variation of a Boston accent, said: "You give me his Dewey decimal info. I'll take care of the guy."

She laughed quietly and rested her head on his shoulder.

Essie hadn't developed much of a dislike for the guards. They didn't know who she was, they didn't know her story. For all they knew, she was dangerous, a murderer. None of them were unkind to her. Any roughness or carelessness was easily attributed to the task at hand. Dragging a resistant human around was physically demanding work.

The only demonstration of kindness she'd received since arriving at the compound came from the guards. Occasionally one would let their palm linger over her shoulder when they laid her on the concrete block serving as her bed. A few would ensure she was covered with a blanket.

She had avoided making eye contact or even looking too closely in their direction, being that there simply wasn't a point in trying to make an emotional connection. Gowon would snuff out any budding humility, so it was best not to draw attention to it, for her sake and for the guard's.

The custodial staff lacked any consistency and tended to always keep their eyes lowered on the task at hand. Early on, she'd avoided making eye contact with them as well, but did so by accident after being startled when one unexpectedly entered her cell. She was immediately reminded of the conversation she'd had with Danny when they were plotting her trip to Denver to get Gabe. Their original thought was to have her pose as custodial staff in the housing complex–until Danny discovered that all of the janitorial staff had their vocal cords removed. In addition, she noticed they each wore a metal band that seemed to float over their temples and occasionally illuminated with different colored pinpoint lights. It wasn't unlike a device they used with her. There was a mechanical way the custodial staff went about their work, unaffected by anything around them, like they existed in a continuous Sim session.

Essie watched the digital clock built into the door controls tick through the seconds. 6:20. The guard shifted his weight, the rustling of his uniform echoing down the otherwise silent corridor. If her predictions were correct, *Second Act Doctor Wu* would be the morning "medical/science" staff. He was typically the earliest to arrive so he would be there any moment. Between the three staff, it would be most preferable that he be on duty if she was going to have a chance of getting out of the lab, let alone the building. For one thing, he was the most distractible of the three. He'd get lost in his thoughts, his mathematical calculations, sometimes jolting to awareness, looking at her as though wondering when she got there. He was also the one who left her sitting unattended for long stretches of time. Another reason was that she suspected he was the second in command after *Palpatine*. *Palpatine* seemed to trust him more than the others, as he'd typically capitalize on *Second Act Doctor Wu* being on-staff and not make an appearance until the afternoon. With the others, he typically made an early morning appearance. He'd stick around if he found testing interesting, excusing himself for extended coffee breaks when things began to bore him.

6:21. A repeated clicking echoed down the corridor, followed by an insistent rattling of the metal door handle, then the rushing of the guard growing more distant. A series of beeps pierced the air and then *Second Act Doctor Wu* was muttering about his ID sensor not working. Based upon observation, the sensor was something embedded into each individual's forearm, further validated by input of a frequently changed numeric code. "Why did they get rid of the retina scanners?" he demanded of the security guard.

"They were causing cataracts and blindness."

"Small price to pay not to have to deal with this horseshit."

"You should have been receiving notifications to have your sensor checked—*there.* I got a read on the sensor, but this is going to keep happening unless you get it replaced. It's a quick process, maybe a 5-10 minute stop into the Security office."

Second Act Doctor Wu muttered something in Mandarin. Essie could hear his voice trail off as he settled into the lab, the hum of the lights, the computer revving up.

"If it doesn't work any other time today, just use the numeric code followed by pound, pound, star. That will override the sensor requirement."

"What was the code?"

"9-7-2-7-4-4-1-8."

Ninety-seven, twenty-seven, forty-four, eighteen.

Ninety-seven, twenty-seven, forty-four, eighteen.

"Can't I just use that all the time?"

"What you do is up to you, Doctor, but what we're told is that staff are to use the embedded sensors. The code rotates every couple of days anyway."

Ninety-seven, twenty-seven, forty-four, eighteen.

Essie placed her palm gently over the underside of her upper arm where she'd tucked three narrow syringes. *Second Act Doctor Wu* had the good sense to keep supplies distanced from "the test subject," something *Hillbilly Bob* was not so careful about. During the last two sessions with *Hillbilly Bob*, she'd used his fondness for close interaction to lift two syringes containing a solution designed to trigger a stroke. She knew this because he'd been quite disappointed "they" hadn't gotten around to using the serum before his lunch break. When he returned in the afternoon, joined by *Bobble*, he dismissed the disappearance of the syringes as ineptitude on the part of his colleague.

The third syringe was a mystery pathogen. *Buzzkill* had filled the syringe from a vial with more warnings on it than anything Esther had seen. *Buzzkill* had gone through her protocols, sometimes eyeing the syringe with severe apprehension, like it would detonate at any moment. Ultimately, the session was cut short due to *Buzzkill* suddenly needing to burst from the room to vomit. As the guard escorted Essie back to her room, she purposely tripped, one of the only times she'd actually had the physical strength to walk out of the lab and snatched the syringe off the counter.

Ninety-seven, twenty-seven–twenty-seven? 9-7-2-7. Ninety-seven, twenty-seven, fourteen. No. Ninety-seven, twenty-seven, forty-four, nineteen.

It was an unpleasant, meticulous process of threading the needles through the top layer of epidermis to secure them in place on the underside of her arm, complicated by needing to complete the task under the scratchy blanket provided as her only bedding, as well as a tremor in her hands, no doubt the result of zero calorie intake for what had to have been weeks. For each syringe, she had pinched a small bit of skin and pierced the needles through it, careful not to push the plunger.

She focused her efforts on lowering her heart rate as she waited for *Second Act Doctor Wu* to summon her, a difficult task considering the endeavor she was undertaking. She reviewed her steps again:

1) She would need to be brought into the lab with an extremely low heart rate and appear unresponsive to stimuli. Her hope was that they wouldn't feel the need to use all, or any, of the restraints. Given *Second Act Doctor Wu's* impatience for the inconvenience of needing to request that a guard unlock her ankles so he could do a reflex test, this seemed like a good possibility.

2) Since *Second Act Doctor Wu* also had little patience for uncooperative test subjects, he'd likely inject her with some form of stimulant to wake up her system so he could get to work. She anticipated he might use epinephrine, which she had familiarity, and would be most ideal. Since the low heart rate would have been artificially triggered, she anticipated the extra jolt would make her feel a bit like the Hulk. The effects of the adrenaline were short-lived, however, so she needed to act fast.

3) *Second Act Doctor Wu* would need to be neutralized quietly, either by being knocked unconscious, or by being injected with one of the syringes. She no longer knew which was which, but it didn't really matter much, she supposed; she just didn't care for the idea of witnessing the physiological response his body would have.

4) They'd switched her from medical gowns to something resembling a prison jumpsuit in the past few days, something about supply issues. The jumpsuit wasn't too far off from the scrubs the "medical/science" crew wore, but she'd need to acquire a lab coat–and shoes, to sell the ensemble.

That was the extent of her plan. There was a restroom attached to the lab room; she'd seen it in the reflection of the mirror on the viewing gallery. She'd been dragged into the shower while she was in and out of consciousness, so she hadn't gotten a very good look at it. (She'd considered creating a situation where she'd need to be showered, but that would only add more people in the room.)

In the reflection, it appeared there might be a breakroom of some kind next to the restroom. She had reason to believe there was also a corridor that led somewhere else. She'd seen custodial staff appear suddenly from there in the middle of a lab session; it stood to reason that they weren't just hovering in the shadows all that time.

She hoped there were objects that could make acceptable weapons, or *actual* weapons, a stairwell, something to help her get to the next challenge in her escape. It would not be a winning plan to return to the corridor, forced to face two armed guards, even empathetic ones. Her plan hinged on there being another way out.

It's better not to feel.
It's better not to think.
It's better not to remember.
Thoughts are the enemy.
Feelings are the enemy.
Memories are the enemy.
The nothingness is peaceful.
The nothingness is safe.

Essie tilted her arm, checking for the syringes, barely able to see them in the dark, the only light provided by the door console and some overhead cameras. She sighed, closing her eyes.

She drew to mind the Bible passage showing a conversation between Jesus and Peter: *"Put your sword back in its place,"* Jesus said to him. *"For all who draw the sword will die by the sword."*

11
day twenty

Luther was hunched forward, his head resting against his fist, when Miles came into the workspace.

"If you're trying to set the course straight for the Ark, maybe we should have someone else on Essie Watch," Miles suggested. "Twelve hours on, twelve hours off while trying to save the world? I told you I can do longer stretches."

"It's motivation for me," Luther replied, his voice tight. "Who would you have do the other watch?"

Miles was considering this question as he approached the monitors, immediately pulling in his breath. He zoomed in on the image on the screen.

Essie was strewn face down across the concrete slab, a blanket tossed over her body from the waist down. Every vertebrae was visible against the snug skin of her back and there were dozens of whip marks that covered her back, continued beneath the blanket, even some on the bottom of her feet.

Her head was also shaved.

"She made an escape attempt," Luther said flatly, pulling in his breath. "An unsuccessful escape attempt, but an impressive one."

Miles sat down on the opposite task chair, her appearance knocking the breath from his lungs.

"She seemed to have a pretty good plan, especially considering what she's been through. Her problem-solving, her mental acuity–" Luther frowned, disliking using clinical terminology when speaking about Essie, being too scientifically fascinated. He quickly typed another few lines on his laptop, then paused, fingers braced over the keyboard. "It's just *unbelievable* that she was still thinking this clearly."

Miles raised his eyebrows, encouraging him to continue.

"She'd been collecting serum syringes. I don't know when exactly; I haven't seen her do it and I knew you hadn't mentioned it."

Miles frowned. "No, I haven't seen her do it."

Luther nodded. "I'm not sure what was in the serum that she used. Whatever it was, it killed Doctor Ling in about fifteen seconds."

"Ling's dead?"

"Yeah."

Miles took a breath. "*Well*, he was injecting it into her; it's only fair, right?"

Luther briefly lifted his eyes, considering the remark, his expression filled with exhaustion and uncertainty, then heard himself recite: "'*Those who use the sword will die by the sword.*'"

Miles nodded.

"She was unconscious when she was brought in first thing this morning, but I think that was an act." He took a deep breath, slowly released it. "Ling injected her with epinephrine to wake her. Considering she was presumably recovered from yesterday's sessions and at baseline–despite her low heart rate and pulse–"

"What was her resting heart rate?"

"Twenty-seven beats per minute."

"She has the ability to slow her heart rate like that?"

"It's a method freedivers use. The heart can be slowed to as low as 10 or 11 beats per minute with considerable training."

"But she didn't train for that, did she?"

He tensed his shoulders. "When I watched her during the early antidote runs, I thought she didn't really play an active role in her recovery. It was all her body's response. When her recovery times got shorter, I assumed it was her body becoming more efficient, sort of like training muscle groups, but now I don't think so. Earlier on, when the pathogen or whatever it happened to be first entered her body, there was chaos with her vitals. First, they'd spike. Eventually there'd be a calm, a steady fall, and then she'd settle into, more or less, a normal range for the rest of her recovery; it would just take some time to get there.

"I think it was her mind–that initial spike? I think her fight or flight response was activated. Even though she knew vaguely what was happening, her mind's instinct was to tense and fight, which made her recovery take longer."

Miles narrowed his eyes on the monitor as Essie's body began to shiver.

"In the later antidote runs, the initial spike started to flatten out and her recovery times started to shorten. It was like she relaxed her mind and let whatever she was facing spread, start to wreak havoc, knowing there was a process that needed to take place."

"I can't imagine having that much self-control to actually *relax* in that situation?"

Luther nodded slowly. "I think she trained her body and her mind. It's a theory, but it aligns with what I saw today."

"Luther, what happens if–" Miles stopped short. "You said her mind serves as a sort of gatekeeper to either allow her body to defend itself—or not."

Luther nodded.

"So, she could choose to *not* have her body defend itself. She could choose to die, if she really wanted to," Miles said, frowning.

Luther scratched his eyebrow and focused his attention on the papers before him. "Theoretically, but I'm not really sure she has that much control. If she *did*–if she could *choose*--" He took a breath. "--I think she would have chosen to die after what happened at the ranch."

Miles considered this, then shook the thought, the images that came to mind, away. "So, Ling injected her with epinephrine," he said in a guiding tone.

"It seemed to power her up like a freight train. I'm not sure how much he injected, but it was immediate. She was acting instinctively, and fast. She got his lab coat and shoes, she found an exit through the bathroom attached to the back of the lab." He frowned. "She's at the White House. I guess it doesn't do any harm to tell you that now."

Miles wasn't sure what he was to conclude from Luther sharing that bit of information so easily all of a sudden, but he found his heart weighing heavier in his chest.

"They have her in an area constructed underground beneath the West Wing. They refer to it jokingly as 'Area 51.' She's not the first experiment carried out there."

"Isn't that where the presidential bunker is? Beneath the West Wing?"

"Among other things."

"Where did she end up? The Oval Office?"

"Not quite. There was actually a corridor that would have led her across the South Lawn beneath the helipad. It apparently exits into a small, secured parking area on the southeast side of the property. It would have been highly unlikely she'd completely escape the grounds, *but*–it would have given her a better chance." He shook his head, imagining her bursting out into the parking lot, having no idea where she was. Where would she have gone? There would have been a security gate, but would the guards there have had any idea who she was? Their main assignment was to keep unauthorized individuals *out*, perhaps they wouldn't have been so cautious with someone trying to leave. But then what? She'd be in the middle of the District, the border surrounding the city secured. She could have hidden somewhere, laid low, and *maybe*...but where? He could have called upon Christopher Loop, who was residing in a hotel in the District; he was really the only person with some ease of movement, who could have potentially reached her, but it would have required too much explanation. He'd never met the man, and with him likely being under surveillance--no, there was no point in thinking about a scenario that didn't happen, would never happen. He cleared his throat. "There's no way she'd know that. The other option was an elevator, which took her just outside the secondary Situation Room."

"Wasn't there security to operate the elevator?"

Luther nodded. "She cut the ID security sensor out of Ling's arm."

Miles lifted his brow. "*That's* my girl."

"By that point, one of the guards had checked the video feed and realized that Ling was the one in the chair. The building went on lockdown. She really didn't have very many places she could go. She ended up trapped in a stairwell, trying to get out the ground floor emergency exit."

Miles released a breath, imagining Essie beating at the door, desperate to be free. He couldn't think too long about what that must have been like for her being dragged back to her prison cell, knowing she wouldn't have another opportunity to escape once additional security measures were inevitably put into place. "So, Gowon had them shave her head, give her twenty lashes as some kind of punishment?"

"First, they put her into the Sim. Gowon wasn't at the White House at the time; he wanted them to hold off on anything else until he got back," Luther said in a tired, monotonous voice. "The lashings *were* punishment." He decided it wasn't necessary to explain that what Gowon had ordered was actually referred to as scourging. While whipping is used as a punishment, meant to injure rather than kill, scourging was often a precursor, in Roman times, for crucifixion. In scourging, the prisoner is stripped naked, tied to a pole and shackled in such a way that they can't possibly flinch to avoid the impact. They're repeatedly flogged across the back, buttocks and legs with a flagrum. The flagrum Gowon selected from his own collection, was ornamented with metal shards. The sound the straps made when they made impact with her skin was like a blade cutting through thicket. "Afterward he had her back doused in high-concentration hydrogen peroxide."

"Isn't hydrogen peroxide *used* for wounds?"

He shook his head. "It kills bacteria, but it also kills the healthy skin cells around it and makes it tougher to heal. That's why her skin looks so pale around the wounds. Those skin cells are all dead."

Miles swallowed hard, watching Essie shiver more overtly now.

"Gowon had her head shaved before that for brain surgery."

Miles rotated his chin slowly toward Luther. "Did you say brain surgery?"

"He's planning to implant sensors in her brain tomorrow. He wants to be able to do more extensive brain mapping and have the capability for deep brain stimulation." Luther said this flatly and without looking up, his eyes focused on the laptop before him.

"Luther, what does that mean?" Miles asked quietly.

He sighed. "If they can map her brain and they have sensors directly attached, they think they'll be able to shut down defenses and trigger the response they want."

"So they can control her mind."

"Her mind, her brain, her immune system."

"Why? They wanted this level of immune response—and now they don't?"

Luther's eyes drifted up to the monitor as someone entered her cell.

One of the night guards, a lanky man with alabaster skin, had stepped over to Essie and was gently threading her arms through the sleeves of a long-sleeved shirt. Her body was still limp as he lifted it just enough to encourage the material down to cover her torso.

Luther released a staggered breath as he watched the monitor.

"That's your guy on the inside, isn't it?"

Luther didn't respond, propping his chin against his fist.

"Aren't you afraid he'll give himself away if he's too nice to her?"

Luther blinked, his eyelashes releasing streams of tears down his cheeks. He rubbed roughly at his eyes. "That's not him."

"It's *not?*"

Luther released the air he'd been holding in his chest. "Some people working for Gowon aren't doing it by choice, Miles."

"Do we know who that is?"

"It doesn't matter. As soon as Gowon finds out about this–" He shook his head. "He was the one who sounded the alarm this morning, but then he watched what they did to her."

133

Miles swallowed hard. "Would she have had a chance if she'd managed to get out the stairwell?"

Luther winced. "No. She's in the middle of the District. There's no way."

"When did they do the whipping session?"

"An hour ago," Luther said, tightening his jaw.

"Only an hour ago? Those wounds looked like they were healing already. They didn't look great, probably like you said, the dead skin, but–they're healing *fast*."

"Yeah."

"Is her body's response time *improving*? Or is it the fight or flight thing?"

"I think this is different."

"Because it's external injuries?"

Luther pulled in a breath. "What I mentioned, with her breathing? The way she used to tense would slow down the healing so her healing time wasn't getting shorter, she just wasn't delaying it from starting. What I've been seeing with her recovery times recently concerns me."

"Isn't it a good thing if she heals faster?"

Luther thought of the babies in the lab experiencing system overload, how their bodies lost the ability to regulate. Once triggered, they couldn't downshift again or find any sort of homeostasis. "Not if it overwhelms her system."

"Have you noticed any signs that's happening?"

"She had a seizure in the Sim today," he said quietly.

Miles furrowed his brow. "Maybe she was faking that, like how she faked being unconscious?"

Luther gave a shake of his head. "She was in non-standard Sim programming for 9 hours. I've never heard of sessions going on that long."

They'd lost interest in her by the time the seizure happened. At first, they thought she was just responding to the program, but then she started convulsing and making primal, strained noises. Her fever had spiked to over 105 degrees and when they'd pulled her from the pod, her eyes were unfocused and twitching. It went on for too long, well into the time to qualify as status epilepticus, at least eight minutes. In an emergency room setting, if a patient wasn't responding to treatment, wasn't coming out of the seizure, there'd be serious consideration to inducing a coma, as allowing a seizure to continue indefinitely meant the brain wasn't getting enough oxygen, which meant brain death. They'd finally resolved to administer epinephrine, reluctant given what had happened that morning, but the convulsions began to ease.

The color had drained from Miles's face.

"She also went into cardiac arrest when they were whipping her."

There had been little time allowed once she'd come out of the seizure, despite the fact she'd been difficult to rouse. Gowon had arrived during that time and was not sympathetic about her situation. Luther had watched the team drag her to the metal table on Gowon's order, use magnetic cuffs to secure her wrists to the table legs on one side, her ankles to the legs on the opposite side so her back was fully extended, so her skin was stretched and her spine and ribs were visible.

She'd taken more than a dozen strikes, her body stiffening involuntarily. The flagrum had at least six or seven tails, each embedded with metal shards so the impact was multiplied. When her body went slack, it was assumed that she'd passed out from the pain.

Then the alarms started sounding.

She was no longer breathing.

Her heart was no longer beating.

They dragged her body onto the procedure table to shock her heart, which Luther was certain, if she were conscious, would have been absolute agony given that some of the slashes had raked enough flesh away that bits of her spine were visible.

It had taken three progressive shocks to restore her heart to a normal rhythm. Her breaths resumed lethargically. When Ian Jameson, the lead researcher, sharply snapped his fingers in her face, she barely responded, her eyelids struggling to open.

"It appears safe to resume," Gowon had said.

Jameson peered over at him in confusion. "You want us to continue?"

"*Well*, yes."

"Don't deceive yourself into thinking she can't die," Jameson warned as Gowon glared down at her beaten body. "She may have suffered brain damage from the seizure and if she *did*, we don't know what impact that would have on her body's ability to recover."

"Are you saying we should take it easy on her?"

"What I'm saying is that everyone has their limits, including her. Our priority needs to be on the next stage, which can't happen if she's dead."

It was in the next moment that Essie spontaneously curled upward, seized by a coughing fit that resulted in a mist of blood splattering Gowon's crisp dress shirt. She lunged toward her left side, struggling to clear her throat, to breathe.

"Her airway is obstructed; let's turn her on her stomach," Jameson ordered, the technicians springing into action.

Essie immediately vomited over the edge of the table. As she'd been denied food since her arrival, most of what came out was blood, mucus and green bile. The act left her body limp, her breaths heavy. A layer of perspiration beaded on her pale skin. Luther guessed her body was already heating up to fight off infections in the wounds.

Gowon took in the scene with interest, likely drawing the same conclusion.

"It would do her good to have some food," Jameson suggested.

Gowon peered down at his blood-splattered suit, twisting his mouth. "*No*."

"She's lost quite a bit of weight already. More than I'd expected. With the stress her body is under, I wonder if it would be wise to push her further today."

Gowon glanced over to the workstation and asked conversationally about the large jug of hydrogen peroxide on the tabletop.

"They were using it to clean up the floor after Ling," Jameson explained.

He nodded calmly. "Douse her wounds in it."

Jameson had started to give a weak protest, but quickly resolved that he didn't have a choice.

The chemical reaction when the hydrogen peroxide made contact with her gaping wounds was excruciating to watch or hear. The sound produced by the sizzling foam sounded like cooking oil on a hibachi grill. It was so loud it had made it challenging for the researchers to communicate with one another, conversations halted until the chemical ran its course.

Essie's skin shivered. An involuntary whimper escaped her lips.

Gowon had taken a deep, satisfied breath before leaving the room.

Luther watched as Essie pulled the sleeves of the shirt to cover her hands, balled her hands into fists to hold the material in place.

Miles blinked slowly. "When are we getting her out, Luther?"

"I'm working on it," he answered quietly. "I know that's not a great answer, but it's the only one I have right now." He suppressed the words that had been plaguing his mind over the course of the day: *If she lives long enough.* There had been something that felt insincere when he tried to think of her rescue with any level of confidence after what had gone on that day. It almost felt like playing make-believe. He couldn't imagine anything for her beyond the surgery now. It was unfathomable to him what she was about to endure. Her body had strong defenses that would neutralize foreign substances—if they tried to anesthetize her, would it even work? He had found that her body would accept substances that provided some sort of physiological benefit to her, but would it interpret anesthesia as something to accept, or something to rid itself of immediately?

If she wasn't anesthetized, how would they keep her from moving? And if they couldn't fully keep her from moving, there was nothing to keep her from committing a very brutal suicide.

Something else he wouldn't be sharing with Miles had happened after she was captured: She'd swiped a gun from one of the guards who retrieved her from the stairwell, but she hadn't used it to aid in her escape; she had attempted to turn the gun on herself.

137

It was reasonable to think she'd try something again.

Then the question was: Would it kill her?

She wouldn't survive if she forced her body upward, putting her brain in the direct path of a surgical saw blade; there's no way her body could heal itself fast enough, he concluded silently.

It wasn't a comfort. Yes, it would keep her from continued torture, along with anything else Gowon and his scientists were planning. Yes, she'd get to go home to Jesus. She'd get to enjoy eternal life without suffering.

But–he wasn't prepared to deal with her death again. It had overwhelmed him in a way he hadn't expected. There were separate events that occurred outside his control, but her death would be his fault. He hadn't done what he was meant to do. He had failed her.

Her surviving had given him another chance and he'd wasted it. He'd failed her again.

It didn't feel like he'd be offered yet another chance.

He glanced up at his notes on the laptop, considering his upcoming meeting with the council.

It was an act of desperation, but it was necessary, something he should have done the moment he found out Essie was alive. He silently scolded himself for justifying putting it off all this time.

"So, we're really going to sit here and watch them–" Miles muttered, then clamped his hand over his mouth, his hazel eyes wide. He looked very close to needing to vomit when his gaze lifted once again to Essie. "When? When are they planning to do the surgery?"

"First thing in the morning. I'll keep an eye on her. You don't need to watch it."

Silence swelled in the room. The cameras had switched to night mode and it appeared Essie had turned her chin to face the door. Her silver irises showed up as a narrow ring of dark, while her pupils glowed. She blinked slowly, pushing streams of tears down her cheeks.

"Luther?"

He had placed his fingers on the screen, tracing her cheek. He lifted his chin toward Miles to indicate he was listening, though he didn't take his eyes off her.

"Anesthesia isn't going to work on her, is it?"

12

warrior

3 months earlier...

Matteo paced across the altar, claiming a fresh headset for his sermon. "Check, check," he said, lifting his dark eyebrows.

He received a thumbs up from the associate pastor.

"There. That's better. Good *morning*," Matteo said with a slanted smile. He secured the wire microphone around his ear. "Sorry about that. I'm afraid I have a chronic incompatibility with technology." He tucked the battery pack into his back pocket. "As I was saying: Show of hands—who enjoys feeling uncomfortable?"

The church was silent.

"Yeah. No one does. There's a reason it's called a 'comfort zone.' It's *comfortable*. We feel at ease. It's predictable for the most part. I'm going to jump right into things here and start off today with something that is going to make some people really *uncomfortable*."

The congregation members shared some confused, uneasy looks. Luther's eyes panned across the aisle to Essie, who did not look confused, nor uneasy, eyes locked on her dad, mouth turned up at the corners. She sat between Josh and Miles. This particular Sunday was the Sunday before the nanotech device, or "bunker buster," as Essie referred to it, a few weeks before she and Josh became a couple so there was a slight formalness to how they sat beside each other. This was made more amusing, or at least, more dramatic, from Luther's vantage point once he noticed that Gabe was seated across the aisle and a few pews back. He kept stealing glances at Essie, taking focused breaths.

"Who's ever heard of non-believers referring to Christians as being meek?"

Essie's chin lifted.

There were some affirmative shrugs.

"Let me ask this: Does God want us to be quiet and keep to ourselves about our faith?"

"No!" Thomas called out.

"Thank you, Thomas. No. This isn't meant to be just you quietly taking in the word of God. He doesn't want us to be simply consumers. God wants us to be warriors, in whatever way He's called upon us to serve. This doesn't necessarily mean charging into battle. It means to be faithful, *unrelentingly* faithful, steadfast so that our actions, our words exude the spirit of God. What does that mean? It means someone sees you and they say, you know that *Essie Natale?*"

Essie slinked reflexively, tucked herself against Miles's shoulder, never comfortable in the spotlight, apparently unaware her dad had planned to single her out during this particular sermon.

Miles gave her a gentle nudge and nodded to Matteo.

"You can feel the presence of God in her actions, her words."

Miles nodded affirmatively. Josh grinned over at her. Gabe sat more upright.

"It doesn't mean we're perfect. It doesn't mean we don't falter sometimes, but against the backdrop of the rest of the world, it's where you see and feel the love of God in this world."

Miles had wrapped his arm around her, focusing his attention back on the sermon.

Matteo glanced over at them and smiled. "I'm biased, but you're in agreement, Miles?"

"Absolutely," Miles said definitively.

"That's what God wants from each of us. He doesn't need us to declare ourselves as Christians–have you ever met someone who really exerts themselves as being something? I was never really involved in the corporate world, but you know the people with the email signature, the alphabet soup, if you will, of credentials behind their name? John Smith PHD comma MBA comma CDS comma OLC comma CCXB comma QBA comma BSA. They really want you to know just how competent they are. 'See? I have credentials.' Granted the acronyms I didn't make up have some prestige, but what if you know John Smith and your experience is that John Smith isn't so competent as a CDS QBA, or-- what were some of the others? BSA OLC CCXB. Maybe the X is for xylophone? I don't know many 'x' words. But if he's terrible at his job and your overall impression is pretty negative of his competency, what value do you place in all those credentials?" He glanced around, twisting his expression. "It wouldn't mean much, right? I realize most people haven't utilized email as much in recent years, but I think it would be similar to if I signed emails: 'Matteo Natale comma CHRISTIAN,' maybe in all caps. Someone creative can come up with an acronym for that. It's been my experience that people who have to qualify themselves so overtly aren't actually the best representation of the credential. Those who declare or defend that they're a Christian, might not be the best representation of the faith. I'm not suggesting that you deny your faith. That's *bad*.

"When you become a follower of Christ, it's not like you get some certificate, some credentials to tote around. When you go from not having faith to accepting Jesus Christ into your life, there's a change that happens internally. You start living your life differently. You act differently, you speak differently. You *exude* the very nature of Jesus. That's what God wants. He wants it to be so obvious that you're a follower of Christ that it's *unnecessary* to have to qualify yourself further. I'll give you another example–when I met Max–" He motioned to the athletic trainer seated on the end of the fifth row. "--I didn't need him to tell me that he works out. If he had introduced himself and added–'and I lift weights,' I wouldn't have been like, oh *really*? I'd never have guessed it. No. I can *see it*. That's how obvious God wants it to be.

"So, how do we do that? Well, first we need to be allowing ourselves to fully experience the love of God, the Word of our Lord. Love like Jesus. 1 Corinthians 13:4-7 NIV: '*Love is patient, love is kind. It does not envy, it does not boast, it is not proud. It does not dishonor others, it is not self-seeking, it is not easily angered, it keeps no record of wrongs. Love does not delight in evil but rejoices with the truth. It always protects, always trusts, always hopes, always perseveres. Love never fails.*' If we back it up to verse 1, here's an interesting text: '*--if I have a faith that can move mountains, but have not love, I am nothing.*' I'll repeat: '*--if I have a faith that can move mountains, but have not love, I am nothing.*' God wants us to love the way He loves. In fact, what that verse just said is that even if you have faith that can move mountains, it is worthless if you *don't* have love. It's one thing to have faith–that happens here," he said, pointing to his head. "But God wants your heart.

"Sometimes it's difficult to like ourselves, let alone love ourselves. We focus on the negative, by nature. Now, we don't mind pointing the finger elsewhere when put on the spot, but in our own minds, I think we have a tendency to see our own flaws, all the problems, all the things we don't do well. We don't want anyone else to see us how we are, but we see our bad habits, maybe problems with alcohol, drugs, anger. It can be discouraging to think about trying to 'fix' all these things. It's like the mentality of New Year's Resolutions, right? It just gets to be a lot and we slink back into old habits, right?

"Do you know, if you shift your perspective from, 'Oh, I need to be less this or not do that--' and instead make the decision to live more like Jesus, big things are going to start happening? Say, if one of your bad habits is having a temper, a short fuse. You decide you're going to live more like Jesus, think of the old WWJD–remember the rubber bracelets? What Would Jesus Do? When situations come up, you're going to try to approach it as Jesus would. You're not focused on the problem so much, but on your attitude, your response. What do you think is going to happen to your habit of losing your temper?"

There were some murmurs from the congregation.

"You're probably going to lose your temper less, right?" He gave a small smile. "That wasn't in my notes—that's a future sermon actually—I'll call back to it in a couple weeks. I got caught up doing my preaching, left my notes far behind." He cleared his throat, took a sip from his coffee tumbler, glancing at his notes. "Where was I—yes. God wants your heart. He wants you to have faith, absolutely, but He wants your heart—so others feel His love through you. The only way you can do that is to feel the love of God, the love of Jesus, in your heart.

"I've had people say to me, Teo, I'm so far gone. I feel far away from God. I'm too messed up. If that's you, I implore you to adjust your perspective and when you look in the mirror, know that God made you in His image. He loves you, just as you are *right now*. '*--you knitted me together in my mother's womb. I praise you, for I am fearfully and wonderfully made. Wonderful are your works; my soul knows it very well.*' You are God's child and He *adores* you. If God had a refrigerator, your face would be on it. If He was giving a sermon, He'd be beaming about how incredible you are." His eyes flitted over to Essie, smiling affectionately. "You were fearfully and *wonderfully* made.

"'*Before I formed you in the womb I knew you–*'

"You are a child of God. He knows you. He loves you. He knows the *good* inside of you. He knows what you're capable of." He gave a slanted smile. "Uh-oh, here's where He's going to push you to step outside of your comfort zone. '*--and before you were born, I consecrated you; I appointed you a prophet to the nations.*'" Matteo lifted his brow. "God did not intend for you to be idle in your faith. I'll say again: God did not intend for you to be idle in your faith. He never wanted us to simply be consumers. He doesn't want you to just show up on Sundays, put on your church face–'How are you?' 'Well, I'm just fine. How are you?', then leave and kind of shrug and say, 'I thought Pastor Matteo was *alright* today. Not his best, not his worst. He wasn't very funny. I like humor with my weekly dose of God.'" His smile stretched. "That shouldn't be the extent of your faith. Remember: He wants to engage with you here," he said, motioning to his head. "But he really wants to get a hold on your heart. Feel His love. Feel His goodness. So you spread His love and His goodness to others. So, it's not, 'Hi, I'm John Smith, certified church attendee. CCA.'" He lifted his thick eyebrow. "Okay, John, that's great, but that's not what God's after.

"*You* are a part of His plan."

He took another sip of coffee, furrowing his brow. "When my daughter was three, she was a part of the Children's Ministry/Sunday School. Sorry, kiddo, I'm not done shining the spotlight on you today. No one look at that beautiful young lady in the third, no, fourth row. *No one* look."

Miles still had his arm around her and had lifted his hand to shield her from onlookers.

"One day the kids came and sang in church. One of the first songs she memorized, one of the first songs she sang–and choreographed, come to think of it," Matteo said, grinning at Essie. "was based upon Psalms 3:5."

Luther saw Essie give a small nod.

Then melodically, Matteo continued: "*Trust in the Lord with all your heart, Lean not to your own understanding. In all your ways acknowledge Him, And He shall direct your paths.*'"

Josh glanced over at Essie and smiled tightly, giving her tense cheek a light pinch.

"Trust is sometimes thought of as being synonymous with faith, but it's really *not*, is it? I think of faith as being in the head, dealing with all the competing thoughts. I experience trust in my heart. It's one thing to wrap your mind around the Word of God; it's another to wrap your heart around it.

"God made you, God loves you, and God has a plan for you," he outlined, counting out the points on his fingers.

"There are times when God will ask you to do things that are difficult and it might be intimidating but remember that He *knows you*. He made you. Let's add some context. Jesus said: '*I am the light of the world. Whoever follows Me will not walk in darkness but will have the light of life.*' Matthew 5:14-16. You *are* God's child. You have been saved by the grace and mercy of Jesus. You carry the light of Jesus in you. I'll repeat: *You*, you as you are right now. You carry the light of Jesus in you.

"Tell me, when does a lantern shine the brightest?"

"In the dark," Thomas called out.

"In the dark," Matteo repeated reflectively. "There's a song my mom used to sing to me when I was little: 'This little light of mine, I'm gonna let it shine. This little light of mine, I'm gonna let it shine. Let it shine, let it shine, let it shine.' There was more to it when it was used as a children's hymn about when Satan tries to *poof* the light out. Which he does. Evil loves the darkness. How do we combat evil? Well, for starters, we keep shining our light, but what does *that* mean, practically speaking?

"Well, it means we turn to God for the answers. We spread our love out onto others. We armor up. Ephesians 6:14-17 breaks it down: *'truth as your belt, righteousness like a breastplate, shoes of peace, a faith shield, a salvation helmet, and the Bible as your epic sword.'*

"I know sometimes it feels like you're all alone, the darkness is closing in on you, and you feel overwhelmed, but know that if you have the armor of God, nothing is impossible. Actually, I don't like the negative tone of that–if you have the armor of God, *anything is possible.*"

Someone yelled out "Amen!" which, as it always did, brought a smile to Matteo's face.

"In 1st Samuel 17:45, we read David's declaration to Goliath: *'You come against me with sword and spear and javelin, but I come against you in the name of the Lord Almighty.'* This scrawny kid was going up against a giant and he said, I'm good! I have God on my side. Imagine a non-believer hearing that. He probably thought *'You poor, pitiful weakling I'm about to kill. So misguided.'* No spoilers, but does anyone know how the story of David and Goliath ends?" He nodded lightly, then frowned. "Know that if God brings you *to it*, he'll bring you *through it*. We had a guest pastor a few weeks ago who went through so many of the times in the Bible when we read this phrase: Do not be afraid. Fear not. How many times is it said?"

"365," Thomas offered.

Matteo nodded, put his hand back in the air and counted out: "God made you, God loves you, God has a plan for you, and God has always, *will always* have your back. You are armored in God's Word. *Fear not.*

"This world is far from what God originally intended, but have you read the Bible? Evil is nothing new. Even in times like these–or I should say, *especially* in times like these, God calls us to be warriors. Consider the story of Esther. Now, for clarification, I'm shifting to talk about Bible Esther, not my daughter, Essie, who's sitting *right there.*"

Essie gave a shake of her head.

"Last time," he murmured, then quickly added: "--today." He took a deep breath. "Bible Esther–who I'm sure appreciates me referring to her in such a way--was a brave young woman who risked her life to save her people from genocide." He gave an almost imperceptible chuckle before continuing on. "When Mordecai challenged her to rise up, he said: '*Perhaps you were born for such a time as this.*'

"We are in our positions, our communities, and in our spheres of influence for such a time as this – to be a light that dispels darkness and champions righteousness. Each one of us has a special quality or skill or talent or way about us–I encourage you to seek it out and to share it. Maybe God's calling on you to do something that takes you a bit more out of your comfort zone than it seems like others are, but if fear is what's holding you back from fulfilling your purpose, from shining your light? *Fear not.* Think of Daniel in the Lion's Den, David going up against Goliath, Esther risking her life to save her people." Matteo peered over in Essie's direction briefly, giving a thoughtful nod. "What might we accomplish if we unleashed all of the faith and love in this congregation into the community? Into the world?" He smiled lightly as he began to sing again: "Let it shine, let it shine, let it shine.

"Let's leave here today, not just satisfied to have checked off a to-do list item to renew your certified church attendee credential–for another week. My hope is that you leave here renewed in the knowledge that God made you in His image. He loves you as you are. We don't have to be perfect to have Him love us or to serve as His mighty warrior. He wants us to know Him, know His word, feel His love. He's calling you closer.

He's inviting you in, but it's a relationship. You need to invite Him into all areas of your life–and most importantly, into your heart.

"He wants us to be fearless in our faith, in our trust–" He placed his hand over his heart. "--and He wants us to embody the love of Christ in a world in *desperate* need of His light. Remember, the battle is God's, and He has already secured the victory."

13

stand

It was an audible. It was risky. If things didn't go well, there was no back-up plan. It was all or nothing.

The council had agreed to let Luther into their chamber out of goodwill, he imagined.

What he needed was for them to want him to stay.

When Danny approached him with his latest invention, he'd been flabbergasted–by the danger of the tech's application in the wrong hands, as well as the fact that with everything else going on, Danny had managed to design, build, and test it in less than a month.

He had named it Caladrius, and had been insistent the name not be shortened.

He explained: "The Caladrius appears in Roman mythology and is depicted in other medieval interpretations. It's also alluded to in the Bible as being representative of Jesus. It's a snow-white bird that is able to take the sickness of a person into itself, then it flies away, dispersing the sickness and healing both itself and the sick person."

Luther had nodded patiently.

"Hopefully that's not blasphemous, me using the name for this."

Luther shook his head. "What is it?"

Danny slid a trinket box that lay open on the conference room table toward Luther.

Inside was a single translucent disk, no larger than a dress shirt button. "Adhere this to a flat surface and press the center of the ring. It will identify any tech within a 60-foot diameter of where it's activated. The councilmember offices are located on the opposite side of the wall from council chambers so you'll want to activate this as close to that wall as possible."

Luther nodded, not verbalizing his concern about the difficulty he might have getting as close to that wall as Danny wanted; certain council members might be apprehensive about him moving too freely around the chamber.

He would have to figure it out. Danny had worked tirelessly to develop brand new technology, he could certainly figure out a reason to cross 10 feet without being tackled by Security.

"Caladrius will absorb all the data from those devices and transfer it to a cloud server that I specify. Once the transfer is complete, there will be no traces on the devices."

"What about their computers, phones?"

"It'll be like doing a hard reset. Everything will be gone." Danny frowned. "Ideally, Caladrius would identify the 'disease,' like in the myth, and just extract what would be most useful, but I'm afraid I don't have time to develop that sort of coding, and we might not account for other things we *should* be looking for."

"What if they don't have their personal laptops or other devices in the building?"

"If they have any device that has been linked to the laptop or phone or what not in the building–earbuds, a smart watch, a speaker, Caladrius–" He seemed to be tiring of saying the word repeatedly. "--will pull that proverbial string. Even 'wireless connections' have digital links. Anything with a microchip, an internal computer, emits a signal. Any nearby tech can be used to amplify that signal so we'll be able to cover far more than the 60-foot diameter."

"Even if the connection isn't active?"

"Why do you think I use a *manual* wheelchair, Luther?"

"For the muscle tone?"

Danny stared at him, then shrugged. "I'll be able to sift through the data and hopefully I'll have something compelling to broadcast that will allow you a chance to get out of there."

"Before I'm arrested."

"Or killed."

Luther narrowed his eyes.

"Many council members conceal carry," Danny replied, but then his green eyes flinched. "It was a joke. There'd be no point in killing you if the information has gotten beyond the chamber walls. It'd be illogical."

Luther cleared his throat. "How long will you need? For Caladrius to suck out all the sickness, as the myth says?"

A small, appreciative smirk appeared on Danny's face. "Ten gigabytes need about 5 seconds of transfer time. Caladrius allows for ten simultaneous channels of data transfer at a time." He shrugged. "Ideally, as much time as I can get. Minimum? Five minutes. If we can't uncover what we need in 6 *terabytes* of data?" He shrugged. "These are mostly politicians, Luther. I don't anticipate we'll have to do much digging."

*   *   *

Luther had thought about telling the council Essie was alive, providing the evidence, telling them all about the harrowing twenty-six days she'd been in Gowon's custody in his torture chamber. That would certainly spark their interest and provide Danny with the time he needed, but it would also spark questions and distrust. Jonas, no doubt, would demand to know how he knew she was alive, who his contact was. Miller and a few others had contact within the Gowon Administration. The former congresspeople, politicians, could have very well had other contacts. If Gowon got word that he knew about Essie, there'd be a shakeup. He might have her moved. He might have the place swept for bugging equipment. He might figure out Marcus's connection.

No, the fact that she was alive needed to remain a secret.

He needed to capture their interest for five minutes with something so compelling, they wouldn't have a chance to notice anything was out of the ordinary.

Luther stepped into the council chamber, the grandeur of the space immediately causing a swirling in his stomach. He'd been in enough government buildings and foreign embassies that he typically didn't feel the intimidation inflicted by their opulent designs and yet he felt almost reverential, taking in the details of the space.

Dark wood paneling lined the walls, giving the room a timeless and authoritative feel. Elaborate decorative moldings and intricate carvings adorned the woodwork, a testament to the craftsmanship of an earlier era. The subdued lighting cast a warm glow over the room showcased by an ornate chandelier centered in the ceiling. The ceiling alone was something to behold–soaring and adorned with intricate molding and spotlighted historical paintings.

The floor featured a busy patterned carpet, common in courtroom and government settings, meant to discourage occupants from looking at it for too long.

Previously, the chamber was used for state senate activities, but the desks of the senators had long been removed, replaced by courtroom style seating, with the exception of the front row, which was maintained as desks for those called to testify or make presentations to the council members.

The main feature of the chamber was a long semicircular dais jutting out from the wall, made of solid wood carved with embellishments. The dais was lined with a row of plush, high-backed leather chairs facing outward toward the chamber. Each council member's workspace was adorned with a brass nameplate and a small microphone.

As Luther reached the front desk on the right side of the center aisle, he noticed only 8 of the council members were situated in their chairs. Notably, Sadie Parker, Kyle McNeary, and Mark Geoffreys were missing.

Jonas Miller had his eyes fixed on the carpet, a dazed expression on his face.

The door to the right of the dais opened and McNeary and Geoffreys filed out, herded by Sadie, who kept her face neutral as she took her seat. Despite having a vague understanding of Luther's intent, though unaware of the technology's capabilities, she struggled to disguise her discomfort with being so close to the proverbial blast zone.

"Let's go ahead and get started," former Justice Grainger said, assessing his central location on the dais to be indicative of a leadership role on the council.

Luther stood behind his intended seat, scanned through his bulleted note pages, the only personal item he was permitted to carry inside. He cleared his throat a number of times, peered up toward the council. "May I have some water? I usually carry something with me, but my coffee tumbler didn't pass the security inspection."

"Of course," Sadie replied, lifting her brow toward the small hospitality table situated along the wall behind the council members. "Jonas? You're closest. Would you?"

Jonas frowned, lifting his hands off his arm rests to express his resentment to be given such a menial task.

Sadie glared at him, starting to rise up from her chair.

"I've got it, I've got it," he said, waving her off.

Luther stepped closer to the elevated dais. He gripped the edge of the podium, discreetly pressing his thumb to the underside on the heavy carved wood edging. He felt the click of the activation switch and glanced up to the clock. "Could you toss some ice in there? That's a luxury I miss a bit."

"Your accommodations don't have a freezer?" Elwes asked conversationally.

"No, I just have a refrigerator. I have one of those ice chests for long-term storage, but it's small, and it's stocked with fish."

"Not a great flavoring addition to drinks."

"Not really, no."

"Do you enjoy fishing? I don't think we've ever talked about it."

"I don't mind getting out on the water from time to time."

"Back in the day, I did some deep-sea fishing. Nothing like the open water, but even on the lakes around here, it's peaceful, takes my mind off things, which is probably recommended from time to time."

Luther nodded.

Jonas was struggling to use the ice tongs, which had attracted the attention of several members of the council.

"Having a little trouble there, Miller?" Elwes asked, frowning.

"Three cubes enough?"

"Nah, the water to ice ratio is off," Geoffreys remarked, nudging Abe Brink, who was staring at his phone. He turned his phone over on the tabletop, shifting his attention to Jonas, smirking in amusement at the impromptu hazing of Jonas Miller.

There were some suppressed chuckles as Jonas winced, clamping the small tongs around what appeared to be a resistant ice cube.

Luther lifted his eyes to the clock. A minute had already passed.

"How have you been, Dr. Graham, since we met last?" Sadie prompted.

He pressed his lips together. "To be frank with you, Senator Parker, it's been the worst month of my life."

Several council members perked up. Those who had found some amusement at Jonas's expense turned dutifully solemn.

"I understand the turnout for Pastor Natale's funeral was–" Sadie struggled to assign an appropriate adjective.

"That's fine, Jonas," Luther said, turning his attention back to the former state representative. As much as he would like to fill in the remaining few minutes, it wouldn't serve him well to spend that time talking about his friend's death. He could not allow his mind to think of Matteo or the scene at the ranch. He needed to maintain his composure.

Jonas released a sigh, replaced the lid on the ice bin, and carefully carried the tumbler back to his seat. He leaned forward and handed it to Luther, only meeting his eye for the brief moment required to ensure a successful handoff, not wanting to have to repeat the process.

"Thank you for agreeing to have me come in today," Luther remarked, glancing again at the clock before turning back to his seat. Just over two minutes had passed. He took an extended sip of water. He had just opened his mouth to speak when he heard Danny's voice:

"We've got what we need."

Luther frowned, staring at the surface of the desk, his eyes tracing the patterns produced by the wood grain. He lifted his hand to his face, tapped the nanotech device positioned over his ear.

"You heard me. We've got it."

"Dr. Graham?"

Luther was perplexed by the ease that they were able to accomplish the task. Danny was right: These were politicians. They didn't need to do much digging.

"Dr. Graham?" Elwes repeated in a gentle tone.

"What's something worth dying for?" Luther asked, furrowing his brow, peering over his shoulder at the council.

His question was met with silence.

He lifted his brow. "I'm actually asking."

"Dr. Graham, this council was under the impression you had something to present," Grainger groaned. "Not have a philosophical discussion."

"I *do*. Have something to present." He tapped the desk conclusively, turning on his heel to face the council. "Our country was founded by people who were willing to risk everything to declare independence from England. Throughout history, people have faced situations that call for an incredible amount of bravery and there have been those who have risen to the occasion.

"During the Holocaust, a Polish priest by the name of Maximilian Kolbe found himself at Auschwitz Concentration Camp. To deter people from trying to escape, there was a rule in place that if anyone tried to escape, 10 men would face starvation. Franciszek Gajowniczek was one of the men selected after a man attempted to escape–as Gajowniczek cried out in anguish, Kolbe volunteered to replace him. He said, this man has a wife, a child. Choose me.

"Jack Phillips, a wireless operator on the *Titanic*, remained with the ship as it sank to make distress calls that ultimately saved the lives of thousands of people. There were also 35 engineers aboard the *Titanic* who continued to work and kept the electricity, the lights would remain on, so the ship could be seen and so the passengers wouldn't panic.

"9/11, firefighters, police rushed into buildings to save complete strangers and some sacrificed their own lives to do this. The heroes that day weren't all police or firefighters. Rick Rescorla was a security officer in one of the Twin Towers. He led people down the staircases singing Cornish songs to boost morale. He's believed to have saved 2,500 people, but he died when the tower collapsed. Benjamin Keefe Clark was a chef in the towers. When the plane hit, he didn't try to escape and save himself. He went to work, getting people out of the tower, including someone in a wheelchair. He didn't think, he just did, and he saved hundreds of lives.

"Five years ago–A church was bombed in Wallace, Colorado–the place was smoldering. A 15-year-old searched tirelessly for three days, first pulling out people, including children, and tending to them, then helping recover bodies. Then pieces of bodies.

"Four years ago–a canister of sarin gas was thrown into the Children's Ministry classroom at a church just down the road from the church bombing. The door was barricaded, the children inside trapped. The 16-year-old doing the lesson didn't think twice. She got the children into the storage closet and gave them instructions to pry open a return HVAC vent so they could get outside. She then sealed up the door from the outside and threw herself over the canister and the escaping gas, absorbing the poison into her body, saving the children.

"That same girl, age 18, discovered that her body generated antibodies with the potential to save, but to generate it, she would have to endure unimaginable suffering and pain, the recovery lasting days. She didn't hesitate. She even went *against* medical recommendations and started adding in extra sessions because she understood that each session would save *that* many more people. She spent thousands of hours in indescribable amounts of pain. She suffered 120 *excruciating* deaths.

"The antidote directly saved the lives of 337,596 people with far-reaching benefits for hundreds of thousands more.

"Same girl, age 19, found out her childhood friend would not be rescued from Mandatory before the Ark deadline. He was written off as too 'damaged' by the Sim programs, the mission too risky even for our best trained MET team. Up until then she couldn't leave the Ark because if she was discovered, it would put everyone's lives at risk. I was desperate to no longer see her suffer so I *lied* to her. I told her she wasn't generating the antibodies anymore; her body wasn't operating the same anymore. I wanted her to stop. I *needed* her to stop. But what did that headstrong girl do? She figured that she was only putting *her* life at risk at that point—so she went in *on her own*, and she got him out. A mission deemed too risky for a trained *military team*, but she was determined. While there, she was given the vaccine. If what I told her was true, she would have died. She thought she was going to die. But she didn't care. She couldn't leave him behind.

"Esther Natale was the bravest person I've ever met—and I've studied history. I know the stories of history's heroes. I've worked with military, police, MET teams, I've worked with some incredibly courageous people. Time and time again, she threw herself on the grenade, not because she wanted recognition for it. She absolutely did *not* want recognition, did not want the spotlight.

"I asked her once *why*. Why did she throw herself on that sarin gas canister, why did she run into the proverbial fire to save her friend, why did she put herself through torture. *Why*. And she told me very simply: if you have an opportunity to help people, you should do it."

Sadie Parker nodded slowly, wiping at her eyes.

"Essie Natale was willing to sacrifice her life for the people of the Arks, not knowing that several of the people who wouldn't be alive if not for her, would in turn, *use her* as a bargaining chip for their own selfish ambitions."

Jonas briefly lowered his eyes, pressing his lips together, a stream of tears rolling down his cheek.

"If you're not willing to sacrifice yourself for the people of the Arks, you are not worthy to *lead* the Arks." He frowned, beginning to pace. "No one voted for any of you to be on a council. No one even voted for this council structure. You appointed *yourselves* to your positions—and for what purpose?"

"We are doing our best during unprecedented times," Mays argued tightly.

"What about the years before that? Most of you were sitting congressmen, senators, governors—and you did nothing. For years you *sanctimonious* assholes turned a cheek to what was happening in the world. You refused to stand firm. You conceded to social pressures. To scrutiny. You caved under pressure. You took bribes, hush money. You *empowered* Samuel Gowon and the current regime."

Sadie Parker swallowed hard, nodding.

"They were *so* confident that no one would rise up against them that they very steadily removed every personal freedom we've ever known and murdered nearly 100 million people without batting an eye. Even *then*, you didn't stand up against them. Oh, you may have talked a big game, posted to social media, threw your fist in the air and feigned outrage, but you did *nothing*.

"And *now*, when you have the opportunity, the resources to put a stop to the tyranny, you want to run away." Luther shook his head slowly. "Make no mistake: the New World Order will *not* show mercy because you rolled over and showed your belly. No matter what Gowon's promised you."

"*Mr. Graham.*"

"What *has* Gowon promised you? Safety? Money? Power?"

"How *dare* you," Grainger growled.

"How dare I? How dare you. You sit up there above everyone else and think yourselves wise and more righteous than all your sheep, right? Well, I may not have the relationship with God that I would like, but my dear friend, Matteo, he sure as hell did, and something he told me blew my mind. Now, I grew up with faith, with religion, but something that just simply hadn't fully resonated with me before was this: God's mercy? Jesus's love? Neither are things I have to *earn*. It just *is*. There is nothing I can possibly do to make myself more righteous than I am right now. So you might be self-righteous, but you're no better than anyone else. And what you've *done,* or *not* done? What you've allowed when you could have done something? That's between you and God. Maybe your heart is truly connected with God, but that's for Him to sort out.

"Others might not agree with me on that. Some might *not think* we should leave it up to God. Some might like a say *now.* They'd like to judge you for themselves, determine if you're worthy, if you can be trusted with their lives, their children's lives. Knowing what I know? They have plenty to be concerned about."

"Are you *threatening* us?"

"We are the Ark's high council. I'm not sure you want to be doing that," Grainger stammered.

Luther narrowed his eyes. "People crave justice and what people have lost as a result of your actions, or inactions, when you've insisted you sit where you sit? They may not want to wait for the justice of God. At the *very least*, if you are not acting in the interests of the people, as *the people* decide, you do not belong where you sit."

He paced in front of the dais, nodding. "There's always the possibility that you really think you're acting in the best interests of our people—in which case, if we're not all dead in the very near future, I'll see you when the clocks strike 13, Comrades." He gave a small, searching smile. "How did *that* one end? 'But it was all right, everything was all right, the struggle was finished.'

"The truth is you were never *in* the fight, were you?"

Grainger slammed his fist down on the desk. "Mr. Graham, you will *stop* this now. Can we get Security in here?"

Danny chuckled angrily in Luther's earpiece. "Throw a tantrum all you want; we're already broadcasting you *son of a bitch.*"

Luther swallowed hard, nodding, glancing down to the button on his shirt, where a pin-sized camera was positioned. "Do you plan to tell the people what this 'high council' has decided? That you've chosen to surrender?"

"We have *not* surrendered. We are simply seeking a diplomatic solution."

"Tell me, would you have also negotiated with Hitler and Stalin?"

"That's preposterous."

"*Is* it? Combined they killed maybe 20-40 million people. Gowon? Nearly 100 million. Minimum. That we know of. And he's just getting started, yet he has confirmed friendly contact with individuals on *this council*."

Silence swelled in the chamber.

He took a steadying breath. "One of the many things we lost to tyranny was a voice. The politicians served themselves rather than the people they were meant to represent. I was under the impression things would be different here. I'm guessing most of the people within the Arks probably feel the same way."

"We represent the people," Mays asserted proudly.

Danny chuckled in his ear. "Oh, I'm going to enjoy *this*."

Luther nodded. "Indy, activate Throne Room display."

When the display activated, the images reflected in the eyes of the council members. Luther glanced over his shoulder, taking in the live feed of their distraught faces, on the same monitor where they'd watched Essie take what he thought was her final breath.

On the right half of the display was the live feed. On the left, Danny was rapidly sharing content, snippets of emails, transcripts.

"Wow, that *is* a clear, clear picture, isn't it? *That is impressive.* Look at the high council sitting up there like kings and queens."

"What *is* this? Is this *broadcasting* outside of here?"

"You were scanned when you came in. How do you have a communication device?"

"Well, I *thought* about abiding by your rules," Luther said, twisting his expression. "And then I remembered at least a third of you are responsible for the death of my best friend and his daughter, that you are putting the lives of millions of people at risk—and *then* I decided I didn't really care about abiding by your rules, which only serve you. The people have a right to know who all of you are and where your allegiances lie. And it would appear that they're going to find out."

"What are you talking about, Dr. Graham?"

Luther's eyes narrowed. "What was it you said to me, *Justice* Grainger? 'If you have nothing to hide, you have nothing to fear?'"

Grainger's brow flinched.

"You said your actions represent the will of the people. Let's see if they agree."

part two

14

sunset

It had been nearly three months since Josh had been to his parents' house. He didn't anticipate how difficult it would be making that final turn, the Natale Ranch, now occupied by Renee and Thomas's family, visible to the right, smoke billowing out from the chimney, different vehicles parked in the driveway, the group of horses Essie had named for the Pevensie children in the *Narnia* books now occupying the main paddock.

Essie had been gone 79 days. In some ways, it felt like ages longer. In other ways, it felt like the wound hadn't even begun to scab.

As he made the turn, he saw the barn door swing open. For a moment, his heart swelled in his chest as he imagined Essie emerging from the barn. When Renee stepped into view instead, all the air seemed to be vacuumed from his lungs. He veered the pickup into a gap between apple trees on the side of the road and immediately dropped out of the truck cab, chest heaving, heart racing.

When he finally arrived at his parents' house, he was nearly a half-hour late. His dad was sitting on the front porch steps sipping his coffee when Josh pulled in, clearly wanting to get a read on him before having him come inside. His dad's analysis was brief, however, and he quickly abandoned his coffee cup on the step, in favor of embracing him.

His mom was sitting on the floor of the living room amidst a plethora of baby toys when they came inside. She gave a tight smile, suppressing an abundance of emotion.

Josh approached quietly, holding a velvety soft elephant plush in his hand.

"Say 'hi' to your brother," his mom said dotingly to Hannah, who turned in his direction, immediately positioning herself on all fours.

"She's *crawling*?"

His mom nodded. "Hold out your hands."

He crouched down a bit closer and extended his hands toward her. "Let me see what'cha got, Hannah Banana."

Hannah wobbled on her chubby hands and knees, mainly interested in the plush, but she allowed him to pick her up. She was very curious about his beard, touching it delicately with her palm, clearly uncertain about the texture. Her face had lost a bit of baby chub, looking more toddler-like, and her attention seemed more focused.

Sara resisted the urge to descend upon him and instead rose to her feet. "You stay," she directed. "My back locks up if I sit on the floor too long. Do you think you'll be able to stay for dinner?" she asked hopefully, despite that being the main component of their plan.

Josh nodded, gazing down at Hannah, who had tucked herself into his arms, squeezing the plush elephant against her chest.

"Is *that*—" his mom started to ask, motioning to the plush. She covered her face with her palm.

"Gelato," he said quietly. "Essie would want Hannah to have him."

Sara pinched her brow, nodding. "I'll just check on dinner then," she said with a bit too much enthusiasm. "If you're staying? You're staying, right?"

"Yeah, Mom. I'll stay for dinner if it's alright?"

She turned toward the kitchen, nodding, patting her hand against her chest to calm herself.

His mom had tried to be gentle as she broached the topic of Essie at dinner. She began by talking about Luther giving speeches. He gathered that there had been a shake-up in Ark leadership, concluding that perhaps the Arks were finally having an electoral process. His parents had gone in person to a number of rallies–and they'd acquired an old television to be able to watch Ark news coverage. It was the first time they'd had a television in the house in a decade. His mind kept wandering as his mom was talking; it was taking a lot of effort and energy to be around people, in general, but it was difficult being in that house, knowing if he glanced out the front window, he'd see the ranch, if he peered north, he'd see the overlook where the grave sites were located.

His seat at the dinner table provided an ideal view of both the front window and the fireplace. He tried to focus his attention on the latter, but the reprieve only lasted so long. Essie was everywhere to him. He could picture her in the living room, tucked close to the fireplace, wearing her reindeer Christmas pajamas, a Santa hat with antlers, and a pair of fuzzy red socks. His mom had been absolutely delighted to host everyone last minute when they'd made it to the Ark, including Gunner and Miles. Exhausted from the trek, both of them, along with Matteo, had wound up falling asleep on the living room couch. Before retiring to bed with his dad, Sara had encouraged Essie to go stay in the under-construction nursery, since there was a daybed in there, but she'd remained out in the living room, watching the fire, arms wrapped around her knees.

Josh had released a short *psst* from the recliner to get her attention and she had quickly gotten up, snuggled in next to him in the chair. It only took her a few moments to fall asleep and she slept until after sunrise and everyone else was already up, finally stirring when she smelled breakfast.

"It always seemed like a natural step for him to be a leader," his dad was saying.

Josh attempted to re-center himself, not clear on what his parents had told him so far. They had been focused on Luther, on political rallies, there was something about an election.

He had always thought Luther should have a more prominent role in the Ark since he had, to Josh's knowledge, come up with the idea,

168

seeing the need, he had networked, campaigned, and ultimately established the resources, making all of it possible. He'd suspected Luther's reluctance to be a leader had something to do with protecting Essie. With that no longer being a concern, it seemed that perhaps Luther was finally stepping into that role. In a way, he knew Essie would be glad he was finally taking a stand.

His mom mentioned that Luther had been talking about Essie at the events and rallies, specifically the work she had done with the Phoenix Initiative, and that was enough to set his mind off again, thinking about her going through the antidote runs. He thought of their argument after he'd witnessed it for the first time, the one time in their lives she'd been genuinely furious with him. Because he hadn't been there for her. She needed him and he wasn't there.

No. There was so much more beyond that. The Christmas Eve spent snuggling on the recliner came after that. All their long conversations. Those weeks she stayed out at the cabin and he got to hold her in his arms. They'd gotten past it. They'd returned to being best friends again. More than that, they had been in love.

It was when his mom used the phrase "all her sacrifices," that Josh jolted to attention and immediately felt physically ill.

"I can't believe what Essie did. I always knew she was an incredible girl, but I had *no idea* what she put herself through."

Luke gazed across the table at Josh, jaw tight.

Sara shook her head. "We owe *everything* to that girl." She clutched her hand to her chest, eyes panning to watch Hannah playing on the floor. A tilt of her head seemed to say what she couldn't: that she now knew they wouldn't have had Hannah if not for Essie. Tears streamed from her eyes. "All of us took the antidote or immunity serum or whatever they want to call it. All of us. If we *hadn't?* Not to mention that she risked her life to get Gabe out of Denver? *She–*" She shook her head, braced her hand over her heart. "We owe her *everything.*"

"Did you ever even *meet* Essie?" Josh said suddenly, his voice tight and bellowing. "She would have hated to have you thinking you owed her *anything.* She didn't do anything for the recognition; she did it because it was the right thing to do. That's all. She wanted *nothing* for herself. No recognition. No special treatment. She wanted absolutely nothing but a quiet life." He could hear her voice murmur: *A bit of land with a pretty view, a cozy place to live; a quiet life.* That's all she wanted. His eyes filled with tears as he recalled her equating the sight of him as being acceptable as the "pretty view." He made eye contact with Hannah, who was seated in her highchair to his left, slowly running her starfish hand through her pureed dinner, which appeared to be sweet potatoes. Her face was furrowed in concern, her blue eyes very round.

He could see Essie walking around the house holding Hannah when she was an infant, singing to her, stroking her back in gentle circles. He remembered how quickly Hannah had become attached to Essie, and vice versa.

Essie hadn't gotten to see how much Hannah had grown in the past 3 months.

She'd never see her grow up.

Perhaps worst of all, Hannah wouldn't remember Essie except through secondhand memories and photos.

Josh felt his heart twist in his chest like a rag being rung out. He stood and moved quickly toward the front door.

When he got outside, he gulped down the air like he'd just broken through a water surface. While still not able to take a deep breath, he directed his feet toward the overlook. He walked solidly–until he rounded the corner and took in the sight of the two grave markers. He immediately spun away, dropping to his knees.

A primal, broken cry echoed across the hills, seeming to reverberate off the mountains in the distance. It was as his throat became dry and his lungs expelled their last bit of oxygen that he realized the cry had come from him.

He lifted his eyes to the horizon–the mountains draped in a soft orange glow, the forest of trees that held within it the same creek that ran alongside his cabin, the distant glacier lake where Essie liked to take Bree on their sunrise rides. He took several breaths.

Just as he had managed to slow the rapid beat of his heart, his eyes fixed on a field of wildflowers set before him. He stood and began carefully moving down the embankment.

Sometime later, once he'd climbed back up to the overlook and settled onto the tree stump, he placed a wildflower bouquet on each gravestone, letting his fingers graze over her etched name. He found himself being lulled by the motion and managed to slow his breathing.

He cleared his throat, preparing himself for the story he was about to share.

"I've been thinking about that day at the train station, when Gabe kissed you." He swallowed hard, lifting his eyebrow. "*I know, I know.* It's not what I thought it was." He pictured how she looked that day–wearing her jean overalls, a raglan shirt with–yellow sleeves?--her golden brown hair tied in two braids. Her face still had a soft youthfulness about it, her eyes round and worried. "Back then I tormented myself thinking it was your first kiss–and even *you* had said that the reason he did it was because you were worried about those jerks at the market in town, how they'd tease you. You thought they'd steal your first kiss." He furrowed his brow. "But I realized recently that you'd actually already had your first kiss." He swept his palm over the gravestone, removing some dirt and dry leaf bits. "It wasn't some big, dramatic, *romantic* moment like what they show in movies, but that day was more than *just* the day you had your first kiss, more than *just* the day *I* had my first kiss. It was *also* the day I realized I was in love with you." He took a breath, gazed out again at the view, and began.

When he'd finished, he glanced to his left at the two simple stone gravestones, the bouquets of wildflowers he'd placed on each. "*That's* the story I should have shared when we had the service for you. I wish I had reminded you about that day when you were here." He nodded. "This is not an ornamental apology bouquet," he said softly, recalling how she had been adamant that he only bring her flowers that he'd picked himself, and *only* if he'd done nothing wrong. "I'll tell you that story when we see each other again. It's a good story. One of my favorites."

171

Sometime later, as the sun sank lower in the sky and the warmth of the day had given way to a dusk chill, Josh decided that he should be getting back to Fenway at the cabin. He was just about to stand when he heard the displacement of dirt over his shoulder.

For a moment, he considered that it could be a bear. With that thought came the image of Essie smiling across at him as they went to lock down the barn after her dad spotted a bachelor bear near the overlook. She had teased Josh, seeing that he was single himself, about "watching out for those *bachelors*."

He was fairly certain a bachelor bear was not approaching him given the uncertain approach of the footsteps, fairly certain he wasn't about to be mauled to death, and he found himself oddly disappointed. Recently he'd felt a longing for death, a strange frustration that he wasn't in frequent mortal peril. Not because he wanted to die, but because he longed to see Essie again. Josh pictured her tight cheeks, the sprinkling of freckles across the bridge of her nose, her cheekbones, the ease of her smile, her silver eyes gazing into his, the looks she reserved only for him. He briefly indulged in the thought of arriving in Heaven, where she was waiting for him. She'd tuck a bookmark to hold her place in whatever she happened to be reading, rise to her feet, tilting her head questioningly. He'd shrug and say, "You *know*, you were right about those bachelors." She'd nod and give some endearing version of an "I *told* you so."

He took a deep breath and pushed himself off the ground, resolving he'd have no choice but to face whoever was approaching the overlook.

He expected it to be Gabe or his dad. He doubted his dad would allow his mom to make the trek, particularly after dusk and particularly after his outburst in the living room. It very well could have been Renee, if she'd spotted him from the ranch. She'd certainly been asserting herself as the vet clinic coordinator, making it impossible to turn down any case assignment. In any case, Josh intended to shun away any attempt at conversation, whoever it was, walk directly to his truck and drive home.

That was until he turned on his heel and found himself looking at Luther Graham.

15

no return

Luther could see the wear of the past few months on Josh's face. He was no older than 22? No, 23 now. He remembered a dialogue about Josh having a late summer birthday. Still. With his patchy, overgrown beard, long hair, dark, sunken eyes, he almost looked middle-aged, though he looked more physically imposing, his shoulders broader, his arms more muscular than the last time he saw him, picking up Essie for a day of fishing.

He allowed the memory to pour over him of Josh pulling up in the pickup, the truck that was still a crumpled heap of metal along the abandoned airfield, Essie excited to greet him. She'd paused, thrown her arms around Luther's neck, and told him she loved him.

He could feel the warmth of her embrace—and then, taking in the sight of Josh, he felt the chill of the early evening again.

Josh had looked ready to leave when Luther approached, but the moment he saw him, Josh had taken a step back, assuming a rigid, protective stance next to Essie's grave.

"I don't mean to intrude," Luther offered.

Josh frowned, clearing his throat, attempting to ease his stance, raking his fingers through his shaggy hair. "I didn't know you came out here."

Luther pursed his lips, shaking his head with regret. "I've only come out here once or twice. I struggle with cemeteries."

Josh glanced at the stones out the corner of his eye.

"I actually came here to find you."

Josh furrowed his brow.

"I went to your cabin first."

The German Shepherd the team had brought back from a MET assignment thankfully recognized Luther as he stepped up to the front door. Luther had already presumed based upon the lack of vehicle in the drive that Josh wasn't there, but he knocked anyway, which confused the dog.

The cabin seemed to be in good shape–the first time he'd been to the old Scouts camp, things had looked pretty worn and dilapidated, but the exterior of not just Josh's cabin, but all the vacant cabins appeared to have been pressure washed and sealed, the steps rebuilt and sturdy. Each cabin had a five-foot-high stack of firewood on their covered porches, prepped and ready for the winter, should anyone decide to occupy them.

Luther had been covertly checking in on Josh over the past few months through the receptionist at the large animal veterinary office where he was employed. Both conveniently and inconveniently, this contact was Renee Shaw, the Worship Band leader at church. He wasn't sure what Essie had shared with Renee about him, but for only meeting her maybe once, Renee seemed quite fond of him. In any case, Renee seemed very willing to share whatever information he'd asked for about Josh. She'd gone on to talk about how she had been convincing him to take assignments, even the basic ones that could easily be taken on by a technician, claiming "There just isn't anyone available" or "We're just so short-staffed," sharing Luther's assessment that Josh needed to be kept busy. Occasionally he'd hear her voice tighten when she mentioned Essie by name. She'd then clear her throat and redirect the conversation back to Josh.

As Luther waited outside the cabin, giving a reasonable amount of time for a person to answer the door considering the entire cabin was probably 500 square feet, he glanced over his shoulder and took in the setting. Based upon the state of the camp, the pristinely restored cabins, it appeared Josh had done a fair job keeping *himself* busy during the time when Renee wasn't sending him to do well visits with livestock and horses.

Resolved that he would need to look elsewhere for Josh, Luther had reached his hand up to the window where the dog had her nose pressed, attempting to get a sniff of him through the glass. As he did, his eyes fell upon a side table positioned beside a reading chair. On it were two leatherbound Bibles, stacked one on top of the other and two photo frames. The first was a white stone frame he recognized from Matteo's office at Calvary. The picture was taken of Matteo carrying 3-year-old Essie on his hip, both bundled for the cold, walking through a Christmas tree lot. Essie was awestruck, her big eyes reflecting the twinkling lights all around them. Matteo was smiling affectionately at her as she took in the trees and lights.

The other frame contained a photo of Essie at about age 8 wedged between the West brothers. She had her arms clamped around each of their necks, tugging them close, all three wearing wide smiles.

"Why did you want to find me?" Josh asked, his voice low.

Assessing Josh's worn appearance even in the filtered sunset light, Luther found he needed to brace himself for the conversation he was about to have with him, despite having played it through his mind a number of times.

Josh looked suddenly impatient to leave, directing his boots toward the path that led back to his parents' house.

"Essie's alive."

The impact of those two words was immediate. Josh's body stiffened.

"Essie's alive," Luther repeated, relieved and overwhelmed to be able to share that information with him.

Josh looked confused and uncertain.

"There's not a way to ease into telling you that."

"You told me she was dead," Josh said finally, his voice thick. He stopped to swallow. "You stood in that cabin—" His throat constricted,

175

tears welling in his eyes. "You looked me in the eyes and you told me–
You said you *saw* her."

"I *did*. I thought I was telling you the truth, Josh."

"When did you find out?"

"About 30 minutes later." Luther furrowed his brow. "I thought
about telling you. To say it was for your own good sounds patronizing,
but honestly, that was my intent. For the most part. *And* hers."

Josh considered this. "You thought I'd do something drastic."

"I *knew* you'd do something drastic. And I wouldn't blame you."

Josh's attention drifted. He stared off toward the mountain view,
clearly processing things.

Luther allowed the silence to stretch, stealing a glance at the place
where Matteo was buried. The site was outlined with stones, a small piece
of granite about the size of a sheet of paper etched with a cross by a local
artisan serving as the grave marker. It was simple; he'd seen more
extravagant grave sites done for beloved pets, but it was enough, he
supposed. He felt a constriction in his chest, tears beginning to brim his
eyes. "The council believed she was dead. I thought it was best that they
continued to think that."

Josh blinked, nodding slowly.

"Gowon took her with help from people in the Ark. I'm not sure if
that's something anyone has told you. I've been doing a lot of public
addresses lately shining a light on some things, including her
kidnapping."

Josh lifted his eyes.

"They were Ark operatives working off orders from council
members, who didn't realize her significance. They were trying to work
out a negotiation with Gowon's people for themselves, their families.
They had been told that Gowon is Essie's father, they justified what they
were doing."

The color faded from Josh's cheeks.

"She's *not* his daughter. It was a tactic they used. They filtered the
information through Christopher Loop so the council would believe it.
Gowon fathered hundreds of children he put into the labs, but she was

not one of them. You've met some of them though," he added conversationally, then retreated.

Josh shook his head. "I couldn't care less who her biological father is, Luther."

He nodded. "It's not important. They're all dead; the people who took her. Gowon had them killed the second they delivered her."

"But what you said? Her injuries? Was that the truth?" His voice was nearly a whisper.

"Crushed spinal column, pelvis, ribs, lung collapse, perforated organs, and a traumatic brain injury—presumably. Yes."

Josh closed his eyes briefly. "She healed from all of those things?"

"I wouldn't believe it if I didn't see it myself."

He took a steadying breath.

"It was going to do you no favors to tell you she was alive if there wasn't a chance that we'd be able to get to her."

Josh furrowed his brow. "You're saying there's a chance now."

"Yes."

Josh stared at him, his eyes filled with intensity. He suddenly doubled over, his breaths releasing in staggered sobs.

Luther stepped toward him. "Why don't you take a seat? Catch your breath?" He'd just placed his hand on his back when Josh turned abruptly and hugged him. He didn't realize how much he'd missed human contact until that moment. He felt a bit taken off guard by the gesture, chuckling nervously.

Essie was the last person to give him a hug. She'd thrown her arms around him and squeezed gently. "Love you, Luther," she'd said, smiling over her shoulder as she took off to greet Josh for their date.

Josh hugging him felt like an extension of Essie.

Luther took a slow, deep breath.

"She's alive," Josh whispered, his warm breath muffled against Luther's shoulder.

Luther patted him on the upper back, nodding, as he took a step back. He was finding it difficult to generate words. He regretted breaking the embrace.

The silence stretched.

Josh's breaths began to steady. He glanced up at the darkening sky, the porch lights now illuminated at the West's house.

"I imagine you probably wanted to be getting back to Fenway," Luther said, thankful his brain had managed to remember the dog's name.

Josh nodded. "I can't leave her loose because of the wildlife. I didn't want to bring her here."

"We'll talk more at your place."

*   *   *

They walked in silence back to the West's house where the orchard truck was parked. The lights were on inside, but there wasn't any movement in the living room.

Luke West sat on the porch steps, leaning forward over his knees, hands folded in prayer. When he lifted his chin, it was apparent that he was startled to find Luther walking alongside his son.

"Evening, Luke."

"*Luther*," he said, rising to his feet. He floated his arms out to the sides, peering out toward the overlook, the driveway, the lack of a second vehicle.

"How's that beautiful little girl of yours?" Luther asked, ignoring the implied question of how he'd arrived undetected.

"Getting big. Crawling now–" Luke peered over his shoulder toward the house and back. "Sara fell asleep putting her to bed."

"Oh, I would have liked to have seen them. Sara's doing well?"

Luke secured eye contact with Josh, narrowing his eyes questioningly. "Yeah, you know," he said, frowning.

"Luke, would you mind *not* sharing around that I was here? I don't want to impose on you, but it would be better if this just stayed between us."

"Of course." Luke shoved his hands in the pockets of his jacket, straightening his posture after Luther gave him a fraternal hug, something he'd never done before. Once Luther rounded the back of the truck and climbed into the passenger side, out of view from the house, Luke turned toward Josh. "Wait up, just a second."

Josh stood rigidly.

Luke put his palm on his son's cheek. "You alright?"

Josh clenched his jaw, gave a short nod.

"What's this all about?" He glanced pointedly toward the truck.

Josh cleared his throat. "There was something of Luther's that I ended up with."

Luke frowned. Many things his son was, but a convincing liar was not one of them. He nodded just the same. "*Oh*. Would you mind coming by and checking on the colt tomorrow?"

Josh gave an uncertain nod. "If I can't, I'll make sure Hutch does. But I'll try," he added.

Luke tugged him in for a hug. "I love you, Josh."

*   *   *

It was a short 10-minute drive from the West's house to Josh's cabin, but it felt ages longer. Luther could feel the questions, the thoughts, the fears percolating in Josh's mind. Small talk just wasn't a reasonable expectation.

Luther stole some glances over at Josh, who gripped the steering wheel tightly. At one point he watched him look up into the rearview mirror and tilt his head as though not recognizing his own reflection.

Fenway was ecstatic to be released from the cabin, but was very efficient at relieving her bladder, scurrying back inside, setting to work to sniff every inch of Luther's pant legs as he took a seat on the dated plaid couch.

Josh watched the dog from his seat in the reading chair, his mind clearly elsewhere. He suddenly jolted from his thoughts and frowned, glancing over at the photo frames, the Bibles. "It's been 79 days, Luther."

Luther nodded slowly. "I know." His voice was controlled and quiet.

"Why haven't we gone in to get her?"

Luther scratched his fingers along Fenway's back, smiling automatically when she responded by walking herself in a circle, nudging her head under his palm and having a seat on his foot. He cleared his throat, neutralized his expression. "We didn't have the resources–or the support. The mission isn't like anything any of the MET teams have faced. We had to be sure we had a plan with a high probability of success. If we fail, we won't have another chance."

Josh nodded slowly, his breaths heavy. "What's happening to her, Luther?"

"It's not going to help you to know all the details."

"I'm already imagining the worst."

"Then it's not going to comfort you to know that it's worse than anything that you could have possibly imagined."

Josh's chin rotated toward him, eyes wide. "Please just tell me."

Luther took a breath. "The worst kinds of torture, Josh. Mental. Physical. Several weeks ago, they tried surgically implanting probes onto her brain." He lifted his eyebrows, still not entirely able to fathom what she had endured, despite seeing much of it with his own eyes.

Despite their previous conversation, when Luther showed up to cover the day of the surgery, Miles never left. He positioned himself at the secondary workstation, buried his face in his hands, murmuring prayers throughout the day. At first, Luther had been concerned about him being there in case things went the way he feared they might, but in the end, it was comforting to have Miles nearby.

"Deep brain stimulation has been used for people with neurological conditions and movement disorders, but their intent was to implant the probes so they could trigger certain responses in her brain."

"Did it work?"

He shook his head. "Her body identified the probes as threats and defended itself."

"How?"

"Best guess is that her brain produced an acid to dissolve them."

Josh pinched his brow.

180

"There was nearly nothing left of the probes. I have no other explanation than that." Luther nodded reluctantly, omitting for Josh as he had done for Miles (who had kept his chin turned away during the actual surgery) how she had suffered a series of seizures during the procedure, how alarming this was considering the extended seizure she'd experienced the day before, that typically a prolonged seizure is associated with brain death, that despite her seeming to have recovered, a part of him wondered if she really had, if there was memory loss or other damage that just wasn't obvious. "The response her body had to the procedure—it was meant to protect her, but it nearly killed her. She recovered from it, but they decided it was too risky to go in that direction with her."

Jameson had suggested that they'd taken things too far with her, considering she was having uncontrolled physiological responses—seizures, cardiac arrest. This was when he and Gowon began to discuss options if she continued to demonstrate that she was no longer an ideal test subject.

Josh took a deep breath. "You said there's now a plan to get her?" His eyes were very round.

"Yes." Luther cleared his throat. "*Before*, any mission would have been rogue, at best. The goal of Ark leadership *had been* to assimilate back with the States without any fundamental changes made. We didn't have resources or support and it had a high probability of failure."

Josh steeled himself, his jaw tightening.

"But *now*, the Ark has new goals. More ambitious goals."

"Which are?"

"To seize control of the U.S. Capitol, take out Samuel Gowon and his entire regime."

"Overthrow the government."

"Yes."

Josh's eyes narrowed. "That's a complete course reversal."

"Yes."

"Does the Ark have the resources to pull that off?"

"We always did. In *addition*, we now have foreign nations who support what we're attempting to do, as far as overthrowing Gowon. Well, *covertly* support, but generously so."

"You said you were keeping the fact that Essie's alive from the council? How does that play out?"

He gave a small smile. "I forget that news doesn't travel around the Ark very easily, particularly with you living off the grid."

Josh frowned.

"The Arks have new leadership in place. The council structure is gone."

Josh's eyes darted around. "Who's the new leadership?"

"*Well*," Luther began, sweeping dog fur off his pant leg. "In anticipation of this mission being a success, it was decided that we should have a working government structure in place to handle things in the interim until we can carry out the full electoral process. An executive branch essentially–President, Vice President, and a Cabinet. Sadie Parker is acting as VP, the Cabinet is fresh faces–no one from the council. It's experts in the various fields. The *actual* experts, not the lobbyist variety of experts."

"And who's the Ark President?"

Luther drew back his shoulders slightly. "I am."

"You are," Josh said flatly.

"It's a means to an end. I wouldn't have chosen it for myself. All I can hope for is a James Garfield length term to accomplish what needs to be done. Perhaps minus the assassination."

Josh tilted his chin. "Garfield was strong-armed into running for President, right?"

"I forgot you enjoy reading almost as much as Essie." He cleared his throat. "It happened in a similar fashion, giving a rousing speech, though at the time, I wasn't aware it was being broadcast to all the people in the Arks–*and* it was probably a little rougher around the edges than Garfield's speech, to be honest."

Josh frowned. "So, I'm speaking to the *President* right now."

Luther shook his head, lifted his eyes. "You're speaking to me."

Josh leaned forward over his knees. "I would think you'd have security detail."

"I do," he said lightly.

Josh peered around the cabin, lifted his eyebrows.

"It's high tech. Don't worry about it. I'm not even *here* right now, if you can believe that."

"Danny?"

"He says 'hello,'" Luther murmured, pointing to his right ear.

Josh was clearly distracted, his gaze distant. "At what point do we rescue Essie?"

"We'll have an elite team of soldiers whose only objective is to get Essie and get out. All the other action going on should provide adequate cover."

"She's in the District then."

"She's at the White House."

Josh froze, his brow furrowed.

"That's obviously been a major complication. Gowon is not well-liked, despite what the administration, the state news would have you believe. The security to get into the District, let alone the White House, is intense."

Both men fell silent watching Fenway bite persistently at an itch on her leg.

"Luther, you said the brain–" Josh's voice caught. "--the *surgery* was 'several weeks ago.' What's been happening to her since?"

Luther's heart started to race. He took a deep breath. "She started to respond poorly, Josh. It was too much what they were putting her through."

Josh sat more upright.

"Gowon and the lead researcher decided that they wanted more test subjects *in case*–in case she couldn't continue." He paused, swallowing hard, deciding he didn't need to elaborate on the why any further. "They wanted to see if they could replicate Essie's cellular traits for the new test subjects." He scratched his head, displeased with his explanation. "They wanted to see if the traits were *hereditary*."

Josh frowned. "*Luther.*"

"Her body rejected fertility drugs, which historically have been used to harvest eggs, but they *were* successful when they tried in vitro fertilization." He cleared his throat.

"She's pregnant?" Josh asked quietly.

Luther furrowed his brow, resolving that less information was probably better at this point. "8 weeks."

Josh took a deep breath, nodding.

"The baby does *not* have the same cellular structure traits."

Josh narrowed his eyes. "What does that mean? What are they going to do?"

Luther pressed his lips together. "They're waiting until Essie reaches the second trimester. Amniotic fluid through that stage has been shown to have some similarities to pluripotent stem cells and it reaches its maximum volume at the start of second trimester so they're interested in collecting–"

Josh shook his head impatiently. "I don't care about Gowon's mad science. What happens to Essie and the baby when she reaches the second trimester?"

Luther considered telling him that the baby would either be killed or be moved to an artificial womb with an uncertain future, that during the same surgery they were planning to remove Essie's ovaries so they could attempt to harvest the eggs, to see if that offered better success. He quickly determined, to his own tremendous relief, that telling him was not necessary because, whether they succeeded or failed, it would never happen. If they succeeded in the mission to rescue Essie, both she and her baby would be safe. If they failed, there was a contingency plan that would result in the total destruction of the area where she was held. No one would survive the blast.

He lifted his shoulders. "The mission will take place before that happens."

16

righteous

"Thirty-four million, two hundred thousand, four hundred and ninety-seven lives lost." Garrison Chase, the highest rated cable news host, said the words slowly, fully extracting every syllable. He released an extended, thoughtful sigh, looking regretfully down at his note sheet, and shook his head, removing his rectangular glasses as he looked up at the camera again. He gulped, simulating something resembling grief.

It was challenging for him to display anything other than exuberance knowing his broadcast could very well be used for historical reference pretty much until the end of time. "You've seen some of their stories. Tonight, we'll look for answers. How could this have happened? Why? Who is responsible? And how do we move forward from here? I'm Garrison Chase and *this* is *American Truth*."

Given the magnitude of pressure to look his best, he had spent the day bleaching his teeth, having his hair cut, colored and styled, having determined his ordinary tousled look, dyed a medium shade of brown (done in an attempt to look younger than his fifty-three years) was inappropriate. He and his trusted stylist had determined a vice-presidential look was in order. After all, it had been suggested that he could have potential in politics after his coverage of the events of the calculated attacks on the country's citizens. His Q score had spiked after he did personal biographies of a number of victims. He had stood in abandoned homes looking at framed photographs and things he presented as favorite possessions and toys, all editorialized of course. He found most victims had entire families and community units exterminated. This had been problematic until he realized no one would refute his claim that an antique clock had been the centerpiece of the family's mantel, dating back generations, and that despite their need to work endless hours, when the clock struck 6pm, wherever any of the family members happened to be, they shared a meal.

Now he needed trustworthy hair that established an air of wisdom to elevate himself further. Something short, to give the appearance of military experience, but with slightly longer sections on top to make it more nonthreatening. Sitting before the stylist, he had to actively suppress the urge to liken the look he desired to Christopher Loop. For one thing, Loop had a bulk to his physique Garrison had never, could never possess, so comparing the two side-by-side would do nothing but hurt his self-esteem. For a second, Garrison lacked any military experience whatsoever and it wasn't something he felt he could exude with any level of believability. As a result, Garrison had asked for an approachable academic slash war news correspondent look. He had some dye stripped from his hair to provide a graceful and natural progression to salt and pepper.

The studio lights were as warm as always, but he was aware that he had permitted slightly less makeup to further enhance his new persona. He worried this had taken these a step too far when he saw himself on the live monitor. He let his lips part as he watched the solemn show intro play out featuring clips of his past coverage and ending with a waving American flag. He frowned thoughtfully as he went live again.

"Over thirty-four million people is the body count after the single largest attack in history. Initial findings suggest perhaps agents of the insurgents occupying what they've termed 'Arks,' sections of acreage in the northern and southern parts of the country, are responsible for tainting vaccination supplies with a lethal drug that took the lives of tens of millions of people in a matter of weeks. Here's what President Gowon had to say earlier."

President Gowon was much more practiced at looking severe. He stood in front of a lineup of flags. "It is with a heavy heart that I stand here today. So many lives. So many lives needlessly and tragically...ended. And for what? For too long in the world, and in our country, there has been an ever-growing culture of hate." He paused, tensing his jaw and shaking his head. No more. That time has ended. I invite our country persons to band together...and *love*. That's what life is all about, isn't it? Love? We will no longer tolerate any presence of hatred in this country. The age of intolerance, of bigotry, of nationalist extremes is over. The history books will speak of this time in our history as the turning point when America took a stand and declared for all the world to hear: We are better than this. We are better together. We will move forward *together*.

"Today I signed executive actions paying reparations to the groups of Americans most impacted by the attacks on our country through my signature on the HEART legislative package. While this does little to numb the tragedy, the heartbreak, it is the right thing to do–and I will expand these as advised in the coming days and weeks. We will move on together, as a country, but we shall never forget where we have come from and why we must never go back. Thank you."

Garrison opened his mouth to speak as the clip ended, but another video immediately began, showing bodies being hauled into trains, tossed into landfills by uniformed peace officers. He furrowed his brow in manufactured sadness, trying to mask the contempt he felt for not being informed there was a segment added. His eyes panned to the teleprompter, which had gone blank, then to the live shot, which he was grateful he was not in.

"*What the hell?*" he mouthed to the producer, who was preoccupied in the sound booth.

"*The government wants you to believe that the people of the Arks were responsible for the loss of life over the past ten months, that the people of the Arks played a role in the loss of life in the years before. What we have witnessed is an orchestrated government plan that goes back decades, a plan to reduce the population of the United States.*"

The screen flashed rapidly with photos of those killed, each accompanied by a name caption and age.

"*These were moms, dads, children, grandparents, sisters, brothers, neighbors, friends, colleagues. The government chose to kill them.*"

An audio file that was unmistakably President Gowon began to play. "*25%. We're looking for a 25% reduction in the country's population. Minimum. Filter to households where someone voted for the other side.*"

"Voting age and older?"

"*Any* age."

"Sir?"

The screen displayed photos of school age children, teenagers, babies, then switched to a video walk-through of a church, a warehouse, train cars stacked with corpses, buildings ablaze, presumably to burn the bodies.

"*Suicide rates surge after big events like this so that should easily reach our target of 40%, higher ideally,*" Gowon continued. "*With birth rates at an all-time low, we should see a steady decrease over the next ten years.*"

The slideshow of photos continued. "*This isn't the first time the government has murdered its own people, but things are different this time. For those of you living in the former United States, our war is not against you. Our war is with the leaders who never seem to have enough power, who silence us, murder us. Over the next several days, we will reveal all that the government has kept hidden. As this information comes to light, I implore you to gather up what supplies you have, protect those unable to fight, and band together. Today marks the day when we begin to take back our country.*"

Large block letters flashed on the screen: "*RISE UP.*"

The live feed monitor switched to Garrison sitting behind his anchor desk, a stunned, stupid expression on his face. The teleprompter was coming back online, but he found he couldn't focus his eyes on the words. The executive producer waved her skinny arms in the air to get his attention. It was as he looked in her direction that the air current chilled his face. His hands flew to his cheeks and found them soaked with tears.

He tightened his jaw and pointed forcefully toward the monitor closest to him, even though it still displayed his shell-shocked face. "That was—" he stammered, "—my sister. Emerson. Her twin girls." He glanced across at the producer, the only person in the studio who didn't look absolutely stunned. "Did the government *murder them*?"

Cut to black.

17
day eighty-one

The outer door squeaked open, but Miles had long stopped glancing up to greet Luther. He released a breath, his cheek propped up by his fist, and continued to watch Essie sitting in the corner of her cell, knees drawn up to her chest. She swayed backward and forward, as though sitting in a rocking chair. Her eyes were glassy and stared blankly across the room toward the camera integrated within the control panel.

Over the past few weeks, she'd started to mumble unintelligible things under her breath at a higher frequency and since Gowon's people had stopped forcing her to listen to heavy metal or death sounds, he'd actually been able to hear her. There had been times he thought he could make out words, but he couldn't conclude with any certainty if the words were prayers, songs, or even if she was speaking in English. There were times she spoke to the baby in perfect Italian, translated easily by the computer. The mumbling had started to concern him though, as it was typically accompanied by punctuated, abrupt movements and an increase in eye twitches and other acquired tics that didn't appear to be voluntary.

Miles focused his attention on the blueprint of the White House's West Wing expansion building, which he had situated on the tabletop before him. He had been studying every resource he had on the building, on the grounds for weeks and the primary, secondary, and tertiary escape points. He had plotted out plans given any number of circumstances, if Esther had the ability to get around on her own or if she was completely unconscious or incapacitated. He'd even considered that she might be in a mental state where she'd be combative. For that, he had a plan. Not one he cared to spend too much time considering, but he had the means to restrain her; he'd be able to administer a medication cocktail that would sedate her long enough so they could make it to the Armadillo vehicle, so they could get out of the District.

He heard Luther speaking quietly around the corner. He assumed he was finishing a phone call—until he noticed the artificial shadows cast by the lighting seemed to indicate he wasn't alone.

"I'm going to ask one more time. Are you *sure* about this?"

Miles leaned sideways in his seat, trying to see around the old computer server equipment. In the next moment, Josh West came into view.

"Oh, *shit*," Miles muttered, nearly losing his balance in the chair. He had actively avoided Josh over the last three months since finding out about Essie—with the notable exceptions of Essie's dad's funeral, where they were both pallbearers, and Essie's private funeral. Since then, he had essentially moved into the abandoned business complex where the surveillance room was located. He knew after those limited encounters that there was no possible way he would be able to face Josh, knowing Essie was alive, knowing what she was going through.

With Luther stepping in as President and focusing his attention on the larger mission—of seizing control of what once was the biggest superpower in the world—Miles rarely left the room, studying blueprints, making extraction contingency plans, and keeping an eye on Essie. While he'd previously ventured out for groceries or meals and to do laundry when Luther covered, Miles had essentially been on 24-hour watch. He'd stocked up on survival food supplies so he wouldn't have to worry about refrigeration and he'd discovered a former medical clinic downstairs with a full bathroom with washer and dryer, though he'd not showered or done laundry in days. He couldn't remember the last time he'd seen daylight.

He raked his fingers through his overgrown sandy-colored curls, rubbed roughly at his eyes, and assessed the state of his workstation. He turned toward them as they approached.

Josh's expression was decidedly neutral, unfazed when he saw Miles. He'd recently shaved, but his hair was long and bushy. There was a wan appearance to his face, his dark eyes shadowed.

Miles stood, shielding his friend's view of the main monitor, having already cut the duplicate feeds on the other screens.

"Hey, Miles," Josh greeted in a stiff, but friendly tone.

Luther pressed his lips together, noticing the blacked-out screens. "I've given Josh some insight into what Essie's been going through, what her current situation is."

Miles swallowed hard, jaw tight. "You think this is a good idea, Bro?" He made unwavering eye contact with his friend, silently urging him to change course.

"It'll be less of a shock for him on the mission that way," Luther said confidently. He lifted his eyebrows pointedly at the primary monitor.

With apprehension, Miles stepped to the side, opening up the sightlines to the screen. He activated the others as well.

Josh immediately moved closer, lifting his hand toward Essie's shape on the screen, showing an overhead view of her cell.

Miles glared over at Luther, shaking his head.

Luther watched Josh gazing at Essie, then gave a reassuring nod to Miles.

Josh was silent for several moments before speaking. "You said we have someone on the inside. That's how we have access to this?" he asked without turning away from the screen, clearly stifling tears.

Miles sighed, switched camera feeds to the one positioned near the door controls. A close-up of Essie's face filled the screen.

Josh pulled in his breath.

Her silver eyes looked vacant, peering over the top of her arms. There were time periods when Miles had watched her and she barely blinked. For the time being, she appeared to be blinking at a normal, but drowsy rate. Her mouth was moving but was hidden behind her arms.

Her hair had grown a considerable amount in the weeks since her head was shaved, disguising any remaining traces of scars from the failed brain surgery.

"I have to get to a meeting," Luther announced quietly, patting Josh's upper arm. He didn't acknowledge Miles's silent protests before taking leave from the room.

Josh leaned closer to the main monitor, lifting his hand to her cheek. "She's so thin."

Miles cleared his throat. "She lost a lot of weight in the first few weeks when they weren't giving her any food. They were forced to feed her because of the baby." His chest tightened, considering that perhaps he'd incorrectly assumed that Luther had shared that specific detail.

"She knows?" Josh asked, his voice thick. "That she's pregnant?"

Miles released a breath. His initial impulse was to respond with something like: "It'd be impossible for her *not* to know," but he thought better of it. The tone of his remark would have conveyed a small amount of his disgust over how they'd carried out the procedures, how they'd treated Essie throughout all of it, but number one, Josh wouldn't know that; it would just sound like mean-spirited sarcasm, and number two, Josh didn't need to know those details. Not right now. So, Miles replied with a simple: "Yeah. She knows."

Essie's body jolted suddenly, like being startled from sleep. She stood.

Miles stepped in and switched back to the overhead feed on several monitors, zooming out on the control panel camera.

She began to pace, shaking out her hands, chin lowered to her chest. Her breathing was becoming more staggered and uneven.

"This happens," Miles said quietly, meaning it to be reassuring.

Esther paced back and forth across the small space four times, then stopped in the dead center of the room. She winced, tears filling her eyes, her mouth moving more purposefully.

"Is there audio?"

Miles lifted the headset and handed it to him. "Usually, she's just too quiet for me to figure out what she's saying." He silently added that much of the time, there were competing sounds in the room—either death metal or literal sounds of death. "Luther says sometimes it sounds like she's praying. I honestly can't tell if it's English or Italian. She talks to the baby in Italian."

Josh kept his eyes upon her, pushing the headphones more securely over his ears. After a few moments, he was mouthing the words along with her. "She's singing."

Miles narrowed his eyes.

Josh began to whisper the words: "*Spirit lead me where my trust is without borders. Let me walk upon the waters. Wherever You would call me. Take me deeper than my feet could ever wander. And my faith will be made stronger in the presence of my Savior.*'" Sure enough, her lips moved along with the melody of the words.

Essie stood motionless, breathing more deeply now. She peered over her shoulder, turned, and took a seat close to where she had been before, hugging her knees to her chest, staring toward the door.

Josh narrowed his eyes on the screen. "Her tattoo is gone."

The image immediately came to Miles's mind of them clamping Essie into the metal chair, forcing her arm forward across the table, and using a literal blow torch to burn away the tattoo, leaving her forearm beveled and blistered and raw.

The skin had healed in the weeks since, only fading pink splotches remaining.

Miles nodded tightly.

"This is what you've been doing for the last three months." Josh said, tilting his chin toward Miles, his voice quiet.

Miles looked defensively at Essie. Affirming the statement felt unfair, that this scene was not representative of what she had gone through.

This was nothing. What they had just witnessed felt similar to a lion pacing her confinement at a zoo out of boredom, but Essie had been through every form of torture. On several occasions, he thought she had died. On several occasions, she had actually clinically died. Her body's unrivaled ability to repair itself seemed to be a form of torture by itself.

He wasn't sure what Luther had shared with Josh. There probably wasn't a need to share every detail, but not doing so felt unfair to Essie, like it minimized what she'd been through.

Even so, he took in the sight of his friend pressing the headset tightly to his ears, listening desperately for anything Essie felt compelled to say, his breaths heavy, tears brimming his eyes, and heard himself say: "Yeah."

Josh swallowed hard.

"You can have a seat," Miles said, grabbing his coffee tumbler and shifting over to the next workstation.

Josh gave a short nod, lowered himself into the task chair, his eyes shifting briefly to the blueprint of the White House grounds, then immediately back to the screen. "Who's on the mission?"

"Gunner, Danny 5, me, you, and a couple Ark military officers I've been told are non-negotiable."

"Who are they?"

"'A neutral third-party,'" he said, shaking his head. "They're good guys. It could be helpful having them."

"Luther called the team an 'elite task force.'"

"Yeah, he was mainly referring to me," Miles replied, taking a casual sip of what was now room temperature coffee.

Josh was actively regulating his breaths, finally working up to speaking again. "Luther wouldn't tell me much about what's happened to her. He told me about the surgeries, and he told me that they've tortured her."

"*Yeah.*"

"He also said what she's gone through is worse than anything I can imagine."

Miles took a breath and nodded.

"I can imagine some really horrible things," Josh murmured, not taking his eyes off the screen.

Miles frowned. "It's worse."

Josh nodded slowly.

"They've laid off the physical stuff, but they're still pushing her hard psychologically. Sim time mainly. They've advanced the technology; it's

195

more immersive than anything they had for Mandatory." Miles took a steadying breath. "She's actually been doing a little better. She had gotten to a point–I didn't think she'd come back from it."

Josh lifted his eyes.

"She thinks we're all dead–it's probably essential you know that." Miles resituated himself in his chair. "The baby helped, I think–gave her someone else to care about, someone else to be strong for."

Essie took a deep breath, her eyes still staring intensely toward the door.

"The baby," Josh began, his voice wavering. He stopped to clear his throat. "The baby is healthy?"

"Yeah, she is," Miles said quietly. "They don't care about that though."

"Luther said they'd be planning to transfer the baby into an artificial womb after the first trimester."

"If they decide to even bother. I don't imagine they have much use for a perfectly healthy, but 'ordinary' baby." His voice had become constricted. He shook his head. "Sorry."

"You haven't had anyone to talk to about what you've been doing," Josh observed calmly.

"Well, *Luther*. He's been occupied–but he's seen what I've seen." His eyes flitted between the monitors and he braced his hands unnecessarily over the keyboard to give himself something to do. "Luther talked about bringing in Danny and Gunner to switch off with me, but–" He shook his head forcibly.

Josh furrowed his brow. "You didn't want to leave her."

Miles pursed his lips, his hand trembling. "*Couldn't,*" he corrected. "I *couldn't* leave her." He sniffled. "They're good guys, but–I like to think that I have more of a bond with her than them."

Josh nodded slowly, taking very methodical breaths. "You do."

Miles glanced over at him. "I'm sorry I lied to you, Josh."

He gave a small shake of his head and leaned forward toward the monitor. "You think they're going to kill the baby."

"I do."

"And that's all she's living for right now."

Miles took a breath. "Either scenario—if they do an abortion or if they finish growing the baby in a tank—it'll break her. There's been so many things they've done that should have done that and she held on, but—"

"*This* will."

Miles nodded. He decided, for the moment, to resist sharing his suspicion that Gowon would have her captors proceed with killing the baby sooner rather than later. He didn't seem like the sort to be patient to receive results. He'd want to start the process over again as soon as possible. It was perplexing to him why Gowon had waited this long.

On the monitor, they once again watched Essie's body jolt, as though startled from sleep. She pushed herself off the floor and began to pace the room in her normal pattern, shaking out her hands. She walked back and forth across the space four times, then turned back and stopped at the center point of the room, eyes closed, attempting to steady her breathing.

"We're coming for you, Essie," Josh whispered.

It happened suddenly and inexplicably.

Essie's chin snapped upward and her arms dropped to her sides. Her eyes searched the room, looking vivid and alert.

"Is there a microphone on this?"

Miles frowned. "No."

Josh cleared his throat. "We're coming for you, Essie," he repeated.

Her eyebrows pulled together. She was taking longer breaths, turning on the spot, eyes moving slowly around the room, as though scanning a crowd of faces.

Over the speaker came the echo of steps in the corridor.

Essie rotated herself toward the door and planted her feet solidly, waiting. Miles zoomed in on the camera feed that originated in the control panel by the door. He knew it wasn't possible. He knew she was probably just awaiting the arrival of whoever was in the corridor. Based upon the time of day, it was probably someone with a food tray, but there was something different about her stance, her gaze, the way she seemed to zero in on the camera, a questioning look on her face.

The door slid open and sure enough, a guard entered holding a food tray. It was the usual afternoon guard, a sharp-jawed young man with a blonde buzz cut.

The guard appeared surprised to see Essie standing so alertly, frowning as he took in her facial expression. He peered over his shoulder, slowing his steps as he waited for the door to close behind him, apparently interpreting her stance as her preparing to make a break for it.

On the control panel video feed, Essie was paying little attention to the guard. Her eyes were still fixed on the camera, though Danny had assessed and assured Miles multiple times that the camera was undetectable and that she didn't know of its existence.

The guard set the tray down, then retreated to the door. He lifted his palm as though intending to wave goodbye, but reconsidered and quickly left the cell.

Essie resumed blinking the moment the door closed.

"Essie," Josh murmured, but she gave no acknowledgement she'd heard him.

It had just been a coincidence. A really weird coincidence.

She tightened her jaw, turned on her heel toward the dinner tray, which the guard had placed on the otherwise empty wall ledge. It contained two bottles of water, some form of 3-d printed meatloaf, mashed potatoes, broccoli, and three dinner rolls. It wasn't the first time the guard had given her extra servings of the food item she seemed to gravitate to most consistently.

As she propelled her body toward the tray, she began to murmur something.

"It's the Lord's Prayer in Italian," Josh offered, taking a deep breath. He pressed the headphones to his ears.

Miles activated the speaker on the workstation.

"Sia fatta la tua volontá," she repeated after she'd recited the prayer, nodding slowly. *Thy will be done.* "Sia fatta la tua volontá." She took a steadying breath, plucked the dinner rolls from the tray, along with a bottle of water, and returned to the back wall, where she slid her back along the concrete until she was seated once again on the floor, legs folded before her. Her lip quivered as she raised the first roll to her mouth and took a bite. It seemed to be taking great effort for her to chew it. Thick tears were starting to pour from her eyes.

She swallowed down the bite of bread, dropped the rolls into her lap and fell forward over her knees, her shoulders trembling with sobs.

After a few minutes, they could hear her taking another deep breath. As she released the air in a slow, concentrated effort, she released her arms at her sides, and took another ration of air. Deep breath in. *Hold*. Release. And again. Deep breath in. *Hold*. Release.

Miles found himself naturally following the rhythm with his own breathing.

As Essie reached a point of calm, a stillness filled the room. She leaned her head back against the wall, taking another focused breath.

It was then that Josh began to sing, quietly, softly, very close to a whisper. It was a song Miles recognized from a Contemporary Christian playlist Essie had shared with him months earlier as a way to further "infuse Jesus into his life."

> *"'You are not hidden*
> *There's never been a moment*
> *You were forgotten*
> *You are not hopeless*
> *Though you have been broken*
> *Your innocence stolen*
>
> *I hear you whisper underneath your breath*
> *I hear your SOS, your SOS...'"*

*   *   *

When Josh was thirteen, his family had made an infrequent trek to Wallace for a weekend; for a visit and also so his dad could help with some structural work on the church. At that time, Calvary had services

199

on both Saturday evenings and Sunday mornings. They had intended to go to church on Sunday since it was a different pastor preaching on Saturday night, but as they finished an early dinner, Essie had quickly gathered her plate and glass and placed them in the sink. She stepped across the kitchen to her dad and gave him a sideways hug. He kissed her forehead and asked her something in Italian, to which she shook her head.

"Where do you think you're off to?" Luke had asked, reaching out, attempting to tickle her.

She smiled tightly. "I'm singing at service tonight."

Sara had clasped her hand to her chest, checking the state of her damp hair, already in her pajamas. "Why didn't you tell us?"

Teo side-eyed his daughter. "I told you they'd be upset."

"I'm singing the same thing in the morning," Essie replied dismissively, heading for the door.

Josh's mom had, of course, gone on about it, but ultimately things moved on to the planned game night. As dishes were being cleared and cleaned and his dad disappeared for his notoriously long post-dinner visit to the bathroom, Josh had slipped out and gone to the church.

This was an unusual decision on his part, for one thing because, like his mom, he was already changed into pajamas. Another reason was that he wasn't one who typically gravitated to church unless forced. It didn't bother him in the least if his family skipped church on Sundays and he could instead take a nap or have an indulgent breakfast; he even preferred it.

He remembered being surprised at the number of people in attendance for a Saturday night service; the place was bustling. As he entered the sanctuary, his eyes immediately found Essie at the front, speaking with other members of the Worship Band. The first song, an upbeat melody, began and she took her place at one of the side microphones, providing backup vocals. Meanwhile, Josh found a seat at the end of a pew with an unobstructed view, ignoring the glances he'd gotten from the people for his chosen attire, and the fact that he seemed to be in attendance alone.

Based upon the conversation at the house, he anticipated Essie would have more of a featured role singing so he found himself a bit disappointed when someone else, a middle-aged woman took center stage, but he enjoyed watching/hearing Essie sing, regardless. The song ended and the band began to clear from the slightly elevated stage. Announcements played and featured new life groups, prayer teams, outreach programs. The sanctuary fell silent and a pastor Josh had never met took the stage. He talked about how so often people focus on doing a year in review at the *end* of a year, but given all the impact that had taken place in just a few months, all the hearts who had turned to Jesus, the sheer growth Calvary had seen, the worship team had decided to do a special presentation slideshow. He then turned to his right and introduced Essie, saying that she would be providing the musical accompaniment, with assistance from someone on the piano. He said the name of the person, but Josh's mind was fixed on Essie.

She didn't look tremendously different than she had before she left the house, but there was something almost ethereal about her as she stepped up to the microphone in the focused spotlight to the side of the projection screen and began to sing, a slideshow of baptisms, of outreach, of food deliveries to at-need communities, of prayer teams, of worship played behind her.

As a teenage boy, Josh hadn't completely accepted what he'd been taught about living life with God's guidance. He'd felt a little lost, given his age, given the state of the world, given his perceptions of his place in his family. He'd appreciated and respected Essie's faith and he didn't dare question it; they seemed to find plenty of other things to talk about, but despite his best friend being deeply embedded within church activities and having a strong connection with God, he could never seem to find one for himself.

But in that church, in that Saturday night service, he watched Essie sing, he listened to the lyrics she sang with such effortless passion, and something invigorating and pure and hopeful awakened in him. He wanted to know Jesus. He needed to know Jesus.

* * *

In a much different room, his eyes were focused on Essie again, though through the intermediary of a computer screen. He let his voice trail off after a second round of the chorus.

Miles wiped roughly at his eyes, refusing to make light of the moment by making a remark about Josh's singing voice, despite the fact the remark would have been positive. It just wasn't the time for it. He picked a pen up off the desk and quietly retraced the lines on the floor plan, then lifted his eyes to the monitor.

Essie's breaths had deepened, her chest rising and falling heavily. She opened her eyes, gazing across the room, zeroed in again on the precise location of the camera.

She doesn't know there's a camera, he reminded himself silently.

And then he heard her begin to sing, continuing precisely where Josh had left off: "'*I hear the whisper underneath your breath; I hear you whisper, you have nothing left.*'"

Her voice was barely louder than a whisper.

The room fell silent, though Miles could hear the chorus playing in his mind:

I will send out an army to find you
In the middle of the darkest night
It's true, I will rescue you
I will never stop marching to reach you
In the middle of the hardest fight
It's true, I will rescue you
Oh, I will rescue you

After a few quiet moments–by Miles's estimate, the remaining length of the song, Essie twisted the cap off the water bottle, made more difficult by the prominent tremors in her hands. She stopped her effort, placing the bottle back on the floor. She sniffled as she vigorously shook out her hands. She squeezed them into fists, flexing and stretching several times until the shaking had lessened considerably. She picked up the water bottle and quickly twisted off the cap. She took a long swig then rested her head against the wall, closing her eyes.

"We're coming for you, Essie," Josh repeated quietly.

Tears soaked through her lashes and began to slip down her cheeks. She took a steadying breath and gave a small, but distinct nod.

18

'til kingdom come

The day before Essie was taken was the last time Josh had seen her in person.

He had needed to check on a foal just west of the ranch. Afterward, he stopped by to pick her up for their date, which up until the moment he laid eyes on her, was intended to be fishing. It was a surprise then when he parked in the driveway and she was standing–no, not standing–*posing* in her playful way, wearing a flowing white dress that reached her shins, her fishhook patterned boots, and his cowboy hat, which he'd forgotten at the ranch the previous day. She had her boots crossed, standing casually, waiting for him to exit the pickup.

He'd presented her with a bouquet of wildflowers as he approached her, then started to drop to one knee as though he was going to propose. It had been something they'd gone back and forth about, always joking, making light of it, but something was different for him as he stood upright and took in the sight of her, something different for him as she smiled at him from beneath the rim of his cowboy hat.

In that moment, Josh decided it would be the last time he'd tease about a proposal. The next time would be the real thing. For the moment though, he'd play along. He rested his hands on her hips, gazed into her eyes, and whispered: "You *know*, we could have your dad marry us right now."

"We *could* do that, couldn't we?" she said, her eyes widening enthusiastically. "We even have a witness."

He lifted his brow in agreement.

She grabbed hold of his hand and started to tug him across the driveway.

It didn't take much persuasion or strength to twirl her back toward him. She grinned widely. "You're right. You probably need more time to decide how you feel about me."

He scrunched his nose. "80-90 years?"

"It's going to take you *that* long to know how you feel about me? Good *Lord*!"

"I meant that to be charming. You know what? *Now* I've done it," he said, irritated with himself. "Let's lock this thing down *right now*." He took two determined strides toward Teo and Luther, peering over at her. "*You*, my love, look absolutely spectacular. *I* look kind of grungy and dirty, but that's okay. That's normal. We *should* commit our sacred vows to each other *just as we are*."

He reversed course again, dragging her along with him back toward the truck, pleased to see her getting amusement out of it. "On *second* thought, when we do this, we should do it right. *Today*, we fish."

She suppressed a laugh as he led her to the passenger side and opened her door, holding her hand and elbow as though guiding her into a carriage.

He waved to a confused Luther and Teo as he jogged around the bed of the pickup, climbing in on his side.

Essie had removed his cowboy hat and was shaking out her hair as he climbed in, the smell of her shampoo strong in the air. "So, you *do* know you'll have to ask my dad for his permission before any actual proposal takes place."

"Of course I know that."

She furrowed her brow, looking forward through the windshield and the house beyond. "I mean, he's not a *huge* fan of yours so you might want to *really* think about what you're planning to say."

He started to back the truck out of the driveway. As he shifted into drive and accelerated forward, he pursed his lips and said shortly: "I think it went pretty well actually."

Essie whipped her chin toward him, having been waving to her dad and Luther. She narrowed her eyes, trying to get a read on him. Her cheeks tightened as she eased back into the bench seat, draping her hand out the window. She angled her chin toward the window, taking in the scenery, but he saw the dimple in her cheek deepen.

He had felt the strong impulse to pull off to the side of the road and propose then and there; they'd just made the turn onto the forest road that led to the old Scouts' camp and the scenery was quite picturesque. Each time there was a service road turn, he heard a voice telling him to stop.

He could imagine pulling the truck to the side of the road, climbing out, circling determinedly to her side, and opening her door. And he'd just ask, once and for all.

No. It couldn't be a "just" situation; it needed to be thought out a bit more–and he'd need to be sure he actually had the ring for the proposal; it was tucked away in his nightstand in a small velvet box: a double-twisted band etched to look like rope (which reminded him of the tree swing) with a cushion cut moonstone outlined with the same rope pattern interspersed with tiny diamonds.

So they'd gone about their day of fishing, as planned, with her borrowing his clothes, which he somehow found an even more endearing look than the dress. His mind was resolute that he'd propose the following day.

He'd chosen mini golf for their date the next day to keep things relaxed and casual. There was nothing like a little competition to bring out Essie's playful side. If she was focused on winning, on her antics meant to distract him, she wouldn't be expecting a proposal. He didn't want to overthink it and feel nervous; he had the ring in his pocket, whatever moment felt right, whenever he felt the impulse, he'd drop to one knee and ask.

He had the ring in his pocket when he'd arrived at the ranch, when Hwin had reared back in front of the truck, when he'd found Bree dead in the paddock, when he'd unnecessarily checked Teo for a pulse.

90 days later and a proposal seemed needless. For 90 days she'd faced torture, experiments that both Luther and Miles refused to share the details of because they didn't think he could handle knowing. 90 days of hell—and it wasn't over yet.

If he'd proposed the day they'd gone fishing, maybe things would have been different. For one thing, his mom would have inevitably descended despite his dad discouraging her from being too overbearing; she would have been wanting to talk about plans, a dress, unable to contain her enthusiasm. Maybe Essie wouldn't have been out in the paddock alone. Maybe she would have been at the cabin instead. Maybe he would have been with her. He could have protected her.

When they arrived at his cabin to go fishing and he'd retrieved some clothes for her to change into, he could have easily grabbed the ring. He could have proposed while they were fishing; it would have been understated but meaningful. She would have loved it.

No. He couldn't let regret cloud his thoughts. Regret wouldn't change anything about what happened. He needed to clear his mind for the mission ahead.

*   *   *

Ever since Essie was kidnapped, Josh's brain hadn't thought of the actual calendar date; he'd thought in terms of days since she'd been gone. Before he found out she was alive, he was thinking in terms of the number of days he'd been without her in his life—without her smile, without her laugh, without her to hold in his arms. The context of his tracking system shifted once he knew she was alive—to days she'd been held hostage, days she'd been tortured, days she'd probably wished she was dead.

He found out she was alive on day 79.

He convinced Luther to let him see her on day 81.

On day 91, Luther had the difficult conversation with him that he needed to put his affairs in order in the event he didn't make it back to the northern Ark. It took a bit of convincing to get him to agree to leave the surveillance room. It was a comfort to be able to know at a glance that she was alive, selfishly, but he also felt like maybe she could feel his presence?

What got him to finally leave was Miles telling him he'd regret not easing the burden for his parents, if things, as he said, "went screwy." Miles had then remarked that everyone in the world *he* truly loved were either already dead, on the mission, or the reason *for* the mission, but if he *did* have anyone else, he'd feel like it was the least he could do to put things in line. He also said that if he'd had a chance to see his family one last time, he'd take it.

Day 92 was spent in a state of disbelief and uncertainty. Josh had gone to the cabin, sat, and stared, his mind reeling the images of Essie from the previous 11 days, the reality that the mission was 5 days away, that they'd be essentially invading the White House.

He was overwhelmed. He struggled suddenly to wrap his mind around the idea that Essie was pregnant, that it had just been a few months ago she had talked about the "seasons" of life, that she was content to spend endless amounts of glorious time together, not thinking too far ahead; it's why she had struggled with the idea of getting married. She was only 20 at that point, after all.

She was 21 now. She'd turned a year older in the walls of her cell.

On Day 93, Josh sorted through things at the cabin and made a list of things he needed to take care of before they left on the mission. Fortunately, he was never one to have many personal possessions. Most of the things he'd acquired could be utilized by the next cabin occupant. Luther had asked him to set aside items he wanted to be sure made it back to him or would be forwarded to his parents if the mission didn't go as planned. Most items from his childhood, he'd put in a box for his mom, including the photo frame containing the picture of Essie, Gabe and himself as kids. There weren't any items he felt like he truly needed. Everything in his own box were things for Essie: the framed photo of her dad holding her in the Christmas tree lot, her dad's Bible, her own leather softcover Bible, her dad's guitar, the cross-pendant necklace Luther's mom had given her that was discovered in the dirt when Bree's body was hauled away, the clasp broken. He thought about carrying it with him, securing it in his chest pocket since he hadn't had it repaired yet, to have a piece of her with him, but he didn't like the idea that if something happened to him, she might not get it back.

Luther only spoke about the mission in terms of either complete success or complete failure now. There wasn't a middle ground. To him, there wasn't an in-between scenario where Essie made it out without Josh. When he'd questioned Luther about this, Luther had been stern in his response: "You're both getting out of this, Josh. I won't accept anything less than that. She deserves nothing less than that."

The reverse alternative was moot. If they failed, if Essie had been killed, but he was somehow still alive, if any of them were still alive and the battle would clearly be lost, each of them had a cyanide capsule.

Day 94 began before sunrise. Just after midnight, Josh had forced himself to sleep for a few hours.

Before Luther told him Essie was alive, it was typical for Josh to get an early start to his day, usually aided by having gone to bed at an early hour in the evening. He'd allow himself one gulp of hard liquor before settling into bed, the alcohol and the depression coaxing him to sleep most nights by 8. During the day, his brain could resolve Essie's absence by presuming that she was simply busy somewhere else. He could move about with some automation through his normal routines. It was in the evening, just as the sun had sunk low in the sky and the more intimate evening lighting filled the cabin and the subdued sounds of the night forest took over, that his heart felt the weight of his grief fully, and most predictably.

Knowing she was alive made long stretches of sleep impossible, as he was unable to quiet his mind for that long and he had sworn off liquor. He'd been sharing shifts with Miles, which had allowed more frequent trade-offs and knowing he was only going to be separated from seeing her for a short time made it possible for Josh to nap, if only out of physiological need. Back at the cabin, his heart twisted in his chest, his thoughts reeled.

Just after midnight, the cabin was tidy, his belongings packed up, and there was an eerie stillness that surrounded him. He didn't even have Fenway to keep him company. When he started staying at the former business complex where the surveillance room was located, Luther had offered to have Fenway tag along with him since he had better access to open spaces. He liked to joke that if Fenway got hungry, he had some useless, leftover "District swamp creatures" she was welcome to.

Josh laid down on the bed, staring up at the skylight in the ceiling. He narrowed his eyes upon a section of stars visible through the canopy of pine trees. "Denebola," he murmured, his eyes following the invisible line. "Regulus—and the Sickle." Leo the Lion, Essie's favorite constellation in the night sky, not because of the story behind the constellation, which was brief, and misaligned with Essie's love of animals, but for the imagery of a lion. She loved the depiction of Aslan in the *Narnia* movies. She loved Lucy's relationship with him, how he had grown larger in her mind as a result of her growth of faith, representing the importance of him in her life.

He took a deep breath and found himself murmuring the chorus from one of her favorite songs:

So come on, my soul
Oh, don't you get shy on me
Lift up your song
'Cause you've got a lion inside of those lungs
Get up and praise the Lord

He recalled how her voice intensified with each repetition of the chorus.

He took a deep breath, eyes drifting across the quiet cabin. He could see her curled up in the chair across from the bed reading, face illuminated in the soft glow of the table lamp, or if it was a chilly evening, the fireplace.

210

He could see her trying in vain to slip inside the cabin when she expected he was already sleeping, wincing as the door groaned loudly against the floorboards.

He could hear her singing or humming a melody to herself, pirouetting nonchalantly across the floor wearing one of his t-shirts. Despite always being an honest person, Essie was a relentless and unapologetic stealer of his shirts. She'd bring extra clothes to the cabin–she had her own drawer–but she'd always opt to take one of his t-shirts from his dresser when it came time for bed rather than wearing her own clothes. He'd tease her about it from time to time, but he never really minded. There was something incredibly invigorating that happened, a rush of adrenaline surging in his heart, when she appeared wearing one of his shirts, even though he had started to expect it. He indulged in the sight of her in any of his clothes, but nothing could match the sight of her in one of his little league shirts, wearing his last name across her back.

There'd been a guilt about her staying at the cabin, that despite having a very important purpose to allow her some healthy hours of sleep, there was an impropriety to it. For one thing, she'd only stayed out there *before* they were a couple. For another, there would have been an assumption that something was going on that directly opposed their beliefs–even Miles had been alarmed, or at the very least, surprised to learn about it. To counter this and to make sure she had her breathing space to work through things, Josh had been sure not to contribute to any dynamic that might give merit to the idea of impropriety, which included suppressing commentary or flirtatious remarks, anything that could put her on edge. He'd also been careful not to be overly physically affectionate.

With one exception.

It was the night after the incident in Hannah's nursery when Essie had been startled to find him in the process of changing clothes. He'd actually been surprised she'd still come out to the cabin after that. Though it was weeks before she'd actually come around and told him how she felt about him, the incident had left little doubt, at least with his parents, who'd overheard her outburst of surprise.

He'd been sleeping for some time, drifting lightly in a dream. In it, he'd gone to a river and witnessed salmon leaping over the water's surface upstream, something he'd only seen in documentaries. He remembered being amused, even during the dream, by the fact that he had acted confused by Essie's choice of the code name Angler for him since he thought it gave the impression he liked fishing more than he did–and yet, there he was, *dreaming* about fish.

He'd just silently told himself to settle back in the dream, he needed his sleep, busy day the next day, all of that, when he felt Essie shift, curling toward him. That did it. He fully emerged from the dream, mind fixated on the warmth of her body against his, the way her arm draped across his chest, how their bare feet occasionally nuzzled against one another. There was something particularly intimate about it.

He slowed his breaths, trying to coax himself back to sleep.

And then her lips gently pressed against his cheek.

He didn't dare move.

She kissed his lower lip next, a little off-center.

He furrowed his brow. If he opened his eyes, he'd be forcing her to define things–*or* they'd wind up in the middle of a very volatile moment, temptation high, desire high. He decided he should do nothing, respond in no way and continue pretending to be asleep.

And then she kissed him again—very delicately on the lips, her palm resting against his cheek.

He felt his lips reciprocate, his response reflexive.

Their lips parted, her breaths warm, her cheek resting high on his chest. He opened his eyes, his heart racing, expecting to meet her gaze and instead, found that she was asleep.

He tilted his chin to try to get a better look and found that indeed, her eyes were closed and there was even some visible vibration beneath her eyelids.

He was disappointed, but relieved that the moment seemed to have resolved itself. He rested his hand on her back, took a long inhalation of her hair.

Sleep now, he told himself.

It started subtly at first, her fingers beginning to stroke his cheek with a light touch that sent shivers up his spine, then her mouth drew upward at the corners and she moved to kiss him again.

He had two options: Go along with it or wake her.

She might be embarrassed if he woke her—or maybe it would nudge things along? Maybe her subconscious had already decided?

Where would it lead if he just went along with it? Maybe she'd just kiss him a few more times. He'd wake her if it got too far.

Was there really any harm in going along with it for now?

Yes. The answer was yes. They weren't a couple. She needed time. She was sorting through a lot. There was absolutely a whole hell of a lot of harm that could come from "just going along with it."

She kissed him more passionately and he could feel her smile stretch as she did.

Before he realized it, he had reached out his hand to frame her face and was guiding her to continue.

She paused, her cheek turning, perhaps following actions he couldn't see. "Josh," she murmured, in a pleading, desperate tone. She seemed frozen in place. "Josh, *no*. Please come back," she whispered.

He told himself ardently not to make another move and he was resolved in this–until she started to cry. He felt a tear stream down her cheek, just before she buried her face in his chest, and her shoulders started to shake.

"*Please come back*," she said in a breathy squeak.

He immediately put both arms around her. "I'm here," he whispered.

Her eyes opened, her expression alarmed as she lifted her chin, her silver eyes shimmering in the beam of moonlight shining through the skylight.

"I'm here, Essie."

She blinked, furrowing her brow as she took in her positioning, a bit sprawled across him. She sat up abruptly, moved away.

"Ess, it was just a dream."

213

She nodded, but suddenly climbed off the bed. She paced back and forth across the cabin, taking slow, focused breaths.

He was concerned about what had transpired in her dream that had made her so upset. Why had she sounded so hopeless? Where had he gone?

She rolled her shoulders, flexed her hands, shook out her arms–it was something he'd seen her do in Fight Club before climbing into the ring. After pacing a few times across the same stretch of flooring, she stopped and took a steadying breath. She turned on her heel and returned to bed, settling immediately into his arms.

"Better?"

"Uh-hm."

"What did I do?"

She frowned. "I said your name out loud?"

"Yeah."

She shook her head. "It wasn't you."

"*Oh.*"

"I mean, it was *meant* to be you, but you wouldn't have done that."

He wasn't sure if he should press for more information, but he didn't need to ask.

"Do you remember *The Neverending Story*?"

"Vaguely."

"The swamp of sadness where Artax the horse sinks and dies?"

He would have laughed at the randomness of the reference, but there were fresh tears in her eyes. "I remember."

"*I* was in the swamp and I was sinking. You were having me grab onto a branch to pull me out, but suddenly you said you didn't like how the swamp was making you feel and you were afraid if you stayed, you'd fall in and wouldn't be able to get out."

The movie scene had come back to him in vivid detail. He remembered watching it with Essie when she was no older than seven–she had been absolutely traumatized, her face blotchy and streaked with tears by the time the scene ended. His mom was furious with his dad for suggesting the movie.

214

"I *left* you there?"

"It wasn't you."

"I'd never leave you there."

"I know that," she said, wiping her eyes.

He furrowed his brow, confused by why she would have kissed him in the dream–and then he realized–he must have kissed her goodbye. He had kissed her–and then left her there to die.

The entire premise being based in what was meant to be a children's movie was, of course, fantastical, but knowing how much the scene had impacted her as a child, what that experience must have been like for her–it bothered him.

"Essie?"

She nodded, resting her chin on his chest. "It was just a dream, I know. It's silly to get upset about it."

Before he'd even made the decision, he found he had his hand bracing her cheek and he was kissing her. It wasn't impassioned or leading, more like gentle reassurance. As their lips parted, he saw that she had closed her eyes. "I would never leave you in the swamp of sadness."

She slowly opened her eyes. "Now I feel really ridiculous."

"Don't."

Her eyes narrowed. "You kissed me," she whispered questioningly.

"I did. I'm sorry. I know you need time with all that's gone on and I'm not putting any pressure on you to figure things out, but I wanted to make sure you know the Josh in your dream isn't me."

"I *know*. That's what I said."

"I hate that *any* version of me would do that."

She furrowed her brow. "*Josh*." That single syllable carried so much uncertainty. Literally anything could follow. "I *know* you. I'm not about to be fooled by something my subconscious cooks up. You haven't met my subconscious directly, but the *girl's got issues*," she said with a deep slant of her eyebrows, her tone reminding him of her dad giving a sermon.

He gave a light smile.

She sighed. "I'm still sorting through a lot."

"I know."

"I've never let myself process anything–I know it's taking me a long time and I'm sorry for that."

He shook his head. "You need to take whatever time you need. I shouldn't have kissed you right then. I just–"

"*Josh.*" She waited for him to meet her gaze, her eyes becoming very round when he did. She furrowed her brow and moved into him, kissing him delicately. Once and then again. She remained close, letting their lips brush against each other. "Now we're even."

He nodded slowly, deciding he wasn't going to correct her, that she'd already kissed him during her dream.

"Come here," he whispered, wrapping his arms around her. While his initial thought when she first started to stay at the cabin was to assume a big spoon, little spoon situation, she preferred to be nuzzled toward him, his arms hugging her, the weight of him surrounding her.

She gave a satisfied sigh as he tightened his embrace.

He turned his chin to look at her empty side of the bed. He'd washed the sheets several times since she'd been gone, but he'd left the pillowcase she'd used alone. He pulled it close now, burying his face in the fibers, searching for her scent. It was long faded, but knowing it was the pillow she'd used, that it was her head's imprint that had made the natural divot in it–a fear, an emptiness surrounded him.

He peered up at the lion constellation gleaming overhead.

So come on, my soul
Oh, don't you get shy on me
Lift up your song
'Cause you've got a lion inside of those lungs
Get up and praise the Lord

Josh pulled in his breath and began to pray–for Jesus to watch over her, to comfort her, to let her feel His presence so she'd know she wasn't alone.

He woke up just before 4am and moved about with purpose, knowing the tasks he'd set out for the day were non-negotiable. He got dressed, poured some coffee, loaded up the pickup, and drove to his parents' house, more specifically, the barn. It wouldn't have surprised him if his dad had appeared as he was tacking up Hwin; he was an infamously early riser and struggled to sleep through minor disturbances, but as Josh rode off on the Belgian toward the mountains, he hadn't yet appeared.

Hwin hadn't had much saddle time at the Ark in the year she'd been there, mainly due to her skittish nature. He'd taken her for several rides with Essie and Bree and she had done well. After what happened at the ranch, she'd refused to go near the barn and had been loose for a few days. His dad had managed to coax her toward him with food and brought her back to their house. He'd been working with her to build her confidence over the past few months.

Hwin had always been responsive and trusting of Josh, mainly because he was the one to save her life after he'd found her severely entangled in barbed wire lying in a ditch. She seemed pleased to have him as a rider again after so long, reaching her muzzle back every so often to nudge his leg. It wasn't typical behavior for horses; it was something she would have seen Bree do to Essie, to check on her, to alert her to something, to complain about the long duration of the ride. Immediately after Hwin nuzzled his leg, she tossed her head high in the air, shaking out her blonde mane, which he interpreted as her being excited for the ride.

He'd done the trail out to the glacier lake overlook with Essie, but like everything else, there was an uncomfortable excess of breathing space as he set out alone. It was too quiet. He much preferred getting to watch her perched atop Bree, taking in the sights with deep appreciation, despite seeing them most days of the week, leaning forward in the saddle when they were climbing in elevation, being sensitive to the challenges the trail posed for the horse.

It took about 45 minutes to arrive at her favorite overlook, a flat stretch of ground speckled with grassy patches where she'd do her daily devotions, along with some pleasure reading.

He had expected he'd be able to identify the right place easily. What he didn't expect was that in the dried mud, he'd find preserved hoof prints that undoubtedly belonged to Bree–and boot prints with a fishhook imprint in the heel.

Most footprints were lost within days, if not hours, but as he inspected them, he realized the last time Essie had come out to the lake was the morning after a torrential rainstorm, the last rain the area had seen in the nearly three months since. The prints had solidified and evidently no one had been by to trample over them.

Josh dropped out of the saddle, securing Hwin's reins to a tree. He crouched down in the dirt and lightly ran his palm across the prints in the dried mud. He released a huff of air, looked up, gazing across the shadowed glacier lake, the sun just peeking over the eastern horizon, painting the mountains in a radiant orange hue.

He stood and moved back to Hwin, whose stance was rigid. Her nose twitched as she took in the smells.

"Remember this place? They brought us along a few times," he said conversationally, trying to keep the shakiness from his voice. He unlatched a satchel from the right side of the saddle, then repeated the process on the opposite side, along with a small shovel.

Hwin snorted, shifted uneasily as the weight she carried lessened significantly.

Originally his plan had been to spread all of Bree's ashes across the glacier overlook—until he finally picked the ashes up from the veterinary office and they'd weighed over 70 pounds. He'd packed up his belongings intended for his parents in a smaller box than what was needed to hold the ashes. It was simply too much to spread in such a way.

He chose a place off the main trail at the edge of the overlook. Despite the surface being dry, the dirt beneath was soft and aided his efforts. Once he'd dug a large enough hole, he retrieved the satchels, placed them into the ground, once again surprised by the heft.

Bree had been just over 2000 pounds, twice the weight of a Thoroughbred racehorse; it was unfathomable that he had fallen on Essie and she'd survived, that her body was able to heal itself, though he didn't allow his thoughts to linger. He couldn't think of how painful that must have been for her, particularly when Luther struggled to describe the video he'd seen of the aftermath, Essie's appearance, how certain he had been that she was dead.

Josh stared at the canvas satchels in the ground, tears filling his eyes. "I know you were trying to protect her," he began, his voice catching. He wiped roughly at his face with his sleeve. "You loved her so much—and boy, did she love you." He took a breath, remembering how weak Bree had become after his mom rejected him when he was only a day old, how he had refused the bottle. They had considered starting him on tube feedings, but the vet had advised against it, saying that his prognosis was poor, that his body had been in distress for too long.

His dad had made the decision to have Bree put down, requesting the vet arrive just before sunrise the following day, so it would be done and Bree could be taken away before anyone else was awake. When his dad returned to the farmhouse after the vet drove away, the sun just peeking over the mountains, he'd released a long sigh. Josh was sitting at the kitchen island and had avoided his dad's gaze. His mom handed his dad a coffee cup, ran her palm over his upper back reassuringly. She'd suggested they do something out of the house that day, which Josh knew was for Essie's sake. Most of his dad's hesitation with putting the foal down was due to Essie.

"It was quick?" his mom asked quietly.

"Like it didn't even happen."

Josh furrowed his brow, suddenly noticing his dad was holding something in his right hand. "What's that, Dad?"

Luke lifted the bottle, placed it on the kitchen island. "There's two more empty ones in his stall–along with one sleeping, but very tenacious little girl."

Josh had smiled widely, standing up, peering out the window toward the barn.

"I'm sorry it took me so long to get you out here. I know you're already running free in Heaven though. Or, I suppose you Narnians call it Aslan's Country?" He smiled lightly. "You'll see her again one day, I promise. If I can help it, that won't be for a long time though." He sniffled. "Hwin's safe–and spoiled; you don't have to worry about her. Keep watch over Teo though, okay?"

Once he'd covered the grave with dirt, he walked Hwin over. He prepared himself that she wouldn't understand, that the sentiment would be lost on her. She whinnied with uncertainty as they approached Bree's grave together. She sniffed the fresh dirt then threw her head back.

"*Easy*. He's safe now, Hwin."

She nudged her large head into Josh's chest, eyes a bit frenzied.

"I *know*," he said, stroking her cheek. "Bree is safe with Teo. It's okay."

Hwin took a step away, gave a low neigh, then stretched one leg forward, arched her body as low as she could manage. At first Josh thought she was attempting to lie down, but as she held position, he realized she was imitating how Bree would bow to Essie to allow her to more easily get on and off his back. She lowered her head to the ground, nuzzling her nose into the dirt, then stood back up.

The movement had always had its practical purpose, but Josh had always thought it looked like the horse had intended to bow to her. He liked to tease Essie when they were younger that the horse was treating her like she was his Narnian Queen. Now, Hwin had all but confirmed the intent behind it. That it was a sign of utmost respect.

Josh patted the horse's side and took a steadying breath, nodding to the grave. "Until we meet again, Narnian."

He led Hwin around the preserved hoof and boot prints before climbing back up in the saddle and starting back for his parents' house.

Josh stopped at the overlook closest to the ranch to lay a bouquet of wildflowers on each of the gravestones. He allowed some slack in the line for Hwin to graze and he took a seat on the tree stump beside Essie's grave. It was a different sensation seeing it now, knowing she was alive. His heart still ached, knowing the risks ahead, knowing that Essie was far from free, but he didn't fear looking at the gravestone etched with her name anymore.

He searched the ground by his feet, gathered up a few small stones and covered the date of death, a small satisfaction rising in his chest when only her birthdate remained.

His eyes lifted to Teo's grave. His birthday was just a few weeks away; he would have turned 46. For some reason, Josh had always thought of him as being younger than that. His mom liked to tease Teo about "those good Italian genes" giving him thick hair with no signs of receding, healthy, olive skin that never seemed to wrinkle or age.

He thought of the last time he spoke to Teo. It had been at the church two days before he died. Josh stopped in at the end of his workday, making sure there was plenty of time before evening life groups began. Teo didn't have an office at the church at his own insistence, as every bit of available space was needed for children's ministry, what with the influx of new babies and new families in attendance.

Josh found him sitting in the back pew of the sanctuary, laptop on the wood bench beside him, thumbing through the thin pages of his Bible. Essie liked to remark about his animated gesturing and movements in amusement and Josh smiled as he watched Teo tap the page of his Bible excitedly, clearly finding what he was looking for. He set the Bible aside and picked up the laptop, happily tapping out the verse. He lifted his eyebrow closest to Josh, slowly rotating his chin. "Aren't you the kid who made me scrambled eggs this morning?"

"That may have been me."

"How's it going?"

"Good. How about you?'

Teo pressed his thumb and index finger together, gesturing as he spoke: "È una bella vita. It's a beautiful life," he translated, smiling tightly. "I'm afraid you missed my daughter though. They wrapped up rehearsal about 15 minutes ago."

"I'm sorry I missed it. I love hearing her sing."

"You and me both. That's why I'm sitting here rather than back in the more forgiving classroom seating." He set the computer aside, stretching his back as he stood. "We need to commission cushions for these pews. I'm usually pacing at the front, but this is terrible for the lower back. Or maybe I'm just getting old."

"No, they're pretty rough."

Teo smiled lightly. "You two going out again tonight?"

"I think the plan is to grab a pizza and watch a movie."

He nodded. "Classic date night. I like it."

"Did *you* eat?"

"I can't remember who's bringing the food, but it's a catered night for life groups. Barbecue, I think."

"Sounds good."

Teo furrowed his brow, checking his watch.

"Hey, Teo? Can we sit and talk for a minute?"

"Mind if we walk and talk instead?" he asked, wincing.

Josh nodded, started toward the lobby. They stepped out into the fenced field to the north of the church, which contained a large play structure, several lawn games, and a soccer field.

Matteo pointed toward a picnic table, sat himself on the tabletop, placing his feet on the bench. "I guess we can sit. This beats the pews, at least."

Josh sat beside him, gazed out toward the expansive view of the mountains.

"What's on your mind, Kid?"

Josh cleared his throat. "I love your daughter, Teo," he said softly. "I've loved your daughter since the moment I met her."

Teo pursed his lips, nodding, knowing where the conversation was heading.

"She's my best friend, my favorite person in the world, and I want her to be my wife."

Teo took a deep breath, tugged his handkerchief from his chest pocket, gripping it in his hand.

"Posso avere la tua benedizione per chiederle la mano?" *May I have your blessing for her hand?*

Teo nodded, sniffling loudly. "Bringing out the Italian. Well done."

Josh allowed the silence.

"On one condition."

"Okay?"

"Don't tell my daughter I cried like a baby when you asked me." He immediately held up his hand. "Actually, *no*. Don't lie to her. She'll never believe it if you told her I held it together."

Josh furrowed his brow, suppressing a laugh. "Is that a 'yes'?"

"Is it a *yes*? Did you think I'd say '*no*'?" he said incredulously, mopping his eyes. He turned, reached across and patted Josh's chest. "I know your heart, Josh. I *see* Jesus in you. In your actions, in your words, in how you love my daughter."

Josh swallowed hard.

"You're not *perfect*–"

Josh shook his head, frowning.

"Despite what Essie says."

Josh laughed, remembering how she referred to him as "irritatingly perfect," emphasis on the irritatingly.

"You were always a good kid and I've watched you become a good, *good* man. I don't have any concerns or doubt of the type of husband you'll be." He lifted his brow. "It doesn't mean I won't keep an eye on you," he said in a warning tone, then broke into a smile. "But the life I see for the two of you?" He pressed his thumb and index finger together again, gave a gesture like a "chef's kiss," which he'd claimed repeatedly to Essie that he never did. "Bellissimo. Una bella vita." *A beautiful life.*

Josh took a deep breath, eyes scanning each letter of Matteo's name. Three months had passed and he still didn't quite believe that Teo was dead.

"She's alive, Teo," Josh whispered. "I'm sure you've known that, seeing that she's not there with you." He cleared his throat. "We're going in to get her in a couple of days and I'm going to do anything it takes to get her to safety, I promise you that. The way Luther talks about it– either way, she'll be free. Either here on earth with me–or we'll both be there in Heaven with you." He wiped roughly at his eyes. "Don't take this the wrong way, but I hope I don't see you for a long time." He gave a weak smile. "But I miss you, Teo."

The silence stretched as he gazed out toward the mountains, the open fields, the glacier lake in the distance.

He nodded repeatedly. "I don't know what God's plan is for us, but I'm going to trust whatever it is." He frowned. "Pray for us," he said, his voice catching. "We have a lot of life left to live here, Teo. Una buona vita." *A good life.* "Una *bella* vita," he corrected, lifting his eyebrows. *A beautiful life.*

"Thank you for changing the course of my life. Thank you for being an incredible father figure and role model for me. Thank you for bringing the girl of my dreams into my life, for raising her to be a strong, fierce, selfless, magnificent, faithful *lioness.*" He smiled, thinking again of her favorite worship song. "I know we'll see each other again. I hope I make you proud and I hope I can be half the dad that you were to Essie." He nodded conclusively, shifting the dirt beneath his boot. "I love you, Teo."

He turned on his heel and once again took in the view of the mountains, the protected lands, and beyond the forest, the glacier lake. He took in the cloudy, darkening sky, signaling an approaching storm. He took in the vividness of the landscape despite the gray overcast of the sky, a late fall bloom filling the fields with purple bitterroot, blue lupine, and yellow arrow leaf balsamroot. He took in a slow, deep breath, savoring all the scents, committing them to memory: The warm, fresh aroma of pine trees, the earthy bitterness of the freshly watered cornfields, the pungent musk of manure wafting from the exotic animal sanctuary, the brisk sharpness of the chilly breeze, the sweet indulgence of smoked meats at his parents' house, along with some sort of baked goods, likely the result of his mom seeing his truck in the driveway.

Hwin rested her muzzle on his shoulder, releasing a breath.

Josh peered over at her, frowning. "Do all Narnian horses behave like Labradors?"

*   *   *

"Where'd you two head off to?" Luke asked quietly from the entrance to the barn as Josh tucked Hwin into her stall.

"The glacier lake overlook."

Luke stepped forward, nodding. "Pretty spot."

"We buried Bree."

His dad continued to nod. "I bet that feels a little better? To have that done?"

"I should have done that a long time ago."

Luke pulled in his breath, released an extended sigh. "Well, it's done now–it's what Essie would want. That spot? The two of them went out there a lot, right?"

"I found their tracks."

His dad furrowed his brow. "*Really*?"

"It hasn't rained in months."

"Yeah, I guess that's true."

"There's not a horse on the trails with a Bree-sized shoe and Essie's the only person I know with a fishhook design in her boot print." He finished filling up Hwin's water barrel and began winding up the hose. As he did, a rumble of thunder shook the barn. Hwin whinnied at the sound. "They'll probably be washed away after this storm."

Luke frowned. "I'm glad you got to see them."

Josh retrieved a couple of homemade horse treats from the tack counter and returned to the stall, where Hwin eagerly waited. She snatched them from his palm quickly but gently. "Good girl," he murmured.

"Your mom is preparing a feast in the house. Do you think you'd be able to stay for lunch?"

"It was probably presumptuous of me, but I had planned to maybe hang out here today." It occurred to him at that moment that this could very well be the last time he ever got to spend time with them.

Luke furrowed his brow. "You never need an invitation, Josh."

Josh swallowed hard. He could feel his dad's eyes upon him. He tried to inconspicuously turn his chin away to allow a tear to absorb into his cheek.

"Josh, can I–I want to ask you something, but God help me, I really don't want to be wrong."

Josh frowned, considering his response, continuing to stroke Hwin's cheek. The horse nuzzled forcefully into his chest, not satisfied with the proximity. "What do you want to ask?"

"I can only think of a couple reasons Luther would come to find you: One would be if he had a role for you to play in whatever he's planning because of your MET background."

Josh nodded slowly. "And the other?"

His dad took a deep breath, wincing. "If Essie's alive."

Hwin moved to lap up some water and Josh took a step back to avoid getting splashed. "It's both."

His dad's dark eyes became very round. He clamped a hand onto Josh's shoulder. "She's *alive*?"

Josh nodded. "No one can know. There's more to it, but we can't risk tipping off Gowon."

"Gowon has her?"

"Yeah." He pulled in a breath and found he needed to steady himself on the gate. He focused on the warmth of his dad's hand on his back.

"Have you seen her? Is she okay?"

"Luther secured a video feed–" He stopped short. "No one can know that either."

"Josh, I won't tell anyone, even your mother. Let me rephrase: *Especially* your mother."

Josh nodded. "She's been through–" He paused, now understanding Miles's struggle to describe things. He wanted to protect his dad, not spoil the images, the memories he had of Essie, but doing so felt like he was minimizing what Essie had been through.

"Is it like what she went through as a baby?"

Josh considered this and with a harsh realization, heard himself say: "Worse."

That single word seemed to strike Luke right in the heart. He shook his head, suppressing some emotion, but not all. His eyes were brimming with tears. "But you're going in to get her?" he asked with a nod.

226

"Yes."

His dad stepped forward and put both arms around him, tugged him close. In all his life, his dad had never held him so tightly. He took another deep inhalation, sniffling. Finally, his dad took a step back, hands gripping his upper arms. "You go get her—and whatever you need to do to keep the two of you safe? *Do it*," he whispered firmly. "You hear me? Whatever you need to do. As long as you're both safe."

*   *   *

The aroma of various casseroles wafted through the living room. Josh leaned his head back into the recliner headrest, Hannah snuggled against his chest. He gently stroked her back in small circles, the same way he'd seen Essie do, gazing at the framed photos on the mantle, compressed due to the addition of small pumpkins his mom had added to the decor. Each year, his parents' house would make a steady transition from normal decor levels, which given her tastes, was already seen by some as being a bit cluttered. She'd start adding subtle hints of fall, a shift from neutral shades to orange and earthy tones. By early November, typically only the dining table would have any hints of fall/harvest, and there'd be a Christmas tree in the front window, garland draped across every shelf, every door frame. While she appeared behind in her decorating, she'd cleared the spot for the Christmas tree and there were already gifts in shopping bags occupying the coat closet as she looked forward to Hannah's first Christmas.

In addition to being nudged closer together, there were more photo frames than ever before. There was a family portrait from probably eight years earlier–likely the last picture taken of the four of them together, an obligatory photo of each of their children individually, Hannah's obviously the most recent, taken of her sitting on the grassy lawn, clapping her hands together, big open-mouth smile. Gabe was in his early teens in his solo photo, sitting on the farm tractor. Josh's own "solo" photo was taken when he was ten and actually pictured Essie as well, though his mom had never noticed until earlier in the year when he'd pointed it out.

The photo was taken at their hometown's community pool/waterpark. Josh was sitting on the end of a lounge chair in front of the towel-covered chair-back and some tropical foliage. If you looked a little closer, you'd notice the folds of the towels on the chair were a bit unnatural if they were simply draped across the back. They had gone to the waterpark late in the summer season and a cold snap had hit that morning, but everyone still wanted to go. It warmed up mid-day, but once the afternoon clouds rolled in, Essie's jaw was actively chattering. When they arrived back to the chairs, Essie had folded herself in half, pulling her knees to her chest, shivering. He and Gabe had jokingly wrapped her in every towel they had, leaving an opening just large enough so she could see and breathe. If you looked close enough at the photo, you'd see Essie's face shadowed in the heap of towels, crossing her eyes and sticking out her tongue.

His mom sat down on the end of the couch closest to him with her mug of tea. "Do you know how long you'll be away?"

His dad joined them with his coffee, but kept his eyes lowered. "Probably hard to say, right? Depends on the condition these horses are in."

Having assessed that Josh was a terrible, *terrible* liar, Luke had gone ahead of him into the house to provide a cover story to his wife. The story was that Josh had been asked to help with a herd of horses that were spotted just outside the Ark boundaries on the eastern side. They appeared to be owner released, like Hwin, and didn't have tremendous survival instincts so they were malnourished, and some were in rough shape. He'd be a part of the team wrangling them up and doing veterinary exams.

"I'm not sure," Josh whispered.

"But it's outside of the Ark. Is there *protection*?"

"Yeah, we have a surveillance team that will provide cover."

"Gowon doesn't care about them helping out some horses," Luke said dismissively , lifting his eyebrows. "From what we've seen on the news, people are starting to fight back against him. There are riots, uprisings in the cities. He has enough other things to worry about."

228

Miles had mentioned something similar about riots, but Josh hadn't cared much to listen at the time, so this information struck him with more significance than he'd been expecting.

They were about to overthrow the government.

"Big things are about to go down," Luke murmured, nodding. "You can feel it."

Sara looked defensively over at their daughter. "Luke, shh."

"I don't think we're in any danger *here*. I think Gowon's judgment day is near though."

"Do people like him *have* a judgment day?"

"It's probably an expedited process."

Josh thought of Essie's assessment that there should be a quick release trap door to hell for such occasions. "'Pull the lever, Kronk!'" he said quietly, the corners of his mouth curling up.

His mom tilted her chin in confusion.

Luke smiled lightly. "'*Wrong* lever!'"

Josh met his dad's knowing gaze.

"I've got to check on dinner," Sara said, bursting to her feet.

"Yeah, you've been sitting for a whole three minutes," Luke jested.

"Luke, *must you*?!" she stammered, her voice tight.

Hannah's eyes opened and she started to fuss.

Josh moved to stand, gently patting her back.

His dad had already crossed the room. As he approached Sara, she threw her hand out, motioning toward Josh holding a fussing Hannah. "I didn't mean to wake–" She shook her head, resetting herself rigidly. "I know the two of you are lying to me. I'm not an *idiot*. Luke, you say Josh is a terrible liar, but you're absolutely *no better*."

Luke glanced over at Josh.

"My plan wasn't always to be a housewife, you know. I *studied* human behavior. I have a damn PhD, for whatever good it does me."

As Hannah settled back into his chest, Josh thought of his mom's old t-shirt that Essie changed into after Hannah had spit up on her, the first of dozens of times: faded forest green with the ram mascot in the center, Colorado State University surrounding it in collegiate block lettering. The shirt color set off the golden and copper highlights in Essie's long, untamed hair. It had also set off the reddened hue of her cheeks.

"If you feel you need to lie to me for whatever reason, I can't change that, but it still hurts. After everything that's happened–"

"I'm going to the District."

His parents both turned simultaneously to look at him.

"Essie's alive and she's being held at the White House. I'm on the team that's going in to get her."

His mom lifted both hands to cover her mouth, her bright blue eyes filled with tears.

"I just found out she's alive two weeks ago," he qualified further.

"Is she okay? What's happening to her?" she whispered, her voice strained. She lowered her hands over her chest.

Josh swallowed hard.

"It's bad, Sara," Luke murmured.

"You *know* about this?"

"I literally just found out in the barn. We know some of what they did to her as a baby. What Gowon's having them do is worse, Josh said. Probably added in Sim torture, like what happened to Gabe?" He guessed, glancing up for confirmation from Josh.

Josh gave a short nod. "Worse."

Luke's shoulders fell. He leaned heavily against the counter.

His mom rounded the kitchen island, placed her palm on his cheek. "You're going to save her," she whispered.

"We're gonna try, Mom."

"*No.* I can feel it," she said, squeezing his arm, nodding insistently. "You're *going* to save her."

19

three hundred

"People love an underdog story, don't they?" Matteo asked, furrowing his brow. "It seems to be human nature to root for the underdog, the person, the team that seems to be down and out? I think of the 1980 Olympics men's hockey team, who were victorious over the seemingly unbeatable Soviet team, Rocky Balboa, the 2004 Boston Red Sox came back from a 0-3 game deficit to win the ALCS and eventually the World Series, breaking an 88-year 'curse,' the 2016 Chicago Cubs, who won their first World Series in 108 years. Even if it's not your team, your sport, there's just something about rooting for an underdog. It's invigorating to witness what's thought to be a long shot, what's thought to be impossible. It ignites a hope, a belief that the impossible *is* possible, right?" He stopped at the edge of the step and winced. "I feel compelled to ask this question: Is anything *impossible* for God?"

"No," the congregation murmured.

"That's right," he said, pleased. "Now, we've seen God make some interesting decisions, choosing questionable people to carry out His work. Today, we're going to dive into one such story--the story of Gideon.

"So, because the people of Israel had turned away from God, He allowed the Midianites to terrorize Israel for seven years, destroying their land and livestock. Judges 7:12 says the Midianites were '*as numerous as locusts; and their camels were without number, as the sand by the seashore in multitude.'*

"In their desperation, the people of Israel cried out to God and God answered. He chose Gideon to lead the people to victory.

"Now, Gideon took on the role reluctantly. He didn't quite believe it–so he asked God for signs that He was on their side. It was like, 'I think I heard You, but just in case–' First, he asked for a sign that it was really God talking to him. So God sent an angel to deliver the message. Gideon was like, 'Cool, cool, but I'm still not sure.' So Gideon put out a fleece of wool on two consecutive nights, first asking for the fleece to be made wet and the ground to be made dry. When God did just that, Gideon then reversed his request. Can you imagine? Gideon says 'Alright, don't be mad–' Gideon was afraid, he was weak, he clearly had doubts. God knew this and He chose Gideon anyway. Does God make mistakes?" Matteo put his hand to his ear.

"No," the congregation murmured.

"God knows us. God knows our hearts. God knows what we are capable of. Those who see themselves as the greatest, the strongest, the wisest, will have a hard time hearing God's voice above their own high thoughts and opinions. Those who are humble, who have open and receptive hearts, will be able to become God's men–and women–of valor, ready to do His will.

"Do you think God was discouraged by Gideon's requests for proof? Do you think He was starting to reconsider His pick? Do you think He was thinking–'Oh, if I only had an HR council, this guy wouldn't have made it through the screening.'" Matteo smiled lightly. "Does God make mistakes?"

"No," the congregation yelled in unison.

"No. God understood that providing the signs gave Gideon the strength and faith he needed. God refused to give up on Gideon, even when Gideon had given up on himself. He had a purpose for him to fulfill.

"Fast forward to a short time later: Newly armed with the Spirit of the Lord, Gideon stands at the head of an Israelite force of 32,000 warriors. Now *this* is a mighty army to be reckoned with. At this point, Gideon was probably feeling pretty good. Then came a new order from God: Everyone who is afraid should go home. Gideon glanced around and was probably like 'uh-oh.' Maybe even his hand was starting to creep up. Can you imagine being Gideon–he had to send out this order to his soldiers. If you're afraid, go home. No consequences, no repercussions.

"*Why* did God send that order? Well, He knew the battle was already won, but if this army of 32,000 won, Israel would claim the glory of victory, celebrating its own strength instead of rightfully honoring God who was in command.

"Overnight, 22,000 of Gideon's soldiers left. Gideon's confidence fell through the floor. He *was* outnumbered 4 to 1, now he's outnumbered 14 to 1.

"Then God spoke again and said there are still too many." Matteo's eyes widened dramatically and he tensed his face. "That's my take of how Gideon must have been feeling. So Gideon probably sighed and said, 'alright, what would you like me to do now?' and God told him to take his army down to the river. There He would tell him who could stay and who should leave. So they went down to the river. God tells Gideon any of the men who scoops the water into his hands to drink and laps it like a dog can stay. Anyone who bends down and dunks his head in to drink goes." Matteo twisted his expression, nodding apprehensively. "You can imagine Gideon was *not* feeling great. He was probably muttering a bit, like 'What's the deal with the lapping water thing?' Let's address that real quick, because that's struck me as odd the several times I've read this. I don't believe there was something particularly telling about the men who scooped the water and lapped it instead of bending down, but I'm not a soldier. It seems the ones who bent down were leaving themselves vulnerable to attack?" He shrugged. "I think the point was to have a certain number–a few good men. Maybe not good. A few men. 300 men. Against 135,000. He wanted the feat to be so impossible, it would seem laughable to think they could win. Gideon needed to know, the Israelites needed to know, that it was not *their* battle, it was the Lord's battle. God

233

delights in using the small, the seemingly weak, the meek, to do truly mighty things.

"So, Gideon's faith faltered, but who could blame him? Then God instructed him to go down to the Midianite camp with his servant, that he'd hear something that would restore his faith. Gideon was probably a little punch drunk at this point." Matteo put his hands on his hips, pressed his lips together, nodding. "'You want me to just *stroll* on down to the enemy camp–*yeeeah, okay. Fine.*' So he goes. He creeps around under cover of night and brush, but he overhears a Midianite soldier telling his comrade about a dream he had where a Midianite tent was knocked down by a loaf of barley bread. Now, I'm not sure how big a loaf of bread it is we're talking here–but stranger still was the dream interpretation of this soldier's buddy. 'This is nothing else but the sword of Gideon the son of Joash, a man of Israel!' the Midianite soldier cried. 'Into his hand God has delivered Midian and the whole camp.'

"Show of hands–if you were going into battle, would it give you confidence to hear that your opponent was afraid of you?" Matteo nodded. "Yeah, little bit. Add to that that your opponent believes God will deliver you the victory?" Matteo rolled his shoulders. "Yeah, that feels better. So Gideon goes marching back to his army of 300 and says, 'let's do this.'

"The rest of the story is truly remarkable. Gideon took his 300 men and divided them up into 3 groups, 3 locations that surrounded the Midianites' camp. He hands out their equipment: trumpets, jars and empty torches. How confident would *you* be feeling? We're taking on 135,000 soldiers and you're holding a trumpet." Matteo winced. "But Gideon gave the signal and the men blew their trumpets and broke their jars, light streamed out in every direction and the Midianite army went into a mad panic, thinking they were being overrun. They turned their swords on each other first. The surviving Midianites fled in terror leaving all their supplies and many of their weapons behind. Their mighty strength had been overcome by a mere 300 men led by Gideon, a man of God.

"The story of Gideon's 300 reminds us that God does not require vast armies or human strength to achieve His purposes. Instead, He seeks faith, obedience, and trust in Him. It's about God's power working through us. It's the Lord's battle, not our own.

"God's plans for us are greater than we can imagine. Like Gideon, we may face doubts and uncertainties, but God calls us to trust Him. As we step out in faith, embracing God's unconventional plans, we can experience the victory that comes from relying on *His* strength." He furrowed his brow. "Did you catch that? *'His'* strength.

"Everyone has different talents, right? Some people are really smart, some are naturally athletic, some are artistic, some are tremendously brave—I am *none* of those things," he said with a wide smile. His eyes flitted over to Essie briefly, then continued drifting across the congregation. "Who gives you your talent? Who gives you your quote unquote gifts? Were you figuring things out in the womb?" He shook his head. "God made you. God gifted you your talents, your skills. *'I can do all things—'*" He put his hand to his ear.

"*'--through Christ, who strengthens me,'*" the congregation recited.

Matteo nodded approvingly. He furrowed his brow. "You've seen me play guitar up here." He waggled his fingers. "My fingers don't play the strings quite the same as they used to, but it's still a talent. Is that talent my own? Or is a gift from God for me to use as a tool to do His work?"

"You're a tool," Thomas called out.

Matteo's eyes widened. "Well, I was going for the talent being the tool, but—" He made eye contact with Luke then covered his mouth with his hand, chuckling.

The congregation laughed.

"I am *not* going to live that one down." He tensed his jaw, pulled his eyebrows upward in a deep slope. "Where was I going with this?" he murmured to himself. "God works *through* us. He uses our talents, our strengths to do His work. When you're facing a difficult, or even an 'impossible' situation, remember one thing—well, two things, though you have the first one memorized. The second thing is this: Nothing is impossible for God. Can you say that with me?"

"Nothing is impossible for God."

"There's a song–" He smiled to himself, gazing toward the back of the sanctuary. "'*Who am I to deny what the Lord can do,*'" he murmured melodically.

"Sing it, Pastor," someone on the right side of the congregation called out encouragingly.

Matteo grinned. "Nah, we don't want that. Singing is *not* my talent. Even auto-tune can't fix my singing, but that's alright." He gave a confused frown, stepped back to his notes stand. "I'm all over the place with my preaching today."

A few people in the congregation chuckled.

He scanned the page, nodded, and resumed pacing. "Nothing is impossible for God. No matter what the situation. Sometimes we may feel like we come up against walls and insurmountable obstacles; moments when the enemy is working hard to make us doubt ourselves and we become tempted to feel afraid that we don't stand a chance to win the battle. The enemy is telling us that we're weak. And we *might be*, but you know who *isn't*, don't you? God. God loves us. God is on our side." He smiled. "'*Jesus loves me, this I know–*'" He paused. "Singing a lot randomly today."

A single voice joined him when he continued. A voice he recognized. He lifted his eyes to the third row, to Essie. "'*--for the Bible tells me so. Little ones to Him belong; They are weak, but He is strong.*'"

He smiled broadly. "'*Yes, Jesus loves me!*'" He nodded, his eyes glistening in the sunlight pouring into the sanctuary as he set his eyes again on Essie. "She sang that one in Sunday School, too, so you'll have to excuse me," he murmured, sniffling. He nodded, pacing away. "When we face impossible situations in our lives, remember that God is with us. Just as He called Gideon to be a mighty warrior, He calls us to step forward with courage, trusting in His strength to overcome our weaknesses. '*I can do all things through Christ who strengthens me.*'"

20

rogue

"We're not set up for it here," Miles said. "And it's too risky. Danny says it has to be some closed satellite connection."

The team had made the trek to a small military base at the eastern border of the Ark the night before. The plan was to join up with the two operatives on the mission, gear up the vehicle, then start the drive after dinner, putting them in the District early the next morning.

Josh tightened his jaw. "Miles, we leave for the District tonight. I won't have another chance to see her–"

Miles took a deep breath. "We don't need to be looking at her on a computer screen anymore, Josh. We're done sitting around doing nothing; we're going to get her. That's what we need to be focusing on. We need to get our plan set, get our gear set, and then we need to go in there and get your girl–and maybe blow some shit up while we're at it. We're not doing goodbyes or last looks, *just in case*. Absolutely not. We are doing this, Josh. We are *doing this*. We need to focus on making sure that in less than 18 hours, she is safe. Focus on *that*."

Josh swallowed hard, pulled back his shoulders, and nodded.

"*Okay?*"

It was taking some effort for Josh to process the reality that in less than a day, the situation would be resolved. There'd be a final result, a final answer. In 18 hours, they could all be dead *or* in 18 hours, he'd get to hold Essie in his arms.

"Josh?"

He nodded. "18 hours."

"18 hours," Miles repeated. "But *first*, you and I are going for a drink." He lifted his eyes to the pair of Ark special operatives who had been lingering at the conference room door. "Hey Guys, call it a superstition, but we always shared a round before taking off on any MET mission. Figure it's fitting to do that now. Care to join us?"

Josh peered across at Miles and frowned but gave no objection.

Miles Kent hadn't had a sip of alcohol in five months. And they certainly didn't have a pre-mission drinking tradition.

The younger of the two operatives, an average height guy who had the look of a high school wrestler widened his stance. "I'm driving first shift so it's a no for me."

The other furrowed his brow, considering the offer. "Thanks, but I'm going to pass. You guys enjoy though."

Josh waited until they were outside before turning to question him.

Miles drew his index finger to his mouth. "Looks like the weather's going to cooperate for the drive," he said, taking in the cloudless sky. He patted the side of the dark gray armored six-wheeled vehicle that they'd be taking from the base to the District. "How do you like our ride?"

Josh peered up at the immense vehicle, the reinforcements on the windows, the geometric armored roof panels with their titanium plates. "It's intense."

"Yeah, it's called an Armadillo, modeled after something they had in Halo?"

"Is that the old shooter video game?"

"Yeah, welcome to the future."

They walked onto the bar patio of the nearby barbecue restaurant, just across the street from the base, and sat at a high-top table overlooking the stone fireplace waiting area and an expansive view of cornfields.

"I forget. Are you a lager or ale guy?" Miles asked, pulling a phone-sized device with a large display from his vest and sliding it toward the center of the table.

Josh immediately moved to look at the device, but Miles waved his hand over it, raising his eyebrows. "Lager," Josh answered.

"Yeah, me, too. I like my beer hoppy. They look short-staffed. I'll go grab our drinks from the bar."

Josh took a deep breath, looking out over the lake set among the cornfields. It reminded him of the lake they'd stumbled upon during their drive back to the Ark. It had been set along the ransacked town's main road where they discovered a young family murdered on the sidewalk. Essie had discovered the youngest child, an infant, actively dying. She'd taken her in her arms and sang to her until her final gasp of air.

Essie had been struggling with her faith and had broken down in fury after Miles took the baby away. She'd raged against God in a way Josh had never seen from her.

Josh ended up dragging Essie into the lake to wash the child's blood from her skin and clothes, to try to help her find some calm, not realizing just how frigid the water would be. He'd held her in his arms for God knows how long, her breaths deepening and echoing against his neck.

"I put in for the appetizer sampler, too," Miles said as he slid back onto his bar stool, placing a mug of beer before each of their places.

Josh nodded toward the view. "It's nice out here."

"Yeah, it's pretty, isn't it? Gabe's going to med school out this direction, isn't he?"

"Yeah, I think it's just north of here."

Miles twisted his expression. "You're *sure*?"

"Pretty sure," Josh replied, suddenly doubting himself. He tried to picture a map from one of his old history textbooks. "I mean, I haven't gotten to—"

"Oh, shoot, sorry, Dude." Miles pulled a small square card from his chest pocket. "Stick that over the back of your cheekbone by your ear."

Josh stared down at the small clear disc adhered to the card. He peeled it off and attached it as Miles instructed.

"Danny, give our boy a little check-check."

"Angler, do you read?"

Josh winced.

"*Oh,* crank that down a bit," Miles remarked.

"Better?"

Josh nodded.

"You can talk, Dude."

"Danny?"

"Ah, *there* you are."

"We just ordered some food–do you want something?" Miles asked, peering across the parking lot toward the main barracks and the Armadillo parked outside.

"Nothing greasy."

"They have salads."

"Chicken Caesar?"

"You got it. Is the campfire elder Gunner there with you?"

"I don't know what the campfire elder part is all about, but yes. He says he's fine."

"Tell him I'll bring him a burger."

There was a delay and then Danny came back with: "He says thank you."

"So, we're good here?"

"Yeah, you're in your own little bubble there. Just keep the device out. It's doing its job."

"Let us know if something changes."

"Yep."

Josh frowned. "What's going on?"

Miles tapped his fingers on the table. "The whole mission plan we just went over in there?"

"Yeah?"

"It's bullshit." He cleared his throat, reaching for the salt and pepper shakers. He lined up the paper napkins in a vague representation of the

White House grounds buildings. "In there, we talked about you going in with Tweedle Dee and Tweedle Dum over on the east parking lot side, going through the tunnel that cuts across beneath the South Lawn, correct?" He set up the saltshaker as Josh.

Josh nodded.

"The path you're taking is quicker with less security. They're planning to have the three of you get to Essie first, then immediately take you out. Non-lethally, if possible."

Josh blinked.

"What we talked about in there was having *me* clear a path along the outer corridor so we could double-back and have a clear route back to the Armadillo. There's a lot more guards along the exterior, which they rightly assumed would take me more time." He guided the pepper shaker along the lined up napkins, stopping in the corner. "They're actually planning to take an exit out the west side of the property, where another vehicle would be waiting to take Essie. The idea would be to make it look like Creature had Essie moved before we got there. They'd come back and play dumb when I finally made it to her cell. Make it seem like Essie was lost to the wind, basically." Miles took in Josh's expression. "Now here's the *real* mission plan."

Josh's shoulders relaxed slightly.

Miles relocated the pieces back to their starting positions, this time pulling out a small bottle of hot sauce to represent Essie. "The security in the exterior corridor is going to get pulled back to a more central location just before we arrive, leaving my path completely clear. *I'll* get to Essie first."

Josh nodded, watching the pepper shaker unite with the hot sauce.

"Meanwhile, *you* would have taken out our ops friends–" He tossed two Splenda packets in the center of the South Lawn. "--beneath the helipad. It's a nice safe spot, given all the other activity that will be going on. There's gonna be a lot of destruction happening, but they should be protected there. They're good guys, they're just following orders."

Josh pictured the imposing Chad ("Coach") and slight but quick Dawson ("Ferris"). He was suddenly very thankful he'd kept strength training a part of his daily routine.

"Thankfully you trained like a prison inmate during your isolation from society. I don't imagine it'll be too difficult for you to take them out. *Especially* since you'll have a little assistance from the Dans."

Josh wondered briefly what new tech the Dans had invented. He assumed it was something effective but non-lethal. That detail wasn't particularly important to him just yet. "So, I take them out and then catch up with you?"

Miles nodded, moving the saltshaker toward the pepper and the hot sauce. "Then we haul ass back down the corridor to the Armadillo."

Josh frowned questioningly. "Who's giving the orders to Coach and Ferris?"

Miles took a deep breath. "Luther."

Josh narrowed his eyes.

"Sadie Parker thinks it's too risky to have Essie out in the world 'unprotected.'"

"She wants to lock her up, too."

Miles gave a short nod. "Luther agreed with her assessment to pacify her. He didn't want to risk her making a stink about it and risking the mission. He told her he just wanted to make sure Essie was safe, but that he saw her point that complete 'freedom' was never going to be an option."

"And she bought that?"

"*Yep.*" He gave a small smile. "There were some profane words coming out of Luther's mouth that day, let me tell you."

"Does she have other motivations?"

"You mean to *use* Essie?"

Josh's body stiffened, then he nodded.

"We didn't *think* so. Danny had vetted her, tracked her activity and communications. She seemed genuinely concerned about just keeping Essie safe." He took a deep breath. "More *recently*, as the mission has gotten closer, she's started to develop an interest in possible medical

242

applications, given how successful the vaccine's been. She seems to have positive intentions, but–" Miles shook his head angrily. "It's not gonna happen. In less than 18 hours, Essie will be free. Not *sort of* free. Not under 'protective custody.' *Free.*"

Josh nodded again.

Miles lifted his eyebrows. "You doing okay?"

"They don't take her. No matter what."

"They're not laying a finger on her. I *promise* you that." He began tidying up the table. "What I've laid out is the only part of the plan I want you focusing on. It's a lot more intricate than this. There are other moving parts in play that are gonna ensure our success. Other players who want Essie to be free almost as much as we do." Miles glanced toward the bar and back. "Focus on taking out the ops guys and getting to Essie. That's *it*. This time tomorrow, Essie will be safe. Keep your mind focused on that."

Josh took a deep breath. There was more to think about that came after the mission, but he couldn't think of that now. Miles was right. He needed to focus on the next 18 hours. He straightened his posture. "I'm good."

Miles leaned forward on his elbows, furrowing his brow. "Tell me about when you first met her. I'm not sure you ever told me."

Josh straightened his posture, clearing his throat.

"You were pretty young, right? Do you remember?"

"I remember," he replied, already picturing the dreary afternoon sky that lurked over the farm that day. "Not a great day leading up to it actually. My parents had been arguing. Gabe and I didn't know Teo very well since he had been living in Texas. I wanted to run off and play, but our mom insisted we be there to greet him. At that point, we just thought it would be him."

Miles furrowed his brow, seeming to have a question, but remained quiet.

"As Teo's truck pulled in, my dad had a death grip on my arm because I was being a pain, my mom was upset with him for the death grip on my arm, Gabe was being smug because I was in trouble. That was the scene Teo was pulling up to."

"How old were you guys?"

"I was 5, Gabe was 6–almost 7. Essie was almost 3."

"Wow."

"Teo got her out of the back seat and she was just *so—shy*."

Miles adjusted on his seat, smiling fondly.

"She hadn't been around other kids; she hadn't gone to Children's Ministry or anything yet at that point." He cleared his throat, taking a sip of beer. "My parents were in shock. Teo's wife had just died so they were expecting they'd be consoling him–he hadn't told them about Essie."

"How did his wife die?"

Josh took a breath in. "She killed herself."

Miles frowned. "Shit."

"They were best friends growing up," he murmured, the reality of that hitting him fully for the first time. He recognized the parallel Teo must have seen with he and Essie. He could imagine the pain Teo felt when she died, but Josh felt an uneasiness when he considered the fact that she'd chosen to leave him, she'd chosen to die. "She had some mental health stuff–her parents died when she was a teenager, she was abused by the relatives she went to live with. When they got married, she and Teo went through several miscarriages, two stillbirths."

"*Shit*."

"Yeah."

"Wait, so Luther saved Essie from the lab, then he just *happened* upon Teo? They didn't know one another before?"

"Teo was moving back to Colorado to work for Calvary. He stopped off at a gas station diner and when he came out, Luther introduced himself."

Miles narrowed his eyes. "*That's* when Teo met Essie? When he 'adopted' her?"

"Yeah."

"*Wow*," he breathed, frowning.

"So, my mom was being a little *much* with Essie; actually, my dad was, too. To me it looked like she was getting overwhelmed by everything—" He stopped and chuckled to himself, wincing a bit. "So I made a silly face at her. At first, she was looking at me like I had three heads, like she was very, very concerned about my mental state. She'd had limited interactions with people at that point and she certainly had never had some weird kid make faces at her."

Miles pursed his lips, thinking of her life before, how strange everything must have been for her.

"She tucked herself behind her dad and I thought I'd scared her. My parents did, too." Josh's mouth curled upward at the corners. "As soon as she saw I was getting in trouble for whatever they thought I'd done, she stepped out into the open, twisted her face and stuck her tongue out at me."

Miles smiled.

"Then I walked over and asked her if she wanted to go play."

"She said 'yes,' I take it?"

He nodded. "I showed her the tree swing first. She'd never seen one so she thought the wooden seat was for her to stand on. I pushed her anyway. Gently, but I'm actually really surprised Teo or my parents didn't intervene."

"Yeah," Miles agreed, lifting his eyebrows. "Your mom always seemed to be an honorary helicopter parent when it came to Essie."

The corners of Josh's mouth turned upward. "Essie had this huge smile on her face, big dimples, the whole time—*and then* she fell."

"Nice job, West."

"Yeah. Her foot slipped and she fell pretty hard. Smacked the wooden seat, landed on the ground."

Miles puffed out his lower lip.

Josh's cheeks tightened. "So the parents were all panicking and starting to descend and Essie was sitting on the ground just absolutely stunned about what happened–and then she burst out laughing."

"*Laughing?*"

"Like a really infectious belly giggle. I went to help her stand up and asked her if she was okay and she said she was, but–" He furrowed his brow, his smile continuing to stretch. "--She had only maybe said the word 'hi' up until that point and then she burst out with 'I may have broken my butt.'"

Miles grinned, picking up his mug. "That's really stinkin' adorable."

Josh lifted his brow.

"And in that moment, you'd found the one whom your soul loves."

Josh narrowed his eyes. "Miles, did you just quote the Bible?"

He wavered his hand. "More or less. I've had a lot of time on my own, Bro. I didn't bring any other reading material to the surveillance room. I read the Bible 4 times in 3 months."

"4 times?"

Miles chuckled. "No offense to God, but I think I need *Harry Potter* or something after that. The Old Testament is *intense*."

The food was delivered and Josh suddenly looked uneasy about eating.

"I don't know why I ordered food. I don't have much of an appetite," Miles murmured, leaning back in his chair.

"We can bring it back for Gunner."

Miles nodded. "Did you suspect anything about what Essie had been through before she met you?"

Josh considered the question. "I think I started to have a sense about things, but it was later on. We were just so young. I didn't know she couldn't sleep at night until a year or two later. Gabe would wait until after I fell asleep to leave our room."

Miles frowned.

"Essie would stay at our house most summers and as she got older, more often. She stayed in Gabe's room and he was supposed to sleep on the bunk in my room. One of the first nights she spent at our house, he heard her awake and went in to check on her. He offered to read to her and snuggled with her and she was able to fall sleep. So that became their routine. Each night, she'd ask him to read to her and each night, she'd fall asleep snuggled against him until eventually it was just something they

246

did. Most of the time she'd fall asleep where he couldn't get out without waking her so he just stayed." Seeing the expression on Miles's face, he added: "At the lab, she was either strapped to a metal table—" He pulled in his breath. "—recovering from the latest experiment—or she was in an empty padded room. That's where she lived, that's where she was expected to sleep. She described it to me once." He shook his head, his voice trailing off.

He remembered the details she'd included—the random deflated beach balls (which had probably originally been meant for some sort of enrichment, but had gone unused until they were intentionally popped by one of the lab technicians to startle her), the rounded rectangular copper tinted windows, one with a strip of tinting peeled off. She'd described how she was mostly alone there, which is "selfishly" how she preferred it. If there was another child there with her, it was typically an infant sprawled helplessly on his or her back, struggling to breathe or already actively dying. Before she told him about it, he had thought the videos of her recovering from sarin gas were the worst thing imaginable, but then the realization struck him as she described that room, that she had no reprieve. The researchers would inflict unthinkable horrors upon her, she'd endure the torturous recovery, and then she'd be brought back to that room to watch dozens of other babies suffer and die.

Those were her earliest memories. Those were the images, the sounds, the smells that came rushing back to her at night.

She had never known the comfort of having another person sleep so close, to be able to hear their steady, healthy breaths.

At one point, he felt jealousy toward Gabe for having been the one, for a time, to provide comfort to Essie, but once he had a clear picture of where she had come from, he only felt gratitude that his brother had been there for her.

"She'd always struggled to sleep at night on her own."

Miles frowned. "*That's* why she started staying at the cabin with you."

Josh nodded slowly. "She'd try to sneak in naps during the daytime, but at that point, she was also dealing with–" He stopped short, deciding bringing up the "bunker buster" would require significant explanation. "She was dealing with other things at the time and it was getting to where she was really struggling to function during the day. So that was our solution–to have her stay out at the cabin."

Miles frowned. "That must have been tough for you–you weren't in official couplehood or anything."

Josh arched his eyebrow. "I got to hold Essie in my arms every night; I loved it. I hated the reason why she couldn't sleep on her own, but I loved having her there."

Miles nodded slowly. "Were you afraid you'd accidentally grab her butt in your sleep or something?"

Josh smiled lightly, gazing across at the lake. "I was *so* paranoid. Not about grabbing her butt *specifically*." He chuckled, shaking his head.

"Like, *this* is okay, this is friendship," Miles said, holding his hand out in front of his chest. He lowered it, made a cupping gesture. "--*this* is crossing a line."

Josh took another sip of beer. He thought of the day she threw the birthday party for the little girl from church when her body was fighting so hard to protect her from the impending explosion in her abdomen. When she'd napped before the party, she'd clung to him with a desperation that had never been in character for her, like the horrors of her past were literally trying to drag her back to their chambers.

"Hey, Josh?"

Josh lifted his chin.

"18 hours," Miles said, taking a deep breath. "18 hours from now she'll be safe, once and for all."

Josh nodded conclusively, running his thumb under his eyes.

Miles sat back in his chair, gazing out at the view. "God, I bet she was really stinkin' cute at that age. When you first met her?"

The day she first came to the farm, she was wearing a pair of overalls a woman from Calvary had given her. There had been a rip in one of the knees, which the woman had repaired by sewing on a small floral print square of fabric. Essie's hair was a wild mane of waves his mom hadn't attempted to tame yet. Her silver eyes were big and round and unlike anything he'd ever seen. The moment she'd decided that Josh wasn't, in fact, crazy, that he was acting out of good nature, her eyes lit up and her lips pinched upward at the corners, revealing her dimpled cheeks.

He nodded. "Adorable."

Miles took in Josh's appearance. "*You're* looking much more presentable, by the way. I'd forgotten what a handsome guy you are when you're not cosplaying as a middle-aged lumberjack."

21

possible

Annette gazed out the window to the darkening sky, a rolling wave of thunder rattling the curio cabinet behind her. There had been little distinction between the night and the dawn. The gradient had simply shifted to a lighter shade of gray.

Typically, she liked to have her coffee on the balcony, but a chill in the air had kept her inside, folded into the armchair just inside from the French doors, a large ceramic mug braced in her hands.

There was also irrefutable evidence that an invasion was imminent. News coverage had claimed attempts were made by the insurgents themselves to penetrate the District border weeks earlier to no avail, the coverage intending to make the Arks seem feeble and without fundamental resources to carry out such an endeavor.

The recent formation of groups on all sides of the District border, however, had gone unreported. The development seemed organic yet coordinated. They had set up camps a short distance from the border and done nothing to engage with security covering the border gates. They were simply waiting.

She placed her mug back on the otherwise untouched breakfast tray on the coffee table, balling her hands into fists as she crossed her arms over her stomach. Her eyes flitted up to the television monitor, then over to the grandfather clock. She watched the seconds count down to the top of the hour. At precisely 8am, the monitor switched on of its own accord. After a brief delay, the Presidential seal appeared and Gowon stepped up to a podium.

Annette stood and made her way to the bathroom to begin to get ready for the day.

*   *   *

Miles stared out the window of the Armadillo, given its name for its geometric armored exterior, vaguely shaped like the carapace of an armadillo. He turned slowly back inside. "I'm relatively new to the faith. Is this how God gives endorsements?"

"*Jesus,*" Gunner muttered, as a brilliant burst of lightning fired down from the sky and made impact with the ground several miles ahead.

"We may have wandered into Revelations," Danny called from the communications cubby. "Based on what I'm seeing on the monitors? There's crazy geothermal activity right now, storms brewing off the coast, atmospheric disruptions? *Meteorites.* Actual, traceable, measurable meteorites."

"Let me know when the tornadoes start touching down," Miles remarked with a grin. "'I gotta go! Julia, we've got cows!'" he added in his best female southern accent.

Coach narrowed his eyes at him.

"It's from *Twister,*" Miles explained. He pressed his lips together, nodding as though to the beat of a song no one else could hear. He took a steadying breath. "We should pray."

Coach and Ferris exchanged a look.

"Have you two accepted the free gift of salvation from our Lord and Savior Jesus Christ?" Miles asked, lifting his eyebrows at the two operatives.

They both nodded with a fair amount of uncertainty.

"It's good to feel right with Jesus at this particular juncture." Miles sat upright suddenly, startled by a sharp crack of lightning, followed by rolling thunder. "Let's pray."

Josh leaned forward over his knees.

Miles tapped his comm button. "You can stay put, Danny and Gunner, but we're going to have a little prayer if y'all want to listen in." He lifted his brow at Coach and Ferris, encouraging them to lean toward the center of the Armadillo. He then joined his hands and bowed his head.

"Dear Heavenly Father, Today, we are heading into the unknown. We don't know exactly what awaits us, what challenges, but we are faithful to you. Please watch over us, set our course, give us wisdom and strength, and hey, if you're interested, we could use You on our team. Old Testament wrathful God would be helpful, or you know, Revelations Jesus riding in valiantly on a white, noble steed? A truly inspiring image. There's a really amazing gray and white dappled Percheron running around up there in Heaven. If you're flexible on color, he'd also be a good pick."

Josh nodded.

"We need You, Jesus. Please continue to remind us in our hearts as we press on that there's nothing You can't do. You *are* the Way Maker. Through you, *all* things are possible. Guide our paths, give us strength. Our mission is driven by love, the strongest force of all, and that comes from You and You alone. No one demonstrates Your love like Essie. She's the best of us, Jesus. Help us bring her to safety once and for all. We trust in your presence, knowing that with Your grace, there's nothing and no one who can stop us. We pray this in Jesus' name. Amen."

22

carry me home

When Essie was eleven years old, she asked her dad about what happens to people after they die. She had been reading some theology books discussing purgatory and how a journey to Heaven involved passage through flames meant to cleanse a person's sins away to make them worthy of Heaven.

She remembered him pursing his lips as she described what she'd read, waiting patiently, as he always did, to allow her to say everything that was on her mind. Usually her questions had some brevity. She had learned early on that she could get more information out of him about his opinion the less prompting she provided. In this case, however, she had been greatly troubled by the claim.

"Jesus made me righteous. He made you righteous. We made all believers righteous. That's it. That's the ultimate gift. We get the gift of eternal life without having to deserve it or do anything more to earn it than to just accept Jesus Christ. These churches are claiming that there's another step before we can earn Heaven and if we don't quite reach the levels needed to be accepted into Heaven, we would then endure further suffering, equal to our level of sin, *before* we could then *earn* passage into Heaven. It's *infuriating*," she had stammered, pacing back and forth in their living room as her dad plated up dinner. "And what's *worse* is that they act as though believers need to worry about earning their way to

Heaven while they're here on Earth. It's totally manipulative. They're motivating people with the threat of suffering. No wonder people turned away from church, if it just makes you feel bad about yourself, if it feels like nothing you do will ever be enough? Because it won't. Absolutely no one is worthy of Heaven, of eternal life. *Everyone* is a sinner. We can't get around that. But they would have people believe God is an angry God who's out to get them, catch them in their sins. They don't get the idea of a loving Father." She'd motioned to him. "Do people *not* understand what a Father's love *is*?"

Matteo had furrowed his brow. "Maybe not. Maybe that's part of the problem?"

She frowned. "That makes me sad for people."

"Me, too."

"I mean, I just have to think of how you love me and I understand God's love."

Matteo froze. Slowly, the corners of his mouth crept upward.

"I suppose it's a difficult thing for people to understand if they haven't felt it before," she said regretfully.

He nodded toward the table and watched her fold herself onto the elephant cushion of the dining chair she'd occupied since she was three years old.

"Okay, so back to the topic at hand," she said, waving her hand in front of her face.

"Yes."

"Jesus earned us Heaven already. He died for us. It's done. The motivation to follow God's Word on Earth is to know Him better, to live like Jesus, to serve God, and to feel blessed while we're here."

Matteo placed a plate of fettuccine before her, took a seat to her left. "I made you authentic Italian tonight. Bon appétit."

"I mean, do I have my information right, Daddy?"

He smiled. "You *do* have your information right."

She frowned, nodding slowly. "Did you just claim this was *authentic* Italian cuisine?"

His lips pulled further upward.

"And you said 'Bon appétit'?"

He raised his eyebrows.

"Well, I'm not going to give you a hard time because I enjoy alfredo sauce immensely–and I love you for making it for me." She gave a light smile. "*But* if you start speaking French, you're going to need to learn how to make croissants."

"Sara West knows how to make croissants."

Her jaw fell open. "She's been holding out on me."

Taking her hand in his, Matteo briefly gave thanks.

She sighed deeply as they released hands. "I'm bothered by this idea of purgatory, of waiting for the end of times." She had decided against sharing that the idea of it felt eerily familiar to her. "How soon after we die do we go to Heaven?"

He began twirling pasta onto his fork. "Immediately."

She furrowed her brow. "The second our bodies die? Boom, we're with Jesus in Heaven?"

"Yes."

Essie stabbed her pasta, twisted a large helping around her fork, and nodded approvingly. "That's *so* cool." She packed the pasta into her mouth and smiled tightly when she noticed him watching her, cheeks puffed out like a chipmunk.

Matteo pressed his lips together, shook his head. "Ti amo, mia dolce ragazza."

It took great effort and a bit of time for her to manage the bite, but once she had, she smiled widely. "I love you, too, Daddy."

* * *

There was seething, relentless, excruciating pain...and then there was nothing.

Just like that. Like a light switch.

Ever since, the experience had been a sensation of nothingness; she was drifting in darkness.

255

It was as though she had slipped into a trap door in her mind where she was safe from feeling anything. No pain. No fear. Just nothingness forever.

It's better here.
It's better not to feel.
It's better not to think.
It's better not to remember.
Thoughts are the enemy.
Feelings are the enemy.
Memories are the enemy.
The nothingness is peaceful.
The nothingness is safe.

She let the nothingness surround her.

She hoped it would continue to insulate her from feeling anything more.

Thoughts are the enemy.
Feelings are the enemy.
Memories are the enemy.
The nothingness is peaceful.
The nothingness is safe.

She felt the sudden, vague sensation of her body, her mind waking up.

She fought it. She didn't want to feel anything anymore, but it was like swimming against the current; she kept feeling her mind being forced toward awareness, toward pain.

First, she felt the air fill the brittle confines of her lungs. Her breaths came in sharp, constricted jolts.

Next, she felt her heart hammering unevenly in her chest.

Her head pounded.

There were surges of heat, of cold, of ravenous pain clawing through every part of her body.

The pain was worse than any of the Phoenix Initiative antidote runs. When she woke from the antidote runs, she had people she loved. There was something to look forward to.

That was gone.

They were gone.

They were all dead.

It was only her.

All at once, the memory of star gazing at the West's farm came rushing back to her, and the physical pain ebbed away.

They were all lying on their backs in the cool grass just outside the horse paddocks. She was situated between her dad and Josh, with Gabe and Luke on the other side of him. They did this on several occasions, but this was the first instance that she could remember.

While pointing out constellations, Luke shared the story of Queen Cassiopeia in his typical animated fashion. As the Greek astrology story goes, Cassiopeia boasted to everyone that she was the most beautiful woman in the world. Evidently, she offended the wrong people because while other Greek gods were featured as valiant constellations, Cassiopeia was banished to the sky, hung upside down by her ankles. The story earned some giggles as Essie and Josh speculated that Cassiopeia seemed the sort to have one of those dresses with 15 layers that looked like cupcake wrappers. They hoisted their feet in the air, calling out in highbrow British voices for assistance. *"Excuse me, Sir. I cannot see!"* and *"Can you not see how beautiful I am?"*

When they'd finally been able to move on and the laughter became more subdued, Luke decided against more stories that would rile them up. He pointed out Orion's Belt, the Big Dipper, Little Dipper, Cygnus, Scorpius, Leo the Lion, which Essie had decided was her favorite. When Gabe challenged her selection, saying it looked like a pirate hook, she wasn't deterred.

"You're not looking *close enough*, Gabe," she had explained, pointing toward the constellation. "Look at his majestic mane–see where the sky is darker and kind of swirly? That's the shadow of his mane. Then he has his giant paws in the air. He's jumping up."

"What do you think he's jumping up *to*?" Luke asked dotingly.

"A tree. Lions *love* trees. That's where he likes to take his naps."

"Lions *do* sleep a lot."

"I'd love to snuggle with a lion. They'd be so warm and cozy."

"*Yeah*, until he decided to–" Gabe stopped speaking abruptly when Luke smacked him on the side.

"Do you think Leo the Lion has a wild mane like your hair?" Luke teased.

"I don't have a *mane*," she said defensively. She turned to Josh. "Does my hair look like a mane?"

Josh furrowed his brow. "Well, it's kind of big and wavy like a mane–and it's a similar color."

She ran her hands briefly over the top of her hair, seemingly to tame it, and laid back down abruptly.

"It's not an insult, Essie," Josh whispered reassuringly, but it did not appear to set her at ease in the least. He propped himself up on his elbow. "What do you love about lions?"

She frowned. "They're strong and brave–"

"And loyal and fun-loving," Josh continued.

"And according to you, excellent snuggle buddies," Luke added.

Essie glanced over to Gabe, who said nothing to refute the claim. There was a bit of hurt in her eyes.

"*Hey*," Josh said quietly to get her attention. "All those things you love about lions? I could describe you the same way. It makes sense you have the hair to match."

She pressed her lips together, tucked her hair behind her ear.

"Essie, our little *lioness*," Luke murmured.

She grinned, her cheeks red.

"You just have to work on your roar," Josh challenged, lifting his eyebrow.

"I'm not going to *roar*, Josh."

"Why?" he asked incredulously.

"Go for it, girl," Luke added. "Well, actually, we probably don't want to spook the animals. Let's plan a roar development session for daytime hours tomorrow."

Satisfied, Essie laid back down.

At some point as they continued to gaze up at the sky, she settled against her dad's arm and fell asleep. She woke just after her dad lifted her off the grass and wrapped her arms sleepily around his neck. She rested her chin on his shoulder, taking in her surroundings, including Luke, Gabe, and Josh, who had fallen in step behind her dad. She remembered Luke smiling sweetly at her, giving her nose a gentle *boop* as they moved toward the house and she struggled to keep her eyes open.

They were gone.
They were all dead.
It was only her.

She could still feel the rocking sensation as her dad carried her, though she knew it was all in her mind, a reverberation of a memory.

Still.

She wouldn't mind it being the last thing she remembered, the last image, the last sensation she'd have as she drifted from this life toward Heaven.

With the small whisper of a voice, she began to pray: "Caro Gesù, lascia che questa sia la fine. Per favore lasciami morire. Per favore lasciami stare con loro, per favore lasciami stare con Te."

Dear Jesus, let this be the end. Please let me die. Please let me be with them, please let me be with You.

The dream, the memory had faded and she could no longer feel the presence of her dad, of Luke, of Josh, of Gabe. She could no longer feel the cool night air.

She felt only pain. Ceaseless pain. In her heart. In her mind. In every part of her body.

She began to hiccup on sobs as she felt her torso being raised, which triggered a rapid fire of sharp jabs through her chest, her back. There was a brief wave of heat and then a light compression. The sensation repeated, as her head was lifted.

It was difficult to isolate the feeling to be able to identify what could be causing it, especially with the competing sensations seething through her muscles, her bones, her veins, but she could feel when her body was released and placed back on the concrete slab.

"Come on, Esther," a low, smooth voice coaxed. She heard the voice, but she didn't understand its presence, didn't understand its message, didn't understand who could possibly be saying it. No one here knew her.

She could feel the concrete slab more firmly beneath her shoulders now. She could feel the chill of the room. She could smell the foul, stale odor of the most recent tray of food, along with her own unwashed skin.

All at once, her blood vessels constricted. Her skull screamed with pressurization, threatening to split apart. She tensed, crying out in a prolonged, desperate sob.

They were gone.
They were all dead.
It was only her.

"Gesù, per favore lasciami tornare a casa. Per favore lasciami morire."

Jesus, please let me come home. Please let me die.

The rush of blood surging toward her arms, her legs, caused her body to stiffen. She could hear her voice whispering over and over again: "Per favore lasciami morire. Per favore lasciami morire."

A warm, heavy hand rested on her forehead. "You're getting out of here."

She was startled by the proximity of the voice, by the sudden weight of the air around her, startled by the promise he was making. She shook her head forcibly. "No," she heard herself plead in a strained, broken voice she didn't recognize. "Non voglio più essere qui. Per favore lasciami morire," she whimpered, her mind drifting back toward darkness. *I don't want to be here anymore. Please let me die.*

"Just hold on a little longer," the voice murmured, thick, rough fingers stroking her cheek. "Roger. Ten ninety-eight."

"Per favore, lasciami morire così posso stare con loro," she whispered, desperate for the darkness.

Please, let me die so I can be with them.

"Esther, they're coming to get you."

She shook her head furiously, tears flooding her eyes. "Per favor, lasciami morire."

The nothingness is peaceful.
The nothingness is safe.

"Say again–" the voice said, changing direction.

There was a hum of another voice, but it was too low for her to understand.

"Songbird, Angler and Sugar are on their way to get you."

The cooling sensation she had felt seeping through her limbs began to pool in her chest. As it did, she tried to process the man's words.

It was a trick. Another program. Another cruel tactic.

The cool liquid she felt pooling in her chest felt familiar. She'd experienced it before. It was just as her brain identified it as epinephrine, the liquid seemed to burst and was like a shock to her heart. Her eyes flew open, her breath caught in her chest.

"*There* you go," the voice murmured encouragingly.

She had been haunted for much of her childhood, her life, with generalized nightmares from the earliest years of her life. There typically wasn't a defined enemy or individual inflicting the suffering upon her; it was just simply happening.

When there *was* a face, it was the face of the man standing over her now, the man who had his palm bracing her cheek, the man looking at her with what appeared to be affection.

She felt as though she should lunge at him, scream at him, fight him, but she found her body unable to move, her jaw tensing, her lip quivering.

261

"You're going to live a long life far away from here," he said, his muted brown eyes brimming with tears, his brow lifting. "I *promise* you that."

The sounds around her suddenly seemed amplified–the constant drip down the corridor echoing against the stone floor, the churning of equipment on the other side of her cell's wall, the flowing of water through piping nearby. And now, a voice echoed loudly through the earpiece of the man standing over her, a voice she knew.

It isn't Miles.
Miles is dead.
I watched him die.
This is a trick.
I watched him die.
Miles is dead.

She could feel her mind slipping toward nothingness again.
She longed for it.
She longed to escape the pain she felt burning through her heart.

They're all dead.

It's better there.
It's better not to feel.
It's better not to think.
It's better not to remember.
Thoughts are the enemy.
Feelings are the enemy.
Memories are the enemy.
The nothingness is peaceful.
The nothingness is safe.
Everyone is gone.
Everyone is dead.
It's only me.
It's better not to feel.

It's better not to think.
It's better not to remember.
Thoughts are the enemy.
Feelings are the enemy.
Memories are the enemy.
The nothingness is peaceful.
The nothingness is safe.

His name is Marcus, her brain announced abruptly. Her eyes opened again and she narrowed her gaze upon the man lingering above her, checking her vitals. Her body continued to seethe with pain, but there was something beyond it that she could feel racing toward her.

His name is Marcus.

He hated her, she remembered that. Before she'd acquired an understanding of "danger," mainly because there was no contrasting environment of "safe" in her young world, she knew his words, his attitude toward her were dangerous. She had only known threats, but she knew she should be most fearful of him. The others were dutiful in their work while he reveled in her suffering.

The day Luther saved her, she was meant to be killed.

Marcus was meant to kill her.

Marcus took her to the room with the fire.

Marcus broke her body.

Each snap of each bone in her body had brought an intensity to his eyes.

Her cries had seemed to invigorate the fury within him.

And then, inexplicably, she didn't cry anymore. She didn't feel anymore.

There had been a nothingness then, but it had been different than the nothingness she'd felt herself slipping to now. It wasn't a nothingness at all. It had been a stillness. A peacefulness.

While Marcus had continued to batter her body, a calm had washed over her and the pain had ebbed away. She had felt cradled. It was a sensation unfamiliar to her. Those who tended to her accidentally held her in this manner on occasion, but at that moment, she had no fear of

263

being cast aside. She felt arms around her and she felt safe for the first time in her life. She breathed easier.

Open your eyes, Little One.

The voice had come from inside her own mind, but it didn't belong to her.

She trusted it, but she knew doing as He said would cause the pain to return.

When she did open her eyes, Marcus was gone and Luther was looking in on her. He already looked panic-stricken so she tried to suppress an outward reaction to the pain raging through her body. He lifted her and held her snugly to his side, not with the same level of comfort she had felt moments earlier, but she knew she was safe.

Sometime later, Luther brought her to her dad. Days or weeks could have separated those moments, but they flowed together in her mind.

She had heard the same voice in her mind as she sat in the car seat in the back of her dad's pickup truck. She had felt the same cradled comfort.

Open your eyes, Little One.

When she had laid eyes upon the stranger who would become her dad, the feeling of comfort, of safety didn't leave. She watched as he focused intently on the road. He glanced over his shoulder and smiled lightly when he discovered her watching him. She felt peace pour through her in that moment and she didn't want there to be anything that came before.

She came to know Jesus through her dad. She believed the first time he spoke His name. She knew Jesus was the one who had held her. In the middle of the turmoil when her body was broken, He cradled her in His arms.

The nothingness around her now was not a comfort. It was not safe. It was empty. It was void of life, of love.

It's better not to feel.
It's better not to think.
It's better not to remember.
Thoughts are the enemy.

Feelings are the enemy.
Memories are the enemy.
The nothingness is peaceful.
The nothingness is safe.
Everyone is gone.
Everyone is dead.
It's only me.

She felt her body writhe with the returning pain as she fought against the nothingness trying to seize control of her mind.

They would not want me here.

Her skull simmered with pain.

Thoughts are the enemy.
Feelings are the enemy.
Memories are the enemy.
The nothingness is peaceful.
The nothingness is safe.

Marcus used their code names. He wouldn't know their names.

She heard a piercing scream at the same moment she gritted her teeth, though she didn't know if it was her own voice or an echo in her memory.

The nothingness is dangerous.
The nothingness is Hell.
It's better to feel. It is better to think.

She could feel the concrete slab beneath her back again.

It is better to remember.

She could hear the gunshots. She could feel Bree, the beautiful mammoth of a horse, falling on her, crushing her.

Bree was dead.

She remembered her body being dragged out from beneath him. She remembered hearing her dad shout from the front steps. As his body fell lifelessly to the ground, she tried to cry out, but no sound emerged from her throat.

It's better not to feel.
It's better not to think.
It's better not to remember.
Thoughts are the enemy.
Feelings are the enemy.
Memories are the enemy.
The nothingness is peaceful.
The nothingness is safe.

Her lungs contracted painfully, releasing what sounded like a strained wheeze.

It's better to feel.
It's better to remember.
He would not want this for me.

She felt warm tears fill her eyes, soaking her cheeks.

Open your eyes, Little One.

She tried to settle her breathing.

"Come on. Open your eyes again," Marcus said quietly, but urgently.

Her head felt pressurized, her skull felt like a sheet of thinning ice, threatening to splinter and split apart. She blinked slowly, her heart continuing to race.

"You need to sit up," he told her firmly.

She felt herself sit upright with some level of automation. She felt her legs flex and stretch seemingly of their own accord, her bare feet gliding over the cold floor. Her torso, her neck, even her head felt constricted and stiff. She tried stretching her shoulders without any relief.

As her breaths stretched, she felt her heartbeat settle into a rapid, but steady rhythm. She took in the sight of Marcus before her, trying to make sense of his presence.

His eyes darted toward the corridor, then he took a breath, placed his hand over her forearm, which was turned upward in her lap, over the part where her tattoo had been. "Turn left," he whispered. "Up the steps there's an open door that leads to a field. Get to the other side of that field. Do you understand?"

She nodded.

"You *run* and you don't look back." Marcus hesitated as she made eye contact with him, seeming to debate whether he should say something more. Finally, just as an explosion struck the building behind them, rumbling the concrete foundation, the walls, he patted her arm, got to his feet, and disappeared out the open door.

Essie stood, wincing as a high-pitched shriek filled her ear drums, as her legs hesitated to support her. Her bare, dirty feet gripped the floor as she moved toward the doorway. She expected it to close just as she reached it, but her eyes panned over to the control panel and found the lights dimmed.

She lifted her eyes as she crossed the threshold into the corridor, peering to the left, in the direction he'd instructed her to go. Sure enough, there was a stairwell. She'd seen it many times. Just beyond the stairwell, just one floor up, she could see daylight.

You need to run now.

23
jericho

Miles pulled off his goggles, which had allowed his eyes to adjust immediately to the low lighting of the stairwell, shook out his hair, soaked by the rain in his brief jaunt from the Armadillo. The room where Essie was being held was thirty paces from the southwest corner of the building. He had entered the entry closest to the south*east* gate of the White House, his route utilizing the underground corridors. He determined that it would offer a safer return trip, avoiding a run across the exposed grass field between buildings.

Originally, he'd thought it best that both he and Josh take on the Ark soldiers, staying in one group entering the compound, but he had preferred to better the odds of getting Essie out. Josh was more skilled at hand-to-hand combat. He was larger, bulkier. Still, Miles now second-guessed his decision to have Josh face both operatives on his own. What if they took him out first?

No. Miles had seen the determination in Josh's eyes as the White House came into view. There was nothing, absolutely nothing that was going to keep him from getting to Essie.

Gunner would step in if something happened to either one of them. He was the ace in the hole.

They were getting her out. There was no other choice in the matter. If Sadie Parker's operatives were successful in their mission, Essie was going to be no better than where she had been. Perhaps there'd be less torture, perhaps there'd be better food, but she'd be studied in a lab, locked away for the rest of her life.

The heavy door clicked closed behind him. He confirmed his entry point into his comm unit, receiving confirmation from Gunner, who was currently acting as cover, watching video feeds provided by nano drones that were tracking their movements, their progression in the mission.

Miles settled his gaze briefly on the narrow stairwell window, preparing himself to make his descent, stealing a glance at the sky.

One of the last times he saw Essie before they'd departed the Ark, she was folded on her side on the concrete floor, her body rigid. She was coated in blood; he could practically smell the rusty odor through the camera. Her breaths had escaped in strained squeaks.

She had been praying for death. Repeatedly, desperately, praying for death.

The murder of her child broke her. She had previously acquired tics from the torture, but the effect that procedure had on her state of mind was immediate and devastating.

She had released a blood-curdling scream when they dragged her into the medical chamber to perform the abortion, kicking, flailing, doing anything to keep them from strapping her to the table. She begged and pleaded–but not with anyone in the room. She pleaded to God to watch over her child, she begged Him to take away all of her child's pain and inflict it instead upon her.

It was the most chilling thing he'd ever witnessed, in the months he'd been observing her, in the length of his life, as her words rushed out and her voice turned hoarse.

The moment it had been done, she had fallen silent, an eerie stillness filling the chamber. The technician had actually paused what she was doing to check to see if Essie was conscious.

The next time her face was visible to Miles, her eyes stared off without focus, she wasn't blinking at a normal rate, and she suddenly looked very pale and weak.

The fight had left her.

This breakdown, this vulnerability and suggestibility was what the so-called "scientists" had been working toward so there was no relief, no time allotted for grief or for recovery. They immediately set to work, delighting as they at last made progress.

It had all been very real to her. He had seen it all unfold through her eyes.

But it wasn't.

Gowon had seen what he had: that Essie's single remaining purpose was to protect that child. He suspected if that was literally ripped away, she'd be a much more agreeable test subject. And if she died, they had her baby, who was everything Gowon had hoped she would be; a comparable, if not preferred replacement.

It's why Miles couldn't let Josh see her before they left.

The last memory Josh had of her, she'd been sitting in her usual place on the floor, leaning against the back wall, whispering to the baby in Italian in a doting voice that gave no indication she was afraid or that they were being held in such conditions. Josh had translated that she was trying to determine if the fluttering she felt in her abdomen was indigestion or kicks; she'd been skeptical, saying she thought it would be too soon to feel kicks. Josh had actually laughed out loud when she observed lightheartedly that it might be early, but her farts "don't feel like *that*."

He couldn't let that memory be overridden by the sight of Essie being carried to and from the medical chamber, her body limp, her stare as vacant as a wax statue.

For the entire drive to the District, Miles had visualized reaching her in that cell, taking her hand in his and telling her she was safe, that she was with them now, that she and her baby, they were *safe*. Just before they arrived, he'd had his first and last communication with the contact inside, who was trying to stir her. He'd heard her crying out in agony in the background. She'd gone quiet when Babel conveyed the message to her that he and Josh were on their way, but he wasn't sure what to make of that.

All he wanted to do was scoop her up in his arms and run for the Armadillo, get her somewhere safe and far from the borders of the District.

He didn't imagine she had the strength to even lift her head or secure a hold around him so he fully expected it to be a challenging jaunt.

It was with bewilderment then that he watched her suddenly burst out of the open southeast corridor door into the rain, running at breakneck speed across the South Lawn of the White House.

He pressed his comm transmission button. "This is Sugar. I have eyes on Songbird. Gunner, watch my six on Entry Alpha. Delta Team return to Armadillo for immediate departure. Confirm. Over." Coach and Ferris should have been disarmed by that point.

The sound of another round of explosions in the distance caused the ground to shake.

Respond, Josh. Come on.

Miles retraced his steps, climbed the short flight of stairs to the exterior door and made a hard turn toward the center lawn. He took off running, his gear bouncing against his back. The ground was muddy from the rain; he had to focus on keeping his balance as he ran. "Angler, do you copy? *Over.*" *Screw it.* "Delta Field Team, *check in.*"

Static.

Essie's legs were propelling at a faster pace. It was unfathomable how she was managing it, given the weak state of her body.

He yelled her name, pushing himself harder.

Her attention had been focused straight across the field, but her eyes shifted over to him, her face tensed in disbelief, the rain beating at her face. Her path started to deviate toward him. Her voice cracked as she screamed his name.

He desperately wanted to drop his gear, but he didn't want anything to delay reaching her. "Danny, do you have locations on Delta Field Team? Over."

Nothing.

He allowed one breath before pressing his comm button again. "Gunner, do you have a visual on Delta Field Team? Over," he yelled.

"Negative."

Just as Gunner's voice came through, something green flashed in Miles's peripheral vision. A flare? He spun his chin toward the back of the White House as the Truman Balcony and Oval Office exploded in a fiery inferno.

Essie's eyes briefly peered over her shoulder to the blast, but she continued to close the distance.

Three more strides...

Two...

One...

She collided into his chest, throwing her arms tightly around his neck, the force of the impact knocking him slightly off balance. "*Joely?*" she squeaked in a breathy gasp.

He nodded, securing his arms around her, trying to catch his breath, made more difficult by the fact that he was actively crying.

Across the lawn, in the center fountain area, he watched the hatch creak open. Josh popped out of the opening, climbing the spiral stairs from the tunnel that connected the West Wing to the east parking lot.

Miles sighed, rotating their bodies so Essie would see Josh over his shoulder--and then he felt the first jolt shake her body.

Then another.

It took until the third gunshot for him to process what was happening.

Her fingers trembled against his neck, her breaths staggered.

"Essie?" he heard himself say in a pleading tone. Her body was starting to fall limp in his arms, her pale face braced in confusion. He tightened his hold around her as she started to fall, his eyes lifting.

Josh was running for them, his face desperate and mournful, yelling something, but Miles couldn't hear him. A deafening silence had swelled around him and everything seemed to be moving forward in slow motion.

This was not how it was supposed to happen. *This can't be happening,* he insisted silently.

And then he watched as Josh was shot twice in the chest, bursts of blood filling the air as he fell in suspended animation.

Gunner appeared suddenly to Miles's right, briefly resting his hand on his arm, which was enough to snap everything to present. Gunner drew his gun and was firing toward the rooftop of the West Wing, hitting the sniper on the second shot. He continued on and dropped to the ground next to Josh. He immediately slung him over his shoulder and motioned insistently at Miles, signaling him toward the Armadillo.

Miles hoisted Essie's legs into a cradle hold, tilting her body toward his chest, and turned on the spot.

Another explosion struck the West Wing of the White House and the attached structures, including the place directly above where Essie had been held, began to crumble.

24

away

"Ark Command, Ark Command, this is Sugar, Delta Team. Over."

"Roger. Go ahead, Sugar. Over."

"We have taken heavy fire, heading toward extraction point Charlie. I repeat: Delta Team has taken heavy fire, we are heading toward extraction point Charlie. Over."

"Copy. Have you secured Phoenix? Over."

"Phoenix DNB. Over."

There was a prolonged delay. "Say again. Over."

"Phoenix—" Miles heaved a great sigh before continuing, finger still pressed on the comm button. His voice was tight, filled with suppressed emotion when he continued: "Sniper fire, multiple rounds. Over."

Josh panned his eyes over to where Miles crouched on the floorboards of the Armadillo. He didn't recognize the voice of the person on Comm.

"Report status of Delta Team, over."

"Three aboard. Coach, Ferris MIA at Phoenix extraction point. Angler KIA. Over."

Josh's vision was blurred, as though looking through muddy water. He moved to lift his head, but it felt like there was an elephant sitting on his chest.

Miles glanced over his shoulder, lifted his index finger to his mouth. His blonde curly hair was coated in rain and mud and flopped about sloppily. He had mopped his face clean recently, but hadn't been very thorough, a thick sludgy film coating his neck and ears. He waited impatiently for the delayed response. "Command, do you copy?"

"Affirmative, Sugar. Lay low at Extraction Charlie. It might be a while before we can get resources to you. Over."

"Ten-zero. Over and out." Miles dropped the receiver, moved quickly to Josh's side. "Easy does it, Rambo."

Josh furrowed his brow, made another attempt to sit up.

"Dude, you're going to be up and moving soon, but not yet."

While he couldn't lift his torso, Josh was able to raise his hands, which he found coated with dirt, blood, bits of flesh. There was too much of it. He felt the sudden need to vomit, but swallowed down the sensation along with putrid, metallic crud coating his throat.

"Miles, 3 o'clock," came Gunner's voice from the driver's seat. There was a distant series of explosions. Within a few seconds, the vehicle rumbled. "I said this earlier, but *damn*, it's getting Biblical out there."

The Armadillo was not a smooth-riding vehicle, but the excessiveness of the shaking led Josh to believe that the terrain was either extremely rocky, or the earth was shaking like an erupting volcano.

He tried to piece together the course of events.

His comm stopped functioning after a tussle with the two operatives. The plan, as it had been discussed with the team, was for the soldiers to assist Josh with making a beeline to Essie's location. They anticipated multiple guards at her holding site so it made the most sense. Miles was meant to be clearing the path along the perimeter corridor for her extraction.

The actual plan had Miles reaching Essie first since the strategically placed attacks on the White House would draw much of the security team to where the action was on the other side of the compound. Josh was tasked with immobilizing the two Ark operatives in what Miles had determined would be the safest area of the compound, the tunnel constructed like a bunker in the center of the South Lawn. There was no better place to ride out the total destruction of the White House while unconscious. Josh was then to join up with Miles for the run back to the Armadillo.

Josh had little trouble sedating Ferris, injecting him with a short-acting sedative, but Coach was prepared to put up a fight, deactivating Josh's comm earpiece during the altercation. It had just occurred to Josh that Miles had said he'd have help from the Dans in dealing with operatives when Coach's body suddenly began to spasm, as though being tased, and he dropped unconscious on the concrete floor.

Josh attached his backup comm as he took off down the corridor. When Miles's message came through ordering them back to the Armadillo, he was very near to where Essie had been held. He turned back, remembering seeing a spiral staircase roughly 30 yards back, near where he'd taken out the operatives. He was too fixated on reaching her to answer back on comm. He'd taken the stairs up to ground level, emerged from the exit, and blinked in disbelief as he took in the sight of the remaining structural walls of the White House engulfed in flames. He turned and through the rain, locked eyes with Miles, who held Essie in his arms. It was nearly beyond the realm of comprehension that she was so close.

She saw him. She'd peered over Miles's shoulder. Their eyes had met. He thought he saw her say his name.

In the next moment, she was shot several times in the back.

He had taken a stride or two toward them when he felt a strange sensation pierce his chest. Everything went dark until they reached the Armadillo. Even then, it was just flashes.

Gunner had dragged him onto the vehicle floor. Josh was close to unconscious, but his eyes had responded to the interior spotlights. He had watched Miles carry Essie inside, place her on the cot on the opposite side of the vehicle from where he was now. He had fought his body's impulse to pass out, clambered across the floor toward her, extending his hand to reach her. Everything faded to black.

Josh knew he'd been shot at least twice in the chest, but despite his inability to move and the radiating soreness in his ribcage, it didn't feel like a critical injury. His breathing was almost normal. Miles was certainly not treating him like he was injured, despite him declaring him dead on comm.

His hand flew to his uniform, and found that it, like his hands, was coated in thick blood.

"That doesn't just wash off. Stop fingerpainting with it," Miles grumbled, moving back toward him from the window.

Josh's eyes darted across the vehicle to the opposite cot, where a body was bundled snugly and tethered to the wall.

Miles followed his gaze. "Give her some time. She took *actual* bullets, unlike you."

Josh's eyes widened. He threw his right shoulder toward the center of the Armadillo, hoping to give himself enough momentum to sit up. He crashed to the floor instead, finding himself facing a bloodied pile of clothes, including what was no doubt the clothes she had been wearing. He found he lacked any of the physical strength required to get up again. He released a series of gasps as he continued to try.

"*Dude.* I know you want to get to your girl, but I already got her all cleaned up and cozy."

Josh allowed Miles to half-lift, half-drag him into a seat along the wall, closest to Essie's head. Her eyes were closed, but her mouth sat loosely ajar, her breaths steady and slow. It appeared that Miles had taken more care in wiping Essie's face, her skin pale, but clean.

Josh attempted to speak, though he found it difficult to generate words. It was like his mind had forgotten how vocal cords worked. He lifted his eyebrows pointedly toward Essie.

Miles motioned for Josh to hold on to the handle, waited for him to do so, then released his arm. "I'm sorry. We had to do it this way." He carefully traversed around the blood splatters on the floor to sit across from him.

Josh was once again startled by the amount of blood.

"You were shot with ammunition that contains a neuro-stimulant. It's designed to mimic a gunshot and attacks the nerves, incapacitates the muscles in the surrounding areas for a few hours. We used it to make the point of impact believable. People don't fake getting shot very well, apparently." He pointed toward Josh's chest. "We rigged up your camo with blood pouches, like what they use in the movies. We wanted a really gruesome show."

Josh looked at his hands.

"We used some of your blood from MET team reserves. Maybe all of it by the look of it." He winced.

Josh peered in on Essie.

"Our guy on the inside put turtle shells on her to keep the bullet wounds shallow." He saw the confusion on his friend's face. "A turtle shell is this tech invented by—not *our* Danny, but one of the Dans—it essentially creates an invisible force field. On the highest setting, it *can* actually stop bullets, but it would have shown up on heat mapping. The level he used is undetectable, but it breaks down the bullet as it makes contact with the force field. The guy who shot her was the one to put the turtle shells on her. He knew where to aim," he added, reading Josh's questioning expression.

Josh's brow furrowed.

"It needed to look like she died–or she'd always be in danger," he explained calmly.

Josh attempted to speak again, managing to get out the word "she" before he needed to stop to aggressively try to swallow.

"I've had the neuro ammo explained to me and I still don't totally get it. It's like your body temporarily thinks it's been shot and had a stroke at the same time. That's why you're having trouble talking."

Josh held up three fingers, then pointed toward Essie.

"Why was she shot three times?"

Josh nodded forcefully.

"It was four, actually. Two in the back, one in the neck, one in the back of her skull." Miles took a deep breath. "I thought it was excessive—apparently, they wanted to be sure there was enough 'evidence.' The fragments of the round that make it through the turtle shell ripped things up pretty good."

Josh narrowed his eyes.

"The wounds are rough, but they were already healing when I cleaned them. For what it's worth." Miles frowned. "The guy loaded her with a crazy amount of epinephrine before setting her loose. I set her up on fluids, some freshly defrosted super soldier blood–*hers*," he clarified, nodding pointedly toward the tubes running into the bundle, "along with anesthesia and pain meds the second we got to the Armadillo. Luther said her body would recognize that they would benefit her so they'd actually work–"

Josh nodded. *They would actually work better for her than anyone else.*

"The epinephrine speeds up the healing process and also makes the anesthesia more effective," Miles said with tentative medical authority. "However it works, she's having a *very* solid sleep right now."

Josh swallowed hard, pulled in his breath as he peered in at her again. "Why *didn't* you—" Josh stuttered, pointing at his own chest, inadvertently poking into a glob of blood.

"Why didn't I tell you?" Miles translated, resisting the urge to lecture him again.

He nodded.

"Your reaction needed to be authentic," he said with a sigh. "Apparently *mine* did, too. The plan *had been* for me to carry her out of the corridor and have you both get shot at the Armadillo." He paused. "That's a weird sentence. *Any*way, evidently Luther had a different plan figured out with the guy inside. I certainly didn't expect her to come running out like that."

Josh frowned, his voice raspy: "*Running?*"

"She was booking it across that field like some Jamaican sprinter, Bro. I couldn't believe it. If she has a need for another code name, I'm naming her Bolt." Miles took a deep breath. "I thought that was it. When things went screwy and she got shot out there? I thought that was it." He shook his head. "But she's safe. Essie is *safe.*"

Josh exhaled, allowing the relief to wash over him as he watched her sleeping, each of his hands gripped around a handle, not wanting to accidentally fall into her or do anything else to disrupt her sleep. Never mind the jarring, shaky handling of the Armadillo rattling her around.

Miles smiled distantly, his eyes a bit dazed, the reality of the situation finally sinking in. A few minutes later, Josh had to kick his boot to get his attention. He looked up, frowning.

"Why was *I* shot?" Josh asked in a forceful whisper, motioning to his chest.

Miles leaned forward over his knees. "Because this next part wouldn't work if you were alive." He patted Josh's knee. "Let's get you cleaned up and looking pretty for Essie." He stood and retrieved a towel from a side compartment, soaked it with water from his canteen clipped to the netting. "Start with the shirt. You look like *Carrie* at the prom right now."

Once Josh had managed to shed his blood-soaked shirt, Miles quickly mopped at any obvious spots on Josh's skin, carelessly dropping the shirt next to the bloodied clothes on the floor.

"I hold you in high regard, Josh, but I'm not sponge-bathing you. Do the best you can. You can do a more thorough job later."

Josh was having a significant struggle with his balance and focused on wiping the blood from his upper body from a seated position–hands, his arms, anywhere that might have contact with Essie.

He winced as he settled back into the seat, deciding his pants with their splotches of drying blood would have to do for the time being since he hadn't regained the necessary coordination to change them. Having a fresh MET t-shirt on and moderately clean arms helped. He leaned his head against the wall of the Armadillo, tilting his chin so he could look in at Esther's face in the shadows, catching his breath from the mild exertion. She had shifted more on her side while he was changing.

"It's a shock, just so you know," Miles said, furrowing his brow. "What she's gone through? I know you know a lot of it, but you don't know everything. Most people wouldn't have survived a day."

Josh glanced up.

"97 days she was in there," Miles murmured, shaking his head. He tilted his head suddenly, picking up on a low, growling noise. "Is she *snoring*?" He focused his attention for a few seconds. "No, that's something in the gears or the axle. That would have been adorable if she was snoring that loud, but it's okay. She doesn't need to worry about being adorable."

Though Josh couldn't verbalize it, based upon the parting of her lips, the angle of her neck, it was very possible Essie *was* actually snoring, but there was no way they'd be able to hear it with all the other noise in the vehicle.

"It's going to affect her. There's no way it won't," Miles said severely. "I wish we could have done this mission a long time ago."

Josh took a deep breath in.

"I have to tell you something," Miles said in a low, reluctant voice.

Josh frowned but nodded encouragingly.

Miles spent the next half-hour of the ride telling Josh about the Sim program that convinced Essie they'd performed an abortion. He told him about her struggle, how she'd fought them. He told him about the blood, the tissue, the clots they'd used to convince her it had been done. He grudgingly told him about how much Essie's appearance, her mind had deteriorated in such a short time, how she had pleaded to God for death, how she had started to surrender to the Sim, how the researchers had delighted in finally having access to her mind.

"Look, I know you can't really respond right now, but you *need* to know these things. You need to be ready to deal with whatever state her mind is in." Miles lifted his brow, insistent he get a response of some kind.

Josh nodded firmly.

"She hugged me so tight though, Bro," Miles murmured, shaking his head. "Out there on the field? *So tight.*"

"I'm hearing on comm that Gowon has been taken out," Danny announced, sliding out of the command center cubby behind the driver's seat.

"Halle-freakin-lujah," Miles muttered. "Also, *Danny*? I almost forgot you were here. Where were you on comm earlier?"

"I was busy blowing up the West Wing."

"That was you? Good work," he said, giving him a thumbs up.

"Gowon is dead?" Gunner called back. "Who do we have to thank?"

"*Holy. Shit,*" was the response from Danny.

"Language!" Miles scolded, smiling lightly across at Josh.

Josh released a suppressed chuckle. It was incredibly comforting to have Miles Kent make a joke, to see him smile. It meant he felt confident that things were going to be okay.

After a few quiet moments, Miles pressed his comm button. "Danny, if you're talking, we can't hear you. Who took out that evil effing–"

"Annette Gibbons."

Miles cleared his throat, then in a very professional, measured voice said: "I'm sorry, could you repeat that please?"

"Gibbons did it. Tomahawk to the gut."

"*Shit*, she wasn't messing around, was she?" Gunner remarked.

Miles pressed his lips together, eyes wide. "*That* was a choice."

A nervous laugh came through the radio. "She spilled his intestines. Really, *really* painful way to go."

"Wait, so she had access to a *Tomahawk*?"

"Gowon was a collector."

"That tracks, actually," Miles muttered, actively trying to block the image of the medieval looking tool with its retractable directional blades that Gowon had used on Essie. He frowned. "Wait, was Gibbons on our side the *whole time*?"

Josh couldn't take his eyes off Essie, who still appeared to be in a very deep sleep.

"Is Gibbons alive?" Gunner asked.

"She's in critical condition. Ark medics are tending to her. A Gowon guard shot her."

"I was just starting to like her," Miles pouted. "She can't be older than, what, fifty?"

Josh shook his head. "Don't," he managed to say.

"I'm *kidding*," Miles clarified. He leaned his head against the side panel. "Tomahawk to the gut," he said reflectively, wiping roughly at his face with both palms, his eyes bloodshot. He rested his palms on the top of his head, taking deep breaths. "Not enough, in my humble opinion, but I'll take it."

"Coming up on the airstrip," Gunner called from the front. "How is Luther possibly here? He's supposed to be leading the overthrow of the government."

"If I've learned anything about Luther Graham, it's that the guy can multitask," Miles remarked, sniffling.

Josh moved to stand and Miles was quickly at his side, forcing him back to his seat. "You've been *shot*. Take it easy."

"Hey, Josh?"

Josh glanced up to see Danny rotating toward him, still parked within his cubby.

"I won't be seeing you again," he said matter-of-factly. "I don't do goodbyes though. I just want to say that I hope the two of you will be safe and happy."

Miles smacked Danny on the shoulder. "You don't do goodbyes, Josh can't talk. This worked out well after all."

Josh gave him an appreciative nod. He glanced over at Essie, who he knew would have quite a bit to say.

"I know, Josh," Danny said, having followed his gaze. "You know, a lot of people can say they wouldn't be alive if not for Essie. I can *also* say that, but I'm one of a few hundred who can also say I wouldn't have been *born* if not for her."

Luther had told Josh that she was the start of all of it. If he'd never met her, he would have never even considered saving any of the other babies in the lab, not the ones intended for the experiments, or the ones bound for other labs to be used for parts; Danny being the latter.

"Tell her I love her," Danny said, then abruptly wheeled back into his cubby without saying anything more.

Miles put a guiding hand on Josh's shoulder, navigating him over the heaps of bloodied clothes to the back hatch. He clamped an arm across Josh's chest when he made a move to retreat back to Essie.

"Gunner's going to carry out your girl. You're not lifting *anything* or *anyone* right now."

The sound of a car door caused Miles to turn on the spot once they were outside. "Hey, Luther! Thought you'd be in a bunker right about now."

"Am I *not*?" he asked, fanning out his arms. "Security footage might tell a different story."

"Gotta love the Dans," Miles said, smiling lightly, motioning toward the horizon, where a wall of rain seemed to be lurking unmoving over the District, lightning strikes continuously bursting over the Atlantic Ocean. "Looks like the Big Guy decided not to sit this one out, after all?"

"Meteorites took out the New England & PJM power grids just before you got to the White House."

"You're kidding."

Luther shook his head. "Small meteorites, mind you. Ten thousand of these things reach the ground every year and don't cause any problems. These were--*precise*."

"With excellent timing."

"Gowon was activating the nuclear arsenal. Several missile sites popped up on radar that we hadn't known about."

"So the asteroids saved our lives? Boy, those 90s end of the world movies really got things wrong, didn't they?"

Luther's eyes lifted to Gunner, just emerging from the back of the Armadillo. Essie was tucked against him, her body visibly shivering despite a fleece blanket wrapped around her. It had been a normal and frequent response during her recoveries to get chills, but it was still alarming to see.

Josh took a step toward her, stumbling as his foot gave out, her name emerging in a gasp.

Miles grasped hold of him, set him up right again. "He can't fully talk yet, Luther. That's normal for the neuro-ammo, right?"

Luther frowned. "How many rounds did he take?"

"At least two?"

"That's normal," Danny chimed in through the speaker on Miles's comm unit.

"Yeah, I'm impressed you're standing, to be honest."

"I tried giving him an Essie-pen."

"Yeah, it couldn't hurt, but the neuro-ammo really just has to run its course."

Miles nudged Josh. "I came up with that. You know, like Epi-pen?"

Luther stepped toward Gunner and looked in on Essie. He kissed his fingertips, then applied them gently to her forehead, as though transferring the kiss. He turned around and shrugged. "Goodbyes have never been my strong suit. Maybe it's better this way."

"I'm noticing a trend with this group," Miles remarked, frowning. "Maybe we should unpack this a little. You, me, and Danny will get together, have lunch, chat about it. Maybe start a life group."

Josh narrowed his eyes, unable to verbalize how much Essie would hate not getting to say goodbye, though being unable to speak in full sentences, he wasn't able to ask *what* exactly was going on. He and Luther had a conversation weeks earlier about hypothetically needing to change identities and relocate, like witness protection, but it felt surreal to think that the vague plan he had alluded to was taking effect. It was surreal to think that they were going anywhere but back to the northern Ark. He glanced up at the jet sitting on the taxiway.

"Everything's been arranged. Money, living arrangements, identities," Luther said, reading his thoughts. He pressed his lips together, swallowing hard. "I can't tell you she's going to be the same after what's happened–" He glanced up to Miles who nodded slowly in agreement, scanning the back interior of the Armadillo for any items he might need to grab. "--but I can promise you she'll be safe. You both will."

"*All,*" Miles corrected, securing the back hatch and turning back toward the group. "There are three of them. They'll *all* be safe."

Luther pulled in his breath and nodded. "That's right. *All.*"

Miles wavered his hand. "Miles Luther, Luther Miles, both excellent baby names. Maybe some combination of the two? Not to tilt the scales, but Miles Luther sounds a bit more gender neutral."

Josh stepped forward and managed to lift his arms high enough to give Luther a hug. "Thank you."

Luther patted him on the back. "Take care of each other, okay, Kid?"

Josh nodded, releasing him. His eyes drifted to the plane, then floated between the three men surrounding him, finally settling longingly on Essie.

"Go ride off into the sunset, Bro," Miles remarked, putting his arm around Josh's shoulder.

"You're not coming?" Josh asked, his voice strained.

Miles shook his head, pinching one eye. "Nah, we've got a lot of work to do here, starting with some pyrotechnics to explain why your bodies are missing. Should be fun. I've always been fond of explosives."

Josh frowned.

"I guess you don't need to know the details," Miles said, eyes drifting over to Essie. "Maybe someday I'll come visit though."

Luther cleared his throat.

"You *know*," he said, patting Josh on the back. "I'm probably going to forget this conversation ever took place."

Luther perked his eyebrow at Miles, then once again stepped toward Gunner. He placed his palm over Essie's hand and closed his eyes briefly. He leaned in and kissed her directly on the forehead, whispering something next to her ear. He then patted Gunner appreciatively on the upper arm, gave a nod to Josh and immediately turned to walk toward his own vehicle. He didn't look back.

"We'll see each other again," Miles said confidently to Josh once Luther was out of earshot. "Be good to her."

Josh nodded, swallowing hard. "She'd want you to come with us."

Miles scrunched his nose. "Like I said, we'll see each other again." He took a steadying breath, then stepped abruptly forward and hugged him, squeezing him tightly. "You two are family to me. You know that, right? Her more so, but you get that."

Josh nodded again.

Miles gave him one last squeeze before letting go, stepping toward Gunner, who he offered a fist bump and a winning smile.

Gunner rolled his eyes.

Miles carefully leaned in and kissed Essie's cheek. "You're free, sweet girl," he whispered, then leaned in and said something directly beside her ear. He kissed her again. When he stood and took a step back, his eyes were filled with tears. He sniffled loudly, lifting his eyes to a watchful Gunner. "Oh, come here, you," he said, giving a helpless Gunner a dramatic smooch on the cheek. He then abruptly spun on his heel toward the driver's door, whirled his index finger in the air. "Now get your ugly mugs out of here. I have things to blow up."

*　*　　*

Gunner led the way onto the jet, efficiently getting Esther situated onto a lofty full bed tucked in a small bedroom toward the back of the plane. He laid her on her side facing the aisle, careful that she didn't put pressure on any of her wounds. He then pulled a duvet over her, kissed her delicately on the forehead. "There are lots of blankets in the drawers, a couple of extra pillows," he said, indicating the base of the bed. "Medical supplies are all along the back wall, if you need them."

He started for the cockpit, stopping at the open jetway door, where he released a sharp whistle. Within seconds, Josh could hear the familiar jingle of a collar tag, then the scuffling of paws on the airstairs. Fenway hesitated just a moment once she boarded the plane, head swiveling from the front of the plane to the back. She cautiously sniffed the plush leather recliners, the carpeted flooring. When she picked up on Essie's scent, she became very alert, tracking her through the cabin. When she found her, she leapt up on the bed, releasing a series of nervous whimpers as she nudged her nose into different points of Essie's body, making sure she was really there.

"*Easy*, girl," Josh managed to say, swallowing hard. "Where'd *she* come from?"

"Luther brought her."

Josh smiled lightly at the German Shepherd, who had finally settled, nestled longways along Essie's side. She rested her chin on Essie's hip and lifted her eyebrows.

"We'll take off in a couple minutes," Gunner said, giving a wave to someone outside before sealing the cabin door.

"Are you coming with us?"

"Well, you need a pilot."

part three

25

it is well

There were rushed breaths, her heart beating wildly in her chest. She could feel the rain on her face, on her arms. She could feel Miles holding her snugly against him.

There was pain. Sudden, biting pain. She saw Josh rushing toward them in the moment before everything blurred. There were waves of consciousness.

Miles was tending to her, speaking to her in a delicate tone. telling her that she was safe, Josh was safe. He had secured an IV line in the back of her hand, running his fingers gently, but firmly over the tape holding the line in place. She immediately felt the effects of the medication, her eyes becoming impossibly heavy. As the stretches of darkness in her vision lengthened, she felt her heart panic. She tried to force her eyes to stay open.

"No one's getting to you here, Essie," he whispered, placing his palm over her cheek. "You can sleep now."

She gazed into his eyes and felt her breaths deepening, her heartbeat beginning to steady.

It was moments perhaps before she opened her eyes, and she was looking into Loretta Graham's beautiful face. Her chestnut complexion was flawless, her cheekbones prominent even when she wasn't smiling.

Essie was lying in Luther's childhood bed and his mom was singing a gentle melody to her. Essie was mesmerized by how Lola's full lips stretched when she sang, the confidence of her movements, her words.

"Now you get some sleep, baby," Lola said, running her fingers over Essie's hair. "I'll be right here beside you."

She felt tingles slide up her neck and took a deep breath.

"Come lay down, Essie. We're about to put the movie on."

She peered over her shoulder where Josh and Gabe had just finished setting pillows and blankets on the inflatable mattress in front of the couch. She'd been disappointed when Sara had encouraged them to "settle down." As darkness had fallen across the farm that first day, she'd felt an ache in the pit of her stomach and she'd worried that her new friends would soon be taken from her, that they were temporary. Seeing Josh beckoning her to lie down beside him, she was relieved to know she wouldn't yet be separated from them and quickly tucked herself beside him, her excitement palpable.

He'd then presented her with a small, velvety elephant plush.

"What's this?"

"That's yours."

She frowned. "Mine?"

"Yeah. It was mine and now it's yours. It belongs with you. You get keep it."

She twisted her expression and popped up to her feet to show her dad her new treasure.

"Let's watch the movie," Josh coaxed, and she'd plunked back down beside him, tucking the plush under her arm.

She encouraged Gabe to move closer, then turned to Josh, nudged close to his ear and whispered: "Do I get to keep you, too?"

He furrowed his brow, then smiled.

She mirrored his expression, a warmth surrounding her that far surpassed the weight of the blanket. She took a deep breath.

The air smelled of brownies.

Essie was sitting on the floor as Sara West gently ran a brush through her hair. There was a lulling rhythm to how she did this. She started at the top, gently gliding the brush through the length of hair, her palm trailing behind. If the brush hit a snag, she was quick to remedy the situation, covering the spot that had been pulled. She'd then lovingly take the section of hair in her hand and gently comb through the tangle.

There was a soft way Sara spoke to her in these moments—her voice never lifting above a gentle whisper, complimenting her "beautiful hair," her "sweet face," reassuring her that she would do her best not to have the brush tug too much, then checking to be sure she wasn't hurting her as she worked through a tangle.

Essie closed her eyes, breathing deeply.

Her eyes had drifted closed for only a few seconds. As she blinked, her dad was smiling kindly at her in her attic bedroom at Calvary and was in the midst of singing a version of *Buona Sera* he'd adapted just for her, changing the line: "*And by the little jewelry shop we'll stop and linger While I buy a wedding ring for your finger*" to be "Next to the toy shop we'll stop to jump in a puddle Then buy a new horse plush for you to *cuddle.*" He galloped her favorite horse stuffed animal up the length of her bed and provided an enthusiastic neigh when he reached her neck, nuzzling her cheek before getting tucked in under her arm. "*In the meantime, let me tell you that I love you. Buona sera, signorina kiss me goodnight.*" As he repeated the chorus, pulling the blankets a bit higher, she was smiling ear to ear. He ran his palm over her cheek:

"Buonanotte, Esther Evin. Dormi dolce, mia bellissima ragazza. Dormi dolce."

She giggled as he attached dramatic enunciation to each syllable in Italian. A peacefulness filled the room as he turned on the sound machine to ocean sounds, clicked on the seashell nightlight, then switched off the table lamp. He ensured the covers were pulled up just right, a slight furrow in his brow, then he leaned in close and whispered the same phrase in English:

"Good night, Esther Evin. Sleep sweet, my beautiful girl. Sleep sweet."

There was weightlessness. It was just a brief moment, her exhilaration catching in her chest, and then she felt her body accelerating backward, the scene of the farmhouse whipping across her vision. The next time she'd jump. She focused on taking a breath, not allowing fear to enter her brain. *Just breathe...and jump*, she told herself. *Almost. 3...2...1...*She felt her body part from the swing, felt herself floating, and then the ground, not as soft as it looked, rushed up to meet her. The bounce sent her a bit further and then she found herself lying flat on her back, staring up at the branches of the tree. There was something less forgiving than the grass beneath her legs. She lifted her head and confirmed that she'd reached the driveway. The pain she'd felt seconds earlier dissipated, and she threw her fist in the air victoriously, hearing the boys' audible groans of defeat.

The screen door burst open. "*Esther Evin Natale*, if your dad saw you–" was all Sara had managed to say before Essie had scurried to her feet and taken off running for the pastures, watching her feet propel beneath her, Josh and Gabe close behind.

She had her eyes lowered, using her boot to scratch at her opposite leg. It was her choice. She'd agreed to sing. Slowly, she raised her eyes and took in the scene of the crowded Calvary Church, squinting through the intense spotlight. Her eyes found the back doors. She could still leave. She could still turn to her left, descend the two steps, and quickly take the perimeter aisle to the lobby. It would take just a few seconds. The moment she reached the outside, she could jog home. She wouldn't have to see anyone the rest of the day. She swallowed hard, starting to angle herself in that direction, but then, in the second row, she met Della's watchful eye. She gave Essie a light smile, a small gesture, but with it, she could feel the weight of her arms around her. There was nothing quite like the squeeze of a hug from Della. It had an almost too-tight, constricting quality at first, but in the middle, when she'd acclimated to the intensity, she found herself melting into it, inhaling the scent of wintergreen mints and a flowery perfume.

Della lifted her shoulders, sitting tall in the pew, and gave Essie an encouraging nod.

Essie took a deep breath, drew her own shoulders back, rotated forward again, and stepped toward the microphone.

There was a sudden, rushing motion, she heard her dad's muffled voice speaking the words she'd heard at other baptisms–" In the name of the Father and the Son and the Holy Spirit...", and then she had broken through the surface of the water. She released her nose, an exhilaration filling her as she swept the water from her face.

She struggled to see him through her wild hair whipping all about in the wind. Josh was chasing her, a sly smile on his face. Her heart was racing, knowing she couldn't outpace him. She turned on the spot, hoping a deviation would throw him off and slow him down, but he grabbed hold of her, wrapped his arms around her, narrating in an animated Australian accent. "Oh, she's a fighter. See the flush in her cheeks, the perspiration on her forehead? She's an *angry* little crocodile, this one. I'm not sure how long I can hold her."

She stretched her body long, trying to clamber her way out of his arms, finally turning onto her back, laughing through her breaths.

She floated weightlessly on the stream at the West's farm, her hair billowing out around her on the surface of the water–there, her mind paused, soaking in the peace of the moment, anticipating what followed–Josh appearing unexpectedly and startling her out of her wits. His face had turned beet red when he realized she'd undressed down to only a sports bra and underwear.

Time was rushing forward, the images, the sounds coming faster.

Luke bowed before her, presenting her with a bouquet of wildflowers.

She saw Renee, Thomas, the other kids at Childrens Ministry, gazing up at her, laughing, as she acted out a Bible story.

Bree thundered across an open field, Essie matching the horse's rhythm, keeping steady balance on his back, arms stretched out at her sides.

She wrapped her arms tightly around Josh's shoulders, watching the sun set over the horizon, billowy orange and purple clouds reflecting off the chilly, still surface of the lake.

Sara smiled lightly, filling Essie's arms with a warm bundle. Essie ran her fingers across the folds of the blanket, taking in the delicate features of Hannah's face.

Her dad gazed across at her with a knowing grin sitting in the rocking chairs on their front porch.

She watched as Miles intertwined their fingers and held her hand against his chest, just before he was baptized.

Everything began to slow. She found herself walking across the pastures at the West's old farm. She stepped into the field of wildflowers, where Luke would pick bouquets, running her fingertips along the tops of the stems. The breeze was gentle, lightly lifting the ends of her hair from her back. She closed her eyes, breathing in the cool, damp morning air. She turned to her right, opening her eyes, and found herself just outside the house at Calvary, the porch covered with sprawling vines and plants. The table lamp was on, casting a soft yellow glow upon the ground outside. There was a faint odor of burnt coffee grinds in the air. She turned on her heel and she was standing at the edge of the glacier lake. Bree was shaking off snow from his back, digging out patches of grass from the earth. She gave the horse a gentle pat on his side and continued on. When she lifted her chin, she was standing in the drive in front of Josh's cabin, the creek babbling over her shoulder. She took a deep breath, smelling the pine, the freshness of the chilly water, the earthiness of the chopped firewood. She made a small rotation, and she was standing at the overlook, the Wests' sprawling property to her left, the preserved lands, the animal sanctuary just before her, and to the right, the ranch, and a brilliant sunrise. She turned toward it, closing her eyes, letting the heat, the light seep into her cheeks.

As she heard the scuffle of a boot that could only belong to one person, she felt her lips curl upward.

26

a thousand miles

Esther woke with her face buried in Fenway's thick, coarse fur. She lifted her chin, examining the back of the German Shepherd tucked in close beside her. She rested her hand on Fenway's side delicately, with an edge of apprehensiveness, like she didn't quite trust what she was seeing. She seemed aware that someone was sitting in the chair across from the bed but was reluctant to raise her eyes. Her eyes panned as high as the base of the window across the aisle, which Josh had closed to keep the cabin as dark as possible.

Fenway lifted her head, contorting her body to sniff Essie's face. She gave a light lick and whimpered nervously.

"Shh, Fenway," Josh whispered.

When the Shepherd continued to whimper, slinking her body to try to position herself to have more direct access to Essie, he stood and clicked his tongue, pointing toward the floor.

Fenway gave a low grumbled complaint as she jumped off the bed, taking up position on the chair across the aisle.

Essie nestled her cheek into the pillow, her eyes drifting closed, her breaths turning heavy again.

As he claimed another blanket for her from the overhead bin, he heard a small, wavering voice just over the steady hum of the engines.

298

"Josh?" Her eyes were swollen, her silver irises muted and cloudy, but she made unwavering eye contact, blinking slowly up at him.

He sat down on the edge of the bed, facing her. He reached toward her, gently stroking her cheek, taking in the details of her face. He'd always been so used to her having a mane of wild hair framing her cheeks; he'd never realized how defined her cheekbones were, how big her eyes, how even small movements of her lips, her eyebrows dramatically changed the expression of her face.

It appeared she was once again falling asleep, but just as her eyes began to close, she startled, her breath catching in her chest. She frowned, suddenly alarmed by her confinement beneath the layers of blankets. She twisted her shoulders, trying to free her arms.

"Hold on, hold on," Josh said quickly. "I overdid it. I didn't want you to be cold."

Once her arms were loose, she clambered to sit up.

Miles had mentioned his concern about her having trouble being able to distinguish between the Sim and real life. In the Sim, of course, she had witnessed his death. Miles warned that she might have an unexpected response to seeing him.

Her breaths came out in short, frantic spurts as she pulled her legs beneath her. She had inched further away from him in the process, apparent by the light blood smears left behind on the sheets from her wounds.

"You're safe, Essie," Josh whispered, noticing he'd put up his palms, something he did with skittish animals. He scolded himself silently–and then before he could reconcile what was happening, she had pushed upward onto her knees and crashed into his chest.

He locked his arms around her, thankful some of his strength had returned in the few hours she'd been asleep.

"*Josh*," she gasped, face buried in his neck.

He nodded. He could feel her hands trembling against his neck.

She arched backward to look at him, eyes wide and disbelieving. She took a deep breath, reaching her hand toward his cheek, cautious to make contact. The moment her fingertips touched his skin was euphoric. "Do I get to keep you?" she whispered.

He smiled lightly and nodded.

Essie secured her arms around him again and released an extended sigh as he did the same.

What seemed like moments later, he could feel her breaths deepen.

He had just started to ease her back on the bed when she startled awake, suddenly clinging onto him.

"We have a long flight. You can rest," he whispered.

Essie turned her chin, taking notice of their surroundings. "Where are we going?"

Josh frowned. "I actually don't know. To tell you the truth, I don't really care."

Gunner had mentioned an 11-to-13-hour flight duration dependent on if they needed to make any stops. By his calculation, they still had 6 to 8 hours to go.

She attempted a deep breath. "I think you probably care a little," she whispered.

He shook his head. "I don't care where we end up, as long as I'm with you." He pressed his lips together, watching her chin begin to fall forward. "Come on, why don't you lay back down?"

She nodded, allowing him to help guide her back on the pillow. "Will you stay with me?" she asked in a small voice, her blinks slowing.

"I'm not going anywhere."

"I mean *here*," she said, motioning to the bed.

"If you want me to."

"Of course, I–" She stopped speaking abruptly. She had been tugging for the blankets when her hand brushed across her abdomen. Her palm rested on the firm, rounded bump, her breaths catching. She furrowed her brow. "Am I–" she began to ask, her voice cracking. Her eyes were becoming increasingly uneasy and mournful. "They took her?" she whispered, her lip starting to quiver. "They took her?"

He shook his head. "*No.* She's safe."

Essie released a huff of air, expression freezing. "She's here?" she asked, motioning to her abdomen.

He nodded.

She frowned. "That wasn't real."

"No."

"I watched you die," she said in a strained voice, eyes studying the features of his face with some apprehension now.

He nodded and shook his head in close succession.

"I watched everyone die."

He wanted to reassure her that most was the Sim, but it didn't feel like much of a consolation, given the exceptions.

"My dad," she said, reading his thoughts, her voice thick. "That was real."

He gave a small nod.

"I'm so sorry, Essie," he said softly, knowing there was nothing he could say to lessen her grief.

It wasn't enough. It wasn't close to enough.

She squeezed her eyes shut, tears streaming down her cheeks. She took a steadying breath. "You're here," she whispered.

"Yes."

She nodded slowly. "And she's here," she said, guiding his hand to rest over her stomach.

"She is."

She nodded again, seeming to be getting her bearings. She furrowed her brow, a thought bringing a look of fear in her eyes. "It felt so real," she whispered, her voice breaking.

Josh wrapped his arms around her, exhaling deeply. "You're both safe now, Essie. You don't need to worry anymore."

Miles had described the Sim session in what he had suspected was "sparing detail," but he alluded to it being a gruesome scene meant to convince Essie that they had killed the baby because she didn't have her same genetic traits.

Miles had taken a moment to compose himself before continuing on to tell him that none of it was true. They never intended to kill the baby.

As it turned out, the baby had the same cellular structure, the same prominence of pluripotent stem cells. They had considered transferring the baby to an artificial womb, but decided it was too risky. The reason for the theatrics, the reason they wanted Essie to believe her baby was dead, was because they knew, like Miles knew, like he knew, that it would break her. The baby was the last person she was staying strong for–and as Luther had observed: Essie was more adept at summoning mental strength for other people than for herself. It was how she was able to silence her body's impulse to scream in agony when she endured the antidote runs; it was the reason she had a natural instinct to throw herself literally on a grenade (or sarin gas canister); it was how she was able to rescue Gabe.

He nuzzled in next to her ear. "Would you like to see her?"

She moved slightly away, her eyes very round. She nodded enthusiastically.

The baby's heartbeat echoed through the speaker on the device the moment Josh placed the portable ultrasound wand on Essie's stomach.

"*There* she is," he remarked with a small smile, rotating the screen so Essie could see more easily.

She watched the baby for some time before speaking, her eyes captivated, her chest rising and falling heavily.

"I did get to take a look earlier. I hope you don't mind."

She furrowed her brow, her eyes filled with tears, and gave a shake of her head. Her cheeks pinched upward. "She's just chilling in her hammock there, isn't she?" she said, her voice dry and raspy.

Josh froze the image on the screen and disconnected the wand. "I'm gonna get you some water."

Essie eagerly took the device.

He pulled the bottom of the wrap nightgown across her midsection and secured the tie, then tugged the covers higher over her waist. He kissed her forehead before moving to the storage cabinets along the back of plane that were stocked with emergency medical supplies, some food and drinks. He found a mug and filled it with chilled water from the small refrigerator.

302

When he returned to her side, she still had the ultrasound device braced in her trembling hands. With her arms turned upward, he could clearly see the large, blotchy patch of skin where her intricate cross tattoo had been—the farm's tree swing, the wildflowers, the stack of books topped off with a sketch of her dad's leather-bound Bible, Bree—all burned away.

"She *is* a she, right?" she asked. When he didn't respond, she glanced up, eyes glossy. "In my mind, I just thought of her as a girl."

He gave a light smile. "I did, too. When I first found out? And she is."

Essie continued to gaze at the still image. "Josh, I know she isn't—" she began to say in a small voice, then stopped, shaking her head.

"Isn't what?" he asked, retrieving the tissue box from across the aisle.

"She's not *biologically–*"

Josh sat beside her. "Essie, look at me."

She lifted her gaze, her lips pulling upward, her eyes brightening upon seeing him. "*Hi,*" she said breathily.

"Hi," he echoed. "I want you to know—I love her already." He lifted his eyebrows. "The little player to be named later?" he added, brushing his hand over her stomach. "I love her already."

She set the portable ultrasound aside, placed her hand over his, her pale, slender fingers a sharp contrast to his tan complexion.

Miles had some trepidation when he'd told him about the baby, about the process the "scientists" had taken.

"Luther told you that they used in vitro?" Miles had asked rhetorically, sitting in the surveillance room, tapping his pen nervously.

"Yeah. He said they wanted to do an egg retrieval to see if Essie's traits are hereditary."

Miles stopped tapping the pen, dropped it on the desk. "The egg retrieval wasn't to create *offspring*."

"Then why would they–"

"I mean, *yes*, they wanted to use her eggs, but since *that* didn't work–" He took a deep breath, shook his head. "I didn't know it, but

303

cloning is a really simple process, scientifically speaking. They didn't even actually need *her* eggs."

Josh frowned. "Wait, the baby is Essie's *clone*?"

Miles held up his hand. "Let me get there. So, cloning involves taking an egg–it doesn't matter from who, as it turns out, because the DNA is wiped. It's basically a blank canvas. DNA cells are taken from anywhere on the donor. The DNA is then *infused* into the egg through some 'scientific' slash 'medical' sorcery and then they somehow convince the egg that it's fertilized."

"So, the baby is Essie's clone."

Miles held up his hand again. "They tried this multiple times using artificial wombs–to grow a clone of Essie." He shook his head. "It didn't work. They were able to get the 'fertilized' eggs to the next stage, to start to implant, but then the eggs, like, self-destructed. I think they sensed a threat? Like it sensed that the artificial womb wasn't where it should be, which *sounds*–" He couldn't seem to find an appropriate adjective. "--but that's what happened. It didn't work."

Josh swallowed hard, nodded. "*Okay.*"

"It only worked when they implanted the egg *in* Essie. Because her DNA's the same? *Maybe*?"

So, the baby is Essie's clone, Josh repeated silently.

Miles shook his head as though he'd said the phrase out loud. "Her cells are pluralpotent, right?"

Josh winced at the mispronunciation but didn't correct him. "Yes."

"With the antidote, her cells were influential in whoever the antidote was injected into. Their cells would learn from her cells."

"Right."

"Okay, well in this case, her body's cells *rewrote* the baby's DNA. The genome or sequence or whatever? It made it unique."

"So, the baby *isn't* Essie's clone."

Miles wavered his hand. "She *was*, but now she's not. Based upon how Essie's cells work, they probably would have made improvements, right?"

Josh sat more upright at this suggestion.

"Yes, I *know*, Essie is perfect, but think of it like making the baby stronger physiologically, right? Parents and children typically have a 50% match for DNA, right?"

Josh nodded.

"When they did a comparison of the genome sequencing between Essie and the baby? There was an 80% match."

"So, you're telling me that the baby is 80% Essie, 20% Essie-influenced–"

"Upgrades?" Miles offered.

Josh released a breath. "That's–*incredible*."

"Right? And hey, at least you know there isn't some other guy's DNA in the mix."

Josh narrowed his eyes.

"I mean, that would help *me* to know that." Miles shrugged, relaxing in his chair, relieved to have gotten through the conversation. "It's *Essie's* baby. No one else's. I mean, yours, too, presuming all the happily ever after stuff comes to be. But at least it's not like *half* some other dude's kid?"

"Miles?"

"Yes."

"Stop talking."

Miles nodded, pressing his lips together.

"But thank you for telling me."

"Josh?" Essie said, clearly not for the first time.

He shook away the thought, looking up. "Sorry."

"Are you okay?" she whispered.

He took a deep breath, then kissed her forehead, her nose, her chin, the ticklish spot near her ear. "Yes."

She gave a tight smile, eyes creasing.

He offered a trade of the water cup for the ultrasound, reassuring her they could check in on the baby later.

Her breaths echoed in the cup as she sipped, her eyes beginning to blink slower.

Josh took the cup just as her chin started to drop. He placed it on the table across the aisle.

Essie sank back into the mattress, burrowing her head into the pillow. She gave a small smile as he joined her under the covers, struggling to keep her eyes open. "I'm sorry, I smell," she whispered.

He shook his head, scooting closer to her. "I don't care. Get over here."

She stretched herself across his chest, releasing a deep sigh as he wrapped his arms around her, and her body relaxed against him.

"Is this okay? I don't want to hurt you," he said, hesitating suddenly, loosening his hold.

Her body startled from sleep at the easing of his embrace. "Please don't let go."

He shook his head, tightening his arms again.

With a jingle of her collar, Fenway leapt up to the foot of the bed. She carefully positioned herself against the back of Essie's legs, resting her muzzle on Essie's hip, eyeing Josh nervously.

"She's safe, Fenway. Your human is safe."

*   *   *

Essie slept the remainder of the flight, not even affected a couple hours later when Josh had to slink off the bed to use the bathroom. Since he was already up, he took the opportunity to connect an IV line to deliver fluids and another transfusion of her stored blood to help her body recover. She only stirred once they'd landed.

Gunner emerged from the cockpit and opened the cabin door. The dry, brisk cabin air was swallowed by warm humidity. This sparked the interest of Fenway, who was quite desperate to pee. The Shepherd gingerly eased herself out of Essie's hold, having stolen Josh's spot when he got up earlier, and sprinted to the door.

Esther blinked heavily, staring across the aisle toward the window, the shade now open. The taxiway and small, single terminal building were illuminated by torches and appeared to be surrounded by palm trees and tropical foliage.

Gunner patted Josh on the back, smiling down at her. "Hey, Pretty Girl."

She slowly raised her eyes. Her lips tightened, but her eyes flitted nervously around the cabin.

"If it's not the campfire elder," she whispered, smiling weakly, making a substantial effort not to cry.

Josh's heart sank as he realized her eyes had been searching for Miles.

"I didn't want to make an overhead announcement if you were sleeping but let me be the first to welcome you to Hawaii, where the current time is 8:14pm, current temperature, 71 degrees."

"We're in Hawaii?" she asked, lifting her head, short golden-brown hair poking out messily in all directions.

"*Aloha*," he replied, bending down and kissing her forehead.

Essie smiled lightly as her eyes began to drift closed again.

27

release

When they arrived the evening prior, Josh had paid little attention to the house where they were staying. He had carried Essie in from the Jeep, his strength having returned enough for him to be confident in doing so. He only briefly noticed the intricacy of the carved wood front door, the fresh tropical bouquet on the counter in the high-end kitchen, thinking only of finding the bedroom to allow Essie to get more rest. It was so dark outside that the windows showed only their reflections as he carried her through the kitchen and living room and into the bedroom, located in the far corner of the house.

She needed to stop at the bathroom briefly, insisting she navigate the space on her own, but didn't put up a fight when he scooped her up for the short distance to the bed, immediately tucking herself against him.

It took mere moments to fall asleep after they'd settled under the covers, firmly embraced in each other's arms.

* * *

When Essie woke the next morning to a soft western sky, she found herself nestled into Josh's stomach, her cheek resting on his chest, her arms stretched across him.

She furrowed her brow, her ear picking up on a sound she'd never heard in person before, rhythmic and soothing. She lifted her head, peering across the room, and listened.

The bedroom had a double set of French doors that led to what appeared to be a wrap-around porch as there was an additional exterior door on the outer wall. Beyond the porch was a wide stretch of cream-colored beach and a vast ocean.

This is real. This would not be in my head. "This is real."

Josh startled awake, reaching for her. "Are you okay?"

"There's an ocean out there," she whispered.

He glanced briefly over to the doors, his face visibly relaxed once he processed the setting, once he'd taken in the sight of her, once he'd rested his palm on her cheek.

She closed her eyes, leaning into his hand. It was just as her mind began to drift into darkness that her body suddenly jolted, as though she had been falling. She pulled in her breath, her body stiff, her eyes wide.

"Hey," he whispered, tightening his arms around her. "You're safe."

She struggled to steady her breathing, once again in a state of disbelief about what she was seeing. She noticed her hand had a stranglehold on his shirt and slowly released her grip, frowning. *This is real*, she said silently, flattening her palm, running her fingers across his chest.

It wasn't the nothingness.

She wasn't in her cell anymore.

She was with Josh. She focused on the details of his face, placing her thumb on his stubbled chin. He looked different than the last time she'd seen him, fresh worry lines in his forehead and between his eyebrows, his bone structure appearing more narrowed. *If this was the Sim, he'd look the same*, she told herself. *This is real*. She slowed her breaths, continuing to study his face, using her fingertips to try to lightly smudge the stress lines away. "We're in Hawaii, Josh," she said in wonder.

Josh nodded, peering toward the windows. "Yeah, we are."

"I always wanted to see the ocean," she murmured. "Run wildly into the waves? I feel like that's probably a requirement the first time you visit the ocean?" Her tone was playful, pushing through her sadness and all the other emotions she was sorting through.

He allowed the silence to swell, then as her thoughts seemed to be receding back to her current surroundings, he spoke her name. "Are you feeling up for a swim?" he asked, raising his eyebrow. The suggestion seemed to catch her off-guard, which resulted in a familiar twist of her expression.

She pressed her lips together, falling short of a smile, her eyes becoming distant as she gazed toward the doors. "We should," she decided, turning on her back with a slight wince. She pushed herself upright and rotated her body so her legs dangled over the edge of the opposite side of bed. She flexed her feet, stretched her legs and ankles.

There were splotches of blood on the back of the nightgown Miles had put on her in the Armadillo, mixed with what appeared to be some sort of ointment, likely where she had been shot. Through the thin, jersey material, Josh could see every protrusion of every vertebrae in her spine, every rib. The gown was wrapped across the front, but it appeared the ties had come undone during the night and twisted around her back, the fabric tugging to one side. Through the split, he could see several vague surgical scars across her spine, as well as dozens of what appeared to be hastily healed whip marks, things Miles probably meant when he insisted that Josh "didn't know everything" she'd been through.

There was a patch of new skin on the back of her head, only visible because her hair was still growing in, the healing skin displacing her hair, like a stubborn cowlick.

He suddenly recalled how Miles had remarked about her taking "real bullets," unlike him. *Two in the back, one in the neck, one in the skull.* Four real bullets aimed to chip off bits of flesh, skull, spine, and he had pressured her to go for a swim in the ocean. "Essie, let's go out there some other time," he suggested. "I wasn't thinking."

"No, I like the idea," she said quietly. She stood carefully, stretching her back, running her palm over her abdomen, loosely securing the nightgown ties.

Josh stood and moved quickly to open the French doors for her.

They both released an audible gasp as they took in the scenery outside, the picturesque bay outlined by vibrant ridged mountains, the abundance of tropical foliage that surrounded the house, the crescent shaped, wide stretch of cream-colored sand.

Essie crossed the porch taking soft steps, as though fearful she might wake someone, briefly glancing in his direction before continuing to the wooden side steps that led to an expansive field of grass. She pulled in her breath as the sensation of the cool, wet ground embraced her bare feet. She closed her eyes and took slow, focused breaths, tilting her head back, chin angled toward the sky.

He descended the stairs quietly and stood beside her, scanning their surroundings for signs of threats, in the event they'd been tracked. A hundred yards or so down the beach, a couple had laid out towels, getting an early start on their day. Further down, a man was jogging with his dog. Otherwise, a quiet stretch of beach. No perceptible threats.

That would be an adjustment–the paranoia. The worry. He couldn't spend their life together looking over his shoulder. She deserved better.

"The 'run wildly' part seems essential?" she asked rhetorically, raising an eyebrow, somehow managing playfulness less than 24 hours out of a torture chamber where she'd spent nearly 100 days. The vibrancy had returned to her eyes.

"Essie, we don't have to–I was just–"

She frowned at him. "Just because we don't *have to* do something doesn't mean we shouldn't." She flashed him a smile before taking off for the waves. She was doing her best to hold down the gown, but the back hem continuously flipped around in the breeze. Despite the emaciated appearance of her body, the scars, reminding him of what she had faced for the past few months, he found his mouth pulling upward into a smile watching her, hearing her squeal with laughter, trying and failing to keep the hem secured around her. She finally gave up on modesty and took off toward the water, the gown flapping around and giving him peekaboo flashes of her narrowed, bare backside. She released a censored expletive in shock as she responded to the temperature of the water, but pressed on

311

until she was waist deep. She peered over her shoulder, smiling as he approached the shoreline. "You're never going to catch me *like that*!"

She turned toward the open water and dove into an approaching wave. When she surfaced again, she flipped onto her back, floating atop the calm water, taking in the pastel morning sky overhead.

After taking several focused breaths, she peered out the corner of her eye and released a low giggle when she saw he was in close pursuit, having just disappeared underwater. She dropped her feet back into the water to wait for him.

He resurfaced just before her, sweeping the water off his face with his palm as he took in the sight of her. "'Crikey, she's a *beauty*,'" he said in a thick Australian accent, smiling broadly, the saltwater beading on his face.

Esther bounced off the sandy bottom toward him.

"In *all* my days, I have never–" he continued, but was cut short when she crashed into him, wrapping all four limbs around him firmly.

They indulged in the act of simply holding one another for several moments, but Josh could feel her jaw chattering against his cheek.

"We can come back out here when the sun is warmer," he suggested.

She nodded into his shoulder.

He secured his arms around her, starting for the shoreline.

"Josh?" There was desperation in her tone.

He froze. "What is it?"

"I'm a little naked."

It occurred to him at that moment that his hands had been embracing her bare skin and not the jersey fabric of the nightgown.

He dropped back into the water, amused by her choice of words. "Are there levels of naked?"

He could feel her smile against his cheek. "If there are, I'm top-level naked."

"*Okay.*"

"It came off in the water." Her breath was catching in her chest as her body attempted to warm itself.

He kissed the side of her head, thankful the waves were gentle. "I think I saw some towels on the porch. Are you okay to stay out here for a second while I go get them?" He regretted the suggestion immediately, but other than carrying her sans clothes, there wasn't really another option besides giving her his sopping wet t-shirt.

"Yeah," she breathed, sounding confident. She released her hold on him and crouched in the shallow water. "Hurry," she added with a smile, though her bottom lip was quivering and actively turning a vague shade of blue.

Josh jogged up the bank of sand to the house, continuously checking over his shoulder to make sure she hadn't—disappeared? Drowned? Been kidnapped? Been eaten by a shark?

Yes, it would definitely take some acclimation to rid himself of the paranoia.

He returned carrying two oversized plush towels. He dropped one in the stretch of sand that seemed safe from the tide, then carried the other out to her, wrapping it around her shoulders as she stood. He rubbed her arms briskly, trying to generate kinetic heat, but her jaw still chattered.

They moved toward the dry beach, where he retrieved the second towel, wrapped it around her waist. "Hold it there, okay? I apologize in advance for the indignity of what I'm about to do."

"Wait, *what*?"

He immediately grabbed her around the upper legs and hoisted her up over his shoulder, started moving quickly toward the house. The sound of her giggling his name in his ear was the sweetest sound he'd ever heard.

She released a startled hoot when a gust of wind blew up the towel as he rounded the side of the house to the porch steps, followed by continued giggling and a tightening of her arms around his neck. "What are you *doing*?"

"Getting you to warmth, m'lady!"

28

thank God i do

A bemused Gunner was standing on the back porch with an anxious, whimpering Fenway when Josh and Essie returned to the beach cottage. He frowned questioningly, glancing back and forth between them. "I didn't think the two of you would be up and out already."

Essie greeted him helplessly from over Josh's shoulder, her arms secured under the towel like a strait jacket.

Josh whirled around on the spot so she could see their friend face to face.

"Hi, Essie," he murmured affectionately.

She released a tight giggle as Josh adjusted the towel around her, accidentally tickling her thigh. "Good morning, Gunner."

"My name is Wyatt now, actually."

"Pardon?" Essie asked, her voice sounding strained from her positioning.

Josh eased her to her feet, being sure she was covered by the towels, wishing he'd picked her up more delicately.

"We have new names here."

Essie frowned briefly, her expression breaking into an enthusiastic smile when she met Fenway's watchful gaze. She clicked her tongue and the dog bolted forward, nudging her head repeatedly into Essie's leg.

Josh put his arm around Essie's waist to steady her as she freed one arm. He was irritated by the fact that Gunner had immediately confronted her with this information.

"Did you choose 'Wyatt'?" Essie asked conversationally, scratching Fenway behind the ears. Her voice was still tight from the chilly water, from her continued shivering.

"I did."

She stood upright. "*Well*. Good morning, *Wyatt*."

His cheeks tightened. "I missed that smile."

She shuffled forward, hooking her free arm around his neck, keeping a firm hold on the towel with her opposite hand. "What's your last name?" she asked as they parted.

"Mitchell. I didn't get to pick that."

"Wyatt Mitchell." She considered it. "I like it."

"Thank you, Isabel Nolan."

Josh's chin snapped upward to see her reaction.

"I'm *Isabel* now?"

Gunner nodded. "You *are*. And you appear to have already met Ben Nolan?"

Essie's eyes panned over to Josh. "*Benji*," she said dotingly, then her expression stiffened. "Wait, he's a Nolan, too? Are we married?"

"Licensed, notarized, and witnessed. It was a beautiful ceremony."

Essie pulled up the hem of the towel to wipe at her ear, her face maintaining an indiscernible severity.

"I didn't mean to interrupt the newlyweds," Gunner remarked, lifting his eyebrow toward the beach and back. "I actually wanted to see about getting breakfast. Probably stick to basics–nothing too rich. No competitive eating," he added pointedly, but eyed her exposed collarbone.

She looked uneasy but shook her head. "I just need some clothes."

"I left a duffel with some clothes outside the bedroom door last night. You'll have a lot more options at your new place."

Josh frowned. "*This* isn't the new place?"

"This is an option, but it's only one bedroom plus the loft. It didn't seem like a great fit for the long term–" he began to say, motioning toward Essie's stomach, briefly distracted by the immodest split in the towel. He diverted his attention to Josh. "I just brought you guys here because the other place has stairs to get to the bedrooms. We can check it out after breakfast if you want?"

Essie smiled politely, her gaze distant.

"I'll go wait up front," Gunner offered.

They watched Gunner disappear around the corner of the porch, Fenway hesitating momentarily before following.

"So, *Mrs.* Nolan–"

Her expression deteriorated in an instant. "Don't say that," she said tightly, moving to go inside.

His heart sank. "Essie?"

She shook her head repeatedly, quickening her pace to the bathroom, which revealed a subtle limp in her gait he hadn't noticed before. "I don't think I should go to breakfast today, Josh."

"*Ess.*"

The door closed firmly behind her. A few moments later, Josh could hear the cladder of water in the shower. He peered up at the woodwork on the vaulted ceiling, taking a steadying breath.

It had been too soon, trying to immediately revert to their normal behavior. With what she had gone through? *Selfish bastard*, he scolded silently, shaking his head.

He stared regretfully toward the bathroom door.

*   *   *

Thirteen minutes had passed since the shower turned off, according to the clock on the nightstand. The only sounds to emerge from the bathroom had been delayed trickles from the showerhead.

Josh sat rigidly on the bench at the end of the bed, staring across at the rattan dresser, where he'd curated some outfit options for Essie from the offerings in the duffel. He wasn't sure who had pulled together the clothing, but it wasn't anyone familiar with Essie's typical attire.

His breath was heavy in his chest as he thought about what he should do.

He had considered checking to see if the bathroom door was locked, but he wasn't sure how wise it would be. If it was locked, she'd surely hear him, the lock indicative of the fact that she wanted to be left alone. If it wasn't locked, it might be too imposing of him to just walk in.

It was jarring to go from her playfulness on the beach, even just out on the porch, to this. He knew she was actively suppressing dealing with all the emotions that had piled up for her over the past three plus months, the trauma, the grief; he didn't think confronting her with it all was something he should do. A day of reprieve from feeling so much seemed perfectly reasonable. Merciful.

Selfish, probably.

It was just so much that she was having to come to terms with. He knew that. He had known that since Luther had finally committed to the rescue plan. Josh still didn't know all of what she'd gone through, but he had seen her scars. He knew the reason Miles and Luther had used sparing detail was because they worried he wouldn't be able to handle knowing.

And yet, he'd been content to completely disregard it.

He took another steadying breath, looked up at the bathroom door and stood.

He knocked lightly and slowly pushed the door open.

She was sitting on the tiled shower floor, legs pulled to her chest, arms wrapped around her knees, back close to the wall. Her face was pressed into her narrow kneecaps, and she was staring blankly toward the space in front of her. It was the same way she had been sitting in her cell the first time he saw her on surveillance. The same way she sat the majority of the time when she had been left in her cell. The only difference was she had a towel wrapped around her now.

She gave no indication she heard him come in, continuing to subtly rock her body forward and back.

Josh reached for another towel off the shelf, approached the shower cautiously.

317

Her eyes didn't lift when he stepped inside, and she didn't flinch when he settled the second towel around her shoulders.

He wanted to crouch next to her and wrap her in his arms, but he worried it might be too much right now; it might startle her.

Instead, he sat across from her, carefully positioning his back along the opposite wall, his legs stretched out beside hers, and waited.

She did not shift her eyes. In fact, there had been no discernible change in her at all. She blinked infrequently, but she did blink, if only out of physiological need. Her short hair was damp and looked significantly darker than her natural golden-brown color. It appeared tousled, like she'd attempted to towel dry it at some point. Her limbs had all narrowed, her knees, elbows, knuckles, shoulders sharpened. Before she was taken, she'd had a significant amount of muscle from ranch work and from rejoining the mixed martial arts club at the gym, but it had all atrophied. There just wasn't much to her. It was startling to see.

He regretted playing so roughly, lifting her over his shoulder. It probably hurt, though she would never say so.

Her face lacked any healthy pigmentation, and her cheekbones were far more pronounced than they ever had been before, her eyes, her cheeks sunken.

He hadn't noticed these details before—how gaunt she had become, how emaciated, though now he wondered how it was possible for him not to. He regretted not getting even a small amount of food in her stomach during the flight. There had been broth, bread, microwavable rice in that storage cabinet. It would have been better for her to get something in her system.

He anticipated she might have a sudden and startling stirring from her trance-like state, but it was mercifully a more subtle awakening. First, her eyes lowered from their fixed point, which had just been beside his left ear. Next, her body stopped rocking. She began to blink at a more natural rate, her chin lifting from her knees. She fixed her eyes upon him, her bottom lip shaking. "I'm sorry," she whispered, furrowing her brow.

He took a deep breath, shook his head. "You don't need to apologize for anything."

She twisted her expression as the stream of tears thickened. "Yes, I do. I basically abandoned you out there on the porch."

It was utterly preposterous what she was faulting herself for after all she'd been through. He pulled his legs toward himself and rolled up onto his knees, scooting toward her. "I didn't want to overwhelm you when I came in. Is it okay if I move closer?"

Essie pinched her face. "I know I'm a mess right now, but *please* don't walk on eggshells with me."

Josh frowned. "Ess, I just don't want to–"

"I'm not a spooked *animal*, Josh. Have you *ever* hesitated to hold me when I'm upset?" she asked tightly, seeming to surprise herself with the level of anger in her voice.

"Well, there was that time you kicked me out of your socialist apartment." He immediately regretted saying it.

Her eyes widened. Being that her eyes and the top of her cheeks were the main facial features visible to him, he could only assume her reaction was poor.

She frowned. "I meant the question to be rhetorical, but I'm *sort of* relieved you feel like you can make a jab?" She gave a weak, confused smile.

"No. I'm an idiot, I'm sorry. It just flew out of my mouth. I thought it would be funny for some reason."

"You're only an idiot because you're still not holding me," she muttered, her voice cracking.

He immediately moved closer, wrapped his arms around her.

"I was really scary at the apartment," she murmured after a few quiet moments, her voice muffled into his shoulder.

"You were upset and I hadn't been there for you like I should have."

She took an exasperated breath.

"And also, kind of scary."

She chuckled airily. "That's better."

*　　　*　　　*

319

Essie ended up falling asleep sitting on the shower floor, which shouldn't have been surprising given her sleeping accommodation over the past few months, but Josh knew he wouldn't allow it if he could help it. Keeping her body upright, he managed to stand, then used poor form to lift her off the floor and carry her back to bed. There, he struggled to untuck the covers, as he'd made the bed while she was showering, his tense state apparently translating into tightly wrapped bed covers. As he carefully leaned down to lay her across the fitted sheet, he felt her body lock itself around him.

"Josh?" she whispered, her cheek nuzzled against his.

He leaned back just enough so he could look in her silver eyes, suddenly looking much more alert. She blinked slowly, looking back and forth between his eyes.

"Essie, will you be my wife?"

Her eyebrows lifted in surprise and her lips twitched upward. "I thought you'd never ask."

29

daughter

When Essie emerged from the bedroom the following morning, she was wearing a pair of baggy gray cargo pants that appeared to be struggling to maintain their hold on her hips, a white slim fit surf t-shirt, tight enough to show her protruding baby bump, and a pair of flip flops.

"I'm confused by the clothing options," she said, running her fingers through her short hair.

"We'll have to adapt to island wear, I guess."

"I'm not sure that's what *this* is," she chuckled. "I need a belt. I'm not used to showing so much belly."

"It's a very cute belly though," he said dotingly.

She ran her palm along the protruding bump. "I can't take full credit for that."

"Well, you both are very, very cute."

Essie grinned. They'd taken another look with the ultrasound the previous evening after consuming their second food delivery of the day from Gunner. Dinner consisted mainly of meat, rice, and something called macaroni salad, Essie's new favorite food.

The baby had been curled up into a cannonball pose, sucking on her thumb, her foot occasionally tapping impatiently. Josh tentatively decided on the nickname "Mini-E" for the baby until they could give it more consideration.

Josh glanced down at Essie's stomach playing peekaboo under the t-shirt as she stretched, smiling at her. "Gunner said there's a lot of really amazing food in town, get you some curves to go with that bump."

She pressed her lips together, taking in Josh's appearance. He had selected a pair of khaki shorts, a button-down shirt with a subtle palm leaf pattern, and a pair of leather sandals. It was about as far from his usual outfit as he could get.

"What?"

"I was just thinking," she said in a playful tone.

"*Yes*?" he said, eager to resume their familiar banter. The previous day's events, the influx of real food into her system had seemed to stabilize things for her. She had been a more subdued version of her normal self for the past 24 hours. They'd spent a good portion of the day lying on the lounge chair on the porch, gazing out at the ocean, the afternoon rainstorm, the sunset. She'd slept a lot, attributing much of her sleepiness to the food.

Her expression, which had appeared lighthearted, even flirtatious seconds earlier, suddenly and inexplicably began to deteriorate before his eyes.

His shoulders sank. "Essie. Talk to me," he said, stepping toward her quickly.

She frowned, her body extremely tense. "I was *so* happy just then–I was going to say something about—" She motioned loosely toward his outfit. "I was *so* happy—and then–"

"*Hey*, it's *okay*."

Her eyebrows pulled together. "I was going to say something about your outfit being 'quite the look for you, Josh West,' but then it hit me that that's not even your name anymore. I was just thinking, and yes, it just now occurred to me, that you literally gave up *everything* for me–that your parents are back at the Ark with Hannah, Gabe–that you won't get to see them–" She was speaking rapidly, voice squeaky and hoarse, her gestures turning rigid and wild, her face braced in pain. "And it just occurred to me that I'll never see my dad–" She paused, wiping roughly at her eyes. "My dad won't ever walk me down the aisle, he won't—he

322

won't get to meet—" She drew her hand to her mouth, her frantic eyes brimming with tears.

"I know."

"She won't know him," she said desperately, her voice breaking.

Josh knew what he was about to say would inflict more pain, but he knew it was important he say it; she needed to hear him acknowledge the depth of the loss. "He was the best dad; I can only imagine him as a grandpa."

She nodded, face pinching as tears continued to stream down her cheeks.

"She'll know him through us, through the stories we tell her about him."

"I know," she said, nodding and shaking her head in alternating gestures.

"It's not good enough though."

Her chin lifted.

"It makes me so sad and so angry that she won't have him in her life. That you don't have him. I *hate* that he's gone." His voice was becoming tight and rigid. "I know he's in Heaven, but I want him *here*."

She swallowed hard. "I'm so sad," she managed to say, her voice a whisper, her bottom jaw quivering. "My heart is really happy to be here with you, but at the same time, it hurts *so* much. I've known for months, but—I couldn't—I haven't had a chance—I'm *so sad*."

Josh wrapped his arms around her, her back shaking as she released the sobs she'd been trying to hold in.

After a few minutes, her shoulders had begun to ease, but she couldn't seem to steady the rapid beat of her heart.

Josh took a few deep breaths, recognizing how she, probably subconsciously, might be influenced by his breathing patterns and he wasn't taking very solid breaths himself.

"I'm also really scared that this isn't real, that this is all in my head and I'm going to come out of this and you'll be gone, or—"

"They're going to twist this into some sort of nightmare in the Sim," he thought angrily.

323

She frowned, glancing up. "Yeah," she replied hesitantly.

It took him a moment to realize that he'd said his thoughts out loud, then another to resolve that he shouldn't use a filter with her. With all she'd faced, it seemed patronizing to think she couldn't handle hearing things about what she'd actually experienced.

He gathered her hand in his and placed it against his chest. "Do you feel that?"

She frowned. "Not really, my hands are really shaky."

He lifted her hand and kissed her trembling fingers before stepping forward and wrapping his arms around her again. "Do you feel this?"

She released a long exhale. "Yeah."

"I'm here."

She nodded. "Do this more," she directed, her voice muffled into his chest. "If you could do this nearly constantly, it would be very, very helpful."

He applied gentle compression and he was rewarded with the sound of a breathy sigh beside his ear, an ease of the tension in her shoulders. He kissed her head in the places he could reach.

She sighed. "This is what I would try to imagine."

"This?"

"I'd be alone and cold and in pain and all I wanted was for you to wrap your arms around me. I imagined you referring to it as an 'Essie burrito,'" she murmured, voice turning dainty for her fake Mexican accent.

Warm tears began to fill his eyes. He took a steadying breath. "I like that. 'Essie burrito.'"

"No, you have to do the voice."

"Essie burrito," he repeated.

She nodded.

"You're right, that is better."

"Now, of course, it'd be an Izzy burrito," she said with a short sigh.

"It would," he murmured, giving her a gentle squeeze.

"It helped. Imagining you holding me, thinking of things you would say."

He kissed the top of her head.

"One time I thought I actually heard you. Like it wasn't just in my head. It wasn't an echo of something from my memory, like your voice was actually in the room with me."

He froze.

"I mean, it's not possible, but it helped me at the time."

He took a deep breath. "'We're coming for you, Essie.'"

She tensed and took a step back, looking up at him.

He slowly shook his head, answering her unspoken question. "One of the guards worked with the Arks–Danny helped him set up cameras. Luther and Miles were keeping an eye on you while Luther figured out a rescue plan."

"Marcus," she said quietly.

He frowned.

She shook her head, encouraging him to continue.

"After Luther told me you were alive, I went to the surveillance room. There weren't microphones, there was no way you should have heard me, but we saw your reaction after I said that."

Her eyebrows pulled together. "I *heard* you," she said insistently. "You said you were coming to get me. You *sang* to me."

He chuckled lightly in disbelief, nodding. He remembered the song coming to him out of nowhere. He had visualized her standing at the front of Calvary Church singing it when she was eleven. At the time, he'd had no idea what she had been through as a child, how the song would have especially poignant meaning for her. He just remembered feeling a joy fill his heart, comforted by the thought of a loving God pulling those who felt lost in the shadows back into the light. "*Yeah*, I did sing to you."

She furrowed her brow. "And not very well."

An actual laugh burst from his mouth, but it came out more like a honk.

"I'm kidding," she said quickly. "You sing really well." She smiled lightly, eyebrows slanting comically upward. "*Wait*, is that what your laugh *sounds like* now?

"I'm out of practice."

"Clearly. Thank God I'm here."

He lifted his eyebrows. "Yeah."

She squinted one eye. "I meant that to be silly."

"I know."

She took a steadying breath and tightened her arms around him. "The island look suits you, Josh West," she whispered next to his ear, her breath tickling his neck. Her body stiffened suddenly, just before the chime of the lock key code echoed from the front entrance.

They turned abruptly toward the front door as Gunner stepped inside. His hopeful expression faded as he took in the mood of the room. "You said just to come in, right?"

Josh nodded, pressing his lips together. "Wyatt," he said, then winced.

"It's weird, I know," Gunner remarked.

"Can we have a few minutes?"

Gunner glanced back and forth between them. "Do you want me to just bring you guys something to eat instead?"

"No, I'd like to get out of the house," Essie chimed in, her expression a bit lighter. "I mean, it's a *beautiful* house," she said, motioning to the room, the view.

"No, I get it."

Josh furrowed his brow. "I just need to talk to Essie about something."

"Okay, *well*, you guys can just meet me over there. There's another Jeep in the garage."

"*Oh*. I guess just give me directions?"

"It's a really small town. Go either direction out of the driveway, take the next road, follow that out to the main road, go right, there's a small shopping plaza a quarter mile down on the right. I promise you can't miss it. Look for the sign for Joe's Shave Ice. It's got like a *giant* rainbow. The breakfast place is next to it."

Josh smiled seeing Essie's attention jump at the mention of shave ice. "15 minutes?"

Gunner nodded. "Take your time. I'd like to check out the surf shop anyway. I'll keep an eye out for you," he said and left.

Essie took a deep breath as the door closed. "I can't call you 'Josh West' anymore."

"In *public*. You can call me 'Josh West' when it's just you and me."

She furrowed her brow. "I thought of not being able to call you that--And then I remembered how my dad referred to you as 'The West Kid' and–" She wiped roughly at her eyes, resetting herself, sniffling as she turned away. "I'm fine. We should go. Sunshine and fresh air and mountains of sugar will be good for both of us." Her mind was clearly still reeling. She was visibly struck by another wave of sadness that actually caused her to lurch forward. She grabbed onto the kitchen counter for support, squeezing her eyes shut.

He stepped toward her and began stroking her back. He released a long breath. "This is going to happen, Essie."

"What?"

"Whenever you need to cry, you can. It's *okay*."

She stood upright again. "But I feel crazy to just, out of the blue, burst into tears."

He shook his head. "It's not crazy. You're *grieving*."

She stepped back into his arms, but her tension was not so easily relieved this time.

He felt the staccato release of her breath against his shoulder. "Grief isn't a phase you go through all at once."

Her tears were starting to soak through his shirt.

"There are going to be moments it sneaks up on you–when the pain feels so sharp and piercing, it's like you'll never take a full breath again."

She nodded.

"But you won't have to face any of it alone ever again."

She continued to nod.

"I can't make it easier for you; I wish I could."

Her breathing began to steady. "Tell me," she whispered.

"What?"

She leaned back. "You've experienced grief."

327

He nodded.

Essie lifted her eyebrows. There was trepidation in her eyes. "Tell me."

"Well," he began, hesitating to mention her dad, not wanting to inflict the pain upon her. Saying his name felt like it would have the same effect as putting a dagger in her heart. Then again, he couldn't be afraid to mention him or it might encourage her to suppress her feelings, feel like she couldn't talk about him. "Teo. Of course."

She nodded, her brow furrowing.

"But there was also–"

Her eyebrows pinched upward, her eyes terrified of what he might tell her. "*Who?*"

He shook his head. "You."

She frowned.

He took a steadying breath, the feeling he'd had arriving back at his cabin after Luther told him she was dead rushing back. The way Luther lost his cool, shouted the words "I *saw* her" when Gabe had speculated the claim that she was dead was a lie told him all he needed to know. That it was a painful, torturous death–and she'd suffered. He faced the realization every day, multiple times per day, that she was gone, that what she witnessed, what she'd experienced before her death was horrific, each time no easier to cope with than the last.

"For 79 days, I was told–and I believed–that you were dead." He realized suddenly that his experience probably carried far less significance now. She was dealing with actual grief; his ordeal bordered on the imaginary. Not to mention that she witnessed *his* simulated death; she thought he was dead, too.

She took in his expression, the silence swelling between them. Finally, she said softly: "You thought I was dead for 79 days?"

"It's different now, I know," he said apologetically. "It wasn't even real grief."

"Yes, it was," she said firmly.

He pulled up the corners of his mouth as he felt tears filling his eyes, then nodded.

Essie braced his face in her hands, searching his eyes. "*Why*? You said you were 'told' I was dead–*why*?" She suddenly retreated from the question, shaking her head. "That's a different conversation." She pushed through her toes and hugged him. "I'm sorry."

He held her snugly.

Essie nuzzled her cheek against his. "Wow, I'd forgotten how exfoliating your face is when you haven't shaved," she breathed toward his ear.

He chuckled lightly.

She ran her palms up and down his upper arms, her cheeks flushed. "You started bench pressing tractors in your spare time? Is that what's happening here?" She kissed her way from his ear, across his cheek, then centered herself in front of him, kissing his lips delicately.

"What are you doing?" he murmured, his lips pulling upward.

"I'm allowed to do this now," she said with a mischievous grin, slipping her arms around his neck. She took a backward step towards the bedroom, attempting to draw him along.

"I can't let you do that," he whispered.

She frowned questioningly, her shoulders starting to fall.

He took a step forward and began speaking quietly: "I, Joshua O'Neill West, take *you*, Esther Evin Natale, to be my lawfully wedded wife."

Her cheeks tightened.

"To have and to hold, to love and to cherish all the days of my life."

She swallowed hard. "I, Esther Evin Natale, take you, Joshua O'Neill West, best friend and love of my life–don't *tickle* me–I'm in the middle of my vows–" she said through giggles.

"You one-upping little–"

"Shush," she said, placing her index finger over his mouth. "Wait, what were you going to call me? 'One-upping little' *what*?"

"I actually don't know. I knew you'd stop me."

She grinned. "You know, I *could* drag this out, give a compelling forty-minute dissertation about why I want nothing more than to be the wife of the guy that just called me a 'one-upping little,' well, we don't know, do we?"

"I imagine you could."

"Said without a trace of sarcasm."

"You know I love listening to you talk," he whispered, then kissed her index finger.

Her breathing deepened as he tilted his chin and kissed the top of her hand. Her eyes were fixated upon the place where his lips touched her skin. She lifted her eyebrows happily. "I'm married to Josh West."

"Well, you didn't *quite* finish your vows."

"Yeah, I did."

"No, you didn't."

"In my head, I definitely did."

"Well, out loud, you'd only just begun."

"Well, *you* interrupted me."

"I did. I'm sorry."

"This is very serious," she scolded, her lips tight, her eyes shimmering.

He framed her face with his hand, ran his thumb over her cheek.

She frowned, then continued where she'd left off. "--to be my lawfully wedded husband. To have and to hold, to love and to cherish, all the days of my life."

He nodded, leaned in and kissed her tenderly on the lips. He wrapped his arms around her, just below her hips and delicately lifted her, carrying her the rest of the way into the bedroom.

*   *   *

"I don't think I can call you Benji," she conceded in a whisper a bit later as she stroked the stubble of his cheek, her body tucked alongside him.

He peered over at her, smiling. "No?"

"*Ben.*" She twisted her expression, looked away, then back again. "I love you, *Ben.*"

He winced. "Feels weird?"

"Yeah."

"No matter what our names are, it's still you and me."

"I know."

"And you can still call me 'Josh West' when it's just us."

"Oh, I *intend to.*"

He grinned. "Good."

She took a deep breath, drawing a spiraling shape across his bare chest with her fingertips. "Who picked our names?"

"Luther and I had a conversation a couple weeks ago about the possibility that we'd need to change our identities. He asked me to choose our first names."

She furrowed her brow.

"Ben was my grandpa's name. I really looked up to him when I was little." He smirked. "*He* was also named for Obi-Wan, or *Ben*, Kenobi."

Her lips curled upward. "Well. *Hello there.*"

He smiled broadly. "*How* do you remember that?"

"I *don't know.* Do I get points—or like, space credits—for the reference?"

"Absolutely. Unlimited space credits."

"Well, now that takes all meaning from my prize. *Unlimited space credits,*" she said with a scowl.

"Fine. How many space credits do you think that reference was worth?"

"Well, I'd like currency that works *here* so I can buy shave ice."

He nodded. "Enough dollars for a shave ice for the Kenobi reference."

She frowned.

"Enough dollars for *a week's worth* of shave ice," he corrected.

"Better." She arched an eyebrow. "Do you think Gunner–or Wyatt–went ahead and ate without us?"

"Pretty sure he would have done that by now."

She scrunched her nose.

"You want to go eat soon?"

"*So much*," she said, then frowned. "Okay, so you chose Ben for you for your grandpa and *Star Wars*."

He nodded.

"Where did Isabel come from?"

He cleared his throat, stroking his fingers through her short hair. "Before Hannah was born, I was over at my parents' house and they were discussing baby names. My dad was razzing Teo about how he chose such an old-fashioned name for you."

Her body tensed a bit at the mention of her dad.

"My mom reminded him that 'Esther' had been Rachel's top choice and he chose it to honor her." He took a deep breath. "Then she asked your dad what *his* top choice had been."

Essie froze.

He scrunched his nose. "It was Mildred."

Her eyes creased.

"*No*, it wasn't Mildred," Josh conceded with a grin.

"Thank God," she replied, cheeks tight.

"*Isabel*," he said softly.

She pressed her lips together, tears pooling in her eyes. "Isabel," she echoed finally.

He nodded.

"I like the name. I like how it sounds when you say it."

He smiled. "I do, too."

30

unprecedented

5 years later...

"Garrison, what do you think we should expect from President Graham in this, his second inauguration speech?"

Garrison straightened his posture, pursing his lips. "Well, Chris, I think we can expect something on-brand for him—reverential, powerful, unifying, and Biblical."

"Early in his first term, we both questioned his approach, whether people would be put off."

Garrison leaned toward the monitor to his right, squinting his eyes as he put on his reading glasses. "Four years ago his win margin was twenty-two percent. 58% of the vote. This past November? Thirty-nine. President Graham pulled *68%* of the vote. That's the biggest landslide *ever* in the history of this country."

Chris pressed his finger to his ear. "Sorry, Garrison, we should have expected this. Not wasting any time, President Graham is about to address the nation. Let's listen in."

Luther Graham stepped up to the podium set before a background of snow-covered mountain ridges, dense forest, and sprawling white valleys. He was bundled in a heavy, full-zipper black jacket, his breath visible. "You may have thought you tuned in for my inauguration speech, but what you *actually* tuned in for was my realization that I need to use better inflection in my tone when I'm joking around. For *example*, when I was asked about where to hold this speech, I said Rocky Mountain National Park *as a joke*. Toby Dover, who had asked me even clarified–'Sir'--I can't seem to get him to stop calling me 'Sir,' but he said, 'Sir, I don't know if you remember, but your inauguration is in *January*?' And I said, 'Yeah *and*?'" He grinned, his eyebrows lifting hesitantly. "It's cold here, folks. This is not CGI, there is no green screen. You *are* seeing my breath. Those *are* mountains. I may have just seen a legitimate yeti."

The off-camera audience laughed.

"Oh I do love it here though. I was born and raised in Denver. It's where I went to school, started college. It's where I took an 'opportunity' through the college at Glory Hospital–which, at least as far as I'm concerned, was an abomination to its chosen name. My time there is what set my course, or rather, *God* sent me there to set my course. You know the rest. I never imagined what lay before me, that I would be standing here today."

He took a deep breath. "My Fellow Americans, we have much to do as a nation to build a country that holds true to our core values. The government is not meant to rule its people, it's meant to serve its people. *I* work for the American people. Many people struggle to keep one boss happy; well, I have two hundred million bosses, with more born every day. It's a beautiful thing, isn't it? Life? New life, old life, middle-aged life." Luther paused and gave a reflective smile, his eyes straying from the teleprompter. He tapped his palms gently against the podium and then he took a few steps to his right, confusing the camera operator. "You know, it doesn't feel that long ago when all of this started for me." He began to pace. "I take it back. It doesn't feel that long ago in *some* ways because the memories are so vivid, even now, but in other ways, it definitely feels like it's been that long. I was 24. I was just a kid," he said, frowning. "I thought I knew what I was meant to do with my life: I was going to be a doctor, a Nephrologist. I chose Nephrology, which focuses on kidney function, mainly because my dad died of kidney disease when I was eight years old. I was determined to find a cure. At the time, I remember actually thinking that there was another eight-year-old out there, and I was going to make sure *he* didn't lose *his* dad. I was interested in science, in medicine, sure, but *that* was the quiet part of my goal I didn't talk about." He furrowed his brow. "Do you know who knew that was what was really on my heart?" He pointed upward. "God. For a long time, I thought the path He took me down was an entire course alteration, having nothing to do with the goals I had for myself." He smiled lightly. "I was wrong. He led me to Evin, He presented the opportunity for me to save her life—and because of *her*, we have a cure for most, if not all, known diseases, *including* kidney disease." He paused, taking a steadying breath. "God knows your heart, God knows my heart." His eyes panned across the crowd. "What's on *my* heart now is to restore the sanctity of life, of childhood, to embrace the simplicities of life that make it meaningful, for all Americans. Life, liberty, and the pursuit of happiness. *'It's gonna happen. Just let the Way Maker through.'*

"Thank you for your support, your trust, and may God bless you and your loved ones—and may God bless the United States of America."

"And off he goes," Chris remarked, chuckling to himself, as they watched Luther Graham jog off toward a military vehicle convoy. "What was that you said? 'Reverential, powerful—'"

"Unifying and Biblical," Garrison said, amused.

"I'd say he delivered."

"I should have added 'brief.'"

"Well, with the windchill, it's currently 14 below."

Luther was beckoned back to the podium, where he waved cordially and dutifully to the crowd, to the camera, before being sworn in as President for his second term. After removing his hand from the Bible, Luther gave a winning smile, waved and called out: "Let's get to work!" then was off again.

There was silence as the camera followed him back to the vehicle convoy, then waited for him to climb inside.

"Just making sure there isn't an encore," Chris remarked.

"Exactly. President Graham doesn't seem to believe in excess or showboating, but he sure keeps everyone on their toes."

"Do you miss the parades?" Chris asked.

"Not even a little."

"And off he goes, officially starting his second term in office," Chris narrated, as the convoy pulled away. He sighed. "So, he clearly went off-script."

"I'd be disappointed if he didn't. You know, he gives a fantastic, well-articulated, concise yet rambling speech."

"'Concise yet rambling.'"

"Yes, he had made the decision to remain brief on his past that everyone feels like they know pretty well, but then he decided, *nope*, I need to talk about it."

"It comes off as a commencement speech—a college graduation commencement speech."

"Yes, I can see that. Inspirational. A bit vague."

"Very God-centered."

Garrison nodded.

"Your take?"

"Look, this President has made it very clear that his religion is first and foremost in his life. That's how he makes his decisions, a sort of *Jesus Take the Wheel* approach."

"Which seems to be working."

"Absolutely."

"In fact, with the rapid turnaround of our country, there's a fear that we'll soon forget all that we faced over the past few decades, or that we won't learn from those events. People seem content to put it behind us."

"'Those who cannot remember the past are condemned to repeat it.'"

"Exactly. And that was not, in fact, Winston Churchill, who penned that phrase, but philosopher George Santayana," Christopher added, furrowing his brow. "In your opinion, what do we need to do going forward to make sure that doesn't happen?"

Garrison nodded, his voluminous locks bouncing as he did, delighted to assume the role of interviewee. "We have to dedicate ourselves to remember, to teach the next generation. I *do* think President Graham is a very intelligent leader–the fail safes he's putting into place, things like term-limits, elimination of the two-party–or I suppose it became a one-party system, wasn't it? Decentralized government, comprehensive congressional and judicial report cards based upon voter feedback, which have a direct focus on compensation? A focus on the individual states? It's all very promising to try to prevent anything like what we've experienced over the last few decades. I think transparency and accountability in government is going to be key to building any sort of trust."

"Do you feel like that's possible? Trust in the government?"

"I guess that's sort of a misnomer, 'trust' in government? But I want to believe it's possible, to a degree, with this Administration. Maybe that's the eternal optimist in me."

Chris perked his brow. "But President Graham seems to have that going for him."

"Absolutely."

"It's just a question of everyone else?"

"Well, *yes*. I think it's important to encourage active engagement in the community, in the government. A very, I'll call him, *infamous* former President claimed that 'good people don't get into government.'"

"Given what we know now, it seems like a very accurate observation from our 45th president."

Garrison shrugged. "*Indeed.* I think we're getting to see what happens when they do."

Chris nodded approvingly. "The question remains: How do we *keep* our government honest?"

"That *is* the 10-billion-dollar question. There were things our founding fathers just simply couldn't anticipate. They anticipated a lot, but I think using their guidance, which has proven to be incredibly solid and well-devised, along with our own wisdom we've gained through a few very painful decades, that I believe President Graham and other leaders, are ensuring we institute policies, laws, precedent that will provide a very positive position for the country for many years, many generations to come."

"It's a bit early to speculate, but how do you like his VP's chances in four years?"

Garrison lifted his brow. "Well, four years ago, my response may have been different. After nearly a year of having Sadie Parker as the interim Vice President, it raised an alarm with me that he would call upon a fresh face to step in to replace her."

"I suppose he was only a fresh face *to us*."

"This is true, but he was prominent in his respective state."

"Chip Elwes was formerly a U.S. Congressman from Arizona, currently 52, father to 9 adopted children, married 27 years to Beverly. He was a nonprofit lawyer before becoming a congressman. He actually sat on the Ark Council, along with Sadie Parker. Now, President Graham did *not* mince words about *other* members of the Council."

"No, he certainly *did not*. Elwes and Sadie Parker had been notable exceptions—though the messaging saying that she decided to step away from politics to 'spend more time with her family'--that sounded a bit like a PR spin."

"It did."

"Whatever the truth was, Elwes hasn't missed a step."

"President Graham has referred to him as a 'workhorse,' 'a person of action,' and 'a man of faith.'"

"High praise from this President, though it makes sense. It was revealed during their original campaign that Graham and Elwes actually have a more personal connection. President Graham, as we know, had run an underground one- or two-man operation to save babies from the government lab experiments. It's my understanding that *five* of Chip and Beverly Elwes's children came from those labs."

Garrison nodded. "They also connected through their church? A 'life group'?"

Chris smiled. "It can be risky to choose someone as VP who is *too* similar to oneself—usually there's the thought to use the VP to supplement your own profile, fill a gap to gain more votes from other demographics, but it seems to be working."

"It does. I do predict in four years, voters might be looking for as close a substitute for Graham as they can possibly get."

"You *do*?"

Garrison chuckled. "Well, I'll put it this way: If Elwes has President Graham's endorsement, which certainly seems to be the case at this point, he has *my* vote."

"*Wow*, well that's certainly something. Perhaps our program isn't quite as balanced as we originally thought."

"Oh, I'm sure we'll have something to disagree on."

Annette switched off the television, shrugging on her puffy, cream-colored jacket. She stepped out onto the back patio, trailed by Denali, her Great Pyrenees. They took the gravel path down the grassy hillside, which led to the boat dock, positioned in a nook of a sprawling lake, which had not yet seen its winter freeze.

"Do we have everything *now*, Den?" she asked, stopping alongside the orange, two-person hard-sided kayak she'd already taken down from the storage rack. It was positioned in the launch ramp, her waterproof bag secured in the netting.

Denali placed a paw on the side of the kayak before expertly hopping into the front compartment.

"I'll take that as a 'yes,'" Annette murmured before climbing inside herself.

The hum of the neighbor's small fishing boat began to grow louder just as the kayak glided into deeper water.

Annette reached swiftly for her temple, stretching a finger to press the translucent button for the facial overlay, having forgotten to activate it before stepping back out of the house. Growing out her hair and no longer applying makeup in the way expected of her in the District would have likely been enough to keep anyone from recognizing her, she expected, but the overlay was necessary to cover the severe scarring on the left side of her face from the explosion that had struck in the room adjacent to her White House bedroom. The intensity of the scars was something that would have drawn unnecessary attention and questions as she assumed her new identity as Leah McKinney.

Originally, she had no plan beyond killing Gowon; she didn't anticipate she'd live long past that point.

Murdering Samuel Gowon had ultimately been easier than she'd anticipated, mainly because he absolutely did *not* see it coming. He was unhinged about the Ark's invasion of the District, the off-shore reinforcements, the coordinated cyber-attack–he had just activated, but not yet fired, nuclear defenses—and then the meteorites struck the power grid. When the power grid went down, it caused a wavering pulsation that had frozen him where he stood. Annette had been too distracted by her task to have given anything else much thought.

Samuel had thrown out his arms when the ground shook, as though steadying himself on a boat. The moment he twisted his torso to look for Annette, she had taken her swing.

Samuel really took care of the rest. The Tomahawk had sliced efficiently into his midsection, directly in line with his belly button, as she'd been instructed and as she'd been training. She knew the exact angle needed in the extension of her elbow. When the blade made impact, slicing into his abdomen with a satisfying *whoosh*, she felt a tremendous relief, knowing it was done.

He'd been confused by the act, confused by the weapon lodged in his stomach. He'd stared down at the blade, disbelieving, then peered over his shoulder toward the glass cabinet where it was typically displayed.

She wasn't sure if he pulled it out of his stomach, or if it was dislodged by a reflexive physiological response or muscle contraction, but one moment the Tomahawk was there, the next, it wasn't–but there was much in its place. She didn't have much time to decipher what was spilling out of his stomach–before Samuel collapsed, before Demetri Malick appeared at the door and shot her with what turned out to be non-lethal ammunition–something impacting the nervous system so it simulated the look and feel of an actual gunshot. She'd lost

340

consciousness, awoken hours later in the cabin she now called home, Chris sitting at her side. He had his glasses on and was reading a *Jack Reacher* novel. He casually closed the book, leaned forward, and took her hand.

"I guess my transformation into Harvey Dent is nearly complete."

"You know, you don't strike me as the comic book type," he whispered.

"My brother."

He nodded. " 'You either die a hero or live long enough to see yourself become the villain.'" He gave an amused smile. "Harvey Dent said that."

"Ah."

"You did both. In the ideal order, too."

"Am I dead?"

"Well, Garrison Chase reported it. It must be true."

She smiled, then winced as the expression tugged at the burns on the left half of her face.

The fishing boat was now well within view.

Your name is Leah McKinney, she told herself, then lifted her chin, feeling a much more convincing expression take over her face. She paused rowing to wave to Jim and Sidney, then pressed the button over her ear to answer her phone, letting the kayak drift forward with the remaining momentum.

Chris.

"Well, *hello* to you...yes, I was watching...you know, you aren't supposed to wear your ring on air. People are going to notice...*Okay*, if you say so. The two of you seem to be getting on well...Do you feel like you're close enough as coworkers to tell him to stop shaking his hair like a romance novel cover model?" Her cheeks tensed. "No, I think he looks like he's *trying* to be a romance cover model, not that he actually looks like one...The effect is more ridiculous than when he was trying to mimic *your* look...Oh, yes, he was...What's *your* look? Are you fishing for compliments? Yes, my description of your 'look' would be complementary. Perhaps. Just going out for a row with Den. I will. Yes,

I'm bundled...He has *fur*, Chris. OK. Well, enjoy yourself...Yes...I'm sure...I'll see you tonight."

She took a deep breath, then began paddling more determinedly toward the 40 miles of waterways and wide-open lake.

31
ke ola nani (a beautiful life)

two years later...

Fenway observed the scene from the safety of a dry stretch of sand. In the early days on the island, she enjoyed spirited jaunts through the waves, rolls on her back across the wet sand, but now that she was nearly nine, she enjoyed observing these activities more than partaking in them herself. Along the shoreline, two young dogs bounded through the waves. Occasionally a wave would catch them off-guard as they strained to get a visual on their humans who had treaded into deeper water. The gray pit bull/Australian Shepherd mix, Maverick, had one white leg that looked like he was wearing a knee-high sock, while the rest of his body was primarily gray; his eyes a vivid shade of blue. The brindle and white Great Dane/Lab was named Goose.

Josh let his eyes scan the water until he spotted Essie sitting casually on a surfboard. She had her back to him, her deeply tanned skin providing a vivid contrast to her green bikini, golden brown hair tied in a messy top knot, hands grazing the surface of the water. She sat more upright as a young girl took the drop on a mid-sized wave and popped to her feet on a longboard nearly twice her height. The girl, wearing her bright turquoise rash guard, grinned as she snapped the board to the top of the wave, then glided along the whitewater, snaking around her mom before riding the dissipating wave toward shore, finally dropping herself into the shallow water.

Essie applauded, smiling widely as Vita surfaced with an enthusiastic: "Did you *see* that?"

Josh slowed from a jog to a more casual walk, moving toward the shoreline. "Was that a pro-surfer out there, or what?" he called.

Vita spun toward him, her thick, golden brown braid whipping salt water into the air. "Daddy! I did it!"

He smiled broadly as she ran toward him, her long, muscular legs bursting over the waves. The younger two dogs immediately descended upon her, sniffing and prodding, checking for injuries. Vita's surfboard suddenly popped out of the water and Goose startled, scurrying up the beach to hide behind Fenway.

"Let's untie your board leash before it drags you out," Josh said, kneeling down as his daughter reached him.

"Did you see me?"

"I did. You were *amazing*."

Vita burst into his arms, soaking his shirt. "I can't wait to show Uncle Wyatt."

"Oh, he's going to be *impressed*. I'm not sure how he's going to take getting shown up by a seven-year-old surfing prodigy though."

She scrunched her freckled nose as she took a step back, her dimples prominent, big brown eyes creased. "Mommy said we could go for shave ice after surfing. Do you want to come?"

He frowned. "Do you think I run *for my health*? It's so I can have *more sugar*!" he said dramatically, tickling her. He raised his eyes as Essie walked toward them, surfboard tucked under one arm, feet sinking in the wet sand. She smiled behind her mirrored aviator sunglasses.

Fenway whimpered, cautiously approaching them, wanting to closer to Essie, but not wanting to get wet.

Vita jogged back toward her mom and gave her a hug. "Daddy's going to come along for shave ice."

"I figured he might."

"It's getting to be lunch time. Maybe we should get some lunch and have shave ice for *dessert*?" he suggested, closing the distance.

"I believe you're speaking one of my love languages, Ben Nolan," she replied with a grin, sweeping sand from his face from Vita's enthusiastic embrace.

"Ah yes, food. The sixth love language. Maybe we hit up one of the food trucks?"

She arched her eyebrows suggestively. "Be more *specific*."

"Barbecue chicken plate lunch with white rice and a heaping portion of macaroni salad."

"Oh, I love it when you talk carb loading to me," she said indulgently.

"Why do you call Daddy by his full name sometimes? It sounds like he's in trouble."

Essie twisted her expression. "I don't know, *Vita Marie Nolan*."

Vita's eyes widened fearfully. "I'm outta here!" She ran back toward the water, beckoning the dogs to follow.

Josh smiled at his wife, tucking a loose strand of hair behind her ear. "Crikey! Have a look at this *beauty*, will ya?"

Essie pinched a bit of his t-shirt, tugged him toward her and kissed him.

"Let me get that," he said as their lips parted, grabbing the surfboard from under her arm. "Hey Vita, grab your board, yeah?"

Vita returned, taking in the sight of her mom's tan, round stomach. "Good *gracious*, your belly's gotten bigger since *breakfast*," she gasped.

"Vita!"

Essie shook her head. "She's not wrong. Look at that thing."

Vita placed her hand on her mom's bare belly and gave a light kiss, grinning. "Do you think the new babies will like surfing as much as me?"

"I don't see why they wouldn't. Hey, why don't you go rinse off?"

"Mav! Goosey Goose! Let's go!" Vita called, taking off with her surfboard and the dogs up to the main beach ramadas.

With a firm grip on the board, Josh placed his hand on Essie's stomach. "How are the Bash Brothers treating you?"

She took a deep breath and briefly slumped against him. "I'm *so* exhausted," she whimpered, puffing out her lip. "I woke up needing a nap."

Josh wrapped his free arm around her back so he could support her on the walk across the uneven sand.

"After lunch and my very *own* root beer float shaved ice, I want to stretch out in the hammock for a nice afternoon nap."

He kissed the side of her head. "The lady wishes for a nap and a nap she shall have."

They continued the trek across the sand, Fenway trailing behind.

"When is Wyatt dropping off our son?" Josh asked.

"He was going to take Mattie to lunch when they got back from fishing I think."

"*He's* going to sleep well tonight."

"Oh, I'm sure Mattie will be charged up as usual after lunch."

"I meant Wyatt."

Essie released a drawn out yawn, which threw off her balance.

Josh tightened his arm around her. "You alright there?"

She nodded, peering at him over the top of her sunglasses, her silver eyes shimmering. "Nolan boys are *exhausting*."

"One of us is bad enough. You're a brave woman to grow two at once."

"There's a word for it, but I'm not sure it's 'brave,'" she said with a grin. "*You're* responsible for this. You know that, right?" she teased, indicating her stomach.

"Oh, it's all me huh? The other night you were talking about having *more* babies."

"Yeah, *so?*"

"You haven't finished incubating *these* two."

"I know that. I was just thinking ahead."

"You calculated the earliest possible date range that you could get pregnant again."

"I don't think I did that."

"*No?* February 10th to the 17th. *Approximately.*"

She scrunched her nose. "Well, even if I *did* do that–"

"Which you *did*," he laughed.

"Oh my goodness, I feel like your sons are stealing my brain cells."

Josh ran his palm across her back. "I feel like you're redirecting, but I'll go with it."

She smiled tightly. "Seriously, they are *systematically* stealing my brain cells. Vita had to stop me from putting the cast iron pan in the fridge this morning. Like, I had no thought that anything was wrong. I was trying to clear a spot on the shelf."

"It's okay. It's normal."

"I was *actively* cooking scrambled eggs. Like, the pan was broiling hot, the eggs were *in* the pan. I thought I was putting the milk away."

"Maybe God's telling you that I should do all the cooking and you just need to relax."

"You *know*, I was starting to draw a similar conclusion."

Josh grinned.

As they finally reached the parking lot area, Vita was busy rinsing her legs in the shower while Maverick snapped his jaws at the running water.

"Looks like we're getting a couple more for lunch," Essie observed, nodding toward Wyatt's Jeep pulling into an open parking spot along the far curb.

"Uncle Wyatt!" Vita yelled, abandoning her surfboard and taking off across the dirt lot as he parked.

Essie took a much more leisurely walk toward the Jeep, shoulders back, round belly leading the way. Josh stayed back, keeping the trio of dogs held in a stay position.

Vita jumped up and down outside the driver's side door, eagerly waiting for Gunner to emerge.

"*Hey, guys,*" Essie said, smiling at Gunner, who was listening enthusiastically to Vita's surfing story. Essie ducked down and waved through the windshield at Mattie, who smiled broadly from his car seat in the back, dark curls bouncing around his face. She continued on to open his door.

"How was fishing?" she asked enthusiastically, eyes wide. She was confused when the opposite door immediately closed but shrugged it off as pregnancy brain playing tricks on her.

"We didn't go fishing," Mattie replied with a sly smile.

"You *didn't* go fishing!" she exclaimed for dramatic effect rather than out of concern.

Gunner, who was halfway out his door, put up his hand to pause Vita, who seemed to still be far from the end of all she had to tell him, and peered over his shoulder. "Yeah, something came up, but we made plans to go–you said your schedule's pretty open this week, right, Buddy?"

Mattie nodded, big silver eyes peering over the top of his sunglasses.

"If it's okay with your mom, of course."

Mattie whipped his chin around to look at her with a pleading blink of his eyes.

Essie pursed her lips. "Well, I *don't know!*" she gasped, twisting her expression as though really pondering the question. "Twist my arm," she said, lifting her arm onto his knees encouragingly.

Mattie grabbed on with both hands and cranked her arm like twisting a screwdriver.

Gunner smiled and hopped back out of the Jeep, closing his door.

Vita resumed her story.

"Okay, *fine*, you twisted my arm. And may I say, you are getting *strong*, Mister!"

He giggled. "Mommy, look!" Mattie pulled up his sleeve and tensed his thin arm.

"Oh, *wow!* How are you *doing* this? I have never seen so much muscle on a 3-year-old–wait–*Honey! Mattie's still just three, right?*" she called over her shoulder.

Mattie scrunched his nose. "I'm *three*, Mommy. You're being *silly*."

Essie turned in the open door and caught Josh's eye. "Have you *seen* the muscle on our 3-year-old?" she whispered loudly, jaw falling open.

Josh laughed. "He'll be bench-pressing the Jeep soon."

She widened her eyes, swiveling her chin back to their son. "That is a *horrible* idea. Do *not* bench press the Jeep."

"Okay, Mommy, I won't. I promise."

"So what trouble did you guys get up to then if not fishing?" she asked, tickling Mattie's underarms before unlatching his car seat.

"It's a surprise!" he said, slipping around her to exit the Jeep.

"Mattie helped me with something really important, didn't you, Buddy?" Gunner said, voice immediately behind her.

"Is that right?" Essie asked, frowning at him suspiciously as she turned around.

"We went on a treasure hunt," Mattie announced, looking adoringly up at his uncle.

"A *treasure hunt*," Essie said, eyes wide. "Ye be a pirate?"

"Arrrrg," Mattie growled, squinting one eye.

"*Well*, did you find any treasure?"

" 'Treasure' is such a vague term," a low voice said behind her.

She peered over her shoulder and released a short squeal.

Josh immediately moved in her direction, stopping abruptly when he saw her with her arms wrapped snugly around a man with a mop of sandy colored curls and a very loud Hawaiian print shirt.

Miles put his index finger to his lips, tightened his hold on Essie. "One sec, Bro. Soaking in the love from your better half."

Essie laughed into his shoulder.

"Alright. That's probably enough. It's a small island. You don't want to start rumors," Miles said, taking a step back, his cheeks tight.

Essie glanced over at Gunner and Josh in disbelief, tears streaming from her eyes.

"I'm just kidding. Get over here, you," Miles said, pulling her into a bear hug.

She squeezed her eyes closed, sniffling loudly.

"Is Mommy sad?" Mattie asked, tilting his chin to the side.

"No, Buddy. We call those *happy* tears."

"*Happy* tears!" Mattie exclaimed. "That doesn't make sense."

"I'll let this thing stretch on for a while, girl. You're going to have to tell me when we should break this thing up."

She shook her head, tightening her arms. "Not yet."

32

a bit of land & a pretty view

"Let me get this straight: you gave up the *beachfront* cottage?" Miles asked in the Jeep as they turned down a one-lane road along the river. There were grasslands to their right, occupied by grazing cows, buffalo, and horses. A well-defined and lush mountain range sat just beyond, a tall waterfall pouring down one of the ridges into an unseen reservoir. "I mean, this looks like we're going to see a Brachiosaurus at any moment, but still."

"The cottage has one bedroom and a loft," Josh remarked. "It just wasn't going to be practical."

"Yeah, I guess that's true."

"We do have direct access to the river, which goes all the way to the beach. It actually ends up less than a block from the cottage."

"I did not know that. That's very cool." Miles looked across the bench seat and over the head of three-year-old Mattie, eyeing Essie knowingly. "You look happy."

Josh glanced in the rearview, smiling lightly.

"I am."

Miles lifted his eyebrows. "And besides the fact that you look like you swallowed a watermelon, you look *fantastic*."

"Oh, *other* than that?"

"Yeah, well, it throws off the aesthetic a little, but you somehow make it work." His eyes dropped to her round belly peeking out from beneath her t-shirt and grinned.

"Mommy has *two* babies in her tummy," Mattie said proudly, holding up the appropriate number of fingers.

"You're having *twins*?" Miles asked incredulously. "Oh, yeah, then you look smokin' hot, all things considered."

Essie winced. "You still have the ability to have what sounds to be a compliment come off as a crushing insult."

"It's not an insult at all. The compliment I'd *like* to give I can't say because there are young ears present."

She grinned widely.

"*And* you're married. And that's old me, not new and improved, *redeemed* me."

Josh lifted his hand to his forehead in a faux salute.

"Uncle Cody, I have a goat," Mattie announced proudly.

Miles widened his eyes. "No kid-ding?"

Essie shook her head, suppressing a laugh.

Miles eyed Josh in the rearview. "Come on, Bro. Are you slacking on your dad pun game?"

"What pun?" Josh asked.

"The answer is yes, he's slacking on his dad pun game," Essie whispered. "But I'm not complaining."

Mattie patted Miles on the arm. "His name is Miles. My goat?"

"Miles the GOAT," Miles remarked with a grin.

"Mommy and Daddy named him."

Miles pressed his lips together. "That's a great name. It'd make a great name for, you know, a *human*, but a goat's cool, too."

"He had a worm as a baby so he never got bigger."

"I'm sorry. Did you say a *worm*?"

Josh cleared his throat. "Yeah, he was at a farm in the area and got really sick. They called me in to–uh–" Josh started to explain, peering over his shoulder to his son and winced. "*Anyway*, they didn't want to pay for treatment for him so I offered to take him in. We nursed him back to health and he's doing really well. He just stayed small."

"He's a forever kid," Essie added with a grin.

"Well, he sounds adorable and endearing," Miles said shortly.

Mattie stared at Miles with interest. "He's noisy and chews on the porch steps."

Essie actively suppressed a laugh.

"I *see*," Miles said, turning his attention to take in the view, elevated above the small surf town and crescent bay.

"Here we are," Josh announced, pulling through the gate.

Miles pursed his lips as the stables and paddocks came into view. "Okay, this place does look more like you guys."

Josh pulled the truck along the dirt drive, stopping just before the front porch steps.

Gunner, who had led the small convoy, stretched as he climbed out of his Jeep. Vita, who had insisted on riding with him, struck a Hercules pose in front of the truck as her dad shifted into park. She stuck out her tongue, dyed blue by her choice of shaved ice flavor, and crossed her eyes.

Miles chuckled watching her. "Cute kid."

Gunner snuck up behind her and tickled her sides and she sprang away laughing, running barefoot toward the paddocks.

"I want to go find Miles to show Uncle Cody," Mattie pleaded, flailing in his car seat.

Essie quickly unlatched the belt and helped him climb out through her side. She yawned widely as she joined the rest of the adults gathered between the two vehicles.

"Are we keeping you up?" Miles asked with a smile, eyes dropping to her belly as her t-shirt rode up again.

"As a matter of fact," she began, interrupted by another yawn. She shook it out and sniffled. "Sorry."

"I promised Vita I'd let her show me how she taught Sabine to shake hooves?" Gunner said, brow deeply furrowed.

"Just wait until she gets stronger with the force," Essie said, widening her eyes.

Gunner crossed to the path leading to the stables, murmuring: " 'I'm one with the Force, and the Force is with me...I'm one with the Force, and the Force is with me...'"

Josh grinned. "Vita and I are watching *Star Wars Rebels* together," he explained, noticing Miles's questioning look. "It's a cartoon. About *Star Wars*. Remember Darth Vader? Luke and Leia? Chewbacca?"

"Obi-Wan," Essie added, motioning to Josh before losing herself in another yawn. She wobbled into Josh's embrace, resting her head on his shoulder.

Josh kissed her on the temple. "You should take that nap."

"But *Cody* is here–" she began, motioning toward Miles. Her blinks were becoming slower as her energy plunged. "I should give him a tour and offer him a beverage and be a good hostess and—" She yawned again and nodded. "Yeah, maybe I should take a nap."

"Was that a *kick*?" Miles exclaimed suddenly, twisting his expression as he stared at her exposed belly, her shirt riding up from Josh hugging her.

"*Oh*, could you see it on the outside?"

"What other way would I see it, my love?" Miles asked dotingly.

She rolled her eyes. "My brain is broken."

Josh kissed the side of her head. "Yes, it is. Poor thing."

Essie took a deep breath.

"There it was again!" Miles pointed excitedly to the portion of skin just beside her flattened belly button. "It was just one little spot–Oh my *chestburster,* that's *so weird*."

She scowled at him.

"What? You're going to tell me your brain is broken, but you get that reference?"

"*Alien*."

"When did you ever watch *Alien*?" Josh asked, perplexed.

"Remember when Gabe and your mom were out of town and it was just you, me, your dad?"

"Oh *yeah*. He had his appendix taken out."

"Sweetie, can I just—" Miles asked, reaching his hand toward her. "I don't want it to be rude or weird."

"Oh, *please*."

"Girl, you've got *two* babies in there?" he whispered, settling his palm near where he saw the kick.

"Hence why I look like I swallowed a watermelon."

He scrunched his nose. "Well, you can't name one Miles because everyone will assume you named the baby after the goat–which would be strange."

Essie smiled fondly at him. "Vita means 'life' in Italian," she explained softly. "When Ben asked my dad permission to marry me, my dad told him that we'd have a beautiful life together. Una bella vita. When I found out that's what he said, I knew it would be her name."

His cheeks tightened. "I actually think it's a very cool name. I'm really glad you didn't go the Dorothy or Paulette route."

"Her middle name is Marie after Josh's mom. Sara Marie O'Neill was her maiden name." She placed her hand over his, guiding it to the left side of her belly. "Mattie is Matteo Lucas."

Miles nodded. "He's a very sweet kid. He looks like you, Josh, except for his eyes."

"Yeah, he's got his momma's eyes," Josh said fondly.

"*Oh*, I was thinking it was the judgmental glare that seemed familiar, but now that you mention it, the color and shape are very similar, too." He grinned—and then he felt the jab of a tiny foot against his palm. He released a small huff of air, his eyes brightening.

"The soccer player is Joel Evin," Essie said quietly.

His jaw dropped open as he looked back and forth between them. "*Joel?*"

She smiled.

"I'm just not an 'awww' sort of person or I'd totally say it."

"That's okay."

He waited for the baby to give his hand another jab before speaking again. "You're really naming him Joel?" he asked Essie under his breath. "Do you, like, need to clear it with your lesser half, because I can plug my ears. Actually, *ear*. I can plug *one* ear. Because this was weird at first, but I don't think I can take my hand away–oh, wow, there he goes again. That's like his *actual* foot. I could feel the shape of it."

Josh smiled at the pair of them, lifted his brow. "We decided on names weeks ago."

Miles pursed his lips, nodding slowly, having a difficult time suppressing a smile. "It means a lot to me, you guys." He furrowed his brow. "*You guys* mean a lot to me."

"Bel, I'm gonna see if Mattie needs help finding that goat," Josh murmured, stepping toward the barn, meeting Essie's gaze. He gave her a knowing smile.

Miles watched him walk away. "Does he call you 'Bel'?"

"He *does*."

"That's very sweet."

Essie stepped toward Miles and let herself be clobbered by his embrace. "I'm really happy you're here," she said, her voice muffled by his shoulder. "*Finally.*"

Miles kissed her twice on the forehead. "Oh my goodness, you smell like sunshine and sunblock. It's incredible."

"Better than the last time you saw me."

He pulled in his breath. "We're going to talk about that, huh?"

"We don't have to," she sighed. "Are you okay?"

"You're asking *me* that question," he said incredulously. "Essie, you're the one–" He growled, tightening his arms around her. "You don't have to be so *good*, you know. I should be the one making sure *you're* okay, not the other way around."

"But you did that already, Joely. You watched over me. You made sure I got out."

"That was Luther."

She took a step back. "I'm sorry, was that *Luther* I was running to in the backyard of the White House?"

"That's a different way of describing the South Lawn."

She lifted her eyebrow.

"Seeing you *now* makes me happy." He took in the sight of her. "I mean, look at you. Your life here. *This–*" He nodded, pressing his lips together. "*This* makes everything worth it."

She tilted her chin to the side, widening her eyes encouragingly.

"I lost my way for a while there. I rode the high of you guys getting out–"

She nodded slowly.

"-but I definitely lost my way."

"You're home now, Joely," she whispered.

"Yeah. It feels like it." He took a deep breath, the corner of his mouth twitching upward. "You should go take your nap, you've got to be exhausted," he whispered, releasing her.

"You're staying through dinner, right?"

"Sweetie, I'm local now. I'll be your permanent house guest if you let me."

She froze.

"That's hurtful."

"No, it's not that," she said. "My brain panicked about if we have a clean set of extra sheets."

He grinned. "So *domestic.*"

She rolled her eyes and shook her head.

"I'm bunking in the cottage loft, dear. I'm not exactly roughing it."

Essie pressed through her tip toes and kissed him lightly on the cheek, tousled his sandy colored curls before turning for the house with Fenway close behind.

*   *   *

"Have you seen Renee?" Essie asked. She was sitting sideways in the hammock, gently swaying herself back and forth. Fenway had situated herself underneath, the hammock fabric grazing her back.

Miles finished a sip from his lowball glass with a satisfied *ahh*. He took the Adirondack chair closest to her. "Yeah, she and Mr. Renee seem very happy together."

"Sorry?"

"She and Corey tied the knot. They're starting a whole herd of petite blonde children."

Essie's eyes widened. "Oh, *wow*. Renee is 22."

Miles shrugged. "Crazy huh? So what's in this?" he asked, giving his glass a gentle shake. "You said it's a Ukulele Sunset?"

Essie chuckled. "Hanalei. Hanalei Sunset."

"It's basically POG juice with dark rum and grenadine," Josh replied.

"I'm not local, what's POG juice?"

"Passion fruit, orange, and guava juice."

Essie held up her glass. "Mine is POG and grenadine so I don't feel left out."

"So that's what y'all do in this town? You drink brunch beverages at 8 o'clock at night?" He took another sip. "Don't get me wrong. I'm digging it. Next time, I'll take my Honolulu Sunset Isabel-Style though," he said, giving her a quick wink.

"Oh, sorry, man. I should have asked."

"No, it's fine. It's not like I *haven't* been drinking. But I should do less of it." He scrunched his nose. "So, do you *want* to hear about everybody? I wasn't sure–I know it's got to be tough. I mean, you're literally living in paradise, but still."

Josh glanced over at Essie, who nodded.

"*Okay*. Well, that Gabe character is now a *pastor*."

Josh turned on his heel. "He was planning to go to medical school."

Miles rotated his chin to Essie, lowered his voice to a whisper. "You certainly leave an impact on the men left in your wake. I'm *just sayin'*."

She shook her head. "In my *wake*? What does *that* mean?"

"What do you *think* it means?"

She narrowed her eyes at him. "You know, you always say things like this to me. You did it on the drive to the Ark, you did it in Montana,

357

stirring the pot with your 'third wheel,' 'men left emotionally damaged' club nonsense, implying I was putting vibes out there that I *wasn't*."

"And how did that make you feel?" he said, grinning, clearly enjoying getting her riled up.

"How did it make me *feel*? Frustrated." She motioned across the fire pit toward Josh. "I've been betrothed in my heart to *that* guy right there since I was a little girl."

Betrothed in my heart, Miles mouthed, suppressing a laugh.

Josh grinned behind his rocks glass.

"That *was* pretty adorable how you said that," Miles remarked, pursing his lips. "I shouldn't have phrased it like that; I was just teasing, but it was inaccurate and mean, and I'm sorry."

She furrowed her brow, pushing off the ground with her toes to sway the hammock. She side-eyed Miles, vaguely confused by his course correction, while still bothered by the trace of accusation.

"Does Gabe seem happy?" Josh asked to fill the void.

Miles found himself distracted, peering over at Essie. He turned more definitively in her direction. "*Psst.*"

She looked up.

"If I was going to make an observation on the impact you have on people, it could *only* be positive."

Her cheeks tightened.

He nodded, pleased to see her mood lighten. He cleared his throat. "Yeah. So Gabe's doing well. He actually got married last year."

Josh lifted his brow. "What's she like?"

Miles sighed. "*Well*, let's see. She's pretty, short–she's pretty short," he clarified. "She's shy, I'm not entirely sure about her sense of humor, but she seems nice-ish. I tend to put some people off so I may not have gotten the best read on her."

Gunner smirked.

"*Alexis*," Miles said, enunciating each syllable. "She does *not* like to be called *Allie*, for the record. I learned that the hard way." He glanced over at Essie and smirked. "And Isabel does not approve."

"What? Who said I don't approve?" she asked innocently.

"Your *face*." Miles rotated his chin toward Josh, who was smiling knowingly at her.

"I did nothing with my face."

"You did a *lot* with your face. *Ben*?"

Josh gazed across the firepit at Essie, grinning, his eyes reflective. "I believe the face was unrelated to Gabe's wife."

"What was the face related to? *Gas*?"

Essie's eyes widened. "Do I have resting gas face?"

The trio of men burst out laughing.

Miles shook his head. "*See*? Fart humor is just not something any of us would think we'd want in a woman, but *there you are*, making it adorable."

"As you were saying—" Gunner said.

"Yes, as I was saying–Gabe and Alexis."

"*Not* Allie," Josh interjected, grinning mischievously.

Miles pointed forcefully at Essie, rising up in his chair. "You did the face again!"

"*What*?!"

"I actually did see it that time," Gunner murmured.

"*Ben*? What's the face about?" Miles asked. "You said the name on purpose. Is this like a hypnosis trick? Can you make her cluck like a chicken, too?"

Josh pressed his lips together.

"I *didn't* make a face," she insisted, frowning. "I don't even *know* Alexis."

"'*Not* Allie,'" Miles echoed.

Essie slapped her hand to her face, covering her mouth.

"You felt it that time," Miles pointed out. "You kind of twitched your nose and glared."

"There was a tiny bit of a snarl with your upper lip, too," Gunner observed.

She turned to Josh for help, her eyes wide. "Why am I doing that with my face?" she whispered, a bit frantically.

"I'll tell you later," he replied, suppressing a smile.

"You better not make me cluck like a chicken, Ben Nolan. I know where you live," she muttered, slumping her shoulders.

He shook his head. "It's a good story," he said softly. "It's one of my favorites."

She narrowed her eyes, but seemed to be redirecting her mind back to the conversation at hand. "*Well*, Gabe's always been more on the serious side so a more reserved girl who doesn't care for nicknames might be a good fit for him." She shrugged, her voice lifting to an unnatural pitch at the end.

Josh nodded supportively. "Totally. I agree."

"As long as Gabe is happy, we're happy for him. *Right*?"

"Right," Josh agreed.

"To Gabe!" Miles said jovially, hoisting his glass in the air.

The other occupants at the fire pit raised their glasses slightly less enthusiastically.

"Yeah, so Gabe's preaching. In Florida. I don't think I mentioned that before. He's up in horse country–Ocala? Mom and Dad West moved there, too, with Hannah Banana. I just attended her *8th* birthday party(?) not too long ago. She's such a *cutie*. She has these, like, big blond curls, big blue eyes. Obviously, she got the looks among the siblings."

Essie took a deep breath, the reality of how much time had passed seeming to hit her square in the chest. "When did they move?"

"Five or six years ago? Your parents started up a dairy farm there. There's been a big push for family farms, ranches, get the country back to those roots, cut down on imports, all that."

Essie locked her gaze on Josh, who had steeled his expression. One of the essential parts of their escape had been to have the Arks, the Gowon Administration, anyone who knew anything about Essie's background, her unique traits, to think both she and Josh were dead. Miles and Danny had rigged up an explosion in the Armadillo, which left only trace remnants of those who didn't survive, which included Gunner so that he could serve as their pilot. The only people who knew for sure they were alive were Miles, Danny, and Luther. Everyone else was made to believe that they were dead. It was how it had to be to ensure their safety, to ensure the safety of Vita, and any other children they'd go on to have.

At the beginning, as they acclimated with their new reality, they had bargained in their grief about how "in a few years," they could go to see Josh's parents in secret. Enough time would have gone by, they wouldn't be on anyone's radar. Once Josh had allowed the possibility of a reunion to percolate in his brain, he had concluded that it was too risky. He'd never forgive himself if something happened to Essie or to Vita.

Josh finally broke from his rigid stance, attempting to take a sip from his empty glass. He raised his eyes to Essie, gave her a reassuring smile.

"They're all doing well," Miles added helpfully, recognizing the building tension.

Essie tilted her head to the side, motioned to the space on the hammock beside her, and lifted her eyebrows suggestively at Josh.

Josh placed his glass on the ground, stood, and joined her in the cloth cocoon of the hammock. Fenway fled the area in the midst of the chaos, jogging over to Gunner, who rewarded her with ear scratches.

Miles took a small sip of his drink, the ice cubes rattling around in the glass.

Gunner stood suddenly in response to a buzzing of his wrist. "I'll be back. I'm just going to go take this," he murmured, excusing himself, moving across the grass toward the stables.

"So what took you so long to make your way out here?" Essie asked after a long silence, tucking herself into Josh.

Miles appeared lost in his thoughts, staring blankly at the bit of grass beneath the hammock.

"Miles?"

He looked up, frowning and clearing his throat.

She repeated her question.

Miles eased back in his chair, nodding, recovering from whatever daze he was in. "Well, I worked with Moose for a few years. That work is *obviously* classified."

"You feel special about that don't you?" Essie said with a grin.

"A bit. A bit."

"Well, you should."

He pinched his face. "He wanted someone he could trust to establish new national security agencies. Can't have a government without bureaucracy as it turns out. Scaled back, obviously, from where it was. Sometime in there, I met a girl." He nodded, pressing his lips together. "We were together for a few years."

"Yeah?"

"I thought we wanted the same things, but as it turns out, we *did not.*"

"That's too bad," Josh said.

"Maybe if we'd met a few years earlier, we would have hit it off. Actually, I *know* a few years earlier, we would have hit it off."

"So what happened?"

"Well, I figured out what Pastor Matteo meant when he said that not everyone who claims to be religious has Jesus in their heart."

Josh gave Essie's shoulder a squeeze.

"How long ago did you break up?" she asked.

"A month?"

"Are we your rebound relationship?"

He squinted one eye. "Maybe a little."

Essie nuzzled into Josh, nonchalantly stroking his neck with her fingertips. "So what is it you want, Joely?"

He didn't appear to have heard her. A pained expression had filled his eyes fixed upon her left forearm turned outward toward the light of the firepit, the burns on her skin faded, but still creating unnatural shadows.

She tilted her chin to the side in the same way she'd done to get Josh's attention.

Miles's eyes refocused on her, the memory of her tattoo being blow-torched away dissipating into the night air. He smiled lightly, blinking away the start of tears.

"You said you thought you wanted the same things, but you didn't," she added helpfully. "What is it you want?"

362

"*Well*," he began, speaking in an uncharacteristically soft voice. "I want to sit in a hammock with the love of my life in my arms and a bunch of muddy, barefoot, let's face it, borderline feral, but ridiculously happy children running around."

Silence swelled.

It was a light breeze sweeping down the hill toward the bay that pulled Miles from his trance. He blinked, realizing he was once again staring at her arm.

She lowered her chin, trying to meet his eye. When he did, he smiled affectionately at her. "Sorry. I meant that in a jesting tone." His gaze briefly fell to her arm again, then he became distracted by the condensation on his glass.

During her captivity, she'd made an effort not to have overt responses, even when he knew she was in agony. Sometimes she just couldn't contain it. She'd be lying as still as possible, but he'd zoom in on her face to find she was sobbing silently. Perhaps she had been motivated not to give Gowon the satisfaction of seeing her suffer, but it seemed more likely she suspected that someone–Luther, Danny, Josh, maybe even him–would be watching and she didn't want to make anything worse for them. It's what made it more agonizing for him when she'd started crying out, screaming, begging God for death, because it meant she believed there was no one left listening, no one left to save her, no one left to be strong for.

He sniffled, giving a steady nod, eyes fixed on the fire. "I knew you were safe, but seeing you–*both* of you here, with your awesome kids–" He patted his chest. "It heals something in my heart."

"*Joely*," she whispered in a coaxing, delicate voice.

He opened his eyes, not realizing he'd closed them and Essie was suddenly crouched before him, trying to remove his glass from his clenched hand. He released his grip and watched her place it beneath his chair.

She peered up at him, her eyes round and vibrant, her lips pursed.

He took in her positioning and startled suddenly. "What are you doing crouched down like that? You'll never be able to stand back up!"

363

She winced. "*Yeah*, actually, I think I'm stuck."

Miles leaned forward and wrapped his arms around her and slowly stood, easing her upright again.

She took the opportunity to lock her arms around his neck, hugging him. She sighed. "I'm okay, Joely."

He nodded.

"*I'm okay*," she repeated in a soft, lulling voice.

He sniffled again, gave another nod.

"Look at me," she said, arching backward. She stretched her lips, her cheeks tight, and lifted her eyebrows.

"Yeah, you're adorable, what's your point?"

She grinned. "Joely, excluding my husband because he's–*well*–"

"Josh West," Miles answered automatically, like his name was all-encompassing of what she needed to say.

She gave a slight shrug, then reset herself, twisting her expression. "He's *irritatingly* perfect, isn't he?"

"Well, I wasn't going to say it, but since you pointed it out," Miles murmured.

"Other than my irritatingly perfect husband?" She placed her palm on his cheek. "*You* are the best friend I've ever had."

He furrowed his brow.

"And I was *actually* pretty mad at you for not coming here with us. For a day and a half after we got here, I thought something had happened to you. I thought you died and Josh just didn't want to tell me."

He pouted his lips in sympathy.

"When I finally asked and he told me you decided to stay back–" Her voice quivered. "I mean, I understood, *I guess*–but I–"

Miles released one of his arms, reached up, and wiped away a tear from her cheek.

"I wanted you *here*," she said tightly.

He frowned.

"And I know you did whatever important work you were doing–"

"Establishing limited bureaucracy."

"Establishing limited bureaucracy," she echoed, sniffling. "But I'm really, *really* happy that you're here now."

He nodded slowly, grinning at her. "Me, too."

"I love you, Joely."

"I love you, too," he murmured, leaning down as she moved to kiss him on the cheek. "*As a friend*," he mouthed to Josh, shielding his mouth with his hand to keep Essie from seeing. "*Don't worry about it. There's absolutely nothing going on–*"

Essie narrowed her eyes upon him.

"Sorry," he said, clobbering her in his embrace.

Gunner returned to the campfire, glancing over at the pair of them with interest. "What'd I miss?"

"More happy tears," Josh murmured.

"There were some sad ones in there, too," Miles admitted. "But mostly happy tears today."

Essie patted Miles's chest and moved to rejoin Josh in the hammock. "So where did you come up with the name *Cody*?"

"I didn't. I think it was randomly generated," he said, settling back in his chair. "Wait, did you all get to pick your own names?"

"*Yeah*," Gunner replied. "Well–"

Essie furrowed her brow. "I'm just not sure Cody fits you."

"Uh-oh. She's naming you again," Josh said, giving a good-natured smile to Miles.

"It'll confuse the kids, sweetie."

She grinned. "*Aww, Joely.*"

"Okay, 'Joel' it is. My name is Joel. Say it's my middle name. It'll be fine." He stretched his arms high above his head, giving her a wink over his shoulder at Essie.

"Everything okay?" Josh asked Gunner, who was checking his watch.

"Yeah. It was just about the Men's Group hike of the Coast and the Falls. You're sure you won't be able to come?"

Josh shook his head. "Maybe next time. The babies could come any day now. Are they *turning*?" he asked abruptly.

"Oh, yeah. They do this. They're like stacked over here," she said, motioning to the outside of her stomach, "then they just, like, roll up together—*and then* roll down again."

Josh smiled. "You're so good at growing babies."

Her cheeks flushed. She internalized a remark, then turned to Gunner. "You could take Joely out on the trail with you guys, introduce him around?"

"It may not be the best idea. It's a challenging trail."

"Are you saying I'm not fit enough?"

"I'm *saying* it had thousand food drop offs, dramatic elevation changes."

"Yeah and?"

"It takes twelve hours."

"*Nope*, I'm good hanging at the beach. You have fun though. When does this hike take place?"

"Tomorrow, 5am."

Miles checked his watch.

"Do you need to roll out soon?" Josh asked.

Gunner furrowed his forehead. "We can stay for a little bit longer." His eyes flitted from Miles to Essie.

Miles sighed. "So what's the *dating scene* like out here?" He waved his hand at Josh and Essie. "You two wouldn't know–I'll redirect specifically to the campfire elder."

Gunner shook his head, rolling his eyes.

"The surfer look agrees with you, by the way. You don't look older than 30."

The remark seemed to both please Gunner and confuse him. "It's an island, Joel."

"*So*, small pond, lots of fish?"

Gunner winced.

"I kind of figured hanging out with you guys," he said, directing his remarks to the whole group, "*might* put me in the company of a girl who wouldn't mind an old-fashioned gentleman such as myself."

Essie suppressed a smile.

"Though if *this* guy is still single, I'm not sure what to think of you all's matchmaking abilities."

"*Wyatt's* very serious with a girl from church," Essie said, matter-of-factly.

"*Really*?"

Gunner nodded. "Four years."

"Dude, you spent the entire drive across the island talking about the origin of all the *chickens*."

Essie suppressed a laugh.

"Hurricanes destroyed chicken coops, no natural predators. Ten second story, *tops*. You should have been telling me about your girl, Dude."

"Her name is *Samantha*," Essie said, enunciating each syllable.

"Tell me about Samantha."

Gunner shrugged. "Sam's great."

Miles frowned. "Well, that's informative."

Essie sighed. "She leads the teen youth programs at church. She's a surf instructor. She used to compete when she was a kid. She's tall, she has *beautiful*, flowing blonde hair, *green* eyes, right?"

Gunner nodded.

"She's really nice, laid back—we absolutely adore her." Essie grinned. "She and *Wyatt* are going to have beautiful, very chill babies someday."

Gunner's eyebrow lifted as he finished the contents of his beer bottle.

"That's great, that's great. I'm really happy for you, Bro. She sounds amazing," Miles murmured, leaning over his arm rest toward Gunner. "I have a very serious question though." His face turned severe. "Does she have   a   *sister*?"

33
before

A half hour later, Essie and Josh stood in the driveway watching the Jeep taillights get smaller as Gunner and Miles drove away.

"I missed him," Essie remarked with a sigh, wandering off into the grass barefoot. While the younger dogs continued to doze on the porch, Fenway eagerly followed along, sniffing the breeze.

"Yeah, I did, too." Josh murmured, dousing the fire pit flames to be sure they were extinguished. He noticed the moment Essie paused mid-step; he could see her mind reeling.

She took a focused, steadying breath, eyes fixed on a patch of grass a few feet in front of her.

It happened from time to time: Thoughts, memories, emotions would come to mind without warning and she'd need to take a few moments to let the wave pass over her.

She started the process over again, her shoulders lifting and falling more overtly, as she took in and released a breath. She squeezed her hands into fists then opened them again, then tried shaking them out. She turned on her heel, starting a third attempt to settle her mind.

He furrowed his brow, fanning his arms out at his sides. "Two arms, no waiting."

She nodded quickly and stepped into his embrace.

He took a slow inhalation, which she echoed, though her exhalation was accompanied by wavering huffs of air, as she tried to suppress sobs. "Again?" he coached.

She nodded.

After another attempt of focused breathing, her shoulders started to relax.

"Better," she whispered.

He kissed her forehead. "Do you want to talk about it?"

"No, I'm okay."

He gave a nod, then spoke melodically next to her ear, his face buried in her golden-brown waves: "'*Here comes the sun–do-do-do-do–here comes the sun and I say it's all right–*'"

She tightened her arms around him, smiling tightly as he continued the Beatles lyrics and started to subtly sway their bodies.

Once he'd gotten through all the stanzas he could remember and repeated the chorus one last time, he peered down at her affectionately.

She lifted her chin, cheeks tight.

"Will you sit down with me for a little bit? I want to give you a foot rub and tell you a story."

"A story and a foot rub? What have I done to deserve *this*?" Her eyes sparkled with enthusiasm. "Wait. What story do you want to tell me?"

"One of my favorites."

She lifted one eyebrow. "Does it start with: '*A long time ago, in a galaxy far, far away*'?"

He grinned. "It's the story about the moment I realized I was in love with you."

369

"*Oh.* That sounds nice."

"It *is*," he said and began to walk her toward the hammock. He stretched the fabric and held it steady as she took a sideways seat facing the ocean, then carefully joined her.

"Oh, they're kicking again," she said, grabbing his hand and placing his palm low on her belly.

Josh watched her lips curl upward, anticipating the next kick.

She furrowed her brow, staring at the placement of his hand on her belly, taking in the setting.

"You okay?"

Her smile became distant. "I dreamed of this. The night before I went to Denver? I had a dream of you and me sitting together–gently swaying–You had your hand resting on my pregnant belly. It was on a porch swing overlooking a lake, I think, but–it *feels* the same. *No,*" she corrected. "This feels better."

Josh exhaled deeply, his cheeks tight. "Slide sideways. I promised you a foot rub."

She did as instructed, slipping the small pillow beneath her neck, stretching her legs across him. She closed her eyes, smiling indulgently as he began to massage the arch of her right foot. "So, you're telling me you know the exact *moment* you fell in love with me?"

"Yes. And I'll clarify that I'm just citing the moment I realized I was in love with you in a *romantic* way; I've loved you since the moment we met."

"Consider it clarified. And ditto."

He smiled. "Okay, so when I was fifteen, the town was putting on a dance. Most kids were being homeschooled so it was a chance to give us some–*normalcy,* I guess?"

She nodded lightly.

370

"You were staying with us. I think your dad was doing some outreach work?"

"What time of year?"

"Spring."

"Food distribution and guest pastor sermons in the city. I went once, but I think Luther told him not to bring me there because of surveillance."

It still surprised him how there was no longer hesitation when she spoke about her dad. Sometimes there were still moments when her voice would constrict and tears would pool in her eyes and if they were sitting or lying together, she would nuzzle closer, but she didn't shy away from speaking about him.

He continued to rub his thumbs tenderly in circles on the bottom of her foot, which was silky smooth from the humidity, the natural exfoliation of frequently barefoot walks on sand.

"Okay, so I was staying at your house for a couple weeks and there was a dance. Sorry I interrupted."

"Yeah, so there was a girl named *Allison*, who asked me to go with her to the dance." He grinned, recognizing the moment Essie remembered, her face briefly pulling into a scowl, the muscles in her foot tensing. She tilted her chin, actively searching her memory as he continued the story. "She came over to the farm a few days before the dance. Her mom was a seamstress and had let out the hem on my pants— that was the year I grew like six inches? *Anyway*, Dad, Gabe, and I were out for a ride–I'm not sure why you didn't come along, but you were at the house when she stopped by. She was just supposed to be dropping off the pants and the jacket, but she wanted to wait for me and ended up hanging out with you and my mom for quite some time."

Essie furrowed her brow, her mouth falling slightly ajar.

371

"You remember now."

She gave a small, tentative smile. "Yeah, but go on."

"Now *you* didn't say anything about what went on, but the day of the dance, my mom told me that Allison, who *did not* want to be called 'Allie'–was quite *offended* to being called 'Allie'--she said her name was Allison, *not* Allie–" He paused to peer over at Essie, who was frowning. "Apparently she hadn't been very nice to you."

He was facing a profound struggle with the tie he'd borrowed from his dad while his mom described how Allison had made a face when Essie bounded into the farmhouse, overalls coated with partially dried mud, hair a wild mess. She had been disgusted when Essie devoured a large helping of pineapple upside down cake standing at the kitchen island. Basically, the entire interaction consisted of Allison pointing out qualities, actions, and interests of Essie's that she found repulsive and unacceptable, remarking about how she "could never" do this or be like that. She immediately followed up with a flattering anecdote about herself, creating a stark contrast between the two of them, Allison no doubt portraying herself as the more attractive, dignified, superior of the two.

His mom had regretted not taking a stand for Essie, but she recounted how shocked she had been in the moment.

He had peered out his bedroom window as his mom told him all this, having been all but ready to leave for the dance, except for the tie. He watched Essie lying on the grass under the oak tree, the centerpiece of their circular drive, bare feet propped up on the wide trunk, legs crossed, holding a book open above her.

"How do I look?" he asked a few minutes later, walking across the dirt driveway, fanning out his arms.

Essie had rotated her chin toward him, lifting her brow. "Honestly, I'm surprised your dad let a monkey live at the farm."

372

He remembered feeling his cheeks tighten. "I get it. Because it's a monkey suit." Despite Allison's mom letting out length in the pants, they still felt a bit too short and the sleeves of the jacket definitely were a bit snug.

She lifted her eyebrows. "You look handsome, Josh. Weird, but handsome."

He sighed as he sat himself on the grass, laying down alongside her. "What are we reading?" he asked, checking the cover of the book she was holding.

"*We?* You can't just jump into the middle of a book."

"Well, catch me up. Paraphrase."

She sighed. "Don't you have a dance to get to? A very pretty, albeit *opinionated* date to pick up?" She batted her eyelashes, then rolled her eyes, giving a look of disgust.

"Was that your impersonation of her?"

She scrunched her nose. "No, that was awful. Forget I did it. I was being rude and I wasn't raised to be rude." She released a sigh, closed the book and set it on the ground beside her. "Josh, you should probably get up; you're going to wrinkle your suit."

He shrugged, looking up at the tree branches, furrowing his brow. "Do you ever worry about bird poop, lying under here?"

She frowned. "Well, I didn't *before*," she chuckled, dropping her legs off the tree and sitting up.

He followed her lead and sat up. "They say it's good luck," he offered.

"*Who* does? *Who* says that it's good luck to get pooped on by a bird?"

He shrugged again. "*So*, I have to go to this really boring thing for a little while."

373

She lifted her brows. "Hence the monkey suit."

"Hence the monkey suit," he echoed with a nod. "My mom's making me go since I made a commitment blah, blah, blah, even though the girl is–" He rolled his eyes and released an annoyed huff of air.

Essie's cheeks tightened despite her best efforts and she narrowed her eyes. "Oh, is that how she is?"

"Yeah, I had a really convincing story to get out of it, too. I was just going to call–"

"You can't cancel at the last minute, Josh. That would be *unbelievably* rude."

"And I wasn't raised to be rude either?" he asked with a grin.

"No, you weren't."

He nodded. "As I was saying, I have to go to this really boring dance with this really awful girl."

"How terrible for you."

"I know."

She scrunched her nose. "*Well*, West boys *do* tend to have two left feet so *that* could result in an eventful evening."

He decided against questioning her assessment. "Are you suggesting I step on her toes?"

"*Heavens* no, not on purpose. I'd *never* suggest that."

"No?"

"I'm just saying, pretty pink nail polish *could be* damaged," she said, her eyebrows lifting. She immediately slumped her shoulders. "I did it again. I was rude and callous."

"As I understand it, *she* probably deserves it for how she treated you."

She sighed. "Even so. It doesn't make it right for me to be that way in return. *Also,* I told your mom not to say anything."

"Why didn't you want her to say anything? Actually, why didn't *you* just tell me? I would have canceled days ago."

She shrugged. "Everyone's entitled to their opinion. For some of the things she said, she *may have* had a point."

He frowned. "*What*? No. You know what? I *am* going to cancel at the last minute." He stood, pleased when she clambered to her feet to stop him.

She kept pace as he moved toward the house.

"No one makes my best friend feel like that."

"*Seriously*, Josh, my self-esteem is *not* that fragile," she said, stopping short, frowning at him. She waited for him to turn back. "*Nor* is the rest of me, according to your girlfriend." Her cheeks tensed into a playful smile.

He turned on his heel. "*Oh. That's* how you're going to play this?"

She grinned, trying to anticipate his next move, eyes checking his foot placement. "Don't worry about me. You go to the dance and I'll be here *not* brushing my tangled hair."

He dropped his chin. "She wanted you to *brush your hair*?

Essie nodded. "I know, *right*?"

"But *where* will the birds live?"

She twisted her face as she processed his remark. "Oh. Because it's a *nest*?" She started for him and he took a long backward stride away. "I believe the expression is 'rat's nest,' Josh."

"I know, but that seemed mean," he laughed, starting to jog backward to stay out of her reach.

Her jaw dropped open and she pressed on more determinedly. "*Well*, it sounds like you and your *fiancé* will have *plenty* to talk about!"

"Oh, she's my *fiancé* now?"

"*Yeah. Fiancé.* I'll buy the two of you a set of pans for all those 'fattening casseroles' she's never going to cook."

He stopped abruptly and she crashed into his chest, unable to hit the brakes fast enough. He wrapped his arms tightly around her. "She hates *casseroles*? That's it. Now she's crossed a line."

Essie didn't try to pull away, but her body was tense and she grumbled at him, face buried in his arm.

"You listen here," he whispered toward her ear. "Are you listening?"

She nodded stiffly.

"Never change a thing about you. I mean, I *know* you brush your hair and it just gets really tangled really easily, so if you want to brush it more *often*, that's totally fine."

The volume of her growl increased.

"But there is *nothing* I would change about you, Essie." He grinned, then added quickly: "Even if there *was* something I'd want to change, you're kind of stubborn so I expect change is difficult–*OUCH!* How do you pinch so hard?" he complained through a laugh, still maintaining a firm hold around her. He took a deep breath. "Essie?"

"Yes?"

"You're perfect just as you are. Don't let anyone tell you different."

He felt her body relax against him and found the grip he had been using unnecessary.

"Would you like me to let you go now?"

She nodded.

He began to loosen his hold, then thought better of it. "Oh wait. What's the *magic word*?"

Essie grunted, straining to secure better footing, free herself from his grasp. "Josh, you're such a–"

"A what? I'm such a *what*?"

She managed to free her arms but wound up with his arms wrapped around her torso, his feet firmly planted on the ground behind her. "This isn't a great position for you to be in, Josh."

He glanced down at her foot, primed to thrust back into his groin. "Oh, I'm *aware*."

"I don't want to do this."

"Believe me, I don't want you to do it either. I'm just counting my blessings that you're not wearing shoes."

She laughed under her breath and dropped her foot to the ground. "Truce?"

"Truce." He slowly released her and stood fully upright again, smiling widely.

She turned on her heel, her wild, untamed golden-brown hair glowing in the sunset, her silver eyes beaming at him.

"What's that look?" he asked as he brushed off his tux.

"Nothing."

"*Nothing* huh?" he asked, picking a piece of dry leaf from her hair.

She shrugged, then in one fluid movement, grabbed hold of his tie, which, to her surprise, immediately popped off into her hand. She held the material in her palm, her face twisting.

"I can't tie a tie," he confessed abruptly.

She smiled. "Is this the clip-on tie from when you were a ring bearer when you were, what, eight?"

"Ten," he corrected, his cheeks tight. "What were you even doing? Grabbing a guy's tie like that!"

One moment, he was internalizing his embarrassment of not being able to tie a tie, the next Essie had bounced forward and kissed him. Not in an impassioned way, but in a playful, sweet way.

377

She took a step back, tucked his clip-on tie delicately in his palm, gave him a flash of a smile, and ran off toward the paddocks.

Sitting in the hammock, Essie frowned, considering the memory he'd just shared. "I *did* kiss you."

He nodded, lifting his brow. "You did."

"How did I not remember that?"

"Because it wasn't like a first kiss or big romantic moment for you. You were just being–"

"A *flirt*."

He grinned. "I don't think that's what that was. You were always affectionate with me."

She frowned. "So me kissing you was the moment you fell in love with me?"

"*Realized* I was in love with you in a *romantic* way," he corrected. "And no, not quite."

"Okay, so what was the moment?"

"Well, I still had to go to the dance. The sun had set, it was getting dark. Dad was driving me over to pick up Allison and we were just pulling out of the driveway. I looked out the back window and you were running to get your book you'd left by the tree. I think my mom was calling you in to have dinner."

Essie nodded. "She was smothering me with attention because she thought I was upset."

He smiled, recalling seeing Essie started waving wildly at them as they drove away. "Do you remember what you yelled out as we drove away?"

She smirked. "'Have fun with the old ball and chain'?"

"'Have fun with the old ball and chain,'" he echoed, nodding. "Dad turned to me and asked if you were feeling okay, thinking you meant the

378

comment for him, since *obviously* my mom was standing right next to you."

"Or are there wedding bells already on the horizon for you and this Allie girl?" his dad had asked.

"*Absolutely* not."

"OK, just checking. Would have worn a nicer shirt if I knew I was going to be meeting my son's future wife."

"No, she's back with mom."

His dad had clutched the steering wheel more firmly, raising an eyebrow over at his youngest son.

"I just said that."

"*Yeah*. Yeah, you did."

Josh frowned.

"Did you mean to say that *or*—?"

Josh considered his answer, glancing to the side mirror where the lights from the house looked like distant stars in the darkness. He lifted his brow. "I didn't mean to say it." He actively suppressed a smile. "But I meant it."

His dad drove on, the corners of his mouth turning upward. "Well. *Okay* then."

Fifteen years later, he took in the sight of Essie lying in the hammock across from him, her hand resting on her round belly. One of the babies happened to give a hard kick at that moment, underscoring his thought, his disbelief in what was his reality: the girl he loved from the moment he met her, his best friend, the one who lived in all of his most treasured memories was his wife, was the mother of his children.

She puckered her lips, eyes creased.

Josh grinned. "*What?*"

She sighed deeply, peering affectionately across at him, giving him a knowing smile.

"*Yes*, I've been 'betrothed in my heart,' too."

Her smile stretched. "Thank you for saying it so I wouldn't have to."

He switched to her other foot, gently pressing his thumbs into her arches.

She gave a satisfied sigh, resting her head back.

"*So*, we're about to be outnumbered," he said after a few quiet moments.

"How hard can it be?"

"Going from a family of 4 to a family of 6..."

She waved her hand dismissively, closing her eyes.

"...double diapers, double feedings..."

"Easy peasy."

"...they could be on different sleep schedules..."

Her eyes opened abruptly and she moved to get up, pushing off his leg.

"Where are you going?"

After managing to steady herself, Essie took his hand, gently tugged him to stand. "What's this 'you' business? *We're* going to get some sleep while we still can."

"It's only 9:30."

"And our son wakes with the roosters."

He released a sigh and started to follow. "*Yeah*, alright, you talked me into it." He stopped abruptly. "On one condition."

Before she had a chance to inquire about what the condition might be, he had scooped her up in his arms.

She put her arms around his neck, wincing. "Do you already regret your decision?"

"*Nope*," he said in a slightly strained voice, starting for the house.

"I'm in the normal twins weight gain range, Josh," she said defensively.

"Totally. You look beautiful. Perfect. Pregnancy is such a miracle." He adjusted his hands. "Out of curiosity, what *is* the range?"

She grinned. "37-54 pounds."

"I did *not* know that." He nodded, continuing onward in a determined fashion. "I'm understanding pregnancy exhaustion a bit more though. They're stealing your energy to–*grow*–obviously–" He was starting to get out of breath. "--but *also*–"

"I'm lugging around an extra 47 pounds?"

"*47*," he gasped. "I would never have guessed that."

"I can walk. You're starting to sweat a little bit."

He furrowed his brow, gave a shake of his head. "I'm *good*."

She suppressed a smile and gave him a kiss on the cheek. "Hey, Josh?" she whispered next to his ear.

"Mmmhmm?"

"Remember that time you gave me a piggyback ride to the overlook and you called me a lightweight?"

"*Yep.*"

"That was really funny."

THE DAY *TRILOGY*:

THE RAIN FALLS
THE EARTH SHAKES
THE SUN RISES